ELEPHANT
AND OTHER STORIES

RAYMOND CARVER was born in Clatskanie, Oregon, in 1938 and grew up in Yakima, Washington State. His father was a saw-mill worker and his mother was a waitress and a clerk. After high school Carver took a job at the same saw-mill, but left almost immediately to join his girlfriend who was sixteen at the time and pregnant. He was nineteen when they married. For years writing had to come second to earning a living with his wife in order to support their two young children, although he did manage to attend John Gardner's creative writing course at Chico State College. During this period he worked as a hospital porter, a textbook editor, a dictionary salesman, a petrol station attendant and a delivery man. These experiences and his own increasingly desperate domestic circumstances were frequently the subject of his fiction. He suffered severely from alcoholism and after several separations his wife left him in 1977. Although he published a number of small press books of poetry and one chapbook of fiction in the sixties and early seventies, it was not until the appearance of the story collection *Will You Please Be Quiet, Please?* in 1976 that his work began to reach a wider audience. On 2 June 1976 he gained sobriety and his luck began to change. In 1977 in Dallas, Texas, he met Tess Gallagher, a poet, with whom he shared the last eleven years of his life and whom he married in June 1988. He began to write again and was awarded a Guggenheim Fellowship in 1979. During this prolific period he wrote and published four major collections of short stories including *What We Talk about when We Talk about Love* (1982), *Cathedral* (1984), and *Fires* (1985). He was awarded the prestigious Mildred and Harold Strauss Living Award in 1983, a tax-free stipend of $35,000 a year for five years. His final collection of stories, *Elephant*, was published in 1988 and he was honoured by induction into the American Academy and Institute of Arts and Letters in May of that year. Raymond Carver regarded his poetry as of equal importance to his short stories and his poetry is published in Britain in two collections: *In A Marine Light* (Selected Poems, 1985) and *A New Path to the Waterfall* (1989), the book he finished shortly before his death on 2 August 1988.

Also by Raymond Carver and published
in Harvill editions

Fiction

Will You Please Be Quiet, Please?
What We Talk about when We Talk about Love
Cathedral

Poetry

In a Marine Light (Selected Poems)
A New Path to the Waterfall

Essays, Poems, Stories

Fires

23624

Raymond Carver

ELEPHANT

And Other Stories

Collins Harvill
William Collins Sons and Co Ltd
London · Glasgow · Sydney · Auckland
Toronto · Johannesburg

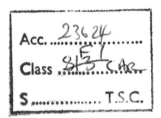
BRITISH LIBRARY CATALOGUING IN PUBLICATION DATA

Carver, Raymond *1938-1988*
Elephant and other stories.
I. Title
813'.54 [F]

ISBN 0 00 271040 4

Grateful acknowledgement is made to the editors of the *New Yorker*
("Boxes", "Whoever Was Using This Bed", "Elephant", "Blackbird Pie"
and "Errand"), *Esquire* ("Intimacy") and *Granta* ("Menudo") in whose
publications the stories in this volume first appeared.

First published in Great Britain by Collins Harvill 1988
This paperback edition first published in Great Britain by
Collins Harvill 1989
Reprinted 1989
© Raymond Carver 1988

Printed and bound in Great Britain by
Hartnolls Limited, Bodmin, Cornwall

Tess Gallagher

We can never know what to want, because, living only one life, we can neither compare it with our previous lives nor perfect it in our lives to come.

MILAN KUNDERA,
The Unbearable Lightness of Being

Contents

Boxes

My mother is packed and ready to move. But Sunday afternoon, at the last minute, she calls and says for us to come eat with her. "My icebox is defrosting," she tells me. "I have to fry up this chicken before it rots." She says we should bring our own plates and some knives and forks. She's packed most of her dishes and kitchen things. "Come on and eat with me one last time," she says. "You and Jill."

I hang up the phone and stand at the window for a minute longer, wishing I could figure this thing out. But I can't. So finally I turn to Jill and say, "Let's go to my mother's for a goodbye meal."

Jill is at the table with a Sears catalogue in front of her, trying to find us some curtains. But she's been listening. She makes a face. "Do we have to?" she says. She bends down the corner of a page and closes the catalogue. She sighs. "God, we been over there to eat two or three times in this last month alone. Is she ever actually going to leave?"

Jill always says what's on her mind. She's thirty-five years old, wears her hair short, and grooms dogs for a living. Before she became a groomer, something she likes, she used to be a housewife and mother. Then all hell broke loose. Her two children were kidnapped by her first husband and taken to live in Australia. Her second husband, who drank, left her with a broken eardrum before he drove their car through a bridge into the Elwha River. He didn't have life insurance, not to mention property-damage insurance. Jill had to borrow money to bury him, and then – can you beat it? – she was presented with a bill for the bridge repair. Plus, she had her own medical bills. She can tell this story now. She's bounced back. But she has run out of patience with my mother. I've run out of patience, too. But I don't see my options.

"She's leaving day after tomorrow," I say. "Hey, Jill, don't do any favours. Do you want to come with me or not?" I tell her it doesn't matter to me one way or the other. I'll say she has a migraine. It's not like I've never told a lie before.

"I'm coming," she says. And like that she gets up and goes into the bathroom, where she likes to pout.

We've been together since last August, about the time my mother picked to move up here to Longview from California. Jill tried to make the best of it. But my mother pulling into town just when we were trying to get our act together was nothing either of us had bargained for. Jill said it reminded her of the situation with her first husband's mother. "She was a clinger," Jill said. "You know what I mean? I thought I was going to suffocate."

It's fair to say that my mother sees Jill as an intruder. As far as she's concerned, Jill is just another girl in a series of girls who have appeared in my life since my wife left me. Someone, to her mind, likely to take away affection, attention, maybe even some money that might otherwise come to her. But someone deserving of respect? No way. I remember – how can I forget it? – she called my wife a whore before we were married, and then called her a whore fifteen years later, after she left me for someone else.

Jill and my mother act friendly enough when they find themselves together. They hug each other when they say hello or goodbye. They talk about shopping specials. But Jill still dreads the time she has to spend in my mother's company. She claims my mother bums her out. She says my mother is negative about everything and everybody and ought to find an outlet, like other people in her age bracket. Crocheting, maybe, or card games at the Senior Citizens Centre, or else going to church. Something, anyway, so that she'll leave us in peace. But my mother had her own way of solving things. She announced she was moving back to California. The hell with everything and everybody in this town. What a place to live! She wouldn't continue to live in this town if they gave her the place and six more like it.

Within a day or two of deciding to move, she'd packed her things into boxes. That was last January. Or maybe it was February. Anyway, last winter sometime. Now it's the end of June. Boxes have been sitting around inside her house for months. You have to walk around them or step over them to get from one room to another. This is no way for anyone's mother to live.

After a while, ten minutes or so, Jill comes out of the bathroom. I've found a roach and am trying to smoke that and drink a bottle of ginger ale while I watch one of the neighbours change the oil in his car. Jill doesn't look at me. Instead, she goes into the kitchen and puts some plates and utensils into a paper sack. But when she comes back through the living room I stand up, and we hug each other. Jill says, "It's OK." What's OK, I wonder. As far as I can see, nothing's OK. But she holds me and keeps patting my shoulder. I can smell the pet shampoo on her. She comes home from work wearing the stuff. It's everywhere. Even when we're in bed together. She gives me a final pat. Then we go out to the car and drive across town to my mother's.

I like where I live. I didn't when I first moved here. There was nothing to do at night and I was lonely. Then I met Jill. Pretty soon, after a few weeks, she brought her things over and started living with me. We didn't set any long-term goals. We were happy and we had a life together. We told each other we'd finally got lucky. But my mother didn't have anything going in her life. So she wrote me and said she'd decided on moving here. I wrote her back and said I didn't think it was such a good idea. The weather's terrible in the winter, I said. They're building a prison a few miles from town, I told her. The place is bumper-to-bumper tourists all summer, I said. But she acted as if she never got my letters, and came anyway. Then, after she'd been in town a little less than a month, she told me she hated the place. She acted as if it were my fault she'd moved here and my fault she found everything so disagreeable. She started calling me up and telling me how crummy the place was. "Laying guilt trips," Jill called it. She told me the bus service was terrible and the drivers unfriendly. As for the people at the Senior Citizens – well, she didn't want to play casino. "They can go to hell," she said, "and take their card games with them." The clerks at the super-market were surly, the guys in the service station didn't give a damn about her or her car. And she'd made up her mind about the man she rented from, Larry Hadlock. King Larry, she called him. "He thinks he's *superior* to everyone because he has some shacks for rent and a few dollars. I wish to God I'd never laid eyes on him."

It was too hot for her when she arrived, in August, and in September it started to rain. It rained almost every day for weeks. In October it turned cold. There was snow in November and December. But long before that she began to put the bad mouth on the place and the people to the extent that I didn't want to hear about it any more, and I told her so finally. She cried, and I hugged her and thought that was the end of it. But a few days later she started in again, same stuff. Just before Christmas she called to see when I was coming by with her presents. She hadn't put up a tree and didn't intend to, she said. Then she said something else. She said if this weather didn't improve she was going to kill herself.

"Don't talk crazy," I said.

She said, "I mean it, honey. I don't want to see this place again except from my coffin. I hate this g.d. place. I don't know why I moved here. I wish I could just die and get it over with."

I remember hanging on to the phone and watching a man high up on a pole doing something to a power line. Snow whirled around his head. As I watched, he leaned out from the pole, supported only by his safety belt. Suppose he falls, I thought. I didn't have any idea what I was going to say next. I had to say something. But I was filled with unworthy feelings, thoughts no son should admit to. "You're my mother," I said finally. "What can I do to help?"

"Honey, you can't do anything," she said. "The time for doing anything has come and gone. It's too late to do anything. I wanted to like it here. I thought we'd go on picnics and take drives together. But none of that happened. You're always busy. You're off working, you and Jill. You're never at home. Or else if you are at home you have the phone off the hook all day. Anyway, I never see you," she said.

"That's not true," I said. And it wasn't. But she went on as if she hadn't heard me. Maybe she hadn't.

"Besides," she said, "this weather's killing me. It's too damned cold here. Why didn't you tell me this was the North Pole? If you had, I'd never have come. I want to go back to California, honey. I can get out and go places there. I don't know anywhere to go here. There are people back in California. I've got friends there who care what happens to me. Nobody gives a damn here. Well, I just pray I can get through to June. If I can make it that long, if I can last to June, I'm leaving this place for ever. This is the worst place I've ever lived in."

What could I say? I didn't know what to say. I couldn't even say anything about the weather. Weather was a real sore point. We said goodbye and hung up.

Other people take vacations in the summer, but my mother moves. She started moving years ago, after my dad lost his job. When that happened, when he was laid off, they sold their home, as if this were what they should do, and went to where they thought things would be better. But things weren't any better there, either. They moved again. They kept on moving. They lived in rented houses, apartments, mobile homes, and motel units even. They kept moving, lightening their load with each move they made. A couple of times they landed in a town where I lived. They'd move in with my wife and me for a while and then they'd move on again. They were like migrating animals in this regard, except there was no pattern to their movement. They moved around for years, sometimes even leaving the state for what they thought would be greener pastures. But mostly they stayed in Northern California and did their moving there. Then my dad died, and I thought my mother would stop moving and stay in one place for a while. But she didn't. She kept moving. I suggested once that she go to a psychiatrist. I even said I'd pay for it. But she wouldn't hear of it. She packed and moved out of town instead. I was desperate about things or I wouldn't have said that about the psychiatrist.

She was always in the process of packing or else unpacking. Sometimes she'd move two or three times in the same year. She talked bitterly about the place she was leaving and optimistically about the place she was going to. Her mail got fouled up, her benefit cheques went off somewhere else, and she spent hours writing letters, trying to get it all straightened out. Sometimes she'd move out of an apartment house, move to another one a few blocks away, and then, a month later, move back to the place she'd left, only to a different floor or a different side of the building. That's why when she moved here I rented a house for her and saw to it that it was furnished to her liking. "Moving around keeps her alive," Jill said. "It gives her something to do. She must get some kind of weird enjoyment out of it, I guess." But enjoyment or not, Jill thinks my mother must be losing her mind. I think so, too. But how do you tell your mother this? How do you deal with her if this is the case? Crazy doesn't stop her from planning and getting on with her next move.

She is waiting at the back door for us when we pull in. She's seventy years old, has grey hair, wears glasses with rhinestone frames, and has never been sick a day in her life. She hugs Jill, and then she hugs me. Her eyes are bright, as if she's been drinking. But she doesn't drink. She quit years ago, after my dad went on the wagon. We finish hugging and go inside. It's around five in the afternoon. I smell whatever it is drifting out of her kitchen and remember I haven't eaten since break-fast. My buzz has worn off.

"I'm starved," I say.

"Something smells good," Jill says.

"I hope it tastes good," my mother says. "I hope this chicken's done." She raises the lid on a fry pan and pushes a fork into a chicken breast. "If there's anything I can't stand, it's raw chicken. I think it's done. Why don't you sit down? Sit anyplace. I still can't regulate my stove. The burners heat up too fast. I don't like electric stoves and never have. Move that junk off the chair, Jill. I'm living here like a damned gypsy. But not for much longer, I hope." She sees me looking around for the ashtray. "Behind you," she says. "On the windowsill, honey. Before you sit down, why don't you pour us some of that Pepsi? You'll have to use these paper cups. I should have told you to bring some glasses. Is the Pepsi cold? I don't have any ice. This icebox won't keep anything cold. It isn't worth a damn. My ice cream turns to soup. It's the worst icebox I've ever had."

She forks the chicken on to a plate and puts the plate on the table along with beans and coleslaw and white bread. Then she looks to see if there is anything she's forgetting. Salt and pepper! "Sit down," she says.

We draw our chairs up to the table, and Jill takes the plates out of the sack and hands them around the table to us. "Where are you going to live when you go back?" she says. "Do you have a place lined up?"

My mother passes the chicken to Jill and says, "I wrote that lady I rented from before. She wrote back and said she had a nice first-floor place I could have. It's close to the bus stop and there's lots of stores in the area. There's a bank and a Safeway. It's the nicest place. I don't know why I left there." She says that and helps herself to some coleslaw.

"Why'd you leave then?" Jill says. "If it was so nice and all." She picks up her drumstick, looks at it, and takes a bite of the meat.

"I'll tell you why. There was an old alcoholic woman who lived next door to me. She drank from morning to night. The walls were so thin I could hear her munching ice cubes all day. She had to use a walker to get around, but that still didn't stop her. I'd hear that walker *scrape, scrape* against the floor from morning to night. That and her icebox door closing." She shakes her head at all she had to put up with. "I had to get out of there. *Scrape, scrape* all day. I couldn't stand it. I just couldn't live like that. This time I told the manager I didn't want to be next to any alcoholics. And I didn't want anything on the second floor. The second floor looks out on the parking lot. Nothing to see from there." She waits for Jill to say something more. But Jill doesn't comment. My mother looks over at me.

I'm eating like a wolf and don't say anything, either. In any case, there's nothing more to say on the subject. I keep chewing and look over at the boxes stacked against the fridge. Then I help myself to more coleslaw.

Pretty soon I finish and push my chair back. Larry Hadlock pulls up in back of the house, next to my car, and takes a lawn mower out of his pick-up. I watch him through the window behind the table. He doesn't look in our direction.

"What's he want?" my mother says and stops eating.

"He's going to cut your grass, it looks like," I say.

"It doesn't need cutting," she says. "He cut it last week. What's there for him to cut?"

"It's for the new tenant," Jill says. "Whoever that turns out to be."

My mother takes this in and then goes back to eating.

Larry Hadlock starts his mower and begins to cut the grass. I know him a little. He lowered the rent twenty-five a month when I told him it was my mother. He is a widower – a big fellow, mid-sixties. An unhappy man with a good sense of humour. His arms are covered with white hair, and white hair stands out from under his cap. He looks like a magazine illustration of a farmer. But he isn't a farmer. He is a retired construction worker who's saved a little money. For a while, in the beginning, I let myself imagine that he and my mother might take some meals together and become friends.

"There's the king," my mother says. "King Larry. Not everyone has as much money as he does and can live in a big house and charge other people high rents. Well, I hope I never see his cheap old face again once I leave here. Eat the rest of this chicken," she says to me. But I shake my head and light a cigarette. Larry pushes his mower past the window.

"You won't have to look at it much longer," Jill says.

"I'm sure glad of that, Jill. But I know he won't give me my deposit back."

"How do you know that?" I say.

"I just know," she says. "I've had dealings with his kind before. They're out for all they can get."

Jill says, "It won't be long now and you won't have to have anything more to do with him."

"I'll be so glad."

"But it'll be somebody just like him," Jill says.

19

"I don't want to think that, Jill," my mother says.

She makes coffee while Jill clears the table. I rinse the cups. Then I pour coffee, and we step around a box marked "Knickknacks" and take our cups into the living room.

Larry Hadlock is at the side of the house. Traffic moves slowly on the street out in front, and the sun has started down over the trees. I can hear the commotion the mower makes. Some crows leave the phone line and settle on to the newly cut grass in the front yard.

"I'm going to miss you, honey," my mother says. Then she says, "I'll miss you, too, Jill. I'm going to miss both of you."

Jill sips from her coffee and nods. Then she says, "I hope you have a safe trip back and find the place you're looking for at the end of the road."

"When I get settled – and this is my last move, so help me – I hope you'll come and visit," my mother says. She looks at me and waits to be reassured.

"We will," I say. But even as I say it I know it isn't true. My life caved in on me down there, and I won't be going back.

"I wish you could have been happier here," Jill says. "I wish you'd been able to stick it out or something. You know what? Your son is worried sick about you."

"Jill," I say.

But she gives her head a little shake and goes on. "Sometimes he can't sleep over it. He wakes up sometimes in the night and says, 'I can't sleep. I'm thinking about my mother.' There," she says and looks at me. "I've said it. But it was on my mind."

"How do you think I must feel?" my mother says. Then she says, "Other women my age can be happy. Why can't I be like other women? All I want is a house and a town to live in that will make me happy. That isn't a crime, is it? I hope not. I hope I'm not asking too much out of life." She puts her cup on the floor next to her chair and waits for Jill to tell her she isn't asking for too much. But Jill doesn't say anything, and in a minute my mother begins to outline her plans to be happy.

After a time Jill lowers her eyes to her cup and has some more coffee. I can tell she's stopped listening. But my mother keeps talking anyway. The crows work their way through the grass in the front yard. I hear the mower howl and then thud as it picks up a clump of grass in the blade and comes to a stop. In a minute, after several tries, Larry gets it going again. The crows fly off, back to their wire. Jill picks at a fingernail. My mother is saying that the secondhand-furniture dealer is coming around the next morning to collect the things she isn't going to send on the bus or carry with her in the car. The table and chairs, TV, sofa, and bed are going with the dealer. But he's told her he doesn't have any use for the card table, so my mother is going to throw it out unless we want it.

"We'll take it," I say. Jill looks over. She starts to say something but changes her mind.

I will drive the boxes to the Greyhound station the next afternoon and start them on the way to California. My mother will spend the last night with us, as arranged. And then, early the next morning, two days from now, she'll be on her way.

She continues to talk. She talks on and on as she describes the trip she is about to make. She'll drive until four o'clock in the afternoon and then take a motel room for the night. She figures to make Eugene by dark. Eugene is a nice town – she stayed there once before, on the way up here. When she leaves the motel, she'll leave at sunrise and should, if God is looking out for her, be in California that afternoon. And God *is* looking out for her, she knows he is. How else explain her being kept around on the face of the earth? He has a plan for her. She's been praying a lot lately. She's been praying for me, too.

"Why are you praying for him?" Jill wants to know.

"Because I feel like it. Because he's my son," my mother says. "Is there anything the matter with that? Don't we all need praying for sometimes? Maybe some people don't. I don't know. What do I know any more?" She brings a hand to her forehead and rearranges some hair that's come loose from a pin.

The mower sputters off, and pretty soon we see Larry go around the house pulling the hose. He sets the hose out and then goes slowly back around the house to turn the water on. The sprinkler begins to turn.

My mother starts listing the ways she imagines Larry has wronged her since she's been in the house. But now I'm not listening, either. I am thinking how she is about to go down the highway again, and nobody can reason with her or do anything to stop her. What can I do? I can't tie her up, or commit her, though it may come to that eventually. I worry for her, and she is a heartache to me. She is all the family I have left. I'm sorry she didn't like it here and wants to leave. But I'm never going back to California. And when that's clear to me I understand something else, too. I understand that after she leaves I'm probably never going to see her again.

I look over at my mother. She stops talking. Jill raises her eyes. Both of them look at me.

"What is it, honey?" my mother says.

"What's wrong?" Jill says.

I lean forward in the chair and cover my face with my hands. I sit like that for a minute, feeling bad and stupid for doing it. But I can't help it. And the woman who brought me into this life, and this other woman I picked up with less than a year ago, they exclaim together and rise and come over to where I sit with my head in my hands like a fool. I don't open my eyes. I listen to the sprinkler whipping the grass.

"What's wrong? What's the matter?" they say.

"It's OK," I say. And in a minute it is. I open my eyes and bring my head up. I reach for a cigarette.

"See what I mean?" Jill says. "You're driving him crazy. He's going crazy with worry over you." She is on one side of my chair, and my mother is on the other side. They could tear me apart in no time at all.

"I wish I could die and get out of everyone's way," my mother says quietly. "So help me Hannah, I can't take much more of this."

"How about some more coffee?" I say. "Maybe we ought to catch the news," I say. "Then I guess Jill and I better head for home."

Two days later, early in the morning, I say goodbye to my mother for what may be the last time. I've let Jill sleep. It won't hurt if she's late to work for a change. The dogs can wait for their baths and trimmings and such. My mother holds my arm as I walk her down the steps to the driveway and open the car door for her. She is wearing white slacks and a white blouse and white sandals. Her hair is pulled back and tied with a scarf. That's white, too. It's going to be a nice day, and the sky is clear and already blue.

On the front seat of the car I see maps and a thermos of coffee. My mother looks at these things as if she can't recall having come outside with them just a few minutes ago. She turns to me then and says, "Let me hug you once more. Let me love your neck. I know I won't see you for a long time." She puts an arm around my neck, draws me to her, and then begins to cry. But she stops almost at once and steps back, pushing the heel of her hand against her eyes. "I said I wouldn't do that, and I won't. But let me get a last look at you anyway. I'll miss you, honey," she says. "I'm just going to have to live through this. I've already lived through things

I didn't think were possible. But I'll live through this, too, I guess." She gets into the car, starts it, and runs the engine for a minute. She rolls her window down.

"I'm going to miss you," I say. And I *am* going to miss her. She's my mother, after all, and why shouldn't I miss her? But, God forgive me, I'm glad, too, that it's finally time and that she is leaving.

"Goodbye," she says. "Tell Jill thanks for supper last night. Tell her I said goodbye."

"I will," I say. I stand there wanting to say something else. But I don't know what. We keep looking at each other, trying to smile and reassure each other. Then something comes into her eyes, and I believe she is thinking about the highway and how far she is going to have to drive that day. She takes her eyes off me and looks down the road. Then she rolls her window up, puts the car into gear, and drives to the intersection, where she has to wait for the light to change. When I see she's made it into traffic and headed towards the highway, I go back in the house and drink some coffee. I feel sad for a while, and then the sadness goes away and I start thinking about other things.

A few nights later my mother calls to say she is in her new place. She is busy fixing it up, the way she does when she has a new place. She tells me I'll be happy to know she likes it just fine to be back in sunny California. But she says there's something in the air where she is living, maybe it's pollen, that is causing her to sneeze a lot. And the traffic is heavier than she remembers from before. She doesn't recall there being so much traffic in her neighbourhood. Naturally, everyone still drives like crazy down there. "California drivers," she says. "What else can you expect?" She says it's hot for this time of the year. She doesn't think the air-conditioning unit in her apartment is working right. I tell her she should talk to the manager. "She's never around when you need her," my mother says. She hopes she hasn't made a mistake in moving back to California. She waits before she says anything else.

I'm standing at the window with the phone pressed to my ear, looking out at the lights from town and at the lighted houses closer by. Jill is at the table with the catalogue, listening.

"Are you still there?" my mother asks. "I wish you'd say something."

I don't know why, but it's then I recall the affectionate name my dad used sometimes when he was talking nice to my mother – those times, that is, when he wasn't drunk. It was a long time ago, and I was a kid, but always, hearing it, I felt better, less afraid, more hopeful about the future. *"Dear,"* he'd say. He called her "dear" sometimes – a sweet name. "Dear," he'd say, "if you're going to the store, will you bring me some cigarettes?" Or "Dear, is your cold any better?" "Dear, where is my coffee cup?"

The word issues from my lips before I can think what else I want to say to go along with it. "Dear." I say it again. I call her "dear." "Dear, try not to be afraid," I say. I tell my mother I love her and I'll write to her, yes. Then I say goodbye, and I hang up.

For a while I don't move from the window. I keep standing there, looking out at the lighted houses in our neighbourhood. As I watch, a car turns off the road and pulls into a driveway. The porch light goes on. The door to the house opens and someone comes out on the porch and stands there waiting.

Jill turns the pages of her catalogue, and then she stops turning them. "This is what we want," she says. "This is more like what I had in mind. Look at this, will you." But I don't look. I don't care five cents for curtains. "What is it you see out there, honey?" Jill says. "Tell me."

What's there to tell? The people over there embrace for a minute, and then they go inside the house together. They leave the light burning. Then they remember, and it goes out.

Whoever Was Using This Bed

The call comes in the middle of the night, three in the morning, and it nearly scares us to death.

"Answer it, answer it!" my wife cries. "My God, who is it? Answer it!"

I can't find the light, but I get to the other room, where the phone is, and pick it up after the fourth ring.

"Is Bud there?" this woman says, very drunk.

"Jesus, you have the wrong number," I say, and hang up.

I turn the light on, and go into the bathroom, and that's when I hear the phone start again.

"Answer that!" my wife screams from the bedroom. "What in God's name do they want, Jack? I can't take any more."

I hurry out of the bathroom and pick up the phone.

"Bud?" the woman says. "What are you doing, Bud?"

I say, "Look here. You have a wrong number. Don't ever call this number again."

"I have to talk to Bud," she says.

I hang up, wait until it rings again, and then I take the receiver and lay it on the table beside the phone. But I hear the woman's voice say, "Bud, talk to me, please." I leave the receiver on its side on the table, turn off the light, and close the door to the room.

In the bedroom I find the lamp on and my wife, Iris, sitting against the headboard with her knees drawn up under the covers. She has a pillow behind her back, and she's more on my side than her own side. The covers are up around her shoulders. The blankets and the sheet have been pulled out from the front of the bed. If we want to go back to sleep – I want to go back to sleep, anyway – we may have to start from scratch and do this bed over again.

"What the hell was that all about?" Iris says. "We should have unplugged the phone. I guess we forgot. Try forgetting one night to unplug the phone and see what happens. I don't believe it."

After Iris and I started living together, my former wife, or else one of my kids, used to call up when we were asleep and want to harangue us. They kept doing it even after Iris and I were married. So we started unplugging our phone before we went to bed. We unplugged the phone every night of the year, just about. It was a habit. This time I slipped up, that's all.

"Some woman wanting *Bud*," I say. I'm standing there in my pyjamas, wanting to get into bed, but I can't. "She was drunk. Move over, honey. I took the phone off the hook."

"She can't call again?"

"No," I say. "Why don't you move over a little and give me some of those covers?"

She takes her pillow and puts it on the far side of the bed, against the headboard, scoots over, and then she leans back once more. She doesn't look sleepy. She looks fully awake. I get into bed and take some covers. But the covers don't feel right. I don't have any sheet; all I have is blanket. I look down and see my feet sticking out. I turn on to my side, facing her, and bring my legs up so that my feet are under the blanket. We should make up the bed again. I ought to suggest that. But I'm thinking, too, that if we kill the light now, this minute, we might be able to go right back to sleep.

"How about you turning off your light, honey?" I say, as nice as I can.

"Let's have a cigarette first," she says. "Then we'll go to sleep. Get us the cigarettes and the ashtray, why don't you? We'll have a cigarette."

"Let's go to sleep," I say. "Look at what time it is." The clock radio is right there beside the bed. Anyone can see it says three-thirty.

"Come on," Iris says. "I need a cigarette after all that."

I get out of bed for the cigarettes and ashtray. I have to go into the room where the phone is, but I don't touch the phone. I don't even want to look at the phone, but I do, of course. The receiver is still on its side on the table.

I crawl back in bed and put the ashtray on the quilt between us. I light a cigarette, give it to her, and then light one for myself.

She tries to remember the dream she was having when the phone rang. "I can just remember it, but I can't remember exactly. Something about, about — no I don't know what it was about now. I can't be sure. I can't remember it," she says finally. "God damn that woman and her phone call. *'Bud'*," she says. "I'd like to punch her." She puts out her cigarette and immediately lights another, blows smoke, and lets her eyes take in the chest of drawers and the window curtains. Her hair is undone and around her shoulders. She uses the ashtray and then stares over the foot of the bed, trying to remember.

But, really, I don't care what she's dreamed. I want to go back to sleep is all. I finish my cigarette and put it out and wait for her to finish. I lie still and don't say anything.

Iris is like my former wife in that when she sleeps she sometimes has violent dreams. She thrashes around in bed during the night and wakes in the morning drenched with sweat, the nightgown sticking to her body. And, like my former wife, she wants to tell me her dreams in great detail and speculate as to what this stands for or that portends. My former wife used to kick the covers off in the night and cry out in her sleep, as if someone were laying hands on her. Once, in a particularly violent dream, she hit me on the ear with her fist. I was in a dreamless sleep, but I struck out in the dark and hit her on the forehead. Then we began yelling. We both yelled and yelled. We'd hurt each other, but we were mainly scared. We had no idea what had happened until I turned the lamp on; then we sorted it out. Afterwards, we joked about it – fistfighting in our sleep. But when so much else began to happen that was far more serious we tended to forget about that night. We never mentioned it again, even when we teased each other.

Once I woke up in the night to hear Iris grinding her teeth in her sleep. It was such a peculiar thing to have going on right next to my ear that it woke me up. I gave her a little shake, and she stopped. The next morning she told me she'd had a very bad dream, but that's all she'd tell me about it. I didn't press her for details. I guess I really didn't want to know what could have been so bad that she didn't want to say. When I told her she'd been grinding her teeth in her sleep, she frowned and said she was going to have to do something about that. The next night she brought home something called a Niteguard – something she was supposed to wear in her mouth while she slept. She had to do something, she said. She couldn't afford to keep grinding her teeth; pretty soon she wouldn't have any. So she wore this protective device in her mouth for a week or so, and then she stopped wearing it. She said it was uncomfortable and, anyway, it was not very cosmetic. Who'd want to kiss a woman wearing a thing like that in her mouth, she said. She had something there, of course.

Another time I woke up because she was stroking my face and calling me Earl. I took her hand and squeezed her fingers. "What is it?" I said. "What is it, sweetheart?" But instead of answering she simply squeezed back, sighed, and then lay still again. The next morning, when I asked her what she'd dreamed the night before, she claimed not to have had any dreams.

"So who's Earl?" I said. "Who is this Earl you were talking about in your sleep?" She blushed and said she didn't know anybody named Earl and never had.

The lamp is still on and, because I don't know what else to think about, I think about that phone being off the hook. I ought to hang it up and unplug the cord. Then we have to think about sleep.

"I'll go take care of that phone," I say. "Then let's go to sleep."

Iris uses the ashtray and says, "Make sure it's unplugged this time."

I get up again and go to the other room, open the door, and turn on the light. The receiver is still on its side on the table. I bring it to my ear, expecting to hear the dial tone. But I don't hear anything, not even the tone.

On an impulse, I say something. "Hello," I say.

"Oh, Bud, it's you," the woman says.

I hang up the phone and bend over and unplug it from the wall before it can ring again. This is a new one on me. This deal is a mystery, this woman and her Bud person. I don't know how to tell Iris about this new development, because it'll just lead to more discussion and further speculation. I decide not to say anything for now. Maybe I'll say something over breakfast.

Back in the bedroom I see she is smoking another cigarette. I see, too, that it's nearly four in the morning. I'm starting to worry. When it's four o'clock it'll soon be five o'clock, and then it will be six, then six-thirty, then time to get up for work. I lie back down, close my eyes, and decide I'll count to sixty, slowly, before I say anything else about the light.

"I'm starting to remember," Iris says. "It's coming back to me. You want to hear it, Jack?"

I stop counting, open my eyes, sit up. The bedroom is filled with smoke. I light one up, too. Why not? The hell with it.

She says, "There was a party going on in my dream."

"Where was I when this was going on?" Usually, for whatever reason, I don't figure in her dreams. It irritates me a little, but I don't let on. My feet are uncovered again. I pull them under the covers, raise myself up on my elbow, and use the ashtray. "Is this another dream that I'm not in? It's OK, if that's the case." I pull on the cigarette, hold the smoke, let it out.

"Honey, you weren't in the dream," Iris says. "I'm sorry, but you weren't. You weren't anywhere around. I *missed* you, though. I did miss you, I'm sure of it. It was like I knew you were somewhere nearby, but you weren't there where I needed you. You know how I get into those anxiety states sometimes? If we go someplace together where there's a group of people and we get separated and I can't find you? It was a little like that. You were there, I think, but I couldn't find you."

"Go ahead and tell me about the dream," I say.

She rearranges the covers around her waist and legs and reaches for a cigarette. I hold the lighter for her. Then she goes on to describe this party where all that was being served was beer. "I don't even like beer," she says. But she drank a large quantity anyway, and just when she went to leave – to go home, she says – this little dog took hold of the hem of her dress and made her stay.

She laughs, and I laugh right along with her, even though, when I look at the clock, I see the hands are close to saying four-thirty.

There was some kind of music being played in her dream – a piano, maybe, or else it was an accordion, who knows? Dreams are that way sometimes, she says. Anyway, she vaguely remembers her former husband putting in an appearance. He might have been the one serving the beer. People were drinking beer from a keg, using plastic cups. She thought she might even have danced with him.

"Why are you telling me this?"

She says, "It was a dream, honey."

"I don't think I like it, knowing you're supposed to be here beside me all night but instead you're dreaming about strange dogs, parties, and ex-husbands. I don't like you dancing with him. What the hell is this? What if I told you I dreamed I danced the night away with Carol? Would you like it?"

"It's just a dream, right?" she says. "Don't get weird on me. I won't say any more. I see I can't. I can see it isn't a good idea." She brings her fingers to her lips slowly, the way she does sometimes when she's thinking. Her face shows how hard she's concentrating; little lines appear on her forehead. "I'm sorry that you weren't in the dream. But if I told you otherwise I'd be lying to you, right?"

I nod. I touch her arm to show her it's OK. I don't really mind. And I don't, I guess. "What happened then, honey? Finish telling the dream," I say. "And maybe we can go to sleep then." I guess I wanted to know the next thing. The last I'd heard, she'd been dancing with Jerry. If there was more, I needed to hear it.

She plumps up the pillow behind her back and says, "That's all I can remember. I can't remember any more about it. That was when the goddamn phone rang."

"Bud," I say. I can see smoke drifting in the light under the lamp, and smoke hangs in the air in the room. "Maybe we should open a window," I say.

"That's a good idea," she says. "Let some of this smoke out. It can't be any good for us."

"Hell, no, it isn't," I say.

I get up again and go to the window and raise it a few inches. I can feel the cool air that comes in and from a distance

I hear a truck gearing down as it starts up the grade that will take it to the pass and on over into the next state.

"I guess pretty soon we're going to be the last smokers left in America," she says. "Seriously, we should think about quitting." She says this as she puts her cigarette out and reaches for the pack next to the ashtray.

"It's open season on smokers," I say.

I get back in the bed. The covers are turned every which way, and it's five o'clock in the morning. I don't think we're going to sleep any more tonight. But so what if we don't? Is there a law on the books? Is something bad going to happen to us if we don't?

She takes some of her hair between her fingers. Then she pushes it behind her ear, looks at me, and says, "Lately I've been feeling this vein in my forehead. It *pulses* sometimes. It throbs. Do you know what I'm talking about? I don't know if you've ever had anything like that. I hate to think about it, but probably one of these days, I'll have a stroke or something. Isn't that how they happen? A vein in your head bursts? That's probably what'll happen to me, eventually. My mother, my grandmother, and one of my aunts died of stroke. There's a history of stroke in my family. It can run in the family, you know. It's hereditary, just like heart disease, or being too fat, or whatever. Anyway," she says, "something's going to happen to me someday, right? So maybe that's what it'll be – a stroke. Maybe that's how I'll go. That's what it feels like it could be the beginning of. First it pulses a little, like it wants my attention, and then it starts to throb. Throb, throb, throb. It scares me silly," she says. "I want us to give up these goddamn cigarettes before it's too late." She looks at what's left of her cigarette, mashes it into the ashtray, and tries to fan the smoke away.

I'm on my back, studying the ceiling, thinking that this is the kind of talk that could only take place at five in the morning. I feel I ought to say something. "I get winded easy,"

I say. "I found myself out of breath when I ran in there to answer the phone."

"That could have been because of anxiety," Iris says. "Who needs it, anyway! The *idea* of somebody calling at this hour! I could tear that woman limb from limb."

I pull myself up in the bed and lean back against the headboard. I put the pillow behind my back and try to get comfortable, same as Iris. "I'll tell you something I haven't told you," I say. "Once in a while my heart palpitates. It's like it goes crazy." She's watching me closely, listening for whatever it is I'm going to say next. "Sometimes it feels like it's going to jump out of my chest. I don't know what the hell causes it."

"Why didn't you tell me?" she says. She takes my hand and holds it. She squeezes my hand. "You never said anything, honey. Listen, I don't know what I'd *do* if something ever happened to you. I'd fold up. How often does it happen? That's scary, you know." She's still holding my hand. But her fingers slide to my wrist, where my pulse is. She goes on holding my wrist like this.

"I never told you because I didn't want to scare you," I say. "But it happens sometimes. It happened as recently as a week ago. I don't have to be doing anything in particular when it happens, either. I can be sitting in a chair with the paper. Or else driving the car, or pushing a grocery basket. It doesn't matter if I'm exerting myself or not. It just starts – boom, boom, boom. Like that. I'm surprised people can't hear it. It's that loud, I think. *I* can hear it, anyway, and I don't mind telling you it scares me," I say. "So if emphysema doesn't get me, or lung cancer, or maybe a stroke like what you're talking about, then it's going to be a heart attack probably."

I reach for the cigarettes. I give her one. We're through with sleep for the night. Did we sleep? For a minute, I can't remember.

"Who knows what we'll die of?" Iris says. "It could be anything. If we live long enough, maybe it'll be kidney failure, or something like that. A friend of mine at work, her father just died of kidney failure. That's what can happen to you sometimes if you're lucky enough to get really old. When your kidneys fail, the body starts filling up with uric acid then. You finally turn a whole different colour before you die."

"Great. That sounds wonderful," I say. "Maybe we should get off this subject. How'd we get on to this stuff, anyway?"

She doesn't answer. She leans forward, away from her pillow, arms clasping her legs. She closes her eyes and lays her head on her knees. Then she begins to rock back and forth, slowly. It's as if she were listening to music. But there isn't any music. None that I can hear, anyway.

"You know what I'd like?" she says. She stops moving, opens her eyes, and tilts her head at me. Then she grins, so I'll know she's all right.

"What would you like, honey?" I've got my leg hooked over her leg, at the ankle.

She says, "I'd like some coffee, that's what. I could go for a nice strong cup of black coffee. We're awake, aren't we? Who's going back to sleep? Let's have some coffee."

"We drink too much coffee," I say. "All that coffee isn't good for us, either. I'm not saying we shouldn't have any, I'm just saying we drink too much of it. It's just an observation," I add. "Actually, I could drink some coffee myself."

"Good," she says.

But neither of us makes a move.

She shakes out her hair and then lights another cigarette. Smoke drifts slowly in the room. Some of it drifts towards the open window. A little rain begins to fall on the patio outside the window. The alarm comes on, and I reach over and shut it off. Then I take the pillow and put it under my head again. I lie back and stare at the ceiling some more. "What happened to that bright idea we had about a girl who could bring us our coffee in bed?" I say.

"I wish *somebody* would bring us coffee," she says. "A girl or a boy, one or the other. I could really go for some coffee right now."

She moves the ashtray to the nightstand, and I think she's going to get up. Somebody has to get up and start the coffee and put a can of frozen juice in the blender. One of us has to make a move. But what she does instead is slide down in the bed until she's sitting somewhere in the middle. The covers are all over the place. She picks at something on the quilt, and then rubs her palm across whatever it is before she looks up. "Did you see in the paper where that guy took a shotgun into an intensive-care unit and made the nurses take his father off the life-support machine? Did you read about that?" Iris says.

"I saw something about it on the news," I say. "But mostly they were talking about this nurse who unplugged six or eight people from their machines. At this point they don't know exactly how many she unplugged. She started off by unplugging her mother, and then she went on from there. It was like a spree, I guess. She said she thought she was doing everybody a favour. She said she hoped somebody'd do it for *her*, if they cared about her."

Iris decides to move on down to the foot of the bed. She positions herself so that she is facing me. Her legs are still under the covers. She puts her legs between my legs and says, "What about that quadriplegic woman on the news who says she wants to die, wants to starve herself to death? Now she's suing her doctor and the hospital because they insist on force-feeding her to keep her alive. Can you believe it? It's insane. They strap her down three times a day so they can run this tube into her throat. They feed her breakfast, lunch, and dinner that way. And they keep her plugged into this machine, too, because her lungs don't want to work on their own. It said in the paper that she's *begging* them to unplug her, or else to just let her starve to death. She's having to plead with them to let her die, but they won't listen. She said she started out wanting to die with some dignity. Now she's just mad and looking to sue everybody. Isn't that amazing? Isn't that one for the books?" she says. "I have these headaches sometimes," she says. "Maybe it has something to do with the vein. Maybe not. Maybe they're not related. But I don't tell you when my head hurts, because I don't want to worry you."

"What are you talking about?" I say. "Look at me. Iris? I have a right to know. I'm your husband, in case you've forgotten. If something's wrong with you, I should know about it."

"But what could you *do*? You'd just worry." She bumps my leg with her leg, then bumps it again. "Right? You'd tell me to take some aspirin. I know you."

I look towards the window, where it's beginning to get light. I can feel a damp breeze from the window. It's stopped raining now, but it's one of those mornings where it could begin to pour. I look at her again. "To tell you the truth, Iris, I get sharp pains in my side from time to time." But the moment I say the words I'm sorry. She'll be concerned, and want to talk about it. We ought to be thinking of showers; we should be sitting down to breakfast.

"Which side?" she says.

"Right side."

"It could be your appendix," she says. "Something fairly simple like that."

I shrug. "Who knows? I don't know. All I know is it happens. Every so often, for just a minute or two, I feel something sharp down there. Very sharp. At first I thought it might be a pulled muscle. Which side's your gall bladder on, by the way? Is it the left or right side? Maybe it's my gall bladder. Or else maybe a gall*stone*, whatever the hell that is."

"It's not really a stone," she says. "A gallstone is like a little granule, or something like that. It's about as big as the tip of a pencil. No, wait, that might be a *kidney* stone I'm talking about. I guess I don't know anything about it." She shakes her head.

"What's the difference between kidney stone and gall-stone?" I say. "Christ, we don't even know which side of the body they're on. You don't know, and I don't know. That's how much we know together. A total of nothing. But I read somewhere that you can pass a kidney stone, if that's what this is, and usually it won't kill you. Painful, yes. I don't know what they say about a gallstone."

"I like that 'usually'," she says.

"I know," I say. "Listen, we'd better get up. It's getting really late. It's seven o'clock."

"I know," she says. "OK." But she continues to sit there. Then she says, "My grandma had arthritis so bad towards the end she couldn't get around by herself, or even move her fingers. She had to sit in a chair and wear these mittens all day. Finally, she couldn't even hold a cup of cocoa. That's how bad her arthritis was. Then she had her stroke. And my *grandpa*," she says. "He went into a nursing home not long after grandma died. It was either that or else somebody had to come in and be with him around the clock, and nobody could do that. Nobody had the money for twenty-four-hour-a-day care, either. So he goes into the nursing home. But he began to deteriorate fast in there. One time, after he'd been in that place for a while, my mom went to visit him and then she came home and said something. I'll never forget what she said." She looks at me as if I'm never going to forget it, either. And I'm not. "She said, 'My dad doesn't recognize me any more. He doesn't even know who I am. My dad has become a vegetable.' That was my mom who said that."

She leans over and covers her face with her hands and begins to cry. I move down there to the foot of the bed and sit beside her. I take her hand and hold it in my lap. I put my arm around her. We're sitting together looking at the headboard and at the nightstand. The clock's there, too, and beside the clock a few magazines and a paperback. We're sitting on the part of the bed where we keep our feet when we sleep. It looks like whoever was using this bed left in a hurry. I know I won't ever look at this bed again without remembering it like this. We're into something now, but I don't know what, exactly.

"I don't want anything like that to ever happen to me," she says. "Or to you, either." She wipes her face with a corner of the blanket and takes a deep breath, which comes out as a sob. "I'm sorry. I just can't help it," she says.

"It won't happen to us. It won't," I say. "Don't worry about any of it, OK? We're fine, Iris, and we're going to stay fine. In any case, that time's a long time off. Hey, I love you. We love each other, don't we? That's the important thing. That's what counts. Don't worry, honey."

"I want you to promise me something," she says. She takes her hand back. She moves my arm away from her shoulder. "I want you to promise me you'll pull the plug on me, if and when it's ever necessary. If it ever comes to that, I mean. Do you hear what I'm saying? I'm serious about this, Jack. I want you to pull the plug on me if you ever have to. Will you promise?"

I don't say anything right away. What am I supposed to say? They haven't written the book on this one yet. I need a minute to think. I know it won't cost me anything to tell her I'll do whatever she wants. It's just words, right? Words are easy. But there's more to it than this; she wants an honest response from me. And I don't know what I feel about it yet. I shouldn't be hasty. I can't say something without thinking about what I'm saying, about consequences, about what she's going to feel when I say it – whatever it is I say.

I'm still thinking about it when she says, "What about you?"

"What about me what?"

"Do you want to be unplugged if it comes to that? God forbid it ever does, of course," she says. "But I should have some kind of idea, you know – some word from you now – about what you want me to do if worst comes to worst." She's looking at me closely, waiting for me to say. She wants something she can file away to use later, if and when she ever has to. Sure. OK. Easy enough for me to say, *Unplug me, honey, if you think it's for the best.* But I need to consider this a little more. I haven't even said yet what I will or won't do for *her.* Now I have to think about me and *my* situation. I don't feel I should jump into this. This is nuts. *We're* nuts. But I realize that whatever I say now might come back to me sometime. It's important. This is a life-and-death thing we're talking about here.

She hasn't moved. She's still waiting for her answer. And I can see we're not going anywhere this morning until she has an answer. I think about it some more, and then I say what I mean. "No. Don't unplug me. I don't want to be unplugged. Leave me hooked up just as long as possible. Who's going to object? Are you going to object? Will I be offending anybody? As long as people can stand the sight of me, just so long as they don't start howling, don't unplug anything. Let me keep going, OK? Right to the bitter end. Invite my friends in to say goodbye. Don't do anything rash."

"Be serious," she says. "This is a very serious matter we're discussing."

"I am serious. Don't unplug me. It's as simple as that."

She nods. "OK, then. I promise you I won't." She hugs

me. She holds me tight for a minute. Then she lets go. She looks at the clock radio and says, "Jesus, we better get moving."

So we get out of bed and start getting dressed. In some ways it's just like any other morning, except we do things faster. We drink coffee and juice and we eat English muffins. We remark on the weather, which is overcast and blustery. We don't talk any more about plugs, or about sickness and hospitals and stuff like that. I kiss her and leave her on the front porch with her umbrella open, waiting for her ride to work. Then I hurry to my car and get in. In a minute, after I've run the motor, I wave and drive off.

But during the day, at work, I think about some of those things we talked about this morning. I can't help it. For one thing, I'm bone-tired from lack of sleep. I feel vulnerable and prey to any random, gruesome thought. Once, when nobody is around, I put my head on my desk and think I might catch a few minutes' sleep. But when I close my eyes I find myself thinking about it again. In my mind I can see a hospital bed. That's all – just a hospital bed. The bed's in a room, I guess. Then I see an oxygen tent over the bed, and beside the bed some of those screens and some big monitors – the kind they have in movies. I open my eyes and sit up in my chair and light a cigarette. I drink some coffee while I smoke the cigarette. Then I look at the time and get back to work.

At five o'clock, I'm so tired it's all I can do to drive home. It's raining, and I have to be careful driving. Very careful. There's been an accident, too. Someone has rear-ended someone else at a traffic light, but I don't think anyone has been hurt. The cars are still out in the road, and people are standing around in the rain, talking. Still, traffic moves slowly; the police have set out flares.

When I see my wife, I say, "God, what a day. I'm whipped.

How are you doing?" We kiss each other. I take off my coat and hang it up. I take the drink Iris gives me. Then, because it's been on my mind, and because I want to clear the deck, so to speak, I say, "All right, if it's what you want to hear, I'll pull the plug for you. If that's what you want me to do, I'll do it. If it will make you happy, here and now, to hear me say so, I'll say it. I'll do it for you. I'll pull the plug, or have it pulled, if I ever think it's necessary. But what I said about my plug still stands. Now I don't want to have to think about this stuff ever again. I don't even want to have to *talk* about it again. I think we've said all there is to say on the subject. We've exhausted every angle. *I'm* exhausted."

Iris grins. "OK," she says. "At least I know now, anyway. I didn't before. Maybe I'm crazy, but I feel better somehow, if you want to know. I don't want to think about it any more, either. But I'm glad we talked it over. I'll never bring it up again, either, and that's a promise."

She takes my drink and puts it on the table, next to the phone. She puts her arms around me and holds me and lets her head rest on my shoulder. But here's the thing. What I've just said to her, what I've been thinking about off and on all day, well, I feel as if I've crossed some kind of invisible line. I feel as if I've come to a place I never thought I'd have to come to. And I don't know how I got here. It's a strange place. It's a place where a little harmless dreaming and then some sleepy, early-morning talk has led me into considerations of death and annihilation.

The phone rings. We let go of each other, and I reach to answer it. "Hello," I say.

"Hello, there," the woman says back.

It's the same woman who called this morning, but she isn't drunk now. At least, I don't think she is; she doesn't sound drunk. She is speaking quietly, reasonably, and she is asking me if I can put her in touch with Bud Roberts. She apologizes.

She hates to trouble me, she says, but this is an urgent matter. She's sorry for any trouble she might be giving.

While she talks, I fumble with my cigarettes. I put one in my mouth and use the lighter. Then it's my turn to talk. This is what I say to her: "Bud Roberts doesn't live here. He is not at this number, and I don't expect he ever will be. I will never, never lay eyes on this man you're talking about. Please don't ever call here again. Just don't, OK? Do you hear me? If you're not careful, I'll wring your neck for you."

"The *gall* of that woman," Iris says.

My hands are shaking. I think my voice is doing things. But while I'm trying to tell all this to the woman, while I'm trying to make myself understood, my wife moves quickly and bends over, and that's it. The line goes dead, and I can't hear anything.

Intimacy

I have some business out west anyway, so I stop off in this little town where my former wife lives. We haven't seen each other in four years. But from time to time, when something of mine appeared, or was written about me in the magazines or papers – a profile or an interview – I sent her these things. I don't know what I had in mind except I thought she might be interested. In any case, she never responded.

It is nine in the morning, I haven't called, and it's true I don't know what I am going to find.

But she lets me in. She doesn't seem surprised. We don't shake hands, much less kiss each other. She takes me into the living room. As soon as I sit down she brings me some coffee. Then she comes out with what's on her mind. She says I've caused her anguish, made her feel exposed and humiliated.

Make no mistake, I feel I'm home.

She says, But then you were into betrayal early. You always felt comfortable with betrayal. No, she says, that's not true. Not in the beginning, at any rate. You were different then. But I guess I was different too. Everything was different, she says. No, it was after you turned thirty-five, or thirty-six, whenever it was, around in there anyway, your mid-thirties somewhere, then you started in. You really started in. You turned on me. You did it up pretty then. You must be proud of yourself.

She says, Sometimes I could scream.

45

She says she wishes I'd forget about the hard times, the bad times, when I talk about back then. Spend some time on the good times, she says. Weren't there some good times? She wishes I'd get off that other subject. She's bored with it. Sick of hearing about it. Your private hobbyhorse, she says. What's done is done and water under the bridge, she says. A tragedy, yes. God knows it was a tragedy and then some. But why keep it going? Don't you ever get tired of dredging up that old business?

She says, Let go of the past, for Christ's sake. Those old hurts. You must have some other arrows in your quiver, she says.

She says, You know something? I think you're sick. I think you're crazy as a bedbug. Hey, you don't believe the things they're saying about you, do you? Don't believe them for a minute, she says. Listen, I could tell them a thing or two. Let them talk to me about it, if they want to hear a story.

She says, Are you listening to me?

I'm listening, I say. I'm all ears, I say.

She says, I've really had a bellyful of it, buster! Who asked you here today anyway? I sure as hell didn't. You just show up and walk in. What the hell do you want from me? Blood? You want more blood? I thought you had your fill by now.

She says, Think of me as dead. I want to be left in peace now. That's all I want any more is to be left in peace and forgotten about. Hey, I'm forty-five years old, she says. Forty-five going on fifty-five, or sixty-five. Lay off, will you.

She says, Why don't you wipe the blackboard clean and see what you have left after that? Why don't you start with a clean slate? See how far that gets you, she says.

She has to laugh at this. I laugh too, but it's nerves.

She says, You know something? I had my chance once, but I let it go. I just let it go. I don't guess I ever told you. But now look at me. Look! Take a good look while you're at it. You threw me away, you son of a bitch.

46

She says, I was younger then and a better person. Maybe you were too, she says. A better person, I mean. You had to be. You were better then or I wouldn't have had anything to do with you.

She says, I loved you so much once. I loved you to the point of distraction. I did. More than anything in the whole wide world. Imagine that. What a laugh that is now. Can you imagine it? We were so *intimate* once upon a time I can't believe it now. I think that's the strangest thing of all now. The memory of being that intimate with somebody. We were so intimate I could puke. I can't imagine ever being that intimate with somebody else. I haven't been.

She says, Frankly, and I mean this, I want to be kept out of it from here on out. Who do you think you are anyway? You think you're God or somebody? You're not fit to lick God's boots, or anybody else's for that matter. Mister, you've been hanging out with the wrong people. But what do I know? I don't even know what I know any longer. I know I don't like what you've been dishing out. I know that much. You know what I'm talking about, don't you? Am I right?

Right, I say. Right as rain.

She says, You'll agree to anything, won't you? You give in too easy. You always did. You don't have any principles, not one. Anything to avoid a fuss. But that's neither here nor there.

She says, You remember that time I pulled the knife on you?

She says this as if in passing, as if it's not important.

Vaguely, I say. I must have deserved it, but I don't remember much about it. Go ahead, why don't you, and tell me about it.

She says, I'm beginning to understand something now. I think I know why you're here. Yes. I know why you're here, even if you don't. But you're a slyboots. You know why you're here. You're on a fishing expedition. You're hunting for *material*. Am I getting warm? Am I right?

Tell me about the knife, I say.

She says, If you want to know, I'm real sorry I didn't use that knife. I am. I really and truly am. I've thought and thought about it, and I'm sorry I didn't use it. I had the chance. But I hesitated. I hesitated and was lost, as somebody or other said. But I should have used it, the hell with everything and everybody. I should have nicked your arm with it at least. At least that.

Well, you didn't, I say. I thought you were going to cut me with it, but you didn't. I took it away from you.

She says, You were always lucky. You took it away and then you slapped me. Still, I regret I didn't use that knife just a little bit. Even a little would have been something to remember me by.

I remember a lot, I say. I say that, then wish I hadn't.

She says, Amen, brother. That's the bone of contention here, if you hadn't noticed. That's the whole problem. But like I said, in my opinion you remember the wrong things. You remember the low, shameful things. That's why you got interested when I brought up the knife.

She says, I wonder if you ever have any regret. For whatever that's worth on the market these days. Not much, I guess. But you ought to be a specialist in it by now.

Regret, I say. It doesn't interest me much, to tell the truth. Regret is not a word I use very often. I guess I mainly don't have it. I admit I hold to the dark view of things. Sometimes, anyway. But regret? I don't think so.

She says, You're a real son of a bitch, did you know that? A ruthless, cold-hearted son of a bitch. Did anybody ever tell you that?

You did, I say. Plenty of times.

She says, I always speak the truth. Even when it hurts. You'll never catch me in a lie.

She says, My eyes were opened a long time ago, but by then it was too late. I had my chance but I let it slide through my fingers. I even thought for a while you'd come back. Why'd I think that anyway? I must have been out of my mind. I could cry my eyes out now, but I wouldn't give you that satisfaction.

She says, You know what? I think if you were on fire right now, if you suddenly burst into flame this minute, I wouldn't throw a bucket of water on you.

She laughs at this. Then her face closes down again.

She says, Why in hell *are* you here? You want to hear some more? I could go on for days. I think I know why you turned up, but I want to hear it from you.

When I don't answer, when I just keep sitting there, she goes on.

She says, After that time, when you went away, nothing much mattered after that. Not the kids, not God, not anything. It was like I didn't know what hit me. It was like I had *stopped living*. My life had been going along, going along, and then it just stopped. It didn't just come to a stop, it screeched to a stop. I thought, If I'm not worth anything to him, well, I'm not worth anything to myself or anybody else either. That was the worst thing I felt. I thought my heart would break. What am I saying? It did break. Of course it broke. It broke, just like that. It's still broke, if you want to know. And so there you have it in a nutshell. My eggs in one basket, she says. A tisket, a tasket. All my rotten eggs in one basket.

She says, You found somebody else for yourself, didn't you? It didn't take long. And you're happy now. That's what they say about you anyway: "He's happy now." Hey, I read everything you send! You think I don't? Listen, I know your heart, mister. I always did. I knew it back then, and I know it now. I know your heart inside and out, and don't you ever forget it. Your heart is a jungle, a dark forest, it's a garbage pail, if you want to know. Let them talk to me if they want to ask somebody something. I know how you operate. Just let them come around here, and I'll give them an earful. I was there. I served, buddy boy. Then you held me up for display and ridicule in your so-called work. For any Tom or Harry to pity or pass judgement on. Ask me if I cared. Ask me if it embarrassed me. Go ahead, ask.

No, I say, I won't ask that. I don't want to get into that, I say.

Damn straight you don't! she says. And you know *why*, too!

She says, Honey, no offence, but sometimes I think I could shoot you and watch you kick.

She says, You can't look me in the eyes, can you?

She says, and this is exactly what she says, You can't even look me in the eyes when I'm talking to you.

So, OK, I look her in the eyes.

She says, Right. OK, she says. Now we're getting someplace, maybe. That's better. You can tell a lot about the person you're talking to from his eyes. Everybody knows that. But you know something else? There's nobody in this whole world who would tell you this, but I can tell you. I have the right. I *earned* that right, sonny. You have yourself confused with somebody else. And that's the pure truth of it. But what do I know? they'll say in a hundred years. They'll say, Who was she anyway?

She says, In any case, you sure as hell have *me* confused with somebody else. Hey, I don't even have the same name any more! Not the name I was born with, not the name I lived with you with, not even the name I had two years ago. What is this? What is this in hell all about anyway? Let me say something. I want to be left alone now. Please. That's not a crime.

She says, Don't you have someplace else you should be? Some plane to catch? Shouldn't you be somewhere far from here at this very minute?

No, I say. I say it again: No. No place, I say. I don't have any place I have to be.

And then I do something. I reach over and take the sleeve of her blouse between my thumb and forefinger. That's all. I just touch it that way, and then I just bring my hand back. She doesn't draw away. She doesn't move.

Then here's the thing I do next. I get down on my knees, a big guy like me, and I take the hem of her dress. What am I doing on the floor? I wish I could say. But I know it's where I ought to be, and I'm there on my knees holding on to the hem of her dress.

She is still for a minute. But in a minute she says, Hey, it's all right, stupid. You're so dumb, sometimes. Get up now. I'm telling you to get up. Listen, it's OK. I'm over it now. It took me a while to get over it. What do you think? Did you think it wouldn't? Then you walk in here and suddenly the whole cruddy business is back. I felt a need to ventilate. But you know, and I know, it's over and done with now.

She says, For the longest while, honey, I was inconsolable. *Inconsolable*, she says. Put that word in your little notebook. I can tell you from experience that's the saddest word in the English language. Anyway, I got over it finally. Time is a gentleman, a wise man said. Or else maybe a worn-out old woman, one or the other anyway.

She says, I have a life now. It's a different kind of life than yours, but I guess we don't need to compare. It's my life, and that's the important thing I have to realize as I get older. Don't feel *too* bad, anyway, she says. I mean, it's all right to feel a *little* bad, maybe. That won't hurt you, that's only to be expected after all. Even if you can't move yourself to regret.

She says, Now you have to get up and get out of here. My husband will be along pretty soon for his lunch. How would I explain this kind of thing?

It's crazy, but I'm still on my knees holding the hem of her dress. I won't let it go. I'm like a terrier, and it's like I'm stuck to the floor. It's like I can't move.

She says, Get up now. What is it? You still want something from me. What do you want? Want me to forgive you? Is that why you're doing this? That's it, isn't it? That's the reason you came all this way. The knife thing kind of perked you up, too. I think you'd forgotten about that. But you needed me to remind you. OK, I'll say something if you'll just go.

She says, I forgive you.

She says, Are you satisfied now? Is that better? Are you happy? He's happy now, she says.

But I'm still there, knees to the floor.

She says, Did you hear what I said? You have to go now. Hey, stupid. Honey, I said I forgive you. And I even reminded you about the knife thing. I can't think what else I can do now. You got it made in the shade, baby. Come *on* now, you have to get out of here. Get up. That's right. You're still a big guy, aren't you. Here's your hat, don't forget your hat. You never used to wear a hat. I never in my life saw you in a hat before.

She says, Listen to me now. Look at me. Listen carefully to what I'm going to tell you.

She moves closer. She's about three inches from my face. We haven't been this close in a long time. I take these little breaths that she can't hear, and I wait. I think my heart slows way down, I think.

She says, You just tell it like you have to, I guess, and forget the rest. Like always. You been doing that for so long now anyway it shouldn't be hard for you.

She says, There, I've done it. You're free, aren't you? At least you think you are anyway. Free at last. That's a joke, but don't laugh. Anyway, you feel better, don't you?

She walks with me down the hall.

She says, I can't imagine how I'd explain this if my husband was to walk in this very minute. But who really cares any more, right? In the final analysis, nobody gives a damn any more. Besides which, I think everything that can happen that way has already happened. His name is Fred, by the way. He's a decent guy and works hard for his living. He cares for me.

So she walks me to the front door, which has been standing open all this while. The door that was letting in light and fresh air this morning, and sounds off the street, all of which we had ignored. I look outside and, Jesus, there's this white moon hanging in the morning sky. I can't think when I've ever seen anything so remarkable. But I'm afraid to comment on it. I am. I don't know what might happen. I might break into tears even. I might not understand a word I'd say.

She says, Maybe you'll be back sometime, and maybe you won't. This'll wear off, you know. Pretty soon you'll start feeling bad again. Maybe it'll make a good story, she says. But I don't want to know about it if it does.

I say goodbye. She doesn't say anything more. She looks at her hands, and then she puts them into the pockets of her dress. She shakes her head. She goes back inside, and this time she closes the door.

I move off down the sidewalk. Some kids are tossing a football at the end of the street. But they aren't my kids, and they aren't her kids either. There are these leaves everywhere, even in the gutters. Piles of leaves wherever I look. They're falling off the limbs as I walk. I can't take a step without putting my shoe into leaves. Somebody ought to make an effort here. Somebody ought to get a rake and take care of this.

Menudo

I can't sleep, but when I'm sure my wife Vicky is asleep, I get up and look through our bedroom window, across the street, at Oliver and Amanda's house. Oliver has been gone for three days, but his wife Amanda is awake. She can't sleep either. It's four in the morning, and there's not a sound outside – no wind, no cars, no moon even – just Oliver and Amanda's place with the lights on, leaves heaped up under the front windows.

A couple of days ago, when I couldn't sit still, I raked our yard – Vicky's and mine. I gathered all the leaves into bags, tied off the tops, and put the bags alongside the kerb. I had an urge then to cross the street and rake over there, but I didn't follow through. It's my fault things are the way they are across the street.

I've only slept a few hours since Oliver left. Vicky saw me moping around the house, looking anxious, and decided to put two and two together. She's on her side of the bed now, scrunched on to about ten inches of mattress. She got into bed and tried to position herself so she wouldn't accidentally roll into me while she slept. She hasn't moved since she lay down, sobbed, and then dropped into sleep. She's exhausted. I'm exhausted too.

I've taken nearly all of Vicky's pills, but I still can't sleep. I'm keyed up. But maybe if I keep looking I'll catch a glimpse of Amanda moving around inside her house, or else find her peering from behind a curtain, trying to see what she can see over here.

What if I do see her? So what? What then?

Vicky says I'm crazy. She said worse things too last night. But who could blame her? I told her – I had to – but I didn't tell her it was Amanda. When Amanda's name came up, I insisted it wasn't her. Vicky suspects, but I wouldn't name names. I wouldn't say who, even though she kept pressing and then hit me a few times in the head.

"What's it matter *who*?" I said. "You've never met the woman," I lied. "You don't know her." That's when she started hitting me.

I feel *wired*. That's what my painter friend Alfredo used to call it when he talked about friends of his coming down off something. *Wired*. I'm wired.

This thing is nuts. I know it is, but I can't stop thinking about Amanda. Things are so bad just now I even find myself thinking about my first wife, Molly. I loved Molly, I thought, more than my own life.

I keep picturing Amanda in her pink nightgown, the one I like on her so much, along with her pink slippers. And I feel certain she's in the big leather chair right now, under the brass reading lamp. She's smoking cigarettes, one after the other. There are two ashtrays close at hand, and they're both full. To the left of her chair, next to the lamp, there's an end table stacked with magazines – the usual magazines that nice people read. We're nice people, all of us, to a point. Right this minute, Amanda is, I imagine, paging through a magazine, stopping every so often to look at an illustration or a cartoon.

Two days ago, in the afternoon, Amanda said to me, "I can't read books any more. Who has the time?" It was the day after Oliver had left, and we were in this little café in the industrial part of the city. "Who can concentrate any more?" she said, stirring her coffee. "Who reads? Do you read?" (I shook my head.) "Somebody must read, I guess. You see all these books around in store windows, and there are those clubs. Somebody's reading," she said. "Who? I don't know anybody who reads."

That's what she said, apropos of nothing – that is, we weren't talking about books, we were talking about our *lives*. Books had nothing to do with it.

"What did Oliver say when you told him?"

Then it struck me that what we were saying – the tense, watchful expressions we wore – belonged to the people on afternoon TV programmes that I'd never done more than switch on and then off.

Amanda looked down and shook her head, as if she couldn't bear to remember.

"You didn't admit who it was you were involved with, did you?"

She shook her head again.

"You're sure of that?" I waited until she looked up from her coffee.

"I didn't mention any names, if that's what you mean."

"Did he say where he was going, or how long he'd be away?" I said, wishing I didn't have to hear myself. This was my neighbour I was talking about. Oliver Porter. A man I'd helped drive out of his home.

"He didn't say where. A hotel. He said I should make my arrangements and be gone – *be gone*, he said. It was like biblical the way he said it – out of his house, out of his *life*, in a week's time. I guess he's coming back then. So we have to decide something real important, real soon, honey. You and I have to make up our minds pretty damn quick."

It was her turn to look at me now, and I know she was looking for a sign of life-long commitment. "A week," I said. I looked at my coffee, which had gotten cold. A lot had happened in a little while, and we were trying to take it in. I don't know what long-term things, if any, we'd thought about those months as we moved from flirtation to love, and then afternoon assignations. In any case, we were in a serious fix now. Very serious. We'd never expected – not in a hundred years – to be hiding out in a café, in the middle of the afternoon, trying to decide matters like this.

I raised my eyes, and Amanda began stirring her coffee. She kept stirring it. I touched her hand, and the spoon dropped out of her fingers. She picked it up and began stirring again. We could have been anybody drinking coffee at a table under fluorescent lights in a run-down café. Anybody, just about. I took Amanda's hand and held it, and it seemed to make a difference.

Vicky's still sleeping on her side when I go downstairs. I plan to heat some milk and drink that. I used to drink whisky when I couldn't sleep, but I gave it up. Now it's strictly hot milk. In the whisky days I'd wake up with this tremendous thirst in the middle of the night. But, back then, I was always looking ahead: I kept a bottle of water in the fridge, for instance. I'd be dehydrated, sweating from head to toe when I woke, but I'd wander out to the kitchen and could count on finding that bottle of cold water in the fridge. I'd drink it, all of it, down the hatch, an entire quart of water. Once in a while I'd use a glass, but not often. Suddenly I'd be drunk all over again and weaving around the kitchen. I can't begin to account for it – sober one minute, drunk the next.

The drinking was part of my destiny – according to Molly, anyway. She put a lot of stock in destiny.

I felt wild from lack of sleep. I'd give anything, just about, to be able to go to sleep, and sleep the sleep of an honest man.

Why do we have to sleep anyway? And why do we tend to sleep less during some crises and more during others? For instance, that time my dad had his stroke. He woke up after a coma – seven days and nights in a hospital bed – and calmly said "Hello" to the people in his room. Then his eyes picked me out. "Hello, son," he said. Five minutes later, he died. Just like that – he died. But, during that whole crisis, I never took my clothes off and didn't go to bed. I may have catnapped in a waiting-room chair from time to time, but I never went to bed and *slept*.

And then a year or so ago I found out Vicky was seeing somebody else. Instead of confronting *her*, I went to bed when I heard about it, and stayed there. I didn't get up for days, a week maybe – I don't know. I mean, I got up to go to the bathroom, or else to the kitchen to make a sandwich. I even went out to the living room in my pyjamas, in the afternoon, and tried to read the papers. But I'd fall asleep sitting up. Then I'd stir, open my eyes and go back to bed and sleep some more. I couldn't get enough sleep.

It passed. We weathered it. Vicky quit her boyfriend, or he quit her, I never found out. I just know she went away from me for a while, and then she came back. But I have the feeling we're not going to weather this business. This thing is different. Oliver has given Amanda that ultimatum.

Still, isn't it possible that Oliver himself is awake at this moment and writing a letter to Amanda, urging reconciliation? Even now he might be scribbling away, trying to persuade her that what she's doing to him and their daughter Beth is foolish, disastrous, and finally a tragic thing for the three of them.

No, that's insane. I know Oliver. He's relentless, unforgiving. He could slam a croquet ball into the next block – and has. He isn't going to write any such letter. He gave her an ultimatum, right? – and that's that. A week. Four days now. Or is it three? Oliver may be awake, but if he is, he's sitting in a chair in his hotel room with a glass of iced vodka in his hand, his feet on the bed, TV turned on low. He's dressed, except for his shoes. He's not wearing shoes – that's the only concession he makes. That and the fact he's loosened his tie.

Oliver is relentless.

I heat the milk, spoon the skin from the surface and pour it up. Then I turn off the kitchen light and take the cup into the living room and sit on the sofa, where I can look across the street at the lighted windows. But I can hardly sit still. I keep fidgeting, crossing one leg and then the other. I feel like I could throw off sparks, or break a window – maybe rearrange all the furniture.

The things that go through your mind when you can't sleep! Earlier, thinking about Molly, for a moment I couldn't even remember what she *looked* like, for Christ's sake, yet we were together for years, more or less continuously, since we were kids. Molly, who said she'd love me for ever. The only thing left was the memory of her sitting and weeping at the kitchen table, her shoulders bent forward, and her hands covering her face. *For ever*, she said. But it hadn't worked out that way. Finally, she said, it didn't matter, it was of no real concern to her, if she and I lived together the rest of our lives or not. Our love existed on a "higher plane". That's what she said to Vicky over the phone that time, after Vicky and I had set up housekeeping together. Molly called, got hold of Vicky, and said, "You have your relationship with him, but I'll always have mine. His destiny and mine are linked."

My first wife, Molly, she talked like that. "Our destinies are linked." She didn't talk like that in the beginning. It was only later, after so much had happened, that she started using words like "cosmic" and "empowerment" and so forth. But our destinies are *not* linked – not now, anyway, if they ever were. I don't even know where she is now, not for certain.

I think I could put my finger on the exact time, the real

turning point, when it came undone for Molly. It was after I started seeing Vicky, and Molly found out. They called me up one day from the high school where Molly taught and said, "Please. Your wife is doing handsprings in front of the school. You'd better get down here." It was after I took her home that I began hearing about "higher power" and "going with the flow" – stuff of that sort. Our destiny had been "revised". And if I'd been hesitating before, well, I left her then as fast as I could – this woman I'd known all my life, the one who'd been my best friend for years, my intimate, my confidante. I bailed out on her. For one thing, I was scared. *Scared*.

This girl I'd started out with in life, this sweet thing, this gentle soul, she wound up going to fortune-tellers, palm readers, *crystal ball gazers*, looking for answers, trying to figure out what she should do with her life. She quit her job, drew out her teacher's retirement money, and thereafter never made a decision without consulting the *I Ching*. She began wearing strange clothes – clothes with permanent wrinkles and a lot of burgundy and orange. She even got involved wih a group that sat around, I'm not kidding, trying to levitate.

When Molly and I were growing up together, she was a part of me and, sure, I was a part of her, too. We loved each other. It *was* our destiny. I believed in it then myself. But now I don't know what to believe in. I'm not complaining, simply stating a fact. I'm down to nothing. And I have to go on like this. No destiny. Just the next thing meaning whatever you think it does. Compulsion and error, just like everybody else.

Amanda? I'd like to believe in her, bless her heart. But she was looking for somebody when she met me. That's the way with people when they get restless: they start up something, knowing that's going to change things for good.

I'd like to go out in the front yard and shout something. "None of this is worth it!" That's what I'd like people to hear.

"Destiny," Molly said. For all I know she's still talking about it.

All the lights are off over there now, except for that light in the kitchen. I could try calling Amanda on the phone. I could do that and see how far it gets me! What if Vicky heard me dialling or talking on the phone and came downstairs? What if she lifted the receiver upstairs and listened? Besides, there's always the chance Beth might pick up the phone. I don't want to talk to any kids this morning. I don't want to talk to anybody. Actually, I'd talk to Molly, if I could, but I can't any longer – she's somebody else now. She isn't *Molly* any more. But – what can I say? – I'm somebody else, too.

I wish I could be like everybody else in this neighbourhood – your basic, normal, unaccomplished person – and go up to my bedroom, and lie down, and sleep. It's going to be a big day today, and I'd like to be ready for it. I wish I could sleep and wake up and find everything in my life different. Not necessarily just the big things, like this thing with Amanda or the past with Molly. But things clearly within my power.

Take the situation with my mother: I used to send money every month. But then I started sending her the same amount in twice-yearly sums. I gave her money on her birthday, and I gave her money at Christmas. I thought: I won't have to worry about forgetting her birthday, and I won't have to worry about sending her a Christmas present. I won't have to worry, period. It went like clockwork for a long time.

Then last year she asked me – it was in between money times, it was in March, or maybe April – for a radio. A radio, she said, would make a difference to her.

What she wanted was a little clock radio. She could put it in her kitchen and have it out there to listen to while she was fixing something to eat in the evening. And she'd have the clock to look at too, so she'd know when something was supposed to come out of the oven, or how long it was until one of her programmes started.

A little clock radio.

She hinted around at first. She said, "I'd sure like to have a radio. But I can't afford one. I guess I'll have to wait for my birthday. That little radio I had, it fell and broke. I miss a radio." *I miss a radio.* That's what she said when we talked on the phone, or else she'd bring it up when she'd write.

Finally – what'd I say? I said to her over the phone that I couldn't afford any radios. I said it in a letter too, so she'd be sure and understand. *I can't afford any radios*, is what I wrote. I can't do any more, I said, than I'm doing. Those were my very words.

But it wasn't true! I could have done more. I just said I couldn't. I could have afforded to buy a radio for her. What would it have cost me? Thirty-five dollars? Forty dollars or less, including tax. I could have sent her a radio through the mail. I could have had somebody in the store do it, if I didn't want to go to the trouble myself. Or else I could have sent her a forty-dollar cheque along with a note saying, *This money is for your radio, mother.*

I could have handled it in any case. Forty dollars – are you kidding? But I didn't. I wouldn't part with it. It seemed there was a *principle* involved. That's what I told myself anyway – there's a principle involved here.

Ha.

Then what happened? She died. She *died.* She was walking home from the grocery store, back to her apartment, carrying her sack of groceries, and she fell into somebody's bushes and died.

I took a flight out there to make the arrangements. She was still at the coroner's, and they had her purse and her groceries behind the desk in the office. I didn't bother to look in the purse they handed me. But what she had from the grocery store was a jar of Metamucil, two grapefruits, a carton of cottage cheese, a quart of buttermilk, some potatoes and onions, and a package of ground meat that was beginning to change colour.

Boy! I cried when I saw those things. I couldn't stop. I didn't think I'd ever quit crying. The woman who worked at the desk was embarrassed and brought me a glass of water. They gave me a bag for my mother's groceries and another bag for her personal effects – her purse and her dentures. Later, I put the dentures in my coat pocket and drove them down in a rental car and gave them to somebody at the funeral home.

The light in Amanda's kitchen is still on. It's a bright light that spills out on to all those leaves. Maybe she's like I am, and she's scared. Maybe she left that light burning as a night-light. Or maybe she's still awake and is at the kitchen table, under the light, writing me a letter. Amanda is writing me a letter, and somehow she'll get it into my hands later on when the real day starts.

Come to think of it, I've never had a letter from her since we've known each other. All the time we've been involved – six months, eight months – and I've never once seen a scrap of her handwriting. I don't even know if she's *literate* that way.

I think she is. Sure, she is. She talks about books, doesn't she? It doesn't matter of course. Well, a little, I suppose. I love her in any case, right?

But I've never written anything to her, either. We always talked on the phone or else face to face.

Molly, she was the letter writer. She used to write me even after we weren't living together. Vicky would bring her letters in from the box and leave them on the kitchen table without a word. Finally the letters dwindled away, became more and more infrequent and bizarre. When she did write, the letters gave me a chill. They were full of talk about "auras" and "signs". Occasionally she reported a voice that was telling her something she ought to do or some place she should go. And once she told me that no matter what happened, we were still "on the same frequency". She always knew exactly what I felt, she said. She "beamed in on me", she said, from time to time. Reading those letters of hers, the hair on the back of my neck would tingle. She also had a new word for destiny: *Karma*. "I'm following out my karma," she wrote. "Your karma has taken a bad turn."

I'd like to go to sleep, but what's the point? People will be getting up soon. Vicky's alarm will go off before much longer. I wish I could go upstairs and get back in bed with my wife, tell her I'm sorry, there's been a mistake, let's forget all this – then go to sleep and wake up with her in my arms. But I've forfeited that right. I'm outside all that now, and I can't get back inside! But say I did that. Say I went upstairs and slid into bed with Vicky as I'd like to do. She might wake up and say, *You bastard. Don't you dare touch me, son of a bitch.*

What's she talking about, anyway? I wouldn't touch her. Not in that way, I wouldn't.

After I left Molly, after I'd pulled out on her, about two months after, then Molly really did it. She had her real collapse then, the one that'd been coming on. Her sister saw to it that she got the care she needed. What am I saying? *They put her away.* They had to, they said. They put my wife away. By then I was living with Vicky, and trying not to drink whisky. I couldn't do anything for Molly. I mean, she was there, I was here, and I couldn't have gotten her out of that place if I'd wanted to. But the fact is, I didn't want to. She was in there, they said, because she *needed* to be in there. Nobody said anything about destiny. Things had gone beyond that.

And I didn't even go visit her – not once! At the time, I

didn't think I could stand seeing her in there. But, Christ, what was I? A fair-weather friend? We'd been through plenty. But what on earth would I have said to her? *I'm sorry about all this, honey.* I could have said that, I guess. I intended to write, but I didn't. Not a word. Anyway, when you get right down to it, what could I have said in a letter? *How are they treating you, baby? I'm sorry you're where you are, but don't give up. Remember all the good times? Remember when we were happy together? Hey, I'm sorry they've done this to you. I'm sorry it turned out this way. I'm sorry everything is just garbage now.* I'm sorry, Molly.

I didn't write. I think I was trying to forget about her, to pretend she didn't exist. Molly who?

I left my wife and took somebody else's: Vicky. Now I think maybe I've lost Vicky, too. But Vicky won't be going away to any summer camp for the mentally disabled. She's a hard case. She left her former husband, Joe Kraft, and didn't bat an eye; I don't think she ever lost a night's sleep over it.

Vicky Kraft-Hughes. Amanda Porter. This is where my destiny has brought me? To this street in this neighbourhood, messing up the lives of these women?

Amanda's kitchen light went off when I wasn't looking. The room that was there is gone now, like the others. Only the porch light is still burning. Amanda must have forgotten it, I guess. Hey, Amanda.

Once, when Molly was away in that place and I wasn't in my right mind – let's face it, I was crazy too – one night I was at my friend Alfredo's house, a bunch of us drinking and listening to records. I didn't care any longer what happened to me. Everything, I thought, that could happen had happened. I felt unbalanced. I felt lost. Anyway, there I was at Alfredo's. His paintings of tropical birds and animals hung on every wall in his house, and there were paintings standing around in the rooms, leaning against things – table-legs, say, or his brick-and-board bookcase, as well as being stacked on his back porch. The kitchen served as his studio, and I was sitting at the kitchen table with a drink in front of me. An easel stood off to one side in front of the window that overlooked the alley, and there were crumpled tubes of paint, a palette, and some brushes lying at one end of the table. Alfredo was making himself a drink at the counter a few feet away. I loved the shabby economy of that little room. The stereo music that came from the living room was turned up, filling the house with so much sound the kitchen windows rattled in their frames. Suddenly I began to shake. First my hands began to shake, and then my arms and shoulders, too. My teeth started to chatter. I couldn't hold the glass.

"What's going on, man?" Alfredo said, when he turned and saw the state I was in. "Hey, what is it? What's going on with you?"

I couldn't tell him. What could I say? I thought I was having some kind of an attack. I managed to raise my shoulders and let them drop.

Then Alfredo came over, took a chair and sat down beside me at the kitchen table. He put his big painter's hand on my shoulder. I went on shaking. He could feel me shaking.

"What's wrong with you, man? I'm real sorry about every-thing, man. I know it's real hard right now." Then he said he was going to fix *menudo* for me. He said it would be good for what ailed me. "Help your nerves, man," he said. "Calm you right down." He had all the ingredients for *menudo*, he said, and he'd been wanting to make some anyway.

"You listen to me. Listen to what I say, man. I'm your family now," Alfredo said.

It was two in the morning, we were drunk, there were these other drunk people in the house and the stereo was going full blast. But Alfredo went to his fridge and opened it and took some stuff out. He closed the fridge door and looked in his freezer compartment. He found something in a package. Then he looked around in his cupboards. He took a big pan from the cabinet under the sink, and he was ready.

Tripe. He started with tripe and about a gallon of water. Then he chopped onions and added them to the water, which had started to boil. He put *chorizo* sausage in the pot. After that, he dropped peppercorns into the boiling water and sprinkled in some chilli powder. Then came the olive oil. He opened a big can of tomato sauce and poured that in. He added cloves of garlic, some slices of white bread, salt, and lemon juice. He opened another can – it was hominy – and poured that in the pot, too. He put it all in, and then he turned the heat down and put a lid on the pot.

I watched him. I sat there shaking while Alfredo stood at the stove making *menudo*, talking – I didn't have any idea what he was saying – and, from time to time, he'd shake his head, or else start whistling to himself. Now and then people drifted into the kitchen for beer. But all the while Alfredo went on very seriously looking after his *menudo*. He could have been home, in Morelia, making *menudo* for his family on New Year's Day.

People hung around in the kitchen for a while, joking, but Alfredo didn't joke back when they kidded him about cooking *menudo* in the middle of the night. Pretty soon they left us alone. Finally, while Alfredo stood at the stove with a spoon in his hand, watching me, I got up slowly from the table. I walked out of the kitchen into the bathroom, and then opened another door off the bathroom to the spare room – where I lay down on the bed and fell asleep. When I woke it was mid-afternoon. The *menudo* was gone. The pot was in the sink, soaking. Those other people must have eaten it! They must have eaten it and grown calm. Everyone was gone, and the house was quiet.

I never saw Alfredo more than once or twice afterwards. After that night, our lives took us in separate directions. And those other people who were there – who knows where they went? I'll probably die without ever tasting *menudo*. But who can say?

Is this what it all comes down to then? A middle-aged man involved with his neighbour's wife, linked to an angry ultimatum? What kind of destiny is that? A week, Oliver said. Three or four days now.

A car passes outside with its lights on. The sky is turning grey, and I hear some birds starting up. I decide I can't wait any longer. I can't just sit here, doing nothing – that's all there is to it. I can't keep waiting. I've waited and waited and where's it gotten me? Vicky's alarm will go off soon, Beth will get up and dress for school, Amanda will wake up, too. The entire neighbourhood.

On the back porch I find some old jeans and a sweatshirt, and I change out of my pyjamas. Then I put on my white canvas shoes – "wino" shoes, Alfredo would have called them. Alfredo, where are you?

I go outside to the garage and find the rake and some lawn bags. By the time I get around to the front of the house with the rake, ready to begin, I feel I don't have a choice in the matter any longer. It's light out – light enough at any rate for what I have to do. And then, without thinking about it any more, I start to rake. I rake our yard, every inch of it. It's important it be done right, too. I set the rake right down into the turf and pull hard. It must feel to the grass like it does whenever someone gives your hair a hard jerk. Now and then a car passes in the street and slows, but I don't look up from my work. I know what the people in the cars must be thinking, but they're dead wrong – they don't know the half of it. How could they? I'm happy, raking.

I finish our yard and put the bag out next to the curb. Then I begin next door on the Baxters' yard. In a few minutes Mrs

Baxter comes out on her porch, wearing her bathrobe. I don't acknowledge her. I'm not embarrassed, and I don't want to appear unfriendly. I just want to keep on with what I'm doing.

She doesn't say anything for a while, and then she says, "Good morning, Mr Hughes. How are you this morning?"

I stop what I'm doing and run my arm across my forehead. "I'll be through in a little while," I say. "I hope you don't mind."

"We don't mind," Mrs Baxter says. "Go right ahead, I guess." I see Mr Baxter standing in the doorway behind her. He's already dressed for work in his slacks and sports coat and tie. But he doesn't venture on to the porch. Then Mrs Baxter turns and looks at Mr Baxter, who shrugs.

It's OK, I've finished here anyway. There are other yards, more important yards for that matter. I kneel, and, taking a grip low down on the rake handle, I pull the last of the leaves into my bag and tie off the top. Then, I can't help it, I just stay there, kneeling on the grass with the rake in my hand. When I look up, I see the Baxters come down the porch steps together and move slowly towards me through the wet, sweet-smelling grass. They stop a few feet away and look at me closely.

"There now," I hear Mrs Baxter say. She's still in her robe and slippers. It's nippy out; she holds her robe at the throat. "You did a real fine job for us, yes, you did."

I don't say anything. I don't even say, "You're welcome."

They stand in front of me a while longer, and none of us says anything more. It's as if we've come to an agreement on something. In a minute, they turn around and go back to their house. High over my head, in the branches of the old maple – the place where these leaves come from – birds call out to each other. At least I think they're calling to each other.

Suddenly a car door slams. Mr Baxter is in his car in the drive with the window rolled down. Mrs Baxter says something to him from the front porch which causes Mr

Baxter to nod slowly and turn his head in my direction. He sees me kneeling there with the rake, and a look crosses his face. He frowns. In his better moments, Mr Baxter is a decent, ordinary guy – a guy you wouldn't mistake for anyone special. But he *is* special. In my book, he is. For one thing he has a full night's sleep behind him, and he's just embraced his wife before leaving for work. But even before he goes, he's already expected home a set number of hours later. True, in the grander scheme of things, his return will be an event of small moment – but an event nonetheless.

Baxter starts his car and races the engine. Then he backs effortlessly out of the drive, brakes, and changes gears. As he passes on the street, he slows and looks briefly in my direction. He lifts his hand off the steering wheel. It could be a salute or a sign of dismissal. It's a sign, in any case. And then he looks away towards the city. I get up and raise my hand, too – not a wave, exactly, but close to it. Some other cars drive past. One of the drivers must think he knows me because he gives his horn a friendly little tap. I look both ways and then cross the street.

Elephant

I knew it was a mistake to let my brother have the money. I
didn't need anybody else owing me. But when he called and
said he couldn't make the payment on his house, what could
I do? I'd never been inside his house – he lived a thousand
miles away, in California; I'd never even *seen* his house – but
I didn't want him to lose it. He cried over the phone and said
he was losing everything he'd worked for. He said he'd pay
me back. February, he said. Maybe sooner. No later, anyway,
than March. He said his income-tax refund was on the way.
Plus, he said, he had a little investment that would mature in
February. He acted secretive about the investment thing, so
I didn't press for details.

"Trust me on this," he said. "I won't let you down."

He'd lost his job last July, when the company he worked for,
a fibreglass-insulation plant, decided to lay off two hundred
employees. He'd been living on his unemployment since then,
but now the unemployment was gone, and his savings were
gone, too. And he didn't have health insurance any longer.
When his job went, the insurance went. His wife, who was
ten years older, was diabetic and needed treatment. He'd had
to sell the other car – her car, an old station wagon – and a
week ago he'd pawned his TV. He told me he'd hurt his back
carrying the TV up and down the street where the pawnshops
did business. He went from place to place, he said, trying to
get the best offer. Somebody finally gave him a hundred

dollars for it, this big Sony TV. He told me about the TV, and then about throwing his back out, as if this ought to cinch it with me, unless I had a stone in place of a heart.

"I've gone belly up," he said. "But you can help me pull out of it."

"How much?" I said.

"Five hundred. I could use more, sure, who couldn't?" he said. "But I want to be realistic. I can pay back five hundred. More than that, I'll tell you the truth, I'm not so sure. Brother, I hate to ask. But you're my last resort. Irma Jean and I are going to be on the street before long. I won't let you down," he said. That's what he said. Those were his exact words.

We talked a little more – mostly about our mother and her problems – but, to make a long story short, I sent him the money. I had to. I felt I had to, at any rate – which amounts to the same thing. I wrote him a letter when I sent the cheque and said he should pay the money back to our mother, who lived in the same town he lived in and who was poor and greedy. I'd been mailing cheques to her every month, rain or shine, for three years. But I was thinking that if he paid her the money he owed me it might take me off the hook there and let me breathe for a while. I wouldn't have to worry on that score for a couple of months, anyway. Also, and this is the truth, I thought maybe he'd be more likely to pay her, since they lived right there in the same town and he saw her from time to time. All I was doing was trying to cover myself some way. The thing is, he might have the best intentions of paying me back, but things happen sometimes. Things get in the way of best intentions. Out of sight, out of mind, as they say. But he wouldn't stiff his own mother. Nobody would do that.

I spent hours writing letters, trying to make sure everybody knew what could be expected and what was required. I even phoned out there to my mother several times, trying to explain it to her. But she was suspicious over the whole deal.

I went through it with her on the phone step by step, but she was still suspicious. I told her the money that was supposed to come from me on the first of March and on the first of April would instead come from Billy, who owed the money to me. She'd get her money, and she didn't have to worry. The only difference was that Billy would pay it to her those two months instead of me. He'd pay her the money I'd normally be sending to her, but instead of him mailing it to me and then me having to turn around and send it to her he'd pay it to her directly. On any account, she didn't have to worry. She'd get her money, but for those two months it'd come from him – from the money he owed me. My God, I don't know how much I spent on phone calls. And I wish I had fifty cents for every letter I wrote, telling him what I'd told her and telling her what to expect from him – that sort of thing.

But my mother didn't trust Billy. "What if he can't come up with it?" she said to me over the phone. "What then? He's in bad shape, and I'm sorry for him," she said. "But, son, what I want to know is, what if he isn't able to pay me? What if he can't? Then what?"

"Then I'll pay you myself," I said. "Just like always. If he doesn't pay you, I'll pay you. But he'll pay you. Don't worry. He says he will, and he will."

"I don't want to worry," she said. "But I worry anyway. I worry about my boys, and after that I worry about myself. I never thought I'd see one of my boys in this shape. I'm just glad your dad isn't alive to see it."

In three months my brother gave her fifty dollars of what he owed me and was supposed to pay to her. Or maybe it was seventy-five dollars he gave her. There are conflicting stories – two conflicting stories, his and hers. But that's all he paid her of the five hundred – fifty dollars or else seventy-five dollars, according to whose story you want to listen to. I had to make up the rest to her. I had to keep shelling out, same as always. My brother was finished. That's what he told me – that he was finished – when I called to see what was up, after my mother had phoned, looking for her money.

My mother said, "I made the mailman go back and check inside his truck, to see if your letter might have fallen down behind the seat. Then I went around and asked the neighbours did they get any of my mail by mistake. I'm going crazy with worry about this situation, honey." Then she said, "What's a mother supposed to think?" Who was looking out for her best interests in this busines? She wanted to know that, and she wanted to know when she could expect her money.

So that's when I got on the phone to my brother to see if this was just a simple delay or a full-fledged collapse. But, according to Billy, he was a goner. He was absolutely done for. He was putting his house on the market immediately. He just hoped he hadn't waited too long to try and move it. And there wasn't anything left inside the house that he could sell. He'd sold off everything except the kitchen table and chairs. "I wish I could sell my blood," he said. "But who'd buy it? With my luck, I probably have an incurable disease." And, naturally, the investment thing hadn't worked out. When I asked him about it over the phone, all he said was that it hadn't materialized. His tax refund didn't make it, either – the IRS had some kind of lien on his return. "When it rains it pours," he said. "I'm sorry, brother. I didn't mean for this to happen."

"I understand," I said. And I did. But it didn't make it any easier. Anyway, one thing and the other, I didn't get my money from him, and neither did my mother. I had to keep on sending her money every month.

I was sore, yes. Who wouldn't be? My heart went out to him, and I wished trouble hadn't knocked on his door. But my own back was against the wall now. At least, though, whatever happens to him from here on, he won't come back to me for more money – seeing as how he still owes me. Nobody would do that to you. That's how I figured, anyway. But that's how little I knew.

I kept my nose to the grindstone. I got up early every morning and went to work and worked hard all day. When I came home I plopped into the big chair and just sat there. I was so tired it took me a while to get around to unlacing my shoes. Then I just went on sitting there. I was too tired to even get up and turn on the TV.

I was sorry about my brother's troubles. But I had troubles of my own. In addition to my mother, I had several other people on my payroll. I had a former wife I was sending money to every month. I had to do that. I didn't want to, but the court said I had to. And I had a daughter with two kids in Bellingham, and I had to send her something every month. Her kids had to eat, didn't they? She was living with a swine who wouldn't even *look* for work, a guy who couldn't hold a job if they handed him one. The time or two he did find something, he overslept, or his car broke down on the way in to work, or else he'd just be let go, no explanation, and that was that.

Once, long ago, when I used to think like a man about these things, I threatened to kill that guy. But that's neither here nor there. Besides, I was drinking in those days. In any case, the bastard is still hanging around.

My daughter would write these letters and say how they were living on oatmeal, she and her kids. (I guess he was starving, too, but she knew better than to mention that guy's name in her letters to me.) She'd tell me that if I could just carry her until summer things would pick up for her. Things would turn around for her, she was sure, in the summer. If nothing else worked out – but she was sure it would; she had several irons in the fire – she could always get a job in the fish cannery that was not far from where she lived. She'd wear rubber boots and rubber clothes and gloves and pack salmon into cans. Or else she might sell root beer from a vending stand beside the road to people who lined up in their cars at the border, waiting to get into Canada. People sitting in their cars in the middle of summer were going to be thirsty, right? They were going to be crying out for cold drinks. Anyway, one thing or the other, whatever line of work she decided on, she'd do fine in the summer. She just had to make it until then, and that's where I came in.

My daughter said she knew she had to change her life. She wanted to stand on her own two feet like everyone else. She wanted to quit looking at herself as a victim. "I'm not a victim," she said to me over the phone one night. "I'm just a young woman with two kids and a son-of-a-bitch bum who lives with me. No different from lots of other women. I'm not afraid of hard work. Just give me a chance. That's all I ask of the world." She said she could do without for herself. But until her break came, until opportunity knocked, it was the kids she worried about. The kids were always asking her when Grandpop was going to visit, she said. Right this minute they were drawing pictures of the swing sets and swimming pool at the motel I'd stayed in when I'd visited a year ago. But summer was the thing, she said. If she could make it until summer, her troubles would be over. Things would change then – she knew they would. And with a little help from me she could make it. "I don't know what I'd do without you, Dad." That's what she said. It nearly broke my heart. Sure I had to help her. I was glad to be even halfway in a position to help her. I had a job, didn't I? Compared to her and everyone else in my family, I had it made. Compared to the rest, I lived on Easy Street.

I sent the money she asked for. I sent money every time she asked. And then I told her I thought it'd be simpler if I just sent a sum of money, not a whole lot, but money even so, on the first of each month. It would be money she could count on, and it would be *her* money, no one else's – hers and the kids'. That's what I hoped for, anyway. I wished there was some way I could be sure the bastard who lived with her couldn't get his hands on so much as an orange or a piece of bread that my money bought. But I couldn't. I just had to go ahead and send the money and stop worrying about whether he'd soon be tucking into a plate of my eggs and biscuits.

My mother and my daughter and my former wife. That's three people on the payroll right there, not counting my brother. But my son needed money, too. After he graduated from high school, he packed his things, left his mother's house, and went to a college back East. A college in New Hampshire of all places. Who's ever heard of New Hampshire? But he was the first kid in the family on either side of the family, to even *want* to go to college, so everbody thought it was a good idea. I thought so, too, at first. How'd I know it was going to wind up costing me an arm and a leg? He borrowed left and right from the banks to keep himself going. He didn't want to have to work a job and go to school at the same time. That's what he said. And, sure, I guess I can understand it. In a way, I can even sympathize. Who likes to work? I don't. But after he'd borrowed everything he could, everything in sight, including enough to finance a junior year in Germany, I had to begin sending him money, and a lot of it. When, finally, I said I couldn't send any more, he wrote back and said if that was the case, if that was really the way I felt, he was going to deal drugs or else rob a bank – whatever he had to do to get money to live on. I'd be lucky if he wasn't shot or sent to prison.

I wrote back and said I'd changed my mind and I could send him a little more after all. What else could I do? I didn't want his blood on my hands. I didn't want to think of my kid being packed off to prison, or something even worse. I had plenty on my conscience as it was.

That's four people, right? Not counting my brother, who wasn't a regular yet. I was going crazy with it. I worried night and day. I couldn't sleep over it. I was paying out nearly as much money every month as I was bringing in. You don't have to be a genius, or know anything about economics, to understand that this state of affairs couldn't keep on. I had to get a loan to keep up my end of things. That was another monthly payment.

So I started cutting back. I had to quit eating out, for instance. Since I lived alone, eating out was something I liked to do, but it became a thing of the past. And I had to watch myself when it came to thinking about movies. I couldn't buy clothes or get my teeth fixed. The car was falling apart. I needed new shoes, but forget it.

Once in a while I'd get fed up with it and write letters to all of them, threatening to change my name and telling them I was going to quit my job. I'd tell them I was planning a move to Australia. And the thing was, I was serious when I'd say that about Australia, even though I didn't know the first thing about Australia. I just knew it was on the other side of the world, and that's where I wanted to be.

But when it came right down to it, none of them really believed I'd go to Australia. They had me, and they knew it. They knew I was desperate, and they were sorry and they said so. But they counted on it all blowing over before the first of the month, when I had to sit down and make out the cheques.

After one of my letters where I talked about moving to Australia, my mother wrote that she didn't want to be a burden any longer. Just as soon as the swelling went down in her legs, she said, she was going out to look for work. She was seventy-five years old, but maybe she could go back to waitressing, she said. I wrote her back and told her not to be silly. I said I was glad I could help her. And I was. I was glad I could help. I just needed to win the lottery.

My daughter knew Australia was just a way of saying to everybody that I'd had it. She knew I needed a break and something to cheer me up. So she wrote that she was going to leave her kids with somebody and take the cannery job when the season rolled around. She was young and strong, she said. She thought she could work the twelve-to-fourteen-hour-a-day shifts, seven days a week, no problem. She'd just have to tell herself she could do it, get herself psyched up for it, and her body would listen. She just had to line up the right kind of babysitter. That'd be the big thing. It was going to require a special kind of sitter, seeing as how the hours would be long and the kids were hyper to begin with, because of all the Popsicles and Tootsie Rolls, M&Ms, and the like that they put away every day. It's the stuff kids like to eat, right? Anyway, she thought she could find the right person if she kept looking. But she had to buy the boots and clothes for the work, and that's where I could help.

My son wrote that he was sorry for his part in things and thought he and I would both be better off if he ended it once and for all. For one thing, he'd discovered he was allergic to cocaine. It made his eyes stream and affected his breathing, he said. This meant he couldn't test the drugs in the trans-actions he'd need to make. So, before it could even begin, his career as a drug dealer was over. No, he said, better a bullet in the temple and end it all right here. Or maybe hanging. That would save him the trouble of borrowing a gun. And save us the price of bullets. That's actually what he said in his letter, if you can believe it. He enclosed a picture of himself that somebody had taken last summer when he was in the study-abroad programme in Germany. He was standing un-der a big tree with thick limbs hanging down a few feet over his head. In the picture, he wasn't smiling.

My former wife didn't have anything to say on the matter. She didn't have to. She knew she'd get her money the first of each month, even if it had to come all the way from Sydney.

If she didn't get it, she just had to pick up the phone and call her lawyer.

This is where things stood when my brother called one Sunday afternoon in early May. I had the windows open, and a nice breeze moved through the house. The radio was playing. The hillside behind the house was in bloom. But I began to sweat when I heard his voice on the line. I hadn't heard from him since the dispute over the five hundred, so I couldn't believe he was going to try and touch me for more money now. But I began to sweat anyway. He asked how things stood with me, and I launched into the payroll thing and all. I talked about oatmeal, cocaine, fish canneries, suicide, bank jobs, and how I couldn't go to the movies or eat out. I said I had a hole in my shoe. I talked about the payments that went on and on to my former wife. He knew all about this, of course. He knew everything I was telling him. Still, he said he was sorry to hear it. I kept talking. It was his dime. But as he talked I started thinking, *How are you going to pay for this call, Billy?* Then it came to me that *I* was going to pay for it. It was only a matter of minutes, or seconds, until it was all decided.

I looked out the window. The sky was blue, with a few white clouds in it. Some birds clung to a telephone wire. I wiped my face on my sleeve. I didn't know what else I could say. So I suddenly stopped talking and just stared out the window at the mountains, and waited. And that's when my brother said, "I hate to ask you this, but –" When he said that, my heart did this sinking thing. And then he went ahead and asked.

This time it was a thousand. A thousand! He was worse off than when he'd called that other time. He let me have some details. The bill collectors were at the door – the door! he said – and the windows rattled, the house shook, when they hammered with their fists. *Blam, blam, blam,* he said. There

was no place to hide from them. His house was about to be
pulled out from under him. "Help me, brother," he said.

Where was I going to raise a thousand dollars? I took a
good grip on the receiver, turned away from the window,
and said, "But you didn't pay me back the last time you
borrowed money. What about that?"

"I didn't?" he said, acting surprised. "I guess I thought I
had. I wanted to, anyway. I tried to, so help me God."

"You were supposed to pay that money to Mom," I said.
"But you didn't. I had to keep giving her money every
month, same as always. There's no end to it, Billy. Listen,
I take one step forward and I go two steps back. I'm going
under. You're all going under, and you're pulling me down
with you."

"I paid her *some* of it," he said. "I did pay her a little. Just
for the record," he said. "I paid her something."

"She said you gave her fifty dollars and that was all."

"No," he said, "I gave her seventy-five. She forgot about
the other twenty-five. I was over there one afternoon, and I
gave her two tens and a five. I gave her some cash, and she
just forgot about it. Her memory's going. Look," he said, "I
promise I'll be good for it this time, I swear to God. Add up
what I still owe you and add it to this money here I'm trying
to borrow, and I'll send you a cheque. We'll exchange cheques.
Hold on to my cheque for two months, that's all I'm asking.
I'll be out of the woods in two months' time. Then you'll
have your money. July 1st, I promise, no later, and this time
I *can* swear to it. We're in the process of selling this little
piece of property that Irma Jean inherited a while back from
her uncle. It's as good as sold. The deal has closed. It's just a
question now of working out a couple of minor details and
signing the papers. Plus, I've got this job lined up. It's definite.
I'll have to drive fifty miles round trip every day, but that's
no problem – hell, no. I'd drive a hundred and fifty if I had
to, and be glad to do it. I'm saying I'll have money in the

bank in two months' time. You'll get your money, all of it, by July 1st, and you can count on it."

"Billy, I love you," I said. "But I've got a load to carry. I'm carrying a very heavy load these days, in case you didn't know."

"That's why I won't let you down on this," he said. "You have my word of honour. You can trust me on this absolutely. I promise you my cheque will be good in two months, no later. Two months is all I'm asking for. Brother, I don't know where else to turn. You're my last hope."

I did it, sure. To my surprise, I still had some credit with the bank, so I borrowed the money, and I sent it to him. Our cheques crossed in the mail. I stuck a thumbtack through his cheque and put it up on the kitchen wall next to the calendar and the picture of my son standing under that tree. And then I waited.

I kept waiting. My brother wrote and asked me not to cash the cheque on the day we'd agreed to. Please wait a while longer is what he said. Some things had come up. The job he'd been promised had fallen through at the last minute. That was one thing that came up. And that little piece of property belonging to his wife hadn't sold after all. At the last minute she'd had a change of heart about selling it. It had been in her family for generations. What could he do? It was her land, and she wouldn't listen to reason, he said.

My daughter telephoned around this time to say that somebody had broken into her trailer and ripped her off. Everything in the trailer. Every stick of furniture was gone when she came home from work after her first night at the cannery. There wasn't even a chair for her to sit down on. Her bed had been stolen, too. They were going to have to sleep on the floor like gypsies, she said.

"Where was what's-his-name when this happened?" I said.

She said he'd been out looking for work earlier in the day. She guessed he was with friends. Actually, she didn't know his whereabouts at the time of the crime, or even right now, for that matter. "I hope he's at the bottom of the river," she said. The kids had been with the sitter when the rip-off happened. But, anyway, if she could just borrow enough from me to buy some secondhand furniture she'd pay me back, she said, when she got her first cheque. If she had some money from me before the end of the week – I could wire it, maybe – she could pick up some essentials. "Somebody's violated my space," she said. "I feel like I've been raped."

My son wrote from New Hampshire that it was essential he go back to Europe. His life hung in the balance, he said. He was graduating at the end of summer session, but he couldn't stand to live in America a day longer after that. This was a materialist society, and he simply couldn't take it any more. People over here, in the US, couldn't hold a conversation unless *money* figured in it some way, and he was sick of it. He wasn't a Yuppie, and didn't want to become a Yuppie. That wasn't his thing. He'd get out of my hair, he said, if he could just borrow enough from me, this one last time, to buy a ticket Germany.

I didn't hear anything from my former wife. I didn't have to. We both knew how things stood there.

My mother wrote that she was having to do without support hose and wasn't able to have her hair tinted. She'd thought this would be the year she could put some money back for the rainy days ahead, but it wasn't working out that way. She could see it wasn't in the cards. "How are you?" she wanted to know. "How's everybody else? I hope you're OK."

I put more cheques in the mail. Then I held my breath and waited.

While I was waiting, I had this dream one night. Two dreams, really. I dreamt them on the same night. In the first dream, my dad was alive once more, and he was giving me a ride on his shoulders. I was this little kid, maybe five or six years old. *Get up here,* he said, and he took me by the hands and swung me on to his shoulders. I was high off the ground, but I wasn't afraid. He was holding on to me. We were holding on to each other. Then he began to move down the sidewalk. I brought my hands up from his shoulders and put them around his forehead. *Don't muss my hair,* he said. *You can let go,* he said, *I've got you. You won't fall.* When he said, that, I became aware of the strong grip of his hands around my ankles. Then I did let go. I turned loose and held my arms out on either side of me. I kept them out there like that for balance. My dad went on walking while I rode on his shoulders. I pretended he was an elephant. I don't know where we were going. Maybe we were going to the store, or else to the park so he could push me in the swing.

I woke up then, got out of bed, and used the bathroom. It was starting to get light out, and it was only an hour or so until I had to get up. I thought about making coffee and getting dressed. But then I decided to go back to bed. I didn't plan to sleep, though. I thought I'd just lie there for a while with my hands behind my neck and watch it turn light out and maybe think about my dad a little, since I hadn't thought about him in a long time. He just wasn't a part of my life any longer, waking or sleeping. Anyway, I got back in bed. But it couldn't have been more than a minute before I fell asleep once more, and when I did I got into this other dream. My former wife was in it, though she wasn't my former wife in the dream. She was still my wife. My kids were in it, too. They were little, and they were eating potato chips. In my dream, I thought I could smell the potato chips and hear them being eaten. We were on a blanket, and we were close to some water. There was a sense of satisfaction and well-being in the dream. Then, suddenly, I found myself in the company of some other people – people I didn't know – and the next thing that happened was that I was kicking the window out of my son's car and threatening his life, as I did once, a long time ago. He was inside the car as my shoe smashed through the glass. That's when my eyes flew open, and I woke up. The alarm was going off. I reached over and pushed the switch and lay there for a few minutes more, my heart racing. In the second dream, somebody had offered me some whisky, and I drank it. Drinking that whisky was the thing that scared me. That was the worst thing that could have happened. That was rock bottom. Compared to that, everything else was a picnic. I lay there for a minute longer, trying to calm down. Then I got up.

I made coffee and sat at the kitchen table in front of the window. I pushed my cup back and forth in little circles on the table and began to think seriously about Australia again. And then, all of a sudden, I could imagine how it must have sounded to my family when I'd threatened them with a move to Australia. They would have been shocked at first, and even a little scared. Then, because they knew me, they'd probably started laughing. Now, thinking about their laughter, I had to laugh, too. *Ha, ha, ha.* That was exactly the sound I made there at the table – *ha, ha, ha* – as if I'd read somewhere how to laugh.

What was it I planned to do in Australia, anyway? The truth was, I wouldn't be going there any more than I'd be going to Timbuktu, the moon, or the North Pole. Hell, I didn't want to go to Australia. But once I understood this, once I understood I wouldn't be going there – or anywhere else, for that matter – I began to feel better. I lit another cigarette and poured some more coffee. There wasn't any milk for the coffee, but I didn't care. I could skip having milk in my coffee for a day and it wouldn't kill me. Pretty soon I packed the lunch and filled the thermos and put the thermos in the lunch pail. Then I went outside.

It was a fine morning. The sun lay over the mountains behind the town, and a flock of birds was moving from one part of the valley to another. I didn't bother to lock the door. I remembered what had happened to my daughter, but decided I didn't have anything worth stealing anyway. There was nothing in the house I couldn't live without. I had the TV, but I was sick of watching TV. They'd be doing me a favour if they broke in and took it off my hands.

I felt pretty good, all things considered, and I decided to walk to work. It wasn't all that far, and I had time to spare. I'd save a little gas, sure, but that wasn't the main consideration. It was summer, after all, and before long summer would be over. Summer, I couldn't help thinking, had been the time everybody's luck had been going to change.

I started walking alongside the road, and it was then, for some reason, I began to think about my son. I wished him well, wherever he was. If he'd made it back to Germany by now – and he should have – I hoped he was happy. He hadn't written yet to give me his address, but I was sure I'd hear something before long. And my daughter, God love her and keep her. I hoped she was doing OK. I decided to write her a letter that evening and tell her I was rooting for her. My mother was alive and more or less in good health, and I felt lucky there, too. If all went well, I'd have her for several more years.

Birds were calling, and some cars passed me on the highway. Good luck to you, too, brother, I thought. I hope your ship comes in. Pay me back when you get it. And my former wife, the woman I used to love so much. She was alive, and she was well, too – so far as I knew, anyway. I wished her happiness. When all was said and done, I decided things could be a lot worse. Just now, of course, things were hard for everyone. People's luck had gone south on them was all. But things were bound to change soon. Things would pick up in the fall maybe. There was lots to hope for.

I kept on walking. Then I began to whistle. I felt I had the right to whistle if I wanted to. I let my arms swing as I walked. But the lunch pail kept throwing me off balance. I had sandwiches, an apple, and some cookies in there, not to mention the thermos. I stopped in front of Smitty's, an old café that had gravel in the parking area and boards over the windows. The place had been boarded up for as long as I could remember. I decided to put the lunch pail down for a minute. I did that, and then I raised my arms – raised them up level with my shoulders. I was standing there like that, like a goof, when somebody tooted a car horn and pulled off the highway into the parking area. I picked up my lunch pail and went over to the car. It was a guy I knew from work whose name was George. He reached over and opened the door on the passenger's side. "Hey, get in, buddy," he said.

"Hello, George," I said. I got in and shut the door, and the car sped off, throwing gravel from under the tyres.

"I saw you," George said. "Yeah, I did, I saw you. You're in training for something, but I don't know what." He looked at me and then looked at the road again. He was going fast. "You always walk down the road with your arms out like that?" He laughed – ha, ha, ha – and stepped on the gas.

"Sometimes," I said. "It depends, I guess. Actually, I was standing," I said. I lit a cigarette and leaned back in the seat.

"So what's new?" George said. He put a cigar in his mouth, but he didn't light it.

"Nothing's new," I said. "What's new with you?"

George shrugged. Then he grinned. He was going very fast now. Wind buffeted the car and whistled by outside the windows. He was driving as if we were late for work. But we weren't late. We had lots of time, and I told him so.

Nevertheless, he cranked it up. We passed the turn-off and kept going. We were moving by then, heading straight towards the mountains. He took the cigar out of his mouth and put it in his shirt pocket. "I borrowed some money and had this baby overhauled," he said. Then he said he wanted me to see something. He punched it and gave it everything he could. I fastened my seat belt and held on.

"*Go,*" I said. "What are you waiting for, George?" And that's when we really flew. Wind howled outside the windows. He had it floored, and we were going flat out. We streaked down that road in his big unpaid-for car.

Blackbird Pie

I was in my room one night when I heard something in the corridor. I looked up from my work and saw an envelope slide under the door. It was a thick envelope, but not so thick it couldn't be pushed under the door. My name was written on the envelope, and what was inside purported to be a letter from my wife. I say "purported" because even though the grievances could only have come from someone who'd spent twenty-three years observing me on an intimate, day-to-day basis, the charges were outrageous and completely out of keeping with my wife's character. Most important, however, the handwriting was not my wife's handwriting. But if it wasn't her handwriting, then whose was it?

I wish now I'd kept the letter, so I could reproduce it down to the last comma, the last uncharitable exclamation point. The tone is what I'm talking about now, not just the content. But I didn't keep it, I'm sorry to say. I lost it, or else misplaced it. Later, after the sorry business I'm about to relate, I was cleaning out my desk and may have accidentally thrown it away – which is uncharacteristic of *me*, since I usually don't throw anything away.

In any case, I have a good memory. I can recall every word of what I read. My memory is such that I used to win prizes in school because of my ability to remember names and dates, inventions, battles, treaties, alliances, and the like. I always scored highest on factual tests, and in later years, in the "real world", as it's called, my memory stood me in good stead. For instance, if I were asked right now to give the details of the Council of Trent or the Treaty of Utrecht, or to talk about Carthage, that city razed by the Romans after Hannibal's defeat (the Roman soldiers ploughed salt into the ground so that Carthage could never be called Carthage again), I could do so. If called upon to talk about the Seven Years' War, the Thirty Years', or the Hundred Years' War, or simply the First Silesian War, I could hold forth with the greatest enthusiasm and confidence. Ask me anything about the Tartars, the Renaissance popes, or the rise and fall of the Ottoman Empire. Thermopylae, Shiloh, or the Maxim gun. Easy. Tannenberg? Simple as blackbird pie. The famous four and twenty that were set before the king. At Agincourt, English longbows carried the day. And here's something else. Everyone has heard of the Battle of Lepanto, the last great sea battle fought in ships powered by galley slaves. This fracas took place in 1571 in the eastern Mediterranean, when the combined naval forces of the Christian nations of Europe turned back the Arab hordes under the infamous Ali Muezzin Zade, a man who was fond of personally cutting of the noses of his prisoners before calling in the executioners. But does anyone remember that Cervantes was involved in this affair and had his left hand lopped off in the battle? Something else. The combined French and Russian losses in one day at Borodino were seventy-five thousand men – the equivalent in fatalities of a fully loaded jumbo jet crashing every three minutes from breakfast to sundown. Kutuzov pulled his forces back towards Moscow. Napoleon drew breath, marshalled his troops, and continued his advance. He entered the downtown area of Moscow, where he stayed for a month waiting for Kutuzov, who never showed his face again. The Russian generalissimo was waiting for snow and ice, for Napoleon to begin his retreat to France.

Things stick in my head. I remember. So when I say I can

re-create the letter – the portion that I read, which catalogues the charges against me – I mean what I say.

In part, the letter went as follows:

Dear,

Things are not good. Things, in fact, are bad. Things have gone from bad to worse. And you know what I'm talking about. We've come to the end of the line. It's over with us. Still, I find myself wishing we could have talked about it.

It's been such a long time now since we've talked. I mean really *talked*. Even after we were married we used to talk and talk, exchanging news and ideas. When the children were little, or even after they were more grown-up, we still found time to talk. It was more difficult then, naturally, but we managed, we found time. We *made* time. We'd have to wait until after they were asleep, or else when they were playing outside, or with a sitter. But we managed. Sometimes we'd engage a sitter just so we *could* talk. On occasion we talked the night away, talked until the sun came up. Well. Things happen, I know. Things change. Bill had that trouble with the police, and Linda found herself pregnant, etc. Our quiet time together flew out the window. And gradually your responsibilities backed up on you. Your work became more important, and our time together was squeezed out. Then, once the children left home, our time for talking was back. We had each other again, only we had less and less to talk about. "It happens," I can hear some wise man saying. And he's right. *It happens*. But it happened to us. In any case, no blame. *No blame*. That's not what this letter is about. *I want to talk about us*. I want to talk about *now*. The time has come, you see, to admit that *the impossible* has happened. To cry *Uncle*. To beg off. To –

I read this far and stopped. Something was wrong. Something was fishy in Denmark. The sentiments expressed in the letter may have belonged to my wife. (Maybe they did. Say they did, grant that the sentiments expressed *were* hers.) But the handwriting *was not her handwriting*. And I ought to know. I consider myself an expert in this matter of her handwriting. And yet if it wasn't her handwriting, who on earth *had* written these lines?

I should say a little something about ourselves and our life here. During the time I'm writing about we were living in a house we'd taken for the summer. I'd just recovered from an illness that had set me back in most things I'd hoped to accomplish that spring. We were surrounded on three sides by meadows, birch woods, and some low, rolling hills – a "territorial view", as the realtor had called it when he described it to us over the phone. In front of the house was a lawn that had grown shaggy, owing to lack of interest on my part, and a long gravelled drive that led to the road. Behind the road we could see the distant peaks of mountains. Thus the phrase "territorial view" – having to do with a vista appreciated only at a distance.

My wife had no friends here in the country, and no one came to visit. Frankly, I was glad for the solitude. But she was a woman who was used to having friends, used to dealing with shopkeepers and tradesmen. Out here, it was just the two of us, thrown back on our resources. Once upon a time a house in the country would have been our ideal – we would have *coveted* such an arrangement. Now I can see it wasn't such a good idea. No, it wasn't.

Both our children had left home long ago. Now and then a letter came from one of them. And once in a blue moon, on a holiday, say, one of them might telephone – a collect call, naturally, my wife being only too happy to accept the charges. This seeming indifference on their part was, I believe, a major cause of my wife's sadness and general discontent – a discontent,

94

I have to admit, I'd been vaguely aware of before our move to the country. In any case, to find herself in the country after so many years of living close to a shopping mall and bus service, with a taxi no farther away than the telephone in the hall – it must have been hard on her, very hard. I think her *decline*, as a historian might put it, was accelerated by our move to the country. I think she slipped a cog after that. I'm speaking from hindsight, of course, which always tends to confirm the obvious.

I don't know what else to say in regard to this matter of the handwriting. How much more can I say and still retain credibility? We were alone in the house. No one else – to my knowledge, anyway – was in the house and could have penned the letter. Yet I remain convinced to this day that it was not her handwriting that covered the pages of the letter. After all, I'd been reading my wife's handwriting since before she was my wife. As far back as what might be called our prehistory days – the time she went away to school as a girl, wearing a grey-and-white school uniform. She wrote letters to me every day that she was away, and she was away for two years, not counting holidays and summer vacations. Altogether, in the course of our relationship, I would estimate (a conservative estimate, too), counting our separations and the short periods of time I was away on business or in the hospital, etc. – I would estimate, as I say, that I received seventeen hundred or possibly eighteen hundred and fifty handwritten letters from her, not to mention hundreds, maybe thousands, more infor- mal notes ("On your way home, please pick up dry cleaning, and some spinach pasta from Corti Bros"). I could recognize her handwriting anywhere in the world. Give me a few words. I'm confident that if I were in Jaffa, or Marrakech, and picked up a note in the marketplace, I would recognize it if it was my wife's handwriting. A word, even. Take this word *"talked"*, for instance. That simply isn't the way she'd write "talked"! Yet I'm the first to admit I don't know *whose* handwriting it is if it isn't hers.

Secondly, my wife *never* underlined her words for empha-
sis. Never. I don't recall a single instance of her doing this –
not once in our entire married life, not to mention the letters
I received from her before we were married. It would be
reasonable enough, I suppose, to point out that it could
happen to anyone. That is, anyone could find himself in a
situation that is completely atypical and, *given the pressure of
the moment*, do something totally out of character and draw a
line, the merest *line*, under a word, or maybe under an entire
sentence.

I would go so far as to say that every word of this entire
letter, so-called (though I haven't read it through in its en-
tirety, and won't, since I can't find it now), is utterly false. I
don't mean false in the sense of "untrue", necessarily. There
is some truth, perhaps, to the charges. I don't want to quibble.
I don't want to appear small in this matter; things are bad
enough already in this department. No. What I want to say,
all I want to say, is that while the sentiments expressed in the
letter may be my wife's, may even hold *some* truth – be
legitimate, so to speak – the force of the accusations levelled
against me is diminished, if not entirely undermined, even
discredited, because she *did not* in fact write the letter. Or, if
she *did* write it, then discredited by the fact that she didn't
write it in her own handwriting! Such evasion is what makes
men hunger for facts. As always, there are some.

On the evening in question, we ate dinner rather silently but
not unpleasantly, as was our custom. From time to time I
looked up and smiled across the table as a way of showing
my gratitude for the delicious meal – poached salmon, fresh
asparagus, rice pilaff with almonds. The radio played softly
in the other room; it was a little suite by Poulenc that I'd first
heard on a digital recording five years before in an apartment
on Van Ness, in San Francisco, during a thunderstorm.

When we'd finished eating, and after we'd had our coffee and dessert, my wife said something that startled me. "Are you planning to be in your room this evening?" she said.

"I am," I said. "What did you have in mind?"

"I simply wanted to know." She picked up her cup and drank some coffee. But she avoided looking at me, even though I tried to catch her eye.

Are you planning to be in your room this evening? Such a question was altogether out of character for her. I wonder now why on earth I didn't pursue this at the time. She knows my habits, if anyone does. But I think her mind was made up even then. I think she was concealing something even as she spoke.

"Of course I'll be in my room this evening," I repeated, perhaps a trifle impatiently. She didn't say anything else, and neither did I. I drank the last of my coffee and cleared my throat.

She glanced up and held my eyes a moment. Then she nodded, as if we had agreed on something. (But we hadn't, of course.) She got up and began to clear the table.

I felt as if dinner had somehow ended on an unsatisfactory note. Something else – a few words maybe – was needed to round things off and put the situation right again.

"There's a fog coming in," I said.

"Is there? I hadn't noticed," she said.

She wiped away a place on the window over the sink with a dish towel and looked out. For a minute she didn't say anything. Then she said – again mysteriously or so it seems to me now – "There is. Yes, it's very foggy. It's a heavy fog, isn't it?" That's all she said. Then she lowered her eyes and began to wash the dishes.

I sat at the table a while longer before I said, "I think I'll go to my room now."

She took her hands out of the water and rested them against

the counter. I thought she might proffer a word or two of encouragement for the work I was engaged in, but she didn't. Not a peep. It was as if she were waiting for me to leave the kitchen so she could enjoy her privacy.

Remember, I was at work in my room at the time the letter was slipped under the door. I read enough to question the handwriting and to wonder how it was that my wife had presumably been busy somewhere in the house and writing me a letter at the same time. Before reading further in the letter, I got up and went over to the door, unlocked it, and checked the corridor.

It was dark at this end of the house. But when I cautiously put my head out I could see light from the living room at the end of the hallway. The radio was playing quietly, as usual. Why did I hesitate? Except for the fog, it was a night very much like any other we had spent together in the house. But there was *something else afoot* tonight. At that moment I found myself afraid – afraid, if you can believe it, in my own house! – to walk down the hall and satisfy myself that all was well. Or if something was wrong, if my wife was experiencing – how should I put it? – difficulties of any sort, hadn't I best confront the situation before letting it go any further, before losing any more time on this stupid business of reading her words in somebody else's handwriting!

But I didn't investigate. Perhaps I wanted to avoid a frontal attack. In any case, I drew back and shut and locked the door before returning to the letter. But I was angry now as I saw the evening sliding away in this foolish and incomprehensible business. I was beginning to feel *uneasy*. (No other word will do.) I could feel my gorge rising as I picked up the letter purporting to be from my wife and once more began to read.

The time has come and gone for us – us, you and me – to put all our cards on the table. Thee and me. Lancelot and Guinevere. Abélard and Héloïse. Troilus and Cressida.

Pyramus and Thisbe. JAJ and Nora Barnacle, etc. You know what I'm saying, honey. We've been together a long time – thick and thin, illness and health, stomach distress, eye-ear-nose-and-throat trouble, high times and low. Now? Well, I don't know what I can say now except the truth: I can't go it another step.

At this point, I threw down the letter and went to the door again, deciding to settle this once and for all. I wanted an accounting, and I wanted it now. I was, I think, *in a rage*. But at this point, just as I opened the door, I heard a low murmuring from the living room. It was as if somebody were trying to say something over the phone and this somebody were taking pains not to be overheard. Then I heard the receiver being replaced. Just this. Then everything was *as before* – the radio playing softly, the house otherwise quiet. But I had heard a voice.

In place of anger, I began to feel panic. I grew afraid as I looked down the corridor. Things were the same as before – the light was on in the the living room, the radio played softly. I took a few steps and listened. I hoped I might hear the comforting, rhythmic clicking of her knitting needles, or the sound of a page being turned, but there was nothing of the sort. I took a few steps towards the living room and then – what should I say? – I lost my nerve, or maybe my curiosity. It was at that moment I heard *the muted sound of a doorknob being turned*, and afterwards the unmistakable sound of a door opening and closing quietly.

My impulse was to walk rapidly down the corridor and into the living room and get to the bottom of this thing once and for all. But I didn't want to act impulsively and possibly discredit myself. I'm not impulsive, so I waited. But there *was* activity of some sort in the house – something was afoot, I was sure of it – and of course it was my duty, for my own peace of mind, not to mention the possible safety and well-being of my wife, to act. But I didn't. I couldn't. The moment was there, but I hesitated. Suddenly it was too late for any decisive action. The moment had come and gone, and could not be called back. Just so did Darius hesitate and then fail to act at the Battle of Granicus, and the day was lost, Alexander the Great rolling him up on every side and giving him a real walloping.

I went back to my room and closed the door. But *my heart was racing*. I sat in my chair and, trembling, picked up the pages of the letter once more.

But now here's the curious thing. Instead of beginning to read the letter through, from start to finish, or even starting at the point where I'd stopped earlier, I took pages at random and held them under the table lamp, picking out a line here and a line there. This allowed me to juxtapose the charges made against me until the entire indictment (for that's what it was) took on quite another character – one more acceptable, since it had lost its chronology and, with it, a little of its punch.

So. Well. In this manner, going from page to page, here a line, there a line, I read in snatches the following – which might under different circumstances serve as a kind of abstract:

> . . . withdrawing farther into . . . a small enough thing, but . . . talcum powder sprayed over the bathroom, including walls and baseboards . . . a shell . . . not to mention the insane asylum . . . until finally . . . a balanced view . . . the grave. Your "work" . . . Please! Give me a break . . . No one, not even . . . Not another word on the subject! . . . The children . . . but the real issue . . . not to mention the loneliness . . . Jesus H. Christ! Really! I mean . . .

At this point I distinctly heard the front door close. I dropped the pages of the letter on to the desk and hurried to the living room. It didn't take long to see that my wife wasn't in the house. (The house is small – two bedrooms, one of which we refer to as my room or, on occasion, as my study.) But let the record show: *every light in the house was burning*.

A heavy fog lay outside the windows, a fog so dense I could scarcely see the driveway. The porch light was on and a suitcase stood outside on the porch. It was my wife's suitcase, the one she'd brought packed full of her things when we moved here. What on earth was going on? I opened the door. Suddenly – I don't know how to say this other than how it was – a horse stepped out of the fog, and then, an instant later, as I watched, dumbfounded, another horse. These horses were grazing in our front yard. I saw my wife alongside one of the horses, and I called her name.

"Come on out here," she said. "Look at this. Doesn't this beat anything?"

She was standing beside this big horse, patting its flank. She was dressed in her best clothes and had on heels and was wearing a hat. (I hadn't seen her in a hat since her mother's funeral, three years before.) Then she moved forward and put her face against the horse's mane.

"Where did you come from, you big baby?" she said. "Where did you come from, sweetheart?" Then, as I watched, she began to cry into the horse's mane.

"There, there," I said and started down the steps. I went over and patted the horse, and then I touched my wife's shoulder. She drew back. The horse snorted, raised its head a moment, and then went to cropping the grass once more. "What is it?" I said to my wife. "For God's sake, what's happening here, anyway?"

She didn't answer. The horse moved a few steps but continued pulling and eating the grass. The other horse was munching grass as well. My wife moved with the horse, hanging on to its mane. I put my hand against the horse's neck and felt a surge of power run up my arm to the shoulder. I shivered. My wife was still crying. I felt helpless, but I was scared, too.

"Can you tell me what's going on?" I said. "Why are you dressed like this? What's that suitcase doing on the front porch? Where did these horses come from? For God's sake, can you tell me what's happening?"

My wife began to croon to the horse. Croon! Then she stopped and said, "You didn't read my letter, did you? You might have skimmed it, but you didn't read it. Admit it!"

"I did read it," I said. I was lying, yes, but it was a white lie. A partial untruth. But he who is blameless, let him throw out the first stone. "But tell me what is going on anyway," I said.

My wife turned her head from side to side. She pushed her face into the horse's dark wet mane. I could hear the horse *chomp, chomp, chomp*. Then it snorted as it took in air through its nostrils.

She said, "There was this girl, you see. Are you listening? And this girl loved this boy so much. She loved him even more than herself. But the boy – well, he grew up. I don't know what happened to him. Something, anyway. He got cruel without meaning to be cruel and he –"

I didn't catch the rest, because just then a car appeared out of the fog, in the drive, with its headlights on and a flashing blue light on its roof. It was followed, a minute later, by a pick-up truck pulling what looked like a horse trailer, though with the fog it was hard to tell. It could have been anything – a big portable oven, say. The car pulled right up on to the lawn and stopped. Then the pick-up drove alongside the car and stopped, too. Both vehicles kept their headlights on and their engines running, which contributed to the eerie, bizarre aspect of things. A man wearing a cowboy hat – a rancher, I supposed – stepped down from the pick-up. He raised the collar of his sheepskin coat and whistled to the horses. Then a big man in a raincoat got out of the car. He was a much bigger man than the rancher, and he, too, was wearing a cowboy hat. But his raincoat was open, and I could see a pistol strapped to his waist. He had to be a deputy sheriff. Despite everything that was going on, and the anxiety I felt, I found it *worth noting* that both men were wearing hats. I ran my hand through my hair, and was sorry I wasn't wearing a hat of my own.

"I called the sheriff's department a while ago," my wife said. "When I first saw the horses." She waited a minute and then she said something else. "Now you won't need to give me a ride into town after all. I mentioned that in my letter, the letter you read. I said I'd need a ride into town. I can get a ride – at least, I think I can – with one of these gentlemen. And I'm not changing my mind about anything, either. I'm saying this decision is irrevocable. Look at me!" she said.

I'd been watching them round up the horses. The deputy was holding his flashlight while the rancher walked a horse up a little ramp into the trailer. I turned to look at this woman I didn't know any longer.

"I'm leaving you," she said. "That's what's happening. I'm heading for town tonight. I'm striking out on my own. It's all in the letter you read." Whereas, as I said earlier, my wife never underlined words in her letters she was now speaking (having dried her tears) as if virtually every other word out of her mouth ought to be emphasized.

"What's gotten *into* you?" I heard myself say. It was almost as if I couldn't help adding pressure to some of my own words. "Why are you *doing* this?"

She shook her head. The rancher was loading the second horse into the trailer now, whistling sharply, clapping his hands and shouting an occasional "Whoa! Whoa, damn you! Back up now. Back up!"

The deputy came over to us with a clipboard under his

arm. He was holding a big flashlight. "Who called?" he said.

"I did," my wife said.

The deputy looked her over for a minute. He flashed the light on to her high heels and then up to her hat. "You're all dressed up," he said.

"I'm leaving my husband," she said.

The deputy nodded, as if he understood. (But he didn't, he couldn't!) "He's not going to give you any trouble, is he?" the deputy said, shining his light into my face and moving the light up and down rapidly. "You're not, are you?"

"No," I said. "No trouble. But I resent —"

"Good," the deputy said. "Enough said, then."

The rancher closed and latched the door to his trailer. Then he walked towards us through the wet grass, which, I noticed, reached to the tops of his boots.

"I want to thank you folks for calling," he said. "Much obliged. That's one heavy fog. If they'd wandered on to the main road, they could have raised hob out there."

"The lady placed the call," the deputy said. "Frank, she needs a ride into town. She's leaving home. I don't know who the injured party is here, but she's the one leaving." He turned then to my wife. "You sure about this, are you?" he said to her.

She nodded. "I'm sure."

"Okay," the deputy said. "That's settled, anyway. Frank, you listening? I can't drive her to town. I've got another stop to make. So can you help her out and take her into town? She probably wants to go to the bus station or else to the hotel. That's where they usually go. Is that where you want to go to?" the deputy said to my wife. "Frank needs to know."

"He can drop me off at the bus station," my wife said. "That's my suitcase on the porch."

"What about it, Frank?" the deputy said.

"I guess I can, sure," Frank said, taking off his hat and

putting it back on again. "I'd be glad to, I guess. But I don't want to interfere in anything."

"Not in the least," my wife said. "I don't want to be any trouble, but I'm – well, distressed just now. Yes, I'm distressed. But it'll be all right once I'm away from here. Away from this awful place. I'll just check and make doubly sure I haven't left anything behind. Anything *important*," she added. She hesitated and then she said, "This isn't as sudden as it looks. It's been coming for a long, long time. We've been married for a good many years. Good times and bad, up times and down. We've had them all. But it's time I was on my own. Yes, it's time. Do you know what I'm saying, gentlemen?"

Frank took off his hat again and turned it around in his hands as if examining the brim. Then he put it back on his head.

The deputy said, "These things happen. Lord knows none of us is perfect. We weren't made perfect. The only angels is to be found in Heaven."

My wife moved towards the house, picking her way through the wet, shaggy grass in her high heels. She opened the front door and went inside. I could see her moving behind the lighted windows, and something came to me then. *I might never see her again*. That's what crossed my mind, and it staggered me.

The rancher, the deputy, and I stood around waiting, not saying anything. The damp fog drifted between us and the lights from their vehicles. I could hear the horses shifting in the trailer. We were all uncomfortable, I think. But I'm speaking only for myself, of course. I don't know what they felt. Maybe they saw things like this happen every night – saw people's lives flying apart. The deputy did, maybe. But Frank, the rancher, he kept his eyes lowered. He put his hands in his front pockets and then took them out again. He kicked at something in the grass. I folded my arms and went on standing there, not knowing what was going to happen next. The deputy kept turning off his flashlight and then turning it on again. Every so often he'd reach out and swat the fog with it. One of the horses whinnied from the trailer, and then the other horse whinnied, too.

"A fellow can't see anything in this fog," Frank said.

I knew he was saying it to make conversation.

"It's as bad as I've ever seen it," the deputy said. Then he looked over at me. He didn't shine the light in my eyes this time, but he said something. He said, "Why's she leaving you? You hit her or something? Give her a smack, did you?"

"I've never hit her," I said. "Not in all the time we've been married. There was reason enough a few times, but I didn't. She hit me once," I said.

"Now, don't get started," the deputy said. "I don't want to hear any crap tonight. Don't say anything, and there won't be anything. No rough stuff. Don't even think it. There isn't going to be any trouble here tonight, is there?"

The deputy and Frank were watching me. I could tell Frank was embarrassed. He took out his makings and began to roll a cigarette.

"No," I said. "No trouble."

My wife came on to the porch and picked up her suitcase. I had the feeling that not only had she taken a last look around but she'd used the opportunity to freshen herself up, put on new lipstick, etc. The deputy held his flashlight for her as she came down the steps. "Right this way, ma'am," he said. "Watch your step, now – it's slippery."

"I'm ready to go," she said.

"Right," Frank said. "Well, just to make sure we got this all straight now." He took off his hat once more and held it. "I'll carry you into town and I'll drop you off at the bus station. But, you understand, I don't want to be in the middle of something. You know what I mean." He looked at my wife, and then he looked at me.

"That's right," the deputy said. "You said a mouthful. Statistics show that your domestic dispute is, time and again, potentially the most dangerous situation a person, especially a law-enforcement officer, can get himself involved in. But I think this situation is going to be the shining exception. Right, folks?"

My wife looked at me and said, "I don't think I'll kiss you. No, I won't kiss you goodbye. I'll just say so long. Take care of yourself."

"That's right," the deputy said. "Kissing – who knows what that'll lead to, right?" He laughed.

I had the feeling they were all waiting for me to say something. But for the first time in my life I felt at a loss for words. Then I *took heart* and said to my wife, "The last time you wore that hat, you wore a veil with it and I held your arm. You were in mourning for your mother. And you wore a dark dress, not the dress you're wearing tonight. But those are the same high heels, I remember. Don't leave me like this," I said. "I don't know what I'll do."

"I have to," she said. "It's all in the letter – everything's spelled out in the letter. The rest is in the area of – I don't know. Mystery or speculation, I guess. In any case, there's nothing in the letter you don't already know." Then she turned to Frank and said, "Let's go, Frank. I can call you Frank, can't I?"

"Call him anything you want," the deputy said, "long as you call him in time for supper." He laughed again – a big, hearty laugh.

"Right," Frank said. "Sure you can. Well, OK. Let's go, then." He took the suitcase from my wife and went over to his pick-up and put the suitcase into the cab. Then he stood by the door on the passenger's side, holding it open.

"I'll write after I'm settled," my wife said. "I think I will, anyway. But first things first. We'll have to see."

"Now you're talking," the deputy said. "Keep all lines of

communication open. Good luck, pardee," the deputy said to me. Then he went over to his car and got in.

The pick-up made a wide, slow turn with the trailer across the lawn. One of the horses whinnied. The last image I have of my wife was when a match flared in the cab of the pick-up, and I saw her lean over with a cigarette to accept the light the rancher was offering. Her hands were cupped around the hand that held the match. The deputy waited until the pick-up and trailer had gone past him and then he swung his car around, slipping in the wet grass until he found purchase on the driveway, throwing gravel from under his tyres. As he headed for the road, he tooted his horn. *Tooted.* Historians should use more words like "tooted" or "beeped" or "blasted" – especially at serious moments such as after a massacre or when an awful occurrence has cast a pall on the future of an entire nation. That's when a word like "tooted" is necessary, is gold in a brass age.

I'd like to say it was at this moment, as I stood in the fog watching her drive off, that I remembered a black-and-white photograph of my wife holding her wedding bouquet. She was eighteen years old – *a mere girl,* her mother had shouted at me only a month before the wedding. A few minutes before the photo, she'd got married. She's smiling. She's just finished, or is just about to begin, laughing. In either case, her mouth is open in amazed happiness as she looks into the camera. She is three months pregnant, though the camera doesn't show that, of course. But what if she *is* pregnant? So what? Wasn't everybody pregnant in those days? She's happy, in any case. I was happy, too – I know I was. We were both happy. I'm not in that particular picture, but I was close – only a few steps away, as I remember, shaking hands with someone offering me good wishes. My wife knew Latin and German and chemistry and physics and history and

Shakespeare and all those other things they teach you in private school. She knew how to properly hold a teacup. She also knew how to cook and to make love. She was a prize.

But I found this photograph, along with several others, a few days after the horse business, when I was going through my wife's belongings, trying to see what I could throw out and what I should keep. I was packing to move, and I looked at the photograph for a minute and then I threw it away. I was ruthless. I told myself I didn't care. Why should I care?

If I know anything – and I do – if I know the slightest thing about human nature, I know she won't be able to live without me. She'll come back to me. And soon. Let it be soon.

No, I don't know anything about anything, and I never did. She's gone for good. She is. I can feel it. Gone and never coming back. Period. Not ever. I won't see her again, unless we run into each other on the street somewhere.

There's still the question of the handwriting. That's a bewilderment. But the handwriting business isn't the important thing, of course. How could it be after the consequences of the letter? Not the letter itself but the things I can't forget that were *in* the letter. No, the letter is not paramount at all – there's far more to this than somebody's handwriting. The "far more" has to do with subtle things. It could be said, for instance, that to take a wife is to take a history. And if that's so, then I understand that I'm outside history now – like horses and fog. Or you could say that my history has left me. Or that I'm having to go on *without history*. Or that history will now have to do without me – unless my wife writes more letters, or tells a friend who keeps a diary, say. Then, years later, someone can look back on this time, interpret it according to the record, its scraps and tirades, its silences and innuendoes. That's when it dawns on me that autobiography is the poor man's history. And that I am saying goodbye to history. Goodbye, my darling.

Errand

Chekhov. On the evening of 22 March 1897, he went to dinner in Moscow with his friend and confidant Alexei Suvorin. This Suvorin was a very rich newspaper and book publisher, a reactionary, a self-made man whose father was a private at the battle of Borodino. Like Chekhov, he was the grandson of a serf. They had that in common: each had peasant's blood in his veins. Otherwise, politically and temperamentally, they were miles apart. Nevertheless, Suvorin was one of Chekhov's few intimates, and Chekhov enjoyed his company.

Naturally, they went to the best restaurant in the city, a former town house called the Hermitage – a place where it could take hours, half the night even, to get through a ten-course meal that would, of course, include several wines, liqueurs, and coffee. Chekhov was impeccably dressed, as always – a dark suit and waistcoat, his usual pince-nez. He looked that night very much as he looks in the photographs taken of him during this period. He was relaxed, jovial. He shook hands with the maître d', and with a glance took in the large dining room. It was brilliantly illuminated by ornate chandeliers, the tables occupied by elegantly dressed men and women. Waiters came and went ceaselessly. He had just been seated across the table from Suvorin when suddenly, without warning, blood began gushing from his mouth. Suvorin and two waiters helped him to the gentlemen's room and tried to stanch the flow of blood with ice packs. Suvorin saw him back to his own hotel and had a bed prepared for Chekhov in one of the rooms of the suite. Later, after another haemor- rhage, Chekhov allowed himself to be moved to a clinic that specialized in the treatment of tuberculosis and related respiratory infections. When Suvorin visited him there, Chekhov apologized for the "scandal" at the restaurant three nights earlier but continued to insist there was nothing seriously wrong. "He laughed and jested as usual," Suvorin noted in his diary, "while spitting blood into a large vessel."

Maria Chekhov, his younger sister, visited Chekhov in the clinic during the last days of March. The weather was miserable; a sleet storm was in progress, and frozen heaps of snow lay everywhere. It was hard for her to wave down a carriage to take her to the hospital. By the time she arrived she was filled with dread and anxiety.

"Anton Pavlovich lay on his back," Maria wrote in her *Memoirs*. "He was not allowed to speak. After greeting him, I went over to the table to hide my emotions." There, among bottles of champagne, jars of caviar, bouquets of flowers from well-wishers, she saw something that terrified her: a freehand drawing, obviously done by a specialist in these matters, of Chekhov's lungs. It was the kind of sketch a doctor often makes in order to show his patient what he thinks is taking place. The lungs were outlined in blue, but the upper parts were filled in with red. "I realized they were diseased," Maria wrote.

Leo Tolstoy was another visitor. The hospital staff were awed to find themselves in the presence of the country's greatest writer. The most famous man in Russia? Of course they had to let him in to see Chekhov, even though "non- essential" visitors were forbidden. With much obsequiousness on the part of the nurses and resident doctors, the bearded, fierce-looking old man was shown into Chekhov's room.

Despite his low opinion of Chekhov's abilities as a playwright (Tolstoy felt the plays were static and lacking in any moral vision. "Where do your characters take you?" he once demanded of Chekhov. "From the sofa to the junk room and back."), Tolstoy liked Chekhov's short stories. Furthermore, and quite simply, he loved the man. He told Gorky, "What a beautiful, magnificent man: modest and quiet, like a girl. He even walks like a girl. He's simply wonderful." And Tolstoy wrote in his journal (everyone kept a journal or a diary in those days), "I am glad I love . . . Chekhov."

Tolstoy removed his woollen scarf and bearskin coat, then lowered himself into a chair next to Chekhov's bed. Never mind that Chekhov was taking medication and not permitted to talk, much less carry on a conversation. He had to listen, amazedly, as the Count began to discourse on his theories of the immortality of the soul. Concerning that visit, Chekhov later wrote, "Tolstoy assumes that all of us (humans and animals alike) will live on in a principle (such as reason or love) the essence and goals of which are a mystery to us . . . I have no use for that kind of immortality. I don't understand it, and Lev Nikolayevich was astonished I didn't."

Nevertheless, Chekhov was impressed with the solicitude shown by Tolstoy's visit. But, unlike Tolstoy, Chekhov didn't believe in an afterlife and never had. He didn't believe in anything that couldn't be apprehended by one or more of his five senses. And as far as his outlook on life and writing went, he once told someone that he lacked "a political, religious, and philosophical world view. I change it every month, so I'll have to limit myself to the description of how my heroes love, marry, give birth, die, and how they speak."

Earlier, before his TB was diagnosed, Chekhov had remarked, "When a peasant has consumption, he says, 'There's nothing I can do. I'll go off in the spring with the melting of the snows.'" (Chekhov himself died in the summer, during a heat wave.) But once Chekhov's own tuberculosis was discovered he continually tried to minimize the seriousness of his condition. To all appearances, it was as if he felt, right up to the end, that he might be able to throw off the disease as he would a lingering catarrh. Well into his final days, he spoke with seeming conviction of the possibility of an improvement. In fact, in a letter written shortly before his end, he went so far as to tell his sister that he was "getting fat" and felt much better now that he was in Badenweiler.

Badenweiler is a spa and resort city in the western area of the Black Forest, not far from Basel. The Vosges are visible from nearly anywhere in the city, and in those days the air was pure and invigorating. Russians had been going there for years to soak in the hot mineral baths and promenade on the boulevards. In June 1904, Chekhov went there to die.

Earlier that month, he'd made a difficult journey by train from Moscow to Berlin. He travelled with his wife, the actress Olga Knipper, a woman he'd met in 1898 during rehearsals for *The Seagull*. Her contemporaries describe her as an excellent actress. She was talented, pretty, and almost ten years younger than the playwright. Chekhov had been immediately attracted to her, but was slow to act on his feelings. As always, he preferred a flirtation to marriage. Finally, after a three-year courtship involving many separations, letters, and the inevitable misunderstandings, they were married, in a private ceremony in Moscow, on 25 May 1901. Chekhov was enormously happy. He called Olga his "pony", and sometimes "dog" or "puppy". He was also fond of addressing her as "little turkey" or simply as "my joy".

In Berlin, Chekhov consulted with a renowned specialist in pulmonary disorders, a Dr Karl Ewald. But, according to an eyewitness, after the doctor examined Chekhov he threw up his hands and left the room without a word. Chekhov was too far gone for help: this Dr Ewald was furious with himself for not being able to work miracles, and with Chekhov for being so ill.

A Russian journalist happened to visit the Chekhovs at their hotel and sent back this dispatch to his editor: "Chekhov's days are numbered. He seems mortally ill, is terribly thin, coughs all the time, gasps for breath at the slightest movement, and is running a high temperature." This same journalist saw the Chekhovs off at Potsdam Station when they boarded their train for Badenweiler. According to his account, "Chekhov had trouble making his way up the small staircase at the station. He had to sit down for several minutes to catch his breath." In fact, it was painful for Chekhov to move: his legs ached continually and his insides hurt. The disease had attacked his intestines and spinal cord. At this point he had less than a month to live. When Chekhov spoke of his condition now, it was, according to Olga, "with an almost reckless indifference".

Dr Schwöhrer was one of the many Badenweiler physicians who earned a good living by treating the well-to-do who came to the spa seeking relief from various maladies. Some of his patients were ill and infirm, others simply old and hypochondriacal. But Chekhov's was a special case: he was clearly beyond help and in his last days. He was also very famous. Even Dr Schwöhrer knew his name: he'd read some of Chekhov's stories in a German magazine. When he examined the writer early in June, he voiced his appreciation of Chekhov's art but kept his medical opinions to himself. Instead, he prescribed a diet of cocoa, oatmeal drenched in butter, and strawberry tea. This last was supposed to help Chekhov sleep at night.

On 13 June, less than three weeks before he died, Chekhov wrote a letter to his mother in which he told her his health was on the mend. In it he said, "It's likely that I'll be completely cured in a week." Who knows why he said this? What could he have been thinking? He was a doctor himself, and he knew better. He was dying, it was as simple and as unavoidable as that. Nevertheless, he sat out on the balcony of his hotel room and read railway timetables. He asked for information on sailings of boats bound for Odessa from Marseilles. But he *knew*. At this stage he had to have known. Yet in one of the last letters he ever wrote he told his sister he was growing stronger by the day.

He no longer had any appetite for literary work, and hadn't for a long time. In fact, he had very nearly failed to complete *The Cherry Orchard* the year before. Writing that play was the hardest thing he'd ever done in his life. Towards the end, he was able to manage only six or seven lines a day. "I've started losing heart," he wrote Olga. "I feel I'm finished as a writer, and every sentence strikes me as worthless and of no use whatever." But he didn't stop. He finished his play in October 1903. It was the last thing he ever wrote, except for letters and a few entries in his notebook.

A little after midnight on 2 July 1904, Olga sent someone to fetch Dr Schwöhrer. It was an emergency: Chekhov was delirious. Two young Russians on holiday happened to have the adjacent room, and Olga hurried next door to explain what was happening. One of the youths was in his bed asleep, but the other was still awake, smoking and reading. He left the hotel at a run to find Dr Schwöhrer. "I can still hear the sound of the gravel under his shoes in the silence of that stifling July night," Olga wrote later on in her memoirs. Chekhov was hallucinating, talking about sailors, and there were snatches of something about the Japanese. "You don't put ice on an empty stomach," he said when she tried to place an ice pack on his chest.

Dr Schwöhrer arrived and unpacked his bag, all the while keeping his gaze fastened on Chekhov, who lay gasping in the bed. The sick man's pupils were dilated and his temples glistened with sweat. Dr Schwöhrer's face didn't register anything. He was not an emotional man, but he knew Chekhov's end was near. Still, he was a doctor, sworn to do his utmost, and Chekhov held on to life, however tenuously. Dr Schwöhrer prepared a hypodermic and administered an injection of camphor, something that was supposed to speed up the heart. But the injection didn't help – nothing, of course, could have helped. Nevertheless, the doctor made known to Olga his intention of sending for oxygen. Suddenly, Chekhov roused himself, became lucid, and said quietly, "What's the use? Before it arrives I'll be a corpse."

Dr Schwöhrer pulled on his big moustache and stared at Chekhov. The writer's cheeks were sunken and grey, his complexion waxen; his breath was raspy. Dr Schwöhrer knew the time could be reckoned in minutes. Without a word, without conferring with Olga, he went over to an alcove where there was a telephone on the wall. He read the instructions for using the device. If he activated it by holding his finger on a button and turning a handle on the side of the phone, he could reach the lower regions of the hotel – the kitchen. He picked up the receiver, held it to his ear, and did as the instructions told him. When someone finally answered, Dr Schwöhrer ordered a bottle of the hotel's best champagne. "How many glasses?" he was asked. "Three glasses!" the doctor shouted into the mouthpiece. "And hurry, do you hear?" It was one of those rare moments of inspiration that can easily enough be overlooked later on, because the action is so entirely appropriate it seems inevitable.

The champagne was brought to the door by a tired-looking young man whose blond hair was standing up. The trousers of his uniform were wrinkled, the creases gone, and in his haste he'd missed a loop while buttoning his jacket. His appearance was that of someone who'd been resting (slumped in a chair, say, dozing a little), when off in the distance the phone had clamoured in the early-morning hours – great God in Heaven! – and the next thing he knew he was being shaken awake by a superior and told to deliver a bottle of Moët to Room 211. "And hurry, do you hear?"

The young man entered the room carrying a silver ice bucket with the champagne in it and a silver tray with three cut-crystal glasses. He found a place on the table for the bucket and glasses, all the while craning his neck, trying to see into the other room, where someone panted ferociously for breath. It was a dreadful, harrowing sound, and the young man lowered his chin into his collar and turned away as the ratchety breathing worsened. Forgetting himself, he stared out the open window towards the darkened city. Then this big imposing man with a thick moustache pressed some coins into his hand – a large tip, by the feel of it – and suddenly the young man saw the door open. He took some steps and found himself on the landing, where he opened his hand and looked at the coins in amazement.

Methodically, the way he did everything, the doctor went about the business of working the cork out of the bottle. He did it in such a way as to minimize, as much as possible, the festive explosion. He poured three glasses and, out of habit, pushed the cork back into the neck of the bottle. He then took the glasses of champagne over to the bed. Olga momentarily released her grip on Chekhov's hand – a hand, she said later, that burned her fingers. She arranged another pillow behind his head. Then she put the cool glass of champagne against Chekhov's palm and made sure his fingers closed around the stem. They exchanged looks – Chekhov, Olga, Dr Schwöhrer. They didn't touch glasses. There was no toast. What on earth was there to drink to? To death? Chekhov summoned his remaining strength and said, "It's been so long since I've had champagne." He brought the glass to his lips and drank. In a minute or two Olga took the empty glass from his hand and set it on the nightstand. Then Chekhov turned on to his side. He closed his eyes and sighed. A minute later, his breathing stopped.

Dr Schwöhrer picked up Chekhov's hand from the bed-sheet. He held his fingers to Chekhov's wrist and drew a gold watch from his vest pocket, opening the lid of the watch as he did so. The second hand on the watch moved slowly, very slowly. He let it move around the face of the watch three times while he waited for signs of a pulse. It was three o'clock in the morning and still sultry in the room. Baden-weiler was in the grip of its worst heat wave in years. All the windows in both rooms stood open, but there was no sign of a breeze. A large, black-winged moth flew through a window and banged wildly against the electric lamp. Dr Schwöhrer let go of Chekhov's wrist. "It's over," he said. He closed the lid of his watch and returned it to his vest pocket.

At once Olga dried her eyes and set about composing herself. She thanked the doctor for coming. He asked if she wanted some medication – laudanum, perhaps, or a few drops of valerian. She shook her head. She did have one request, though: before the authorities were notified and the news-papers found out, before the time came when Chekhov was no longer in her keeping, she wanted to be alone with him for a while. Could the doctor help with this? Could he withhold, for a while anyway, news of what had just occurred?

Dr Schwöhrer stroked his moustache with the back of a finger. Why not? After all, what difference would it make to anyone whether this matter became known now or a few hours from now? The only detail that remained was to fill out a death certificate, and this could be done at his office later in the morning, after he'd slept a few hours. Dr Schwöhrer nodded his agreement and prepared to leave. He murmured a few words of condolence. Olga inclined her head. "An honour," Dr Schwöhrer said. He picked up his bag and left the room and, for that matter, history.

It was at this moment that the cork popped out of the champagne bottle; foam spilled down on to the table. Olga went back to Chekhov's bedside. She sat on a footstool, holding his hand, from time to time stroking his face. "There were no human voices, no everyday sounds," she wrote. "There was only beauty, peace, and the grandeur of death."

She stayed with Chekhov until daybreak, when thrushes began to call from the garden below. Then came the sound of tables and chairs being moved about down there. Before long, voices carried up to her. It was then a knock sounded at the door. Of course she thought it must be an official of some sort – the medical examiner, say, or someone from the police who had questions to ask and forms for her to fill out, or maybe, just maybe, it could be Dr Schwöhrer returning with a mortician to render assistance in embalming and transporting Chekhov's remains back to Russia.

But, instead, it was the same blond young man who'd brought the champagne a few hours earlier. This time, however, his uniform trousers were neatly pressed, with stiff creases in front, and every button on his snug green jacket was fastened. He seemed quite another person. Not only was he wide awake but his plump cheeks were smooth-shaven, his hair was in place, and he appeared anxious to please. He was holding a porcelain vase with three long-stemmed yellow roses. He presented these to Olga with a smart click of his heels. She stepped back and let him into the room. He was there, he said, to collect the glasses, ice bucket, and tray, yes. But he also wanted to say that, because of the extreme heat, breakfast would be served in the garden this morning. He hoped this weather wasn't too bothersome; he apologized for it.

The woman seemed distracted. While he talked, she turned her eyes away and looked down at something in the carpet. She crossed her arms and held her elbows. Meanwhile, still holding his vase, waiting for a sign, the young man took in the details of the room. Bright sunlight flooded through the open windows. The room was tidy and seemed undisturbed, almost untouched. No garments were flung over chairs, no shoes, stockings, braces, or stays were in evidence, no open suitcases. In short, there was no clutter, nothing but the usual heavy pieces of hotel-room furniture. Then, because the woman was still looking down, he looked down, too, and at once spied a cork near the toe of his shoe. The woman did not see it – she was looking somewhere else. The young man wanted to bend over and pick up the cork, but he was still holding the roses and was afraid of seeming to intrude even more by drawing any further attention to himself. Reluctantly, he left the cork where it was and raised his eyes. Everything was in order except for the uncorked, half-empty bottle of champagne that stood alongside two crystal glasses over on the little table. He cast his gaze about once more. Through an open door he saw that the third glass was in the bedroom, on the nightstand. But someone still occupied the bed! He couldn't see a face, but the figure under the covers lay perfectly motionless and quiet. He noted the figure and looked elsewhere. Then, for a reason he couldn't understand, a feeling of uneasiness took hold of him. He cleared his throat and moved his weight to the other leg. The woman still didn't look up or break her silence. The young man felt his cheeks grow warm. It occurred to him, quite without his having thought it through, that he should perhaps suggest an alternative to breakfast in the garden. He coughed, hoping to focus the woman's attention, but she didn't look at him. The distinguished foreign guests could, he said, take breakfast in their rooms this morning if they wished. The young man (his name hasn't survived, and it's likely he perished in the Great

War) said he would be happy to bring up a tray. Two trays, he added, glancing uncertainly once again in the direction of the bedroom.

He fell silent and ran a finger around the inside of his collar. He didn't understand. He wasn't even sure the woman had been listening. He didn't know what else to do now; he was still holding the vase. The sweet odour of the roses filled his nostrils and inexplicably caused a pang of regret. The entire time he'd been waiting, the woman had apparently been lost in thought. It was as if all the while he'd been standing there, talking, shifting his weight, holding his flowers, she had been someplace else, somewhere far from Badenweiler. But now she came back to herself, and her face assumed another expression. She raised her eyes, looked at him, and then shook her head. She seemed to be struggling to understand what on earth this young man could be doing there in the room holding a vase with three yellow roses. Flowers? She hadn't ordered flowers.

The moment passed. She went over to her handbag and scooped up some coins. She drew out a number of banknotes as well. The young man touched his lips with his tongue; another large tip was forthcoming, but for what? What did she want him to do? He'd never before waited on such guests. He cleared his throat once more.

No breakfast, the woman said. Not yet, at any rate. Breakfast wasn't the important thing this morning. She required something else. She needed him to go out and bring back a mortician. Did he understand her? Herr Chekhov was dead, you see. *Comprenez-vous?* Young man? Anton Chekhov was dead. Now listen carefully to me, she said. She wanted him to go downstairs and ask someone at the front desk where he could go to find the most respected mortician in the city. Someone reliable, who took great pains in his work and whose manner was appropriately reserved. A mortician, in short, worthy of a great artist. Here, she said, and pressed the

money on him. Tell them downstairs that I have specifically
requested you to perform this duty for me. Are you listening?
Do you understand what I'm saying to you?

The young man grappled to take in what she was saying.
He chose not to look again in the direction of the other room.
He had sensed that something was not right. He became
aware of his heart beating rapidly under his jacket and he
felt perspiration break out on his forehead. He didn't know
where he should turn his eyes. He wanted to put the vase down.

Please do this for me, the woman said. I'll remember you
with gratitude. Tell them downstairs that I insist. Say that.
But don't call any unnecessary attention to yourself or to the
situation. Just say that this is necessary, that I request it – and
that's all. Do you hear me? Nod if you understand. Above
all, don't raise an alarm. Everything else, all the rest, the
commotion – that'll come soon enough. The worst is over.
Do we understand each other?

The young man's face had grown pale. He stood rigid,
clasping the vase. He managed to nod his head.

After securing permission to leave the hotel he was to
proceed quietly and resolutely, though without any unbecom-
ing haste, to the mortician's. He was to behave exactly as if
he were engaged on a very important errand, nothing more.
He *was* engaged on an important errand, she said. And if it
would help keep his movements purposeful he should imagine
himself as someone moving down the busy sidewalk carrying
in his arms a porcelain vase of roses that he had to deliver to
an important man. (She spoke quietly, almost confidentially,
as if to a relative or a friend.) He could even tell himself that
the man he was going to see was expecting him, was perhaps
impatient for him to arrive with his flowers. Nevertheless,
the young man was not to become excited and run, or otherwise break his stride. Remember the vase he was carrying!
He was to walk briskly, comporting himself at all times in as
dignified a manner as possible. He should keep walking until

he came to the mortician's house and stood before the door. He would then raise the brass knocker and let it fall, once, twice, three times. In a minute the mortician himself would answer.

This mortician would be in his forties, no doubt, or maybe early fifties – bald, solidly built, wearing steel-frame spectacles set very low on his nose. He would be modest, unassuming, a man who would ask only the most direct and necessary questions. An apron. Probably he would be wearing an apron. He might even be wiping his hands on a dark towel while he listened to what was being said. There'd be a faint whiff of formaldehyde on his clothes. But it was all right, and the young man shouldn't worry. He was nearly a grown-up now and shouldn't be frightened or repelled by any of this. The mortician would hear him out. He was a man of restraint and bearing, this mortician, someone who could help allay people's fears in this situation, not increase them. Long ago he'd acquainted himself with death in all its various guises and forms; death held no surprises for him any longer, no hidden secrets. It was this man whose services were required this morning.

The mortician takes the vase of roses. Only once while the young man is speaking does the mortician betray the least flicker of interest, or indicate that he's heard anything out of the ordinary. But the one time the young man mentions the name of the deceased, the mortician's eyebrows rise just a little. Chekhov, you say? Just a minute, and I'll be with you.

Do you understand what I'm saying, Olga said to the young man. Leave the glasses. Don't worry about them. Forget about crystal wineglasses and such. Leave the room as it is. Everything is ready now. We're ready. Will you go?

But at that moment the young man was thinking of the cork still resting near the toe of his shoe. To retrieve it he would have to bend over, still gripping the vase. He would do this. He leaned over. Without looking down, he reached out and closed it into his hand.

Also available as Harvill Paperbacks

GIUSEPPE TOMASI DI LAMPEDUSA
The Leopard
"A novel of exceptional stature.
One may claim for it classic status"
FRANK KERMODE

JORGE AMADO
The Tent of Miracles
"Not only is Jorge Amado one of the greatest writers alive,
he's also one of the most entertaining"
MARIO VARGAS LLOSA

MIKHAIL BULGAKOV
The Master and Margarita
"A masterpiece... a classic of twentieth century fiction"
New York Times

FYODOR DOSTOYEVSKY
The Double
"Comic, uncanny and profound"
JOHN BAYLEY

PETER MATTHIESSEN
Far Tortuga
"Unique... original... enormously haunting"
WILLIAM STYRON

BORIS PASTERNAK
Doctor Zhivago
"The first work of genius to come out of Russia
since the Revolution"
V.S. PRITCHETT

GEORGES PEREC
Life a User's Manual
"One of the most singular literary personalities
in the world"
ITALO CALVINO

SALVATORE SATTA
The Day of Judgment
"A great European novel"
SUSAN SONTAG

ALEXANDER SOLZHENITSYN
The First Circle
"A majestic work of genius"
Sunday Times

Harvill Paperbacks are published by Collins Harvill,
a Division of the Collins Publishing Group

I have always loved writing. I am fascinated by the effects of words – how choosing a slightly different word can conjure an entirely different spell. Language is much more important than mere communication. It's what makes humans different from other animals. Stories are important but much more important and interesting is how the story is told.

I spent a *very* long time trying to write a novel that was good enough to be published. The eventual publication of *Mondays are Red* was the realisation of a dream. It was life-changing. Then, of course, I simply had to do it again, so here is *Fleshmarket*, a very different book. It was inspired by a tour round Surgeons' Hall in Edinburgh and hearing the true and truly chilling story which forms the basis for the opening chapter. It grew into the story of *Fleshmarket* when I asked myself, as all writers do, 'What if . . . ?'

I love writing for teenagers, young people, young adults, whatever you want to call them. They are open to new ideas, they can cope with a multi-layered story, they respond to unusual language, they question, they demand to understand, and at the same time their imaginations are still free. In their imaginations, they can fly. For a writer, that is an unmissable opportunity.

Nicola Morgan

www.nicolamorgan.co.uk

Other titles available from Hodder Children's Books

NICOLA MORGAN

Hodder
Children's
Books

A division of Hodder Headline Limited

A Catalogue record for this book is available
from the British Library

ISBN-10: 0 340 85557 6
ISBN-13: 9780340855577

Typeset in Bembo by Avon DataSet Ltd,
Bidford-on-Avon, Warwickshire

Printed and bound in Great Britain by
Bookmarque Ltd, Croydon, Surrey

The paper and board used in this paperback by Hodder Children's Books
are natural recyclable products made from wood grown in sustainable
forests. The manufacturing processes conform to the environmental
regulations of the country of origin.

Hodder Children's Books
A Division of Hodder Headline Limited
338 Euston Road
London NW1 3BH

With huge thanks to my two experts: Richard Rodger,
Professor of urban history at the University of Leicester,
and Rev John Weir Cook, Church of Scotland Minister.
Their expertise and support were invaluable and any mistakes
that remain are my fault. Special thanks to Chris Kloet,
my editor, for her enormous influence on the shape of this
story, for telling me what I often did not want to hear,
and for the inspirational book of old Scots songs.
And finally, thanks to my daughters and especially to
Harry, my husband, for putting up with it all.

The Doctor

O dinna fear the doctor,
He comes to mak' ye weel,
To nurse ye like a tender flower,
And your wee head to heal;
He brings the bloom back to your cheek,
The blithe blink to your e'e –
An't werena for the doctor,
My bonnie bairn might dee.

O wha would fear the doctor!
His pouthers, pills an' a';
Ye just a wee bit swither gi'e,
An' then the taste's awa'!
He'll mak' ye sleep as sound's a tap,
And rise as light's a flee –
An't werena for the doctor,
My bonnie bairn might dee,

A kind man is the doctor,
As mony poor folk ken;
He spares nae toil by day or night
To ease them o' their pain;
And O he lo'es the bairnies weel,
An' tak's them on his knee –
An't werena for the doctor,
My bonnie bairn might dee.

Alexander Smart

Prologue

Edinburgh, the Infirmary, 1822

The woman walked slowly into the room, her stiff skirts rustling in the sudden silence. A man, in long black coat and firmly pointed collar, came towards her and led her across squeaky floorboards towards the table. He did not look at her face. She did not look at the table.

She kept her eyes down so that she need not study the crowds ranged around the walls of the vast, cold room. More than three hundred people, her husband told her proudly later. All come to watch her operation. All hoping to learn something that would help others.

Her left breast, where the tumour was, swelled against her arm. If she did not have this operation, the tumour would grow and spread and eventually she would die, her lungs rattling with fluid and her bones brittle with pain. She had seen it happen to her mother.

What the surgeon had not told her, in his need to persuade another patient to endure his knife, was that the chances were high that she would die anyway.

Another man came towards her, again not meeting her eyes, his collar squashed into his thick neck and a jewel of moisture on his wispy moustache. He led her to the table. Behind, her husband carried the baby, two years old, too young to understand. She could hear a dog's scratchy claws tap-tapping on the floorboards, rising above the curious murmurs of the crowd.

'Lie down here. Please,' said the man, pointing to the large oak table in the middle of the room. Under the table sat a bucket, half full of pinkish water, with two worn scrubbing brushes nearby. The table was not completely dry.

The woman placed her back to the edge of the table and with her hands tried to lift herself on to it. She had to jump two or three times before she could reach high enough but after some awkward wriggling, in front of all these watchers, she was sitting on the edge of the table. She hoisted her legs up on to it, trying to keep her dignity, smoothing her skirts down and holding her feet tightly together. She shivered and cold sweat chilled her armpits. She lay down on the damp wood, arms rigidly beside her.

She looked at the ceiling and grew colder. A large spider hung briefly on its thread above her face. Watched her watching it. It scuttled back towards the safety of its web. The sunlight threw flickering shadows, which danced drowsily across the dull ivory plaster. The loud murmuring of the spectators lulled her and she could almost believe that this was not going to happen.

No one had spoken her name since she entered the room. Maybe she was not really there? Where was her husband standing? Where was her baby, her curly-haired, diamond-eyed daughter? She was glad her older child, Robbie, had not been allowed into the room. But she must not scream, or he would hear from outside and not understand that this was something which must be done, this cutting into his mother while she lay awake on the table. In front of all these peering bushy-faced men.

Suddenly she heard the sound of the door opening, the hushing, and slow footsteps tapping a smooth semibreve beat across the floor. The dog barked.

'Make that dog be quiet!' came a voice of strange musical richness. It was a young voice, liquid, honey-smooth.

Through glazed eyes, a distant part of the woman's brain took in the man's pock-marked ugliness, his gummed unseeing eye. Yet there was something comforting in this ugliness, something unthreatening. He had been ill-treated by life and yet he chose to be here with her, to help her.

The voice continued, from close by her, softly, 'You will need to undress yourself. Otherwise, how can I perform my task?' His perfume washed over her. Floral. Roses, sweet, heady.

Obediently, but blushing hot red, she sat up awkwardly. Her breast hurt as her arm brushed against it and she felt again the angry mass of the tumour. She fumbled with the buttons and struggled to free her arms. No one helped. It would not have been proper.

The young surgeon carefully tucked his lacy cuffs out of sight, under his soft mulberry coat, its buttons glinting. He checked that the chain of his time-piece hung in a perfect arc across his front. The other man held an apron for him. The surgeon bent his head and the apron was slipped over his neck and tied behind him.

Unseen eyes wandered over her nakedness. A breath of chill air brushed her exposed chest. She shivered. The room waited.

'Just one side. One side is sufficient,' said the surgeon. She mumbled her apology, as though she should have known. As she lay down once more, half-covered now, aware of her own acrid sweat, she saw him take from a deep place within his apron some metal instruments. Three sharp knives and some things like scissors, amongst a fistful of metal objects with unknown purposes.

The woman found herself breathing faster. She did not know anyone who had had surgery before, but she knew that it must hurt. She had tried to imagine how much, had reassured herself by saying, 'If someone else can bear it, I can bear it too. It is only pain. We are made to bear pain. Men bear worse than this on the battlefield.' Her knees were locked, her lower back arched off the table, her fingers clenched tight as walnuts.

Someone put a thin white cloth, a handkerchief, over her face. She did not know why. She could still see through it. It smelt of moths and tobacco, clinging to her skin like a cobweb. Now several men came closer, two on each side of her. The ghost of a face loomed over hers. She smelt their pipe breath, the dark sweat of their bodies, heard the rustling of their stiff clothes. Strong male hands grasped her wrists and ankles. Fingers held her head. She started to struggle, her breathing fast, her chest bursting.

'Be calm. I have not started yet. Stay very still and very calm. It will soon be over. My usual time is one and three quarter minutes. You can bear it for so short a time. Childbirth takes longer than that. Be very calm and breathe slowly and deeply.'

His voice barely reached her terror. She wished someone would hit her on the head, knock her out. Her body was not hers. It pounded with fear. Blood spat through her heart. Air trapped itself in her chest. Her teeth hurt. Tears squeezed between clenched eyelids.

Then, through all this fear came the voice of her baby. 'Mammy, Mammy, not cry Mammy,' and tears were in the words. Her mother's love drowned everything else and she turned towards where her baby's voice came from. She spoke from under the cloth.

'Do not fret, little one. Your mammy's well. All is well. I will be with you soon.'

Silently she shrank back down into herself and waited for what was to come.

The pain was one shattered scream, shooting into a million splinters in her ears. Something was stuffed between her teeth. Every muscle in her body, every joint, jerked into spasm. Something rasping was inside her, scraping against the bones in her chest, digging into her, tugging, ripping. She felt blood flow around her back and blackness flooded over her, suffocating.

As if in a dream she flew towards a white light, stretched from head to toe on a silver arrow, twisting unbreathing, spiralling, silent screaming. Somewhere else, down there, behind, was the pain, but she was outside it, watching it and hearing it. As long as she could hold her breath, she would not be down there. She could hold her breath for ever, for ever and ever and ever. She could stay out here, up here, and never go back. Stay in the knife-sharp angel whiteness, never breathing again. How easy it would be, how dizzyingly easy just to float away. She watched with detached pity the dwarfed figure of herself pinned on the table in the room below, like a beautiful but damaged butterfly specimen not quite dead.

Outside the room, her son, only eight years old, clenched his ears between his hands. He crouched in a ball and rocked and rocked and rocked, to lull the sound of his mother's scream. She saw him from above and reached out for him, held him in her heart, flew with him, floating free together, and then, suddenly, simply, she let him fall. She dropped him. Something closed inside her and she let him go. As he fell alone, a part of her cried for him but did not properly feel the crying. She knew there was a reason for crying but she could not grasp what it was before it had gone. Now she was in a place where nothing seemed as strange as it should.

The arrow reached the top of its path, slowed, hovered, turned and began to arc back down to earth, away from the light and silence. Back to the pain. Dragged into reality, she felt once more the cold hardness of the table. She was burning, ice hot.

Some more tugging at flesh that did not feel part of her, some more clenching of her jaw so tightly that a tooth cracked down the middle, and then the voice said, 'Finished. A good job, I believe you will all agree. This woman came to us today with a large tumour of the breast and she will leave us cured of her cancer.'

The men around the room clapped and the noise of their admiration rose like wind in a graveyard. The woman was helped to a sitting position by someone. Steadying her dizziness, biting back the sick faintness which threatened to disgrace her, she lifted her legs off the table and stood up. Someone behind her wrapped bandages around the heavy pad that was pressed to the place where her breast had been. She gasped.

Composing herself, the woman stood, curtseyed to the surgeon, curtseyed to the rows of faceless watchers, and followed her husband and baby out of the room. She held her head high but looked at no one.

The dog followed behind, scratch scratching on the wooden floor.

The surgeon dropped the instruments into the bucket of cold pink water and strolled over to speak to a friend in the audience, wiping his hands on a large handkerchief. A young man picked up the instruments and shook them in the water. He lifted them out again and carried them dripping to the surgeon. Using his handkerchief, the surgeon dried them. He held one knife up to the light for those close to him to see the brilliant sharpness of its blade. He spat on it and polished it on his sleeve. It sent a diamond of light dancing on to the ceiling and everyone laughed when the light landed like an angel on the door as it closed behind the grateful woman.

Footsteps echoed through the towering corridors, as the woman walked, smooth as marble, unbreathing, followed by her silent family. No one could touch her. She touched none of them. She was different. Robbie, young as he was, felt it. He had felt her pain as though it was his. It had burned him and left its mark. The mark was the empty space where his real mother had been. The place where she had left him.

The first day after surgery, the woman felt weak. An apothecary instructed that she should be kept quiet. The authorities gave special permission for straw to be spread outside the house to deaden the clattering and clashing of hooves and carriages.

On the second day, she felt stronger. She asked for chicken broth and her husband brought it to her himself, glad to see that she was on the mend. He handed the baby back into her care with relief and went to his work. Important work, which Robbie did not understand but which gave them increasing prosperity and comfort. Robbie, watching his mother constantly, fearfully, was pleased she was getting better too. When his mother was better, everything would be all right again. They could carry on as they had been before. Looking forward.

On the third day, she felt merely tired and somewhat absent. Her breast – or the place where her breast used to be – was painful and red. Hot to touch. Two pink spots flushed her cheeks. The apothecary told her that this was her body healing itself. Her husband was pleased again – her pink cheeks made her look pretty – young and fresh. As a rose.

On the fourth day, she did not know his name. Did not recognize her trembling son with his eyes so wide and wet. Could not care about her baby's hungry cries. Threw her sweat-soaked blankets off, rattled with bone-deep cold, screamed at the snakes writhing before her eyes, vomited, clawed moaning at the blackening rash that crept over her body.

On the fifth day, she died.

1

Six Years Later – February 1828

Robbie lingered. Daylight was disappearing and the February wind needled through the open-weave cloth of his jacket. But he did not want to go home yet. Here, near the Royal Park, the air was fresher, the wind wafting the scent of the sea instead of the pig-swill reek of the Old Town. He stopped to watch the workmen on the new railway, in noisy humour as they finished work for the day. He could just see through the trees the cavernous hole in the hillside, where each day more rock, blasted by gunpowder, was carried away by horse-drawn rail wagons.

He turned his collar up and hunched his shoulders, thrusting his fists into sagged pockets. He wondered if his father would be home. No point in wondering if he would bring any food, or money. There had been a time – and it seemed a long time ago – when Robbie had relied on his father, when it seemed as though the three of them could manage together. The fire had destroyed more than buildings. It had changed everything. Again.

If it had not been for the fire, Robbie would have had better work than ferrying deliveries for a baker. And a better life to go with it.

He shivered. His sleeves were too short and the material thinned by use. He was hungry. He had bread in his pockets, of course – a whole fresh bannock, still warm. Mr Brown had given it to him. But Robbie would not eat it until he came home and could share it with Essie and their father.

Robbie's work was done for the day, his last delivery – to the Sheep Heid tavern in Duddingston – safely unloaded and the barrow returned to the bakery near the Palace. The looming peak of Arthur's Seat towered behind him and he remembered, as he could not avoid doing each time he passed this spot, the bonfire that had enflamed the sky for King George's visit. But he pushed it from his mind. It was a time better forgotten completely.

He should go home.

He made his way quickly towards the Old Town, leaving Holyrood Palace behind him, its windows yellow and warm, music faint within its walls. Darkness fell more heavily and dank perpetual smoke clogged the air. Shadowed people scurried through the unlit streets. Tall black buildings swooned over him and the stench increased. The cobbled pavements were slippery with filth and rotten food. Doorways and corners seethed with bundles – humans lying wrapped and waiting to sleep. Or drunk. Something fell from a window high above, landing with a splash a few feet in front of him. He hurried on through the thickening darkness.

Voices. Laughter from behind him. He turned. Two figures were rounding a corner and were approaching through the gloom, their way lit by a boy carrying a swinging lamp. Gentlemen, Robbie could see that straightaway. Tall hats, elegant canes waving, dark coats falling almost to their knees, stiff upright collars, their necks warmed by thick cravats. One slapped the other on the back with another roar of laughter. Robbie stood aside to let them pass, pressing himself into an empty doorway. The boy ran along in front, the lamp in one hand and a stick in the other, checking for sudden dips or loose cobbles which might catch the gentlemen's elegant feet.

The taller one, Robbie could see now as they passed, wore a plum-coloured coat, lace cuffs flopping from the sleeves, every button gleaming. A jewelled brooch at the throat.

Suddenly one voice, harsh as cymbals, rang out above

15

the other city noises. A sentence, a name, that made Robbie's blood freeze.

'Gad's sake, Dr Knox! Keep your flesh–cutting knife away from me! I could not bear such pain!'

Robbie shrank back into his doorway. His breath stuck in his throat. He felt himself spinning backwards into a dizzy past that he preferred to forget. No longer fourteen, he was eight years old again, bewildered. He was standing outside a room, a huge black studded door blocking his way. He was alone. Everyone else, his whole world, was on the other side of the door and no one had explained why. He heard footsteps along the chilled marble corridor and saw two men striding towards him, until they were towering over him. One of the men had a monstrous face, gouged and pitted by smallpox. Robbie turned away.

'What is this?' asked the pitted man.

'The woman's child, Dr Knox,' replied the other.

The pitted man bent down, till his face was close to Robbie's and Robbie could smell his perfume. Flowery. 'Well, well, young man. Look at me. Come on, look at me. You do not mind my face, do you? What does it matter about my face when I intend to save your mother? Eh? Besides, just look at this coat. Quality. Sheer quality. Took delivery of it only yesterday. Wearing it especially for your mother's operation.' He made a tiny adjustment to the way his coat sat, flicked an invisible something from its breast, breathed in more deeply, pumped out his chest.

Robbie found himself oddly drawn to the man's voice, with its warm musical quality. He looked at the face again. It was stiff, like a mask. Then Robbie noticed something else. One eye was white and blank, dead, unmoving. It was frightening because it could be thinking anything. It looked like veined pig fat. He looked away again.

Dr Knox stood up. 'Well, well. Must not keep the patient waiting. How do I look, Hamilton?'

'Superlative, Dr Knox. As always. No one would guess you had come straight from a cadaver.'

Dr Knox smiled and looked at his fingers for a moment, holding them away from him to focus better. 'Onwards, Hamilton. Goodbye, laddie.'

The door opened, an orchestra of voices rose and hushed as it closed, and Robbie waited. He did not know what for. He strained to hear through the shut door. Nothing. Then perhaps a murmuring rustling, a dog barking, a voice, possibly Dr Knox's voice, silence.

Then Robbie's world was shattered.

The scream was a blade which sliced through him and he joined it, screaming himself as he rocked and rocked and rocked the scream away. Yet he would never rock that scream away. As he floated tumbling in his mother's arms through the lightest whitest void, holding her tightly, never wanting to let her go, she dropped him, without warning, pushed him away, and when he finished spinning he found himself alone. Alone in front of the closed door, with his hands over his ears. His mother had left him.

Now, just as suddenly, he was back in the present again, back on an Edinburgh street, six years later, seeing two gentlemen walk past laughing. One of them was Dr Knox. The surgeon. Six years older too, more bushy-faced, grown more into his skin. The lyrical laughing voice echoed in Robbie's head. The memory of that awful moment had been buried deep in the silt of his mind until now. Occasionally over the years he had heard the man's name but seeing him in the flesh, hearing that voice again, made everything different, and real. He followed them, drawn by an inexplicable fascination. He could hear snatches of words, their voices swelling, ripe with claret.

Dr Knox was speaking now. 'A shocking idea, my dear fellow, shocking. To eliminate pain in surgery? Pain is God's will, God's gift. How could we mere mortals be so bold, so dreadfully audacious, as to consider trying to go against God's will? Pain? We must welcome it, as God's gift to us.' Knox was flinging his lacy arm in the air as he spoke.

Robbie's thoughts spun like oatmeal in the wind. This was something he had tried not to consider. It was too enormous, too confusing for his mind. God was good and yet God had made his mother suffer and had killed her. God had chosen to take his mother from him. And that was God's gift to him. He had heard this message many times before. In the kirk each Sunday, until they stopped going four years ago, and now in the streets sometimes, listening to the preacher in his wooden tent, ranting to a rowdy crowd about God's will and punishment and salvation. And damnation.

Robbie could not think of blaming God. Could not hold such a terrible thought in his head for fear that lightning would strike him dead, or typhus, or the plague sent as a punishment. Was his poverty not already a sign of God's anger with him and his family? That was what the clever preachers said. That poverty was a fair punishment. Somewhere in Robbie's mind a tiny doubt occasionally fluttered, but every time he squashed it dead. Doubt was a sin.

So, he dare not blame God. But what about this man, this Dr Knox? Surely he was to blame? This was the evil man who had killed his mother. And from his mother's death had come the destruction of her family's dreams.

It had been the beginning of the end. Of course, there had been the fire, but first there had been his mother's death. It had changed his world. Yet this man, the cause of it all, this doctor, neither knew nor cared. Here he was, now, six years later, still caring nothing of what he did to people. How could he swagger around in his expensive clothes, while others lived like pigs in filth and stench, their lives hopeless?

The other man was speaking now.

'They will not mind so much, Knox, your patients. Most of your patients are dead before they reach you. One could even say that they have the patience of the dead.'

Dr Knox roared with laughter and stumbled against his companion, as he slipped in the slime. 'How very true, sir. But I treat them all with equal respect. Dead or alive, they all receive my utmost care and attention. However, it is worth noting that it is the living ones who make the most noise. By Gad! All that screaming – it is surely enough to turn me deaf as well as half blind. Now if some of these doctors with their fairy-tale ideas of killing pain could stop a patient's noise, there would be something worth paying for.'

Robbie's heart pounded. He had to follow them. He could not have said why, only that it was impossible not to. If Robbie's life was a prison, Dr Robert Knox was the man who had hurled him into it and thrown away the key with a careless pock-marked sneer. Robbie was drawn to him like any enemy to another.

Following a man in the shadowed streets was not difficult. Tiny alleys, unexpected corners and deep doorways made easy hiding places if necessary. There were other people on the street, too, some hurrying home before the darkness fell completely, others lingering for their own reasons. Even if Dr Knox and his companion had looked round, they would not have seen him. He kept his eyes fixed on the two hats a few steps ahead.

He thought of nothing other than following this man and then . . . Nothing else. No clear thoughts, just an instinct, a feeling of being pulled. He did not notice the chill darkening wind, the cold smurring rain across his face. He forgot that his young sister would be waiting for him, on her own if his father was not there.

The two men turned left. Robbie followed them up a short steep street. He knew where he was. There was Infirmary Street in front of him. And there the hospital where . . . He put the thought from him quickly. They turned left, through some gates. Past the hospital, between the shoulders of buildings, they passed into a tree-frothed square. Surgeons' Square. Calm, peaceful, enclosed. Detached from the rotting streets. Secret. The windows like eyes looking down. The carvings above the doors like noses.

Robbie stayed in the shadows of the buildings at the entrance to the square. He watched the men and their boy cross the square and go towards a building in the left-hand corner. They gave something to the boy and he ran off, past where Robbie hid, and out of the square. In front of the men, the door opened, spilling its orange light on to the steps. They went in and the door closed behind them. Now the square was empty.

As wind rustled the trees that grew in the square, whispering, the glow from the gas-lights danced lazily across the cobbles. The pavements were swept clean. No bundles in doorways here.

Robbie looked at the building. Was it where Knox lived? It did not look like a square where people lived. The buildings seemed too severe for homes. On this one, the shutters were closed, as if it had folded its arms against him. As he walked carefully towards it, keeping to the shadows at the edge of the square, he saw that light was coming from a gap in the shutters of a basement window. Glancing in all directions to make sure he was not watched, he ran over and looked down through the railings. Squinting between the gap, it was hard at first to make out what he was seeing. But as his vision adjusted, he gasped.

He could hardly believe what he saw. He moved his head to the side to see more of the scene through the crack. On a table, spread, pinned, exposed, lay, flat on its back, the body of a man. He could not see the legs, but it was clear that it was human. Now, its waxen yellow flesh hardly resembled any man Robbie had seen.

One hand was fixed to the table, palm upwards, crucified by tall pins. Flaps of its flesh were peeled away, to show purpled lines and a maze of tiny tubes. One eye was missing. But, no! Not missing, just lying on the table beside the body, sliced open to reveal the jelly inside. Most horrible of all – Robbie held his arm over his mouth and breathed through his sleeve – a huge rectangular hole had been cut in the man's belly. From inside it spilled . . . Robbie could not look any more.

He turned and ran, his lips clamped together to keep the scream inside. Out of Surgeons' Square, past the hospital without looking or breathing, or thinking, back down the steeply sloped street, across the Cowgate again and into a narrow alley. He felt safer in the familiar darkness of the side roads, away from carriages and people.

As he ran up the filthy narrow street, the same thoughts spattered his brain: What sort of evil was this? What sort of man could cut up a human body in this grotesque ungodly way? What would the pain feel like, when living flesh was sliced and pinned like an insect? And how could his mother not have died of such pain?

Only when he reached the low entrance to his own close off the High Street, did Robbie stop running. With his hands on his knees, he bent over, gasping, saliva pooling in his mouth. He spat. He turned into the tiny passageway between the buildings. Hearing a noise, he looked down. A rat stared up at him, its thin lips snarled back, its two top needle-sharp teeth crossed over each other like swords. He kicked it away from the pig carcass that it had been eating. That was probably one of the pigs that lived on the ground floor of Robbie's building. Two adults, nine children and four pigs. Or three pigs now. One room. The sewage sludging past their doorstep. And swirling around their tiny smoke-grimed window hummed the smell of it, mixed with the rotten meat stench from the entrails and carcasses of the flesh market which by day filled the bottom of the close and gave it its name. Fleshmarket Close. Often a dog or scrawny cat would drag a stolen pig's ear or the hairy meatless end of a cow's tail to the relative quiet of their staircase and chew it before leaving the remains to the rats and flies.

Knox would not be living somewhere like this. Nor would Robbie if his mother had not died.

At the shared stairs to the upper floors, Robbie

scraped his boots against the bottom step. Exhaustion hit him then and his thigh muscles were shaking as he climbed to the top floor. There was no light but he knew the way by heart, though he still walked carefully, in case something lay on the stairs. He paused and took deep breaths before opening the door, aware that he did not have much food in his pocket.

' 'S Robbie,' he called. Footsteps and scuffling inside as the door opened. Essie's bird-like eyes were diamond-bright, in an eight-year-old's face polished acorn brown with dirt. Her wiry arms were never still and her grubby dress hung off her scrawny body. Essie had the energy of a sparrow. She survived on sparkle. And she could steal like a magpie. Robbie smiled as he moved his hand to touch her wild dark tangle of hair. She wriggled away and screwed up her face.

'Pleased to see me, Essie? Or pleased to see supper?'

'Supper!' Robbie gripped his sister's hair and playfully tightened his fist. 'Supper, supper, supper!' shrieked Essie. 'What's for supper?'

'A feast fit for a king,' proclaimed Robbie, letting her go. 'Guinea fowl, freshly caught from his Lordship's estate, jugged hare in a rich plum sauce with brandy and capers, flavoured with herbs from distant parts of the Orient, delicious strawberries . . .'

'You mean bread? An' tatties?' asked Essie.

25

'Yes, all right, I mean bread. But not potatoes. Sorry. Is he back?'

Essie knew who Robbie meant. She did not answer. 'I got milk. It's warming by the fire.' She went to fetch what they needed for their meal. Bread and milk. And, as always, oatmeal. Not much. February was the worst time to be poor. Food was scarce and expensive.

Their father often did not come back. Sometimes he disappeared for a week at a time. More than once, he disappeared for a month. There was usually a reason. Twice he had been taken by the army press gang and had been lucky to escape. Once, Robbie wondered if he had been in prison. Sometimes, his story was that he was trying to find work, but Robbie had stopped believing that anyone would give him any work worth having. Not with the smell of whisky on his breath and the empty wild tired look in his eyes.

Years ago, before . . . when their mother was alive, Robbie's father had been respected. And, for a time, almost wealthy. He had made sufficient money through brains, hard work and a good education. He had gone into business with some friends and been lucky, though lucky was not how it seemed looking back. Insurance, that was the new craze. People were getting rich in insurance and the opportunities seemed endless. A new world, people called it, and Edinburgh at the forefront.

Edinburgh still was, and many of those people still were rich. But for every one who had moved into grand spacious squares in the New Town, there were others who had lost everything. Robbie's father was one of those. Without rich friends in powerful places, lawyers or professors, when his business failed he had no one to help him.

Robbie and his family should be in the New Town now, not in this stinking midden. That had been the plan. And how near they had come to it. Before . . .

Now, as they dunked their bread in warm, slightly tangy milk, hunched near a smoking fire in one draughty room at the top of a five-storey building, Robbie could not help noticing the plaster crumbling with dampness, the sticky black soot that coated every surface in the room, the crazy muddled shelves of half-broken objects, and the endless sickening smell of dead rats under the floorboards and their own waste in a bucket. One bed between three of them, two stools, a table with a broken leg leaning against the wall, water to be queued for and carried up the slippery stone stairs. In February at least there was clean water to be had but in the summer the public well often ran dry and they eked out a jug of stagnant liquid that grew black with flies. They were always hungry, always exhausted, always weak. In winter their eyes were hollow and their skin flaky under their hair. And itchy. Their spit was black with the smoke that hung over the town. This was not a life. An animal could make a better life for itself than this, thought Robbie.

Essie could smile through it. But Essie knew nothing different. Essie had not had time to dream before their mother died.

That night, as the city slumped into silence in the streets far below, and as the two of them lay head to toe in the bed they shared, and as Essie slept, Robbie found his mind wandering to a time which usually he preferred to forget. Now, with his resentment stirred by the unexpected encounter with Dr Knox, he let himself remember the life that had been taken from him. The life he should still have.

2

A Dream Fit For a King

August 1822. He would never forget it. The city swarming with excitement at King George's visit. Colour and heat and noise.

Everything, every detail, was organized by the famous writer, Walter Scott. Robbie remembered his father explaining that the visit had been Mr Scott's idea in the first place. 'It is the first time for two hundred years that a British king has come to Edinburgh,' said his father proudly as they watched the preparations. 'Mr Scott says it is a way of bringing the Highlanders and Lowlanders together. We live in a new Scotland, Robbie, and Edinburgh is at the forefront.'

The streets, scabbed dry by weeks without rain, were now swept clean by gangs of sweating men. Dozens of carts dragged sand from Portobello beach and spread it on the cobbles. Mr Scott's orders, said Robbie's father, to muffle the sounds of horses and allow the bands to be heard. Each day the Town Criers announced new orders from the great man. Residents to empty their chamber pots and buckets every morning into the public drain, not the cobbles below. Privies, where they existed, to be emptied too, not left until they overflowed. Every window facing a street to have a light shining in it after dark. No jostling during the King's presence. Each bystander to choose a place and stay in it – no pushing.

Mothers rushed to make new dresses for themselves and their daughters. Men who might find themselves in the presence of the King assembled their uniforms – all to a new design, ordered by Mr Scott, of course. Tight white breeches, white waistcoat and blue coat, with a blue and white cockade on a low-crowned hat, to be decorated with heather.

Strange wild-looking men with enormous manes of shaggy red hair swaggered about, swirling in kilts. At first Robbie was frightened by these creatures – everyone had heard about the terrible behaviour of Highlanders. But Mr Scott had invited them, said his father. 'Why do they wear skirts?' asked Robbie. 'I am not sure that I know,' said his mother. 'People are saying that it is all Mr Scott's idea.' Essie hid in her mother's proper skirts as these creatures rolled roaring past, speaking a foreign language of frightening coarseness.

A new wonder – gas lighting. Robbie's father had taken him to watch one day as work began on installing three hundred lights from Holyrood Palace to Dalkeith, the route the King would take each day of his visit. For not a moment of the King's stay must he be in darkness.

A woman who lived near Robbie had been given a special ticket by the Provost. She had been chosen to parade on a balcony reserved for the most beautiful ladies. They were to stand and smile and be smiled at by the King. There was excitement, mixed in no small part with jealousy. Was her nose not slightly too thin? Were her shoulders not somewhat rounded? And everyone knew that the roses in her cheeks were not from God but came from her pinching her face whenever she thought no one was looking.

Scaffolding sprouted up the sides of every building. People who lived on top floors sold tickets for others to perch on roofs. When a half-finished scaffold collapsed amid mangled bones and broken heads, and two young men dead, within a few hours the platform was higher than before.

No one knew which day the King would arrive at Leith harbour and rumours spread like typhus. Every day more people arrived in Edinburgh: Highlanders, Lowlanders, each suspicious of the other. Traders came from London, selling new essentials, their confident manners a marvel to everyone. Strange accents mingled and voices were loud with excitement. The terrible skirl of bag-pipes pierced the air and the city heaved with heat and sweat and breath.

Still, the King had not arrived.

There was another rumour. Robbie's mother was worried: she had heard of a highly unpleasant disease, the Itch, which could be caught from close contact with crowds, especially during celebrations. 'But we need not worry,' she told her husband. 'There is a cure.' And she showed him what an English trader had sold her that day as she walked along the Grassmarket: Barclay's Original Ointment. 'It has come all the way from England, from London no less,' and she gazed wonderingly at the shiny white jar with its clean smooth lid and its elegant, confident lettering.

It was a time for excitement, a time to believe things out of the ordinary.

Then one day, as hot and heaving and noisy as the others, Robbie's father announced that they were going on an outing. A surprise. His mother's eyes shone. They had to put on their best clothes. Two-year-old Elizabeth, Essie for short, had her unruly black curls forced inside a cap and her pinafore changed for a clean one. She fidgeted in her clean white stockings and soft child's slippers. Robbie felt tall and proud in his new grown-up clothes: an iron-brown coat above fawn breeches that stopped just below his knees, and silk stockings which wrinkled at the ankles despite being held up with garters. His new shoes were a little too big and the stockings slippery, so that he had to curl his toes and shuffle slightly to stop them sliding.

They set off, through the bustle and noise. And the colour! Robbie did not know a word for it. It was more than the colours of the rainbow. Sunlight reflected from the reds, the blues, the whites, of clothes and flags and carriages. Ostrich feathers dyed every shade imaginable danced from vendors' barrows and ladies' heads. As they walked towards Princes Street, over the sweeping arches of North Bridge, and as they gazed across at the pale buildings on the other side, the city looked carved out of sand. Sunlight streamed across the pillars and spires and copper domes as though heaven was smiling on this city. To the west, the soft hills cupped it in the hands of God. In the other direction rose Calton Hill, its sides swarming with tiny people struggling to the top to see the herring-silver strip of sea where the King would land. Tents were pitched on slopes, so that people would not miss the spectacle when the King came. And to each side of Robbie and his family, lay the twin protrusions of the castle rock and Arthur's Seat, two sleeping giants guarding them. There could be nowhere like it in the world.

'Hurry, Robbie,' said his mother as Robbie lingered to look. 'We have a surprise for you.' They were heading towards the symmetrical lines of the New Town.

The surprise was a house. A house sitting in the sun, its own black railings shiny, its iron gate open, clean steps going up to the black door, and others going down to a basement. Robbie's mother and father stood together. His hand rested on her back. A tiny sweat shone on her nose. Her cheeks were poppy-bright, her face fragile, as though she might melt away.

'Who lives here?' asked Robbie, not sure why they were there.

'No one lives here,' smiled his father, looking proudly at the house. 'It is not ready. But when it is finished, we will live here.'

Robbie hardly knew what to think. He wanted to see inside. 'May we go in?' How could he live in a house like this, with its own door, and big windows gulping in sunlight? And no filth on the street. A wide street with air flowing through it. Saxe-Coburg Place, it was called, which spoke to him of royalty and foreign courts.

'No, Robbie,' said his mother. 'Not yet. But you can look through the window.' Part of him wanted to run up the steps as a small child might, and stare and stare in wonder. But the other part of him, the one stiff and grown-up in a formal collar and breeches, held back. He walked carefully up the steps, his shoes slipping at the heels and slapping on the stonework. Looking through the railings to the side, he could see into the nearest room on the ground floor. Try as he might, he could not stop his eyes opening wide. It was huge! The ceilings high, the plaster flowing in teardrops around the corners. An enormous fireplace, surrounded by a white carved frame, much wider than the fireplace itself, a ledge above it. The clean straight lines perfect.

He could not imagine living in this house. And yet, the more he thought about it, the more he could see them here, breathing in the space in the huge light rooms.

Essie was wriggling in her father's arms. She was not interested. They walked back towards the Old Town, towards the cluster of ramshackle buildings clawing their way up towards the Castle. Towards the thick yellow pall of smoke that clung like phlegm to the roofs. Robbie was full of questions and he shared his parents' excitement as they answered and added information of their own. They would have water running from a tap in the kitchen, and their own privy outside. Robbie and Essie would no longer share a bed. They would have servants, two, perhaps even three. Gas-lights of their own, fixed to the walls in glass globes, his father explained. A garden, with flowers. Roses – his mother wanted roses.

Robbie's mother looked at his father with pride. This was all due to his success in business, his hard work and his education, she told Robbie. Robbie listened with only a part of himself. He was not interested in how. All he felt was the pure excitement of moving to a new life. Not that he had ever particularly disliked the one he had before, but even he could see now that his old street was narrow and smelt of pigs and fish, while this new one flowed with air from the sea and the hills.

That evening, humid and sticky, they dressed in their best clothes again. Not Essie. Essie was too young. A neighbour came to look after her. Robbie's mother looked fragile as eggshell, in her new silk dress with its skirts the lightest blue of a morning sky. His father stood stiff and proud, rich in plum purple, his arms behind him and his shoulders pulled back, his chin pushed upwards by his thick cravat. And Robbie itched in his sharp-edged collar, the new shiny-buckled shoes now painful where they had rubbed skin away.

A concert. Robbie had never been to a concert before and was not entirely sure that he wanted to. 'This is what we will do when we live in the New Town,' explained his father. When we live in the New Town.

It was a phrase Robbie had heard a dozen times that day. It still sounded far away.

St Cecilia's Hall. A short squalid walk from their street, along cobbles newly cleaned for the Visit, but with the smell merely disturbed and the gutters still overflowing with waste. Robbie's mother hoisted her skirts high above the filth with both hands. Ladies held bottles of smelling-salts to their noses as they passed. Robbie's mother had some, too, and she let her skirts fall to wave the bottle hesitantly beneath her nose, wrinkling it in surprise.

They jostled into the hall. Robbie could not see in this crowd of adults. 'Follow me,' said his father, and with his mother urging him on he pushed blindly through all the people, until they came to the edge of the room. His father helped Robbie climb on to the ledge that formed the base of one of the many half-pillars that were set into the side of the hall, and he leaned into the space between the pillar and the wall. Now he stood taller than his father, and could scan the seething sea of people. He could see the orchestra in their places, lights dancing from their instruments. His father stood close so Robbie could not fall. Robbie could smell his hair, with its warm powdered grease. His mother stood beside her husband, her face shining. She looked hot. But she smiled at Robbie through the noise.

A man was walking to the front of the orchestra. 'The conductor!' whispered his father. The audience hushed and calmed. An eager breathless silence. The conductor raised his arms. And then began an evening Robbie would never forget. Sometimes he closed his eyes to the music and let it just flow through him. But most of the time he watched. He gazed at each instrument and tried to identify the sound it made, tried to imagine that he was the player.

But he did not really imagine himself as a player, did not properly feel the pull, until the music shrank to a whisper and amidst the waves of applause another man came out and stood in front of the conductor. This other man, with wild stormy hair and a long neck, dressed all in stiff black and white, held a violin, its rich amber warmth glowing in the lamplight. After a pause, the man bent his body towards the instrument and into the silence he began to play.

Robbie sank into the song the violin sang. He could no longer smell his father's hair, feel the stiffness of his own new collar. He flew with the music, the sad-sounding up and down swelling of notes whose names Robbie did not know. Sometimes the notes were tiny, fast, the player's fingers flickering over the strings like spiders' legs. Sometimes they were long and sad and lingering, hovering on each note for ever. They flowed from him and through the violin and into the air where they hung like mist. It could not be an instrument of wood and gut, this violin. It had a voice. The voice of a swan, long and white and untouchable.

After the concert, as they pushed their way into the night air, Robbie was dazed.

'Did you enjoy it, Robbie?' asked his father.

'What was his name?' asked Robbie.

Felix Janiewicz. The name was too spiky, too sharp to make such music. But Robbie wanted to play the violin like Janiewicz.

'How I would like to play the violin like him!'

His father laughed as they began to climb the stairs to their home. His mother smiled, a wisp of damp hair dangling from the coils around her head. 'Would you like to learn, Robbie?'

He could only nod. She looked at her husband. 'He could, could he not? We can afford it now.'

'Of course,' said his father. 'You may have lessons when we live in the New Town.' When we live in the New Town.

'Oh, surely we could start a little sooner than that, my dear,' she smiled at her husband. Her silk skirts were drooping now, crushed and limp from the hot crowds.

'Anything for you, my dearest,' said Robbie's father.

Robbie sang within.

39

Inside their small dark home, Robbie's mother stroked sleeping Essie's head and thanked the neighbour.

'You look tired,' her husband told her.

'I am a little,' she agreed. She did. She looked pale, even yellow-tinged. Robbie thought nothing of it at the time.

The next day, King George's ship was sighted from Leith. But the weather was wild – rain and wind after days of heat. The ship could not land.

His mother took Robbie to a shop. A violin-maker's shop. John Blair, stated the sign on the window. A balding, worried man with tiny wire spectacles produced instruments of different sizes and fitted them under Robbie's chin. He made Robbie hold his left arm out straight to see if he could cup the end. He told Robbie that this part was called the scroll. A three-quarter-sized violin was what was needed, decided the man, warming to his task, squinting at Robbie's neck, his fingers, his chin. He had long arms, said the violin-maker. Then Robbie had to choose which one.

'They all look the same to me,' said his mother.

Later, Robbie would learn that this was because Mr Blair modelled his violins on those of the great maker, Stradivarius. But even on that first day, they did not look the same to him. All were a yellow colour, but each with its own features, its own shading and swirling. He touched every one, passing his finger over the shininess until his hand settled on a particular instrument. It spoke to him when he touched it.

To choose a bow, he had to hold the violin and sweep a bow across the strings. The noise was terrible, wiry, and his heart sank. 'Dinnae worry, lad, ye'll soon learn,' smiled the violin-maker. 'Everyone mak's sic a sound a' first.'

Robbie left the shop with his mother, the beautiful violin safely in a box. He could hardly speak.

Before they went home, his mother stopped at another shop. Her eye was caught by something in the window. 'A kaleidoscope, Robbie! I have heard of these. It is the new toy. Would Essie not love one? Shall we buy her one?' Robbie looked through it, amazed at the endlessly different patterns of every colour in the world. Kaleidoscope – that was the word he had wanted to describe the colourful words yesterday. More than the colours of the rainbow.

They bought one for Essie and returned home clutching their parcels.

Robbie's mother brushed against the doorway as they went into their home. She winced, stopped, breathed hard. 'It is nothing, Robbie. Do not fret,' she said.

He was not fretting. He was thinking about his first violin lesson.

That night, the long-awaited bonfire lit up the rain-soaked sky over Arthur's Seat. With the peak invisible against the dark, the glow from the bonfire hung suspended as if by God. They stood outside with everyone else, hours past their bed-time, and watched the firelight in the sky. Finally, a miracle. Even Essie stood still and watched. Above the invisible chimney of the Edinburgh Gas Company, a ring of fire in the shape of a golden crown hung above the city. Was this God's greeting to the King? Everyone agreed that this was the time, this was the place to be alive.

A month later, without Robbie understanding why, his mother had died. From that day everything had changed. There was the fire as well, of course, and their father's bankruptcy, but they came later. It was his mother's death which had begun their downfall. And it was Dr Knox who was responsible for it.

Now, lying cold in bed next to Essie, in their one stinking room on a top floor, the fifth, with stench from below and the rain seeping in from above, it was impossible not to blame the man who had caused it all. Gone was the dream of a beautiful house in the New Town, with its airy rooms in summer and views of distant snow-capped hills in winter. Gone was Robbie's schooling, though he had kept his books and still studied them when he could. As for Essie, she never went to school. She could have gone to a kirk school, except that they did not go to the kirk any more. Their clothes would not have been acceptable. Besides, said their now-dissolute father when furious with whisky, his voice no longer English-sounding but settled in the Scots of his birth, 'God has decided who gaes to heaven and who doesnae – wha' difference would it mak'? He mak's it fair plain wha' he thinks o' us.'

Robbie was worried by this thought. Frightened of how it seemed to match the dark fear lurking inside him. Frightened of what it meant for the future. Because God decided everything. Did He not? What would God think about them not going to the kirk any more? Perhaps He would decide to punish them further?

There was something else that Robbie had lost. He would never forget the day. Maybe a year after the fire, with no money in the house, and more often than not no food on the table, he had come home from his job selling salt around the wealthier houses. He opened the door to their room. He noticed immediately. His eye was drawn straight to the empty place.

'My violin!' he whispered. Essie looked at him and turned away, her lips tight, her eyes slitted with worry.

'Where is my violin, Essie?' he shouted now. Footsteps on the stairs. His father, red faced with exertion, weak from the climb, leaned against the door-frame bleary-eyed.

'Where's my violin?' demanded Robbie.

'Food, will ye look?' said their father. 'Guid food. Breed, and a whole chicken. Apples. Ale for ye, Rabbie – ye're auld enough now.'

'Where is my violin?'

'Would ye no' raither ha'e food?'

Then Robbie knew. His father had sold the violin for food. As he watched Essie hungrily swallowing her supper and his father's eyes gleam as he drank whisky from a cracked glass, the last glass they had, he knew then that this must be the end. The end of any dream.

Three years later, Robbie was usually careful not to dwell on thoughts of what his life might have been like. Tonight, however, as he lay next to curled-up Essie, trying not to think about the emptiness in his stomach, he made no effort to stop himself. Something murky stirred in the silty depths of his mind.

Was it seeing the hospital again? Was it hearing the cello sounds of Dr Knox's voice? Or was it seeing that dissected body bare and split open?

It was seeing Knox, surely? Seeing the man who was the cause of it all and discovering that this man did not know or care what he had done to Robbie and his family.

He felt tears begin to squeeze between his eyelids. He knew there was only one way to drive away these tears. Anger. He heated up the anger he needed, till it boiled. Soon, he could form the anger into a thought. Somehow, anyhow, Dr Robert Knox must know and pay. Know just what he had done, and be sorry for it.

Robbie slept. Tomorrow he would act.

3

Caught

Their father had still not come back by morning. Robbie put the thought of him away. He would turn up. Or not. Whatever, they would manage.

Robbie was the only regular earner in the house and they scraped by on what he earned. His salt-selling job had gone with the rest of that industry. His new job as a delivery boy for a baker took him out of the Old Town, down below the Cowgate, towards the palace. It provided enough to pay the rent, but with very little left over for food. How much money there was for food and other essentials depended on how hard Robbie worked, and how generous he could persuade the customers to be. It helped when he had Essie with him, as he often did in the afternoons. Her smile could usually twist another coin from the toughest customer.

The baker, Mr Brown, was a worried, sweating, smooth-cheeked man, almost entirely bald and shiny-headed. His hands and wrists were criss-crossed with ancient burns from the ovens and the girdle-pans hanging over the fires in the back of the bakery. But he had never burnt a loaf or a pie or a plum cake in his life and his bannocks, his bridies and oatcakes were sought after across the whole of Edinburgh. Robbie's job was to deliver the orders to houses, taverns and other shops or to fetch the supplies that Mr Brown needed.

Robbie worked extra fast that morning. He made more deliveries in eight hours than he normally did in a day. By the time the two o'clock kail-bell rang out from the steeple of St Giles, he had done enough. At the bakery, he fixed a frown on his face as he spoke to Mr Brown. 'I'm awfy sorry, Mr Brown,' – Robbie had long ago learnt to lose his educated accent when necessary – 'it's ma wee sister. She's no right, the day. Wuid ye mind if . . ?'

'Och, awa' wi' ye. I'll see ye the morrow,' and Mr Brown waved a sweaty forearm in Robbie's direction. 'I hope it's no' anything serious? Tha' wee Essie, she's a guid bairn.' Everyone loved Essie. If there were a hundred hungry raggedy children, Essie's bird-bright eyes and crooked-toothed smile would shine out amongst their shadowed faces. She would never be left to starve. Her face was open and warm and her gaze was direct. People wanted to give her things – a cake, a pie, a pastry, anything to feed that smile. Most people did not see that she could bristle, too, and then her eyes were spiky, and her words sharp through her teeth, though she softened quickly. Her sparkle always returned.

'No, it's just a touch o' the cold but ye ken how these things can change on a halfpenny. Thank ye, Mr Brown, sir,' and Robbie ran off.

Leaning into the biting wind, he walked up the hill towards their close. He bought a quarter of crusted cheese to add to the bread he already had from Mr Brown.

Essie grinned, looking up from where she was roughly scraping out the grate.

She made a face at the food, but ate it hungrily enough anyway, tearing at the bread. One tooth was crooked, turning towards its neighbour, but all her teeth were strong and healthy, ivory in her stained face. After a while, she stood up, grabbing her shawl and wrapping it around her head and shoulders. She looked like a miniature grown-up. 'Come on, Robbie. Let's go,' she said. She liked to go with her brother in the afternoons and when their father was away Robbie liked to have her safe with him.

Robbie picked up his jacket and moved towards the door. 'No, Essie, not today. I am not working this afternoon. There is something I have to do.' He started to leave.

Essie followed him down the rickety wooden stairs and the final flight of stone steps out of the building. 'If we had more money, Robbie, we could buy meat – mebbe a wee bit of beefsteak?'

'Food is all you think about! You are not coming with me.' He felt gritty inside, the shrill wind needling him. A thin smurr, almost rain, wetted his face. By now they were through the tiny passageway on to the main street, Essie tagging behind.

'Please let me come.'

'Stop whining!' snapped Robbie, moving faster. 'I say you are not coming and there is nothing you can do about it.' He had a bitter taste in his mouth. Essie looked stung.

Robbie stopped. 'I am sorry, Essie. I have something to do. Something important. I will be back later.'

Essie was still following him. 'But . . .'

'Go home!' Robbie shouted, boiling over. There was a pause as they glared at each other, and then he watched his sister turn and run with furious legs back towards the door. He shouted, 'Sorry, Essie!' but the anger was still too strident in his voice. A few people glanced over. The Highland porter at the corner, waiting in the cold with his sedan chair for a customer, looked at Robbie, then at Essie disappearing. His face was disapproving, and fierce with its huge orange beard. The porter, like everyone else, liked Essie, and he watched out for her where he would have ignored the other ragged children who ran wild through the streets. Robbie almost went after her, almost agreed to work a little more for some beef steak for his sister. But she would come to no harm and he could wait no longer. Maybe he would bring her something later, to sweeten her again. He turned away, put her from his mind, and walked quickly towards Surgeons' Square.

Robbie did not know what he planned to do in Surgeons' Square. He just knew that if he ever wanted to find a way to make Dr Knox know what he had done, he had to go there, to touch and perhaps enter the world of surgeons and knives and bodies. At the moment, he did not know how this might happen. He only knew it must.

Robbie found himself almost running. Twice he bumped into people. Once he was shouted at and someone started to chase after him, but thought better of it. There was something chilling in his face as he ran.

Usually he would have avoided the elegant thoroughfare of South Bridge, its new golden arches sweeping majestically over the midden of the Cowgate below. Usually he would keep to his familiar wynds and dank narrow side streets, but today he ran deliberately amongst the warmly-clothed gentlemen along the gracious new road. Did he not have as much right as they to be there? Entering Infirmary Street from here, he ran straight towards the Infirmary and soon found himself, breathless, in Surgeons' Square. What now? He stood for a few moments, watching people coming and going. No one looked at him. The building where Knox had been the night before, and where the body had lain, stood tall and narrow in the left-hand corner, hiding its gruesome contents behind a gentle elegance. On the right-hand side of the square, he saw two men coming out of a severe building in the corner, their black coats thick against the February chill. Robbie waited till they had walked away. He moved towards this long, low building. The smurr had turned to sleet, slicing across his face. Ice on his eyelashes made him blink. He thrust his raw fingers deep into his pockets.

'Surgeons' Hall', announced the carved stonework above the door. Another man was walking towards it. Robbie walked on but, as the man pushed the door open, he had a glimpse of marble, a huge roaring fire in a grate and something bright as silver, before the door closed.

'Clear off, boy!' Robbie leapt at the voice in his ear. He swung round. A man stood four feet from him, peering from underneath a large black object – an umbrella, the new fashion amongst Edinburgh gentry – his other hand holding a shiny-topped cane raised in readiness. Robbie stepped back. The man glared at Robbie through eyes set deep and steady in a high-domed forehead. His side-burns sprang sideways in a dirty grey froth. Above them his cheeks were red-veined from the cold and a drip gathered at the end of his nose.

Without thinking, and with his heart racing, Robbie blurted out, 'Message, sir. For Dr Knox.' He was ready to run if necessary.

The man's face seemed to darken and his chin jutted forward. 'Dr Knox will no doubt be in his school.' He sneered the last word. Robbie looked blank. 'His anatomy school, boy. The building over there.' He gestured with his cane towards the building where Robbie had seen the body the night before. He spoke mockingly, as though he wanted nothing to do with Knox or his anatomy school.

'Thank you, sir,' said Robbie politely. He turned and walked firmly away towards Knox's building, his anatomy school, conscious of the man's eyes on his back as he went. Would the man wait to see if he went right into the building? But no, the man went towards Surgeons' Hall; the door opened and closed;

and Robbie was alone in the square again.

He stood under the trees in the middle. What now? He looked at the clock high on a steeple lower down the hill. Half-past three. Still some daylight left. He did not feel satisfied. He burned with the need to act. He looked back towards Knox's anatomy school. How could he get in? And what did he hope to achieve? Yet he could not bring himself to leave.

He felt powerless in the shadows of these buildings. Of Surgeons' Hall, and Knox's anatomy school, and not far away the Infirmary where his mother had suffered at the surgeon's hands. At the thought, something ugly spat around his body. His armpits prickled.

In the gathering shadows and icy squalls, Robbie left the square and sheltered in a low doorway in the street outside, his muscles aching with cold. He could not go home. He waited. Watched the entrance into Surgeons' Square.

He did not have to wait long. Soon, the unmistakeable profile of Dr Robert Knox turned the corner and began to walk towards him out of Surgeons' Square. Knox was wrapped against the cold. He too had an umbrella to protect his clothes from the rain. How clumsy and strange an umbrella looked, thought Robbie. Knox's cravat sat high under his neck and a tall hat was set at a careful angle on his head. He stood for a moment, inhaling the air, the steam from a grating rising like hell-smoke around his feet, and then began to walk. Fast. He held a cane in the other hand and used it so forcefully that he seemed to be pulling the ground towards him as he strode.

He came straight towards Robbie.

Robbie's heart beat in his ears. His breathing quickened. As Knox passed by, the sweet smell of floral perfume drifted over him. Robbie held both hands over his mouth. Clenched his lips.

He forced his legs to move.

Robbie followed Knox at a distance. The gathering wind whipped his hair into his eyes. He did not care. He did not care about the freezing rain that spat over his face. Nor about the greying darkness and the fact that he was walking away from home.

He just walked, fast, keeping that tall frame in his view. Once on the main street, suddenly Knox stopped. Turned. Robbie stopped. Stooped and pretended to adjust his boot. Knox waved his cane at an approaching carriage. It clattered to a halt. Knox climbed in and the carriage rumbled off, with Robbie running after it. It was not hard to keep up – the wide street was crowded and the carriage had to swerve round people, other carriages, horses, barrows, dogs, pigs.

He must have followed it for half a mile or more

before it turned into a side street and pulled up in front of a large-windowed house with shiny railings. Knox climbed out, easily, elegantly, paid the driver and went towards the house. It must be his house. Robbie had found where Dr Knox lived. He watched the door swing wide and Dr Knox enter.

Now, for the first time, Robbie began to feel the cold. His lungs hurt as he stood gasping in the icy mist. He stretched the collar of his jacket to cover his mouth, warming the air as he breathed it. The rough homespun material became moist. In this quiet, elegant street, Robbie became suddenly aware of his ragged, filthy appearance. His baggy trousers were torn at both knees, and too short, inches above his ankles. His jacket was also too small, with only one button left and the elbows threadbare. It smelt, he now realized, of ancient dirt and damp fires and meat-grease. He wore his father's shirt, collarless, limp and filthy. His boots were mud-caked, dark with rain. Running his fingers through his hair, he tugged at the tangles. Suddenly, he could smell his own fresh sweat.

He walked through the gate, closing it silently behind him. Stepped softly up the flagstoned path. Winced at the gentle scrunch of his boots on the loose stones beside it. Slowly made his way towards the first window. Soon, he could see through the glass.

Inside, the room blazed with light. On the walls, fixed halfway up, were the glass globes that Robbie knew held gas-lights. A fire burned in the grate. Robbie felt colder. Dominating the room was a huge dining-table, set for ten or twelve people. Silver cutlery and delicate blue and white porcelain plates sat waiting. Cut-glass goblets, three for each place, sparkled under two enormous chandeliers, dripping with dangling crystal and holding too many white candles to count. Everywhere, jewels of light danced from reflecting surfaces, mirrors, silver and gold, as if someone had taken an armful of sunlight and thrown it high into the air.

A maid came into the room. Robbie shrank back a little but still watched. She fussed round the table, picking up pieces of cutlery and holding them to the light, adjusting glasses by a fraction.

There was another window a few yards along. Robbie moved towards it, peered in. He saw it immediately. On a table in the window, an ochre-yellow violin, exposed, facing him, lying on its side. The bow next to it, carelessly laid, as though only recently left. Nearby, a music stand, facing the window. Robbie could almost see the composer's name. The notes looked complicated, flying over the page like insects.

Suddenly, a man walked into view. Picked up the violin and in one easy movement swung it to his shoulder. Knox! Robbie felt that rush again and his heart crashed.

At that very instant, Knox turned, for some invisible reason, towards the window. Robbie was frozen where he stood, as though pinned. For a stretched moment, Knox stared at Robbie and Robbie stared back. Then Robbie reacted, just as Knox did too. Knox dropped the violin, ran to the door of the room. Robbie stepped back, ready to run, and . . . screamed as a man gripped his shoulders with a shout.

Two men had been standing behind him. One now held him, lifting him by his shoulders. Robbie could not see them properly. The man's fingers dug into Robbie's flesh and his muscles would not work. Helplessly, he kicked his legs but his boots only brushed the ground.

At that moment the front door opened and Knox came out. When he saw Robbie dangling like a child, he laughed, leaning against the door-frame.

'Well, well, well,' he drawled. 'What have you found, gentlemen? I confess I do not recall asking you to bring some entertainment to my *petit soirée*.' Knox's pitted face was creased with amusement, and his eyes, or his one seeing eye, stared directly at Robbie. Robbie burned back, furious. He was too old to be held in the air. But the man who held him was much too strong.

'Peering in through your window, Knox, he was. Almost had his grubby nose pressed against your clean glass,' said the man who held Robbie.

'Been watching your maidservant, I should wager,' said the other, his own voice wet with lust for the girl.

'Aye, well, bring him in, gentlemen. We shall see what the lad has to say for himself.'

Robbie was dropped to the ground suddenly and pushed towards the door. He stumbled past Knox, who bowed slightly and clicked his heels together in mock respect. Robbie felt a sudden desire to lash out, to hit this evil, ugly man, but that would achieve nothing.

His thoughts scrambled as he was escorted across the hall and through a door at the end. The smells tumbled him back to a long-ago happier time – an oaky furniture smell, violin rosin, and . . . food! The unmistakeable aroma of roasting pheasant brought him the memory of gravy ripe with plums and suddenly another memory, forgotten until now. His mother, hearing the clattering shout of the wine-seller announcing a new arrival of claret in Leith, sending Robbie out on to the street to buy a jugful to taste. And him bringing it back, trying not to spill a drop, and his mother and father pouring themselves a glass and swirling it around so that through it the flames of the fire danced purple and warm. The memory now so vivid that it was almost unbearable.

Robbie now found himself in a room with a fire burning in the small grate and a comfortable chair to one side of it. One wall was covered from floor to ceiling in books. Another wall had panels painted pale green, with paintings of huge trees and scowling skies and temples. More gas-lights on the walls, their steady flames clean. In the middle of the room sat a huge desk, its surface clear except for an ink-well, and three knives. Each knife was slightly different. One had a thicker blade, fatter, fuller, swelling outwards in the middle before tapering to a point. One was jagged, fierce, like a foxhound's teeth, but long, long and full of power. And the other was tiny, its blade no wider than a fingernail at its widest point, yet so sharp that its silvery edge slid invisibly into nothing. Robbie tore his eyes away.

There was the violin, lying on its back now. He stared at it. It had been in Knox's hands. Yet he wanted to touch its smoothness. Without thinking, he raised his hand and touched the side of his chin, the place where his own violin had used to rest. He realized that the men were watching him and he quickly looked away.

Knox was smiling, his dead eye fixed, his living eye bright and steady. He came towards him. Robbie stepped back. Nearer the desk. Nearer the knives.

'What were you doing, boy, staring into Dr Knox's

window?' It was the man who had held him, his bald head and narrow eyes giving him a cruel face.

Robbie did not answer.

All three men oozed wealth. Their shiny tailcoats gleamed in the firelight above their snow-bright breeches. Their hair was pomaded, the side-curls set perfectly, the smell of scent filling the air. Oriental designs swirled across their jewelled waistcoats, bright like peacocks.

But something still made Knox different from the others. There was something in the way he stood, in the way his jaw sat. He wore power like a cloak.

'Lost your tongue, have ye, boy?' This from the other man, smaller, shorter than Robbie, his head thrown back so that he could appear to look down his nose.

'Nothing.'

'Nothing, *sir*,' said the man.

'I believe the lad was observing my violin,' said Knox.

'No doubt with a view to stealing it,' sneered the bald man.

Knox spoke, his mellow voice hypnotic and soft. 'Well, laddie, you have seen my violin. And now you see the owner of the violin. What do you have to say?' He stared down at Robbie, his lips lightly curled, his nose held high. Robbie stared back, though it took a huge effort to keep his eyes on that strange face. He fixed his gaze on Knox's seeing eye. Its hidden depths swirled, hazelnut and warm. Robbie was being drawn in. He tore his eyes away.

'What do you have to say?' repeated Knox, taking one step nearer and looming his face close. Just as he had done six years before, if he had only remembered.

'Nothing . . . sir,' said Robbie. It was all he could say.

'Nothing? You have nothing to say to Dr Knox?' snapped the smaller man, poison in his nasty little voice.

Knox spoke again, still watching Robbie, with a smile. 'Aye, well, gentlemen, we are not inordinately interested in what the lad has to say, are we? Meanwhile, we have a dinner to enjoy, more guests to greet. What shall we do with this boy, eh? A puny specimen, do you not agree?'

Knox stretched a tapering soft finger towards Robbie. Robbie stepped back, towards the desk again. Knox moved more quickly and prodded him in the chest. 'Puny, he is. No flesh on him at all.' He laughed again.

Robbie's anger rose, boiled over, and in his fury, uncontrolled, he reached out and grabbed a knife, the one with the thicker swelling blade. But in the instant that he felt it in his hand, a numbing fear sliced through his body, and the knife dropped on to the floor. Knox leapt to pick it up. The small man snatched up the other two knives and held them away from Robbie. The other man rushed to grab Robbie, stretching his arms behind his back and locking them together by hooking one of his own arms through them. He forced Robbie's shoulders back brutally, almost paralysing him.

He did not need to. As Knox approached, holding the glinting steel close to his face, Robbie felt the strength drain from him and he hung limp from the man's arm, eyes to the ground, his head swirling with faintness.

Knox held the blade to the light, breathed on it, wiped it on the lace of his cuff and held it to the light again.

'You chose well, laddie. This is a special knife. I designed it myself. It is not for delicate work. It is for . . . Look up boy, look at the craftsmanship of this beautiful instrument.' Robbie did not look up.

The small man shouted, 'Look up boy, when you are told.' Still Robbie did not, could not look up. The man who was holding him gripped his hair and pulled his head back so that he had to look. He closed his eyes. 'Open your eyes!' roared the small man. The large man twisted Robbie's hair until he had to open his eyes.

Knox continued. 'Aye, as I was saying, laddie. A special knife, designed to slice through muscle, sinew, tendon, all in one go. Not so important on a dead body, where speed is not of the essence, but on a living patient, excellent, most excellent for slicing . . .'

He did not finish his sentence. Robbie had collapsed in a spiral of blackness, his shoulders wrenching backwards as he fell forwards, his legs rag-limp. The man let him fall and as he hit the ground he heard the three men laughing.

'Such a delicate constitution we often see amongst young ladies of the upper classes,' said Knox. Shaking away the dizziness, Robbie pushed himself up on to his hands and knees and from there lurched to his feet. At the sight of Knox standing there, with the corners of his mouth turned up and open laughter in his face as his hand gestured courteously towards the door, every emotion Robbie had ever known was balled into purest rage. Their mocking farewells as he ran from the house were fuel to his anger. He stumbled down the steps, the door closing behind him. As he ran down the street, his fury grew.

At first as he ran, his anger had no words or order. It was pure emotion. And it felt red, blazing raw red. But slowly through the bloody mist burned the one clear thought: that Knox must suffer. If he had hated Knox before, now, now that he had faced him and felt his sneer, his hatred was a hundred times as strong. He could not rest until he had brought Knox down into the gutter with all the other filth.

Soon, exhausted, he slowed to a walk. He felt alone. There were still people on the streets, carriages, horses. But even so, he felt alone.

Walking past Infirmary Street again, he allowed himself to think of his mother's death. He had never felt alone before then.

He remembered kind women hugging Essie and the sickly lavender smell of them as they bustled into his house, gathering chubby Essie in their arms, with cries of 'The puir wean.' As for Robbie, he was told to 'Be a man, now, Robbie.' God had called his mother, they said. God wanted her. 'Aye, the guid Lord gives and the guid Lord tak's awa'. And only the guid Lord kens the wa' o' it.' Robbie's heart shrank under these words. They were meant as lessons of comfort and strength but for the first time in his life the words of the Bible did not seem to offer anything. A tiny sinful thought wormed its way into the crack in Robbie's heart: if God was so good, why would He take away a child's mother? The thought had frightened him. He hoped no one would see what was in his mind. He kept silent and his silence looked like strength.

Men would shake his hand and mutter emptiness. Robbie would look at his father, wanting him to say something to make everything right again, but it never happened. His father shut himself away, could not look properly into the eyes of his children, rejected the help offered by kind friends and relations. And after a while those friends and relations had stopped asking. Stopped calling at the close with a fresh bridie or a mill bannock or a fruit loaf wrapped in a clean cloth. Turned away by the silence and the emptiness and the sense of there being nothing they could do to help. 'Pride comes afor' a fall,' grumbled one wifie sourly as she left the house for the last time.

Mostly, Robbie remembered silence in his head. As though the world had stopped but would surely start up again at any moment. There were no words for what he felt and so he said nothing. As for Essie, she cried for a while but not for long. She never stopped playing with her kaleidoscope, though. She never tired of looking through the hole and trying to twist the toy to see the patterns change. 'Scope, scope,' she would demand and Robbie would gently place his hands on her tiny ones and guide the sections round.

They did not move house. Robbie never quite knew why. Once, maybe a month after his mother died, he said something about, 'In our new house,' but his father just looked at him, a desperate empty stare, then looked away, and said, 'There is no new house.' It just was not mentioned again. Robbie began to wonder if it had been a dream.

So for two years they had stayed, the three of them, in their old home, on the first floor of a building off the Canongate, a respectable place to live, not on the ground or top floors where the poorest people stayed. Still the stench and ugliness around them, but no more than anyone else had to bear, even people in well-paid work. They should have been satisfied. No servant lived with them, but a woman came each day to look after Essie and cook for them. Jeannie McKnight, she had been called, and they would never know how much they needed her until she was gone. Robbie carried on at school, learning his Latin and Greek and mathematics. His father wanted him to be a doctor. That was what had been planned for him from the very start, when his mother was alive.

'Study hard, my boy,' said his father, his hand on Robbie's shoulder as he had struggled with his Latin composition one evening. 'Study hard, and you will go to the University. You will be a doctor four years later. Think on that, Robbie. My son, a doctor! We shall be proud of you, your mother and I.'

Robbie did not want to be a doctor. He would do it if he had to, but without his heart being in it. He wanted to play the violin. Wanted to play like Janiewicz. The chance of ever being as brilliant as Janiewicz was almost non-existent, and earning a living as a concert violinist, without contacts or a rich patron to support him, would be next to impossible. But Robbie did not know this and such things meant nothing to him at that age. So, he could dream. He had not planned it or even spoken his dream aloud. To do that would be to destroy it.

He had only had a few violin lessons before his mother died. The teacher, a tiny curled up wiry man, whose back only straightened when he played the violin, his watery eyes white behind bent spectacles, had turned up for the usual lesson the very next day, when their home was dark with grief. He had left immediately, bowing out with his voice full of apologies in a thick German accent. Robbie remembered watching from a window as the man's coat-tails bobbed away round the corner, his white-stockinged legs picking their way carefully through the filth, his battered violin-case held protectively under his arm and his back stooped under its own weight.

For two years, the three of them carried on. They lived almost as though things were just the same and the dreams had never been. The violin lessons started again. He learnt to curl his hand around the strings and slide his finger to find the exact note, and to sweep his bow arm smoothly across one string on its own, up or down according to the signs on the page. When he played, sending the highest squeaking notes swimming through the window towards the distant sky, he could float away with them and leave behind the ugly streets below. He could almost dream again. Could almost forget the empty space inside him, the place where his mother had left him.

Gradually, their father had begun to warm, to smile again when he came home from work with a present, to ruffle Robbie's hair or slap him on the back like a man or take Essie on his knee in front of the fire, jigging her up and down and quietly singing a nursery song:

> 'Come! Say your prayers, my bonnie bairn,
> And saftly slip to bed –
> Your guardian angel's waiting there,
> To shield your bonny head.
>
> O never mind the foolish things
> That clavering Robbie says . . .'

And here Robbie would join in, twisting silly faces at Essie to make her giggle.

> 'They're just the dregs o' ignorance,
> The dreams o' darker days.

Our grannies, and our gran'dads too,
They might believe them a',
And keep themsel's in constant dread
O' things they never saw.

Lie still, lie still, my ain wee bairn,
Sic stories are na true,
There's naething in the dark can harm
My bonnie harmless doo.'

And so things settled into some sort of life: kirk, lessons, their father's work, respectability. They began to live. Not to forget, but to move forward.

Then, two years after their mother had died, just when everything was turning towards something better, the fire. The fire that changed everything again. But Robbie would not think about that. Not now. Now he was nearly home and Essie would be waiting, especially if their father was not back. He quickened his step again.

In the High Street, almost at Fleshmarket Close, he drank water from a well, scooping it from the bucket with his hands and throwing it over his face. Its peppermint coldness took his breath away.

Darkness had fallen already. Shadows scuttled around the tiny unlit cobbled streets of the Old Town. Stallholders had packed away their goods; shops had barred their entrances for the hours of darkness. Vegetable remnants and rotten scraps lay scattered. Robbie picked up some kail leaves and wiped the dirt off with his sleeve. A tavern door opened and two laughing men rolled out, followed by the warm breath of whisky. A woman, too, her tattered skirts hoisted high without shame as she slithered through the filth and stumbled in the doorway, shouting with laughter. The rain had stirred up the smells of human and animal waste.

In Fleshmarket Close, a ground floor window was broken and, as Robbie walked past, a rat ran from it and slipped down the wall. Through the window he glimpsed a single candle casting its flimsy flicker over the exhausted scene inside. A baby weakly wailed, like a kitten in the darkness.

On the stairs he passed one of the women from the fourth floor. A Glasgow woman rented the room and had five other women as lodgers in it. The women shared two dresses between them. They took in sewing and knitted the feet in stockings to pay for their gin. Two of them would wear the dresses when they went to collect or return the sewing. The rest of the time they appeared only in incomplete underclothes or wrapped in a filthy blanket. At first, when Robbie and Essie and their father had moved to this building, they had been shocked by the women's lewd drunken hanging bodies falling out of their underclothes. Now, if Robbie stumbled across one on the stair, he hardly gave her a thought.

Robbie could see from Essie's face that their father was still not home. She had set food on the table and sat waiting, ignoring her own hunger. Her face flashed from fear to relief. Then anger.

'Where've you been?' her eyes blazed at him. He had no good answer. How could he have forgotten his sister? How could he have allowed himself to be drawn away from his home and into the world of Dr Robert Knox?

He put the kail down, held his arms out, walked towards her, trying to warm her with his smile. He moved his hand to scruff her hair but she turned away, thistle-angry. She stabbed at the fire with a stick and it flared up, spitting.

'I'm sorry, Essie.' Then he pointed to the table. 'Look at this! A feast! Well done!'

She said no more as they sat down to eat, Robbie on the bed, Essie on a stool. The other stool empty. Robbie could see that beneath her anger, her clam-tight silence, had been real fear. It lingered in her eyes, and the streaks in the grime around them. It only fuelled his guilt.

From the guilt, there was only a small step in Robbie's mind to the simple cause of all this. If Knox had not killed his mother, none of this would be happening. They would be living comfortable lives in their new house, with time and energy to laugh and plan and dream. Food on the table each day without effort. Fresh air fluttering the curtains through the open windows in summer. A huge fire brightening their eyes in winter. Violin lessons.

'When will he come back, Robbie?' Essie stopped chewing as she waited for the answer, her mouth stuffed with bread.

'Oh, him. Who knows? I have given up wondering. We manage without him, don't we?'

'But what if *you* don' come back? What if you just don' come back one day? I thought . . . today . . .' Something swam in her eyes. She snapped her face away.

'Of course I will come back. How would I not come back?'

Essie looked back at him fiercely, her jaw clenched. 'Promise me you won' go away. Even for one night.' She managed to twist her fear into anger, as though she was ordering him instead of pleading.

'Of course I promise,' said Robbie, believing it.

4

Thief

Next morning, Robbie woke even earlier than usual. His breath froze in the air above him. As he lay with icy feet under the coarse sheet and one thin blanket, his coat on top, waiting for the Cowgate clock to strike five o'clock, he thought of Dr Knox. He burned with the need to act. Yet he seemed to have no power. What could he do to affect a man with the status of Robert Knox, with his wealth, his new house, his expensive clothes, his casual violin lying on its back?

He was still thinking about Knox as he made his way to the bakery in the frozen darkness of the early morning, slapping his hands together and stamping his feet to thaw them. Did Knox and gentry like him ever stop to think about the tired army of people who worked in the ice and rain and darkness to provide the food and services that kept their lives so comfortable?

His mind was not on his work that day. He was slow,

unsmiling. Mr Brown said nothing, but sweated more, pressed his lips together. Robbie missed one of the deliveries and found that it had been given to another boy, who grinned slyly at him. At lunch-time, when the kail-bell on St Giles' Cathedral rang out to mark two o'clock, he went home to get Essie, as he usually did when their father was absent. It was better if she was with him. And she was strong enough to be helpful. Not to mention that her grin and magpie eyes could often twist another halfpenny out of a customer. That afternoon, he and Essie traipsed from house to house with the bread barrow but earned little extra in the way of tips. Robbie's mind was elsewhere and Essie caught his mood.

They were hungry. Starved of energy. Their scalps were itchy, flaking. They had had no vegetables since a kail broth that Essie had burnt four days ago. No meat for longer. Breakfast had been oats mixed with water. Cold water. Fuel for the fire was precious – it took energy to collect and was usually wet.

Essie stopped. Her hand was pressed into her side, rubbing it. 'I'm sore, Robbie. Can we no' stop?' She looked paler than usual, her skin tight over her cheekbones and some of the glimmer gone from her eyes. 'An' my feet are soaked.' She held out her foot and Robbie could see the sole of her shoe hanging off. He had cut a hole in the tips of the shoes some time ago, because her feet kept growing, and now her dirty toes glistened wet and red with cold.

He was suddenly irritated. He should not have to worry about her. His life ought not to be like his. He should be studying for university. Some boys of his age would be there already. He should not have to live from day to day thinking only about the next meal. He tried in vain to push his bitterness aside. Normally he simply did what had to be done and did not dwell on what might have been. But things were different now. His mind was being pulled in unusual ways. 'Go home, Essie. I shall be back later.'

'Why? Where're you going?'

'None of your business. I have to see someone.'

'Who?'

'I told you – it's none of your business. Now go home.'

'It's a girl!' She grinned, the hunger-pains forgotten, her cheeks round again with laughter.

'It's not a girl.'

' 'Tis so,' and she started to flutter her eyelashes and pout her lips.

'Go HOME, Essie! Go away!' Taut with irritation, he kicked a stone and it hit an iron grating with a pistol twang. Heads turned.

Her face flinched into fury. 'You're no' worth her, whoever she is.' And she spun on her foot and ran away, the sole of her shoe splattering in the mud, her dirty skirts tangling in her legs.

Robbie put her from his mind. Essie would come to no harm. She could look after herself. Besides, she liked something to be angry about. He would make it up to her, buy a pie, bring her something. It never took much to smooth her feathers again.

Time to go.

He left the barrow behind some rubbish down a close where pigs grunted in a pen. The stink of a midden was ripe nearby. He would collect it later and return with it to work as though he had never been away.

He set off for Surgeons' Square, choosing the familiar narrow streets. As he came closer, he walked more quickly. This time, he wanted to find his way inside one of the buildings. What did they do in there, those surgeons? Apart from cutting up dead bodies? What life did they lead inside those broad-windowed buildings? One thing was certain – it was not a life spent sharing a building with pigs, and rats crawling out of broken windows and gin-drowsy babies mewling before they died.

Past Infirmary Street he took a side street round to the back of Surgeons' Square and soon found himself behind Surgeons' Hall. He stopped, thought. How could he get in?

As he wondered, he saw two serving-girls. He followed them towards the back entrance. The girls giggled and looked at each other as he nipped in front of them down the steps to the basement and held the door at the bottom open for them, bowing low with a smile as they went past him and through the door. But when he closed the door after them, he did not close it properly. After a minute to let them disappear, he pushed it open again and slipped in, unseen. He followed the dark mildewed corridor, its only light sifting through the tiny windows at ceiling level.

Round a corner, a door, locked. Another on his right. An open door ahead of him. Noise, light, laughter. The kitchen. Hot gravy smells. He slipped past. Another corner, a wider passageway, another door. Up some stairs and through a door at the top. The hall. Empty. Silent, huge. The smell of silver and an enormous crackling fire.

He stared up at the paintings high on the walls. Portraits of men, some seeming newly painted, the firelight leaping from their gilded frames. Serious-looking men with wise eyes and ruddy complexions, not smiling. Red or blue or black polished coats and shining white breeches with gold buttons. The light bounced from their cheeks, giving them a warmth which contrasted with their unsmiling eyes.

He heard footsteps. Quickly he hid in a doorway. A man walked across the end of a corridor, his head buried in a book, his coat-tails swinging.

Robbie took a corridor at the other end of the hall. He opened the first door, slightly. A fug of tobacco and a murmur of quietly talking men. He gently closed the door again.

The corridor turned to the left. He followed it. Three doors on each side of the corridor. All identical. All closed.

Silence. Though in the distance, when he listened carefully, he could hear the distant clattering sounds of servants, haphazard voices, wet wind on the window panes, a sombre sleepy tick from the tall clock behind him. Footsteps. Far away.

Move. No point in standing there. Robbie opened the next door he came to, slowly, cautiously. Nobody. He walked in, looking round, checking each corner, casting his eyes quickly over each tall-backed chair. Nobody.

He was in a library. A smell he did not know, of oldness and difference. Something like tobacco but not. A sort of wood perhaps. And stale air, trapped and heavy and still. Looking round, he saw, from floor to ceiling, row upon row of brown leather books. Most behind glass. In the middle, a table, covered with more books, some cloth-bound in the new fashion, and thinner publications. Journals. Robbie walked over, his feet squeaking loudly on the polished wooden floor. He picked a journal up. Its paper was thick, cream-white. It crackled as he turned the pages.

His eyes darted down the list of articles inside the front cover, haphazardly taking in titles. *Disease and the Poor. On the Methods of Elimination of the Small-Pox. Treatise on the Brain, the Eye, and the Ear. Excision or Amputation. New Principles of Surgery of the Hip Joint.*

He began to read, his mind entranced. It was difficult and he read slowly, stumbling, not understanding half of it. It contained strange words, many of which he struggled with, even with his knowledge of Greek and Latin, and it seemed to open up a new and frightening world. Diseases he had never heard of, ways of dying he had never dreamt about, operations he could not imagine. A world where people died and people lived, people suffered and were saved. Or not. Not his mother. Not at the hands of Dr Knox.

Each time he read the chilling description of an operation with its cold explanation of gruesome techniques, his breath stuck in his throat and he wanted desperately not to read, but he could not stop. His eyes were dragged along the lines. His heart sped as the words took hold and he began to touch the edges of the minds of the men who had written them.

Nowhere did he find anything about the pain the patients suffered. Did these men not consider that? What was a doctor if he did not cure pain?

Was pain really God's will? Now that he was older, he began to hear the questions more clearly. But he was still afraid to consider the answers. What sort of a world was it, where children were robbed of their mothers, and men and women were left screaming on a table, or dead, pinned open for anyone to peer into? Was there an easy answer? That it was God's will and he was not to ask why? Or was there another answer that would make better sense? Or was there no answer anywhere at all?

His thoughts returned to Dr Knox. What had gone through the man's mind when he cut into Robbie's mother's flesh? Anything? The wish that she would stop screaming and let him concentrate? The hope that her blood would not spatter his lacy cuffs? And where was he now? Relaxing at home, smiling at guests, retelling the story of Robbie's fainting? Or at his anatomy school, his spindly fingers deep inside some misused body?

Robbie was just about to put the journal down, his skin cold, when the door suddenly opened. He spun round.

It was the man who had confronted him in the square. The one with the umbrella, the frothy sea-grey whiskers and supercilious voice. And another, tall, ferret-eyed, bald-headed, with a tiny hard tight mouth that pinched itself together like an oyster. Both men, after a moment of surprise, moved quickly towards him, shouting for assistance. He had no time to run. They grabbed him, one at each arm. He was trapped. He would not demean himself by struggling.

The bald-headed man spoke, his thick cravat stuffing his collar full and giving him an air of bull-dog strength.

'What have we here, Professor Syme? A thief?' His little mouth turned up, sneering.

'And a persistent one at that,' agreed Professor Syme. 'I have seen him before. Looking for Knox – for some ungodly reason, I've no doubt. This is not the first time you have been here, is it boy? Running errands for the vile doctor. Stealing for Knox, were you?'

'I've stolen nothing, sir,' replied Robbie.

'But what is this in your hand?'

'I wanted to read it.'

Professor Syme's mouth twisted contemptuously. 'Read it? What would you be doing with reading, boy? A liar, too. And not a good liar, at that.'

'It is soap you should be looking to steal, boy,' said the other man, his face creased with distaste.

By this time, two other men had come into the room and Robbie was surrounded. Men in tail-coats, exuding power, all large-seeming, puffed out by their layers of well–cut cloth, their necks thickened by cravats and tall collars. Everything he was not, in their uniforms of success.

There was nothing he could do. He held his head high.

'Take this filthy creature downstairs, Guthrie, and lock him up,' barked Professor Syme. 'Tell someone to get a constable. Fast. The boy is slippery.'

With one arm twisted painfully high behind his back, Robbie was marched out of the room by two men. Across the hall, back through the door and down the same stairs he was pushed, as though they did not care one jot whether he fell and broke his neck.

He was thrust into a cellar, its wet air thick with mould. The key scraped in the lock, and he was in blackness. What now?

He did not have to wait long to find out. Within minutes, voices outside the door, the key turning again, and light flooding into the cellar. The man called Guthrie entered with two constables, one carrying a lantern, all stooping through the low door-frame.

'Here he is,' snarled Guthrie, unnecessarily.

'Thank ye, sir. We'll tak' him now. Turn ye'sen, boy.' Robbie obeyed, turning his back to them. His hands were grabbed and he felt cold metal snapping round his wrists. Someone pushed his back and he stumbled out of the room.

On his way along the corridor towards the back door, he passed the serving-girls whom he had met on his way in. They stared briefly, then turned aside with small frightened glances, before passing him. Robbie looked at the ground and felt himself blushing.

Outside in the lane, a black windowless carriage waited. He was pushed into it, as passing people stopped and stared. Robbie sank into the darkness of a corner and shrank down inside himself.

As the carriage rattled its way over the cobbles, he could picture the passers-by, stopping and trying to catch a glimpse of whoever was inside. He could see their shadows, like ghosts.

After a few minutes, the carriage came to a halt. A few seconds in the open air were enough to see where he was, even in the gathering darkness of the late afternoon. The Canongate Tolbooth's turrets pierced the scudding charcoal sky above them, its tiny windows black. Next to it, sharing a wall, the new tavern, its noise swelling through the open door. Once inside the Tolbooth, he was pushed along corridors, down worn stone stairs slippery with grease and dirt. He knew he needed to act. Ever since being caught, he had been paralysed, powerless against all these stronger men. Now he had to do something.

He stopped. An angry curse came from the man

behind him, and pain as a foot trod on his heel. He felt himself being pushed violently in the back. He stood his ground and turned.

'Please,' he said, unable to stop the desperation in his voice. 'I didn't do anything. Please just let me go. I didn't do anything!' His voice rose, spiralling with panic.

'It's no' my mess, gawkit laddie,' replied the man, holding a lamp above his head. Nothing in his voice hinted that he cared. It was a cold voice, blank. 'Git a move on, will ye?' And he pushed him again.

'I, I . . . if you let me go, I'll pay you,' pleaded Robbie, not knowing what else he could say.

The man's eyes shrivelled in contempt. 'Pay me, wid ye? Aye, an' wi' what wid ye pay?' He hawked his lips together and spat straight into Robbie's face. The spittle ran down his cheek and over his mouth as his hands were freed and he was pushed into a cell. The tiny narrow door crashed shut behind him.

Robbie turned and beat the door with his fists until they hurt. 'Let me out! Let me out!' he yelled, fear mixed with anger so that he could not tell which was which. But no one came, and he sank to the ground, pressed his forehead into the straw-covered floor and held himself until his heartbeat slowed.

Into the silence came a noise. A shuffling, grunting noise.

Robbie was not alone. He knelt up slowly, froze his breath, strained his eyes into the shadows. Something leapt at him from behind and he felt a cold hand, stinking and leathered, over his mouth. Another hand grabbed his hair and he was pushed face down into the ground. His arms were squashed beneath him. He could not move. He could barely breathe, his mouth and nose pressed into the damp straw. The man, whoever it was, straddled his back and Robbie smelt his rancid breath and felt its warmth against his neck. A whisper, sibilant and wet, forced its way into his ear, 'Hushie, pretty boy, or ye'll no live tae tell the tale.' And the man suddenly bit Robbie's earlobe. Something dribbled down his neck and he squeezed his eyes and mouth shut.

The hand moved from his mouth and he felt it creeping amongst his clothes. He whimpered through his nose. Into each pocket, through every cranny, between each thin layer squirmed the hand. The hand found what it was looking for, a coin, hidden deep in a pocket. Robbie had forgotten it was there. He could have bought food with it. Why had he not bought food with it, instead of letting it be found by this creature?

The man rolled away from Robbie and crawled on all fours over to a corner. Robbie straightened up. He spat saliva from his mouth. And spat again to get rid of the taste, gagging.

He shuffled over to another corner as far from the man as possible, his eyes becoming used to the dark greyness of the cell. Sitting, wedged as deeply as he could into the corner, his knees bent up in front of him to shield his body, he fingered his ear lobe where the man had bitten it. The cold wetness of the wall soaked into his back as Robbie watched the man.

He had never seen such a creature. A tangle of greasy hair fell over its face, so that it was hard to tell which way round the head was. The feet were bare and filthy, the toe-joints thick like knots. The legs and arms were nothing more than bones, draped with sagging brown skin, hollowed. Then the man raised his head and the hair fell back to reveal a face. White eyes, round and wild. The mouth hanging open in a slack-jawed grin, as he held the coin up to stare at it closely. Four brown teeth at the front, like sticks. Suddenly laughing, the man threw his head back, wide-mouthed, and swallowed the coin. Robbie's heart stopped. Here was madness. This was how everything would end. He would surely die here and no one would know. Silently inside himself, a scream swelled and rose until he did not know how he could keep it in.

He slowed his breathing and tried to control his thoughts and calm his body.

The man half crawled, half stumbled away to another

corner. Robbie watched him through partly-closed eyes, wanting and yet not wanting to see what he did. He saw the man press his hands against the wall and move his face closer to the stone. The man's tongue hung out like a dog's and into the silence came the sound of the creature licking the wall, sucking up the mildewed water than ran in slow drips down the ancient stones. When he had drunk his fill, the man crumpled down on to the ground and curled up, muttering to himself in two voices. Occasionally he giggled.

Soon, the man seemed to sleep. Robbie had to stay awake. He tried not to think about the hunger that was eating at his stomach. Or the thirst. He tried not to think about what would happen to him tomorrow.

And Essie! What in God's name would Essie be thinking? Robbie could hardly bear to think of it.

What time was it? After dark, he knew. The cell had become almost completely black and Robbie realized that the earlier dim light had come from an encrusted grating at the very highest point of the cell, opening on to the street. Often, walking past this place, Robbie had heard the cries of grown men rising from the holes at boot level. He had always turned away and thought no more of whose voices they might be.

His sense of powerlessness was overwhelming. It rose in his chest and he screwed up his eyes against it. What have I done? What has Dr Knox made me become?

Though Robbie did not sleep, his night passed in a torpid state somewhere between nightmare and reality. The cold was bone-deep. He tried to shrink as far into the corner as possible. He began not to feel bits of his body. A part of him was trying to stay awake, to plan how to escape and return to Essie. Another, stronger, part of him knew he could never escape. In this stinking hole, dying seemed completely possible.

At some time, during the darkest, most distant part of the night, the time when the heart slows almost to nothing, the time when death most easily worms its way into a sleeping soul, Robbie turned his face towards the wall and dragged his parched tongue against the dripping stones. And as he drank, he cried.

Afterwards, he wrapped himself in his own arms again and tried to rock his fears away. He strained his ears to hear the heartbeat sounds of his city. Everything was muffled by the thickness of the walls. Sometimes he stared at the grating, as though by seeing he could hear better. When he heard the sounds of the scavengers with their carts outside the grating, his face lit up and he tried to catch their words, desperate for any signs of the normal world. But he could make out nothing above the metal scraping of their spades as they shifted the filth of the streets.

He hunched down into himself again and drifted.

Eventually, the blackness through the grating began to soften into a dark greyness. Just as Robbie had decided that morning was approaching, the metal grate of bolts sliding and the lock turning jerked him into wakefulness. He squinted into the blinding glare of a lamp.

'Git up.'

With difficulty, Robbie struggled to his feet. His body was cramped with cold and the sweat had frozen in his clothes. The other prisoner also lurched to his feet, grunting with excitement.

'No' you,' growled the gaoler.

'How's tha'? No' me? When's ma turn, then? Eh?' The voice was cracked from lack of use. The prisoner moved towards Robbie and grabbed him by the arm. Robbie flinched. In the light of the oil lamp, he could see the scabbed face and desperate eyes.

'Get yer haunds off of him, scum. There's a mowbit breed for ye.' The gaoler held out a loaf he was carrying, dangling it just out of reach of the prisoner, who leapt towards it with a cry. The gaoler threw it into the shadows of the cell and the prisoner fell on it, eating it like a wild animal.

'You. Oot,' the gaoler gestured with his head. Robbie did not need to be told twice. He left the cell.

'Go on – up the stairs,' said the gaoler gruffly. 'Ye're free to gae.'

'How's that?' asked Robbie.

'A message came. Fae a genty doctor. Said there'd bin a mistake. Said ye should no' have been arrested.'

Robbie's mind spun. 'What was his name?'

'I dinnae ken. Aye, so I do. Knox. Dr Knox, the message said. Must be a friend o' the magistrate. Ye've higher friends 'n ye shuid. Anyway, awa' wi' ye and dinnae ask questions.'

Robbie left the building with his thoughts swirling. It did not make sense. Why would Dr Knox do that? It could not be true. There must be some mistake.

Robbie would not, could never, feel grateful to Dr Knox. No one wants to be grateful to an enemy. Either the gaoler had got the name wrong, or Dr Knox had some evil intentions of his own, some new way to humiliate Robbie. Either way, it did nothing to Robbie's hatred of the man, except to fuel it further.

Now faint with hunger, Robbie hurried home. The city creaked into wakefulness in the almost darkness. A breeze, sharp and fresh, washed through his head. He put thoughts of Dr Knox behind him and thought only of Essie. What would she be thinking? Would she be all right? He felt a sense of brewing panic as he climbed the familiar stairs, straining his ears for any sounds.

Even before he was through the door, Essie launched herself at him with an animal cry. She beat her fists against his chest. Robbie knew what he had done. He was the person who was meant to care for his sister, and he had not. He had left her, broken his promise.

He tried to grip her arms but she was strong. 'Where've you been?' she shouted, staring up at him, ragged spirals of hair stuck to her face. Her eyes were red, exhausted. 'You've been out all night. Where've you been?'

'I know. I am sorry. I just . . . I was . . . trapped.'

'Trapped?'

Robbie walked to the other side of the room and stared out of the window, his eyes gritty with tiredness. Looking ahead through the greyness, all he could see were the lopsided roofs of other buildings, tumbling together, the gaps between them narrow and crooked like the wrinkles in ancient skin. But if he strained his eyes to the left, he could just make out, in the dark distance, the roofs of the New Town, a gentle glow from their streetlights. He turned back to Essie and told her exactly where he had been.

Essie's eyes opened wide. 'But why'd you steal a book? We've too many books already.'

'I did not steal it,' snapped Robbie. 'I was just looking at it.'

'But what if you do it again? What if you get locked up again? An' what if they don' let you out and you go tae court an' then . . . what if you get hunged?'

'Hanged, not hunged,' said Robbie, with a smile.

'Hanged, hunged, wha' ever!' shouted Essie.

'Because I won't,' said Robbie.

'How d'you ken? Ye don' ken anything.'

'Because I will look after you properly now. I've been foolish, Essie. I'm not going anywhere near that place again, and I will put Dr Knox from my head. I will earn us money for food, good food, plenty of food, and I will study. I will go to university and then I shall have a good job to look after us properly.'

'A doctor?' said Essie. 'You was going tae be a doctor.'

Robbie said nothing. What was the point in being a doctor? If God had ordered the world to include pain, how could he fight against that? No, the only sensible way was to earn some more money to improve their daily lives. Food, warmth, clothes and maybe one day a better place to live. Look no further than that and you will not be let down, he told himself. Even that might be a struggle, but it was worth it. He would throw off the madness of the last few days, walk away from the horror, concentrate on each day.

As he thought it, he could almost believe it. Even thinking it made him feel lighter.

Essie needed him. Not that she would admit it. They needed each other. When she was not helping him, she worked hard herself, doing what she could to help them survive. Often she earned money running errands for the stallholders at the flesh market, or the many other traders who propped their stalls wherever they could.

When he returned in the evenings, Essie would have queued for water from the public well, carrying it in several journeys up the stairs to the fifth floor, her face red with exertion and sweat streaking the dirt on her cheeks. Occasionally, she might have washed some clothes or their sheet, treading them with her feet in cold greyly sudded water. She would have found firewood to add to the pile they tried to keep constantly drying by the fire, or coal if she was lucky and if her pockets had room in them. She would have collected tinder, scraps of dead grass or sticks or even paper, and she would gather it in her pockets and fill their tinder-box with it, leaving it by the fire to dry. If they ran out of tinder, they had nothing with which to start a fire in the evening, and then the cold would settle in their bones overnight and by the morning their sheet would be iced over with frozen breath. The water in their jug would be frozen thick.

She might have picked up some food from the ground by the market stalls, anything from kail leaves or a turnip, to a scrawny pig-rib or fallen piece of oxtail from the flesh market. She was quick like that, and her pockets were deep. Her smile, though not innocent, was clear. No one could resist her fire-bright eyes. Robbie could imagine that if someone caught her thieving, the victim would not call the authorities but would pat her on the head and even give her an extra coin for her daring. Each evening when Robbie came home she would proudly produce what she had won that day – perhaps an apple, or even some cheese. Once a whole portion of beefsteak, suspiciously clean and undamaged.

Each evening, though exhausted, he would still find time to teach Essie her reading. She would scowl and fidget. 'What's the point, Robbie?' she would mutter, twisting her fingers around each other as she struggled to read the long words he gave her.

'The point is so that you can read the Bible,' Robbie would say.

'I ken what the Bible says. Mr Chalmers reads it tae us.'

Recently, Essie had started at Sunday School. It was her own idea. She had stood at the door one day and watched the shiny rows of children happy all together. She'd shouted out the answer to an arithmetic question and the startled teacher, a young wispy man with a weak voice and long fluttering hands, had invited her in. She loved answering the questions more quickly than anyone else, and then running away at the end before the teacher could catch her to ask more about her family circumstances. She had lied already. Dead mother – well, that was true enough – dead father, no brothers or sisters, lived with an aunt and uncle, went to school every day of course, sir . . .

She liked it because it was different from every other day of the week. It did not hurt her hands or make her hungry. There was something sure about it. Something warm and routine. And there was something to eat at the end of it too, quickly snatched before she ran off.

'Why do I have tae read the Bible? I ken what it says,' she would repeat to Robbie.

'It's right, Essie. It's just right,' he said, wearily, not thinking below the skin of the words.

She would just look at him, and her eyes would seem to know more than she was saying. He would turn his eyes away and she would carry on reading, her voice dull. And he would wonder, too, what the point of it was. But one day there just might be a point. If you did not think that, what would you do?

Robbie wished Essie would go to school properly. There was a free school, but it was run by the kirk and they did not belong to a kirk. Besides, their father would not consider asking for charity from the kirk, even if they had belonged. He had heard ministers preach against poverty often enough – it was a punishment from God, they said. He was not blinded or crippled by ill-fortune, so he was not one of their so-called 'deserving poor'.

Sunday School and Robbie's teaching. It was not much, but it would have to do. He must hold on to the idea that there was a point to it all. But it was hard to hold on to, what with the endless daily task of finding food and warmth. Keeping their heads above the pig-swill streets.

Now, his heart lifted as he saw the fire in Essie, that surviving spirit in her coal-bright eyes. He needed her spark. A curl of black hair spiralled over one of her eyes. He moved his hand to brush it aside and she scowled but let him do it anyway.

Together they ate an oatmeal and water brose. Robbie stopped suddenly, dropping his spoon. His hand went to his forehead and he swore. 'Hell's fire! The barrow! Quick, Essie!' He had left the bread-barrow the evening before and had never returned to the baker's shop with it. Surely it would be stolen by now, or swept away with the rubbish by the scavengers whose job was to clean the streets at night.

'Come with me, Essie! Hurry!' He threw her shawl

towards her, grabbed his jacket. They pulled on their shoes and boots and together they ran down the stairs and out into the sleepy charcoal morning. They sped through the early morning crowds, Essie not knowing exactly what it was they were running for. Robbie ran fast, his feet thumping out his prayer, 'Let it be there! Let it be there! Let it be there!' His tongue was dry in his mouth. He would lose his job, surely, if it was gone. Even Mr Brown, tolerant as he was, would never let him get away with that. But with Essie beside him, there was a chance Mr Brown would not be too harsh.

Into the narrow close, round the corner, past a man lying curled against a wall, vomit and blood around his head. Past the midden, and the one privy which served several streets, its low door swinging wide, the pit overflowing. There were the pigs, their snouts buried in rotten turnips. There was the pile of rubbish. No scavengers that night then. Where . . . ? There it was! There was the barrow. Robbie could have sung aloud. Everything was going to be all right. This was a sign. From now on, God was on his side.

The barrow was filthy. It had been underneath a window and someone had thrown the contents of a chamber pot on to it rather than use the midden. They cleaned it as best they could with grass grabbed from the edge of the Royal Park, and hurried to the baker's shop.

Mr Brown's sweaty face greeted them, frowning, flustered. 'How d'ye explain ye'sen, laddie? Where did ye go yesterday?' he spluttered. His hands were on his wide hips, his fingers splayed, dough sticking to them like tatters of flesh. Essie smiled sweetly up at him and he reddened, his lips melting. She spoke, falling into a broader Scots accent as she widened her eyes to him. 'Sorry, Mr Brown. It wis ma faut. I wis no' weel, ye ken, an' Robbie had tae look after me. But I'm a' better. An' I'll help ye all the week long, I will so.' For a moment, Mr Brown simply stood there. Then he softened. There was nothing he could say. He could no more have been cross with Essie than he could have stamped on a blackbird's egg. He was under her spell like everyone else. Mr Brown helped them load the bread on to the barrow, and gave Essie a piece of gingerbread with a sugar rose on it. Her cheeks crinkled as she bit into it. She looked at Robbie and gave him a secret smile.

A weak filtered sun began to whitewash the past few days as they set off on their deliveries.

God was on their side at last, thought Robbie.

5

The Resurrection Men

It was now the beginning of March, and each day grew lighter, brighter as the waking sun trickled its warming fingers across the city. Often, still, the chill wind whipped itself up and the icy rain dripped down bare necks, but these were the final weapons of winter. Now, bulbs began to spray their colours across the grassy spaces. A few fresh vegetables appeared in the haphazard filthy stalls that sprung up like weeds in the shadowed archways. Girls sold daffodils, their cheeks rose-red, their hair floating free, blown like meadow grasses. Spirits lifted.

Robbie threw himself into rebuilding their lives. Each day he worked hard, often with Essie at his side. They earned enough to buy Essie shoes. She leapt around their room, delighted with the stiffness of the new leather, her blackberry curls bouncing past her shoulders now. That day, they had a rabbit, broiled in the broth pot until the flesh dropped away from the bones and the flavour caramelized.

Robbie threw himself into his studying, reopened the schoolbooks which were piled under the bed. Books were among the few possessions their father had not sold. He either thought they were not worth enough, or worth too much.

Robbie kept Essie at her studies, too, though this was a struggle. She could not see the point, but if it meant she had food at the end of it she would do it. She was bright, quick to learn. Sometimes, though, when Robbie looked at her filthy clothes, ragged black fingers and nut-brown face, he wondered how she would ever marry. It was her childlike spirit that drew everyone to her, but what would she be like when she was no longer a child? There was nothing of their mother in her. Essie was all fire and thorns, thistle-sharp and magpie-bright. She had none of their mother's fragile poppy lightness.

He loved Essie. Not that he would ever tell her so. He did not imagine she ever thought of things like that. She was too caught up in living. And she did live, too — much more than survive. Essie threw herself at life, her sparkle darting, too fast to catch.

So, for this short time, their world was steady, warm, solid.

Until the tide changed. It happened late one evening

towards the end of March. The darkness was still that night and gentle for the time of year, the cold wind resting. Essie was at home before Robbie that evening, making the fire, preparing their meal. Robbie had delivered a load of special Easter breads to a large house at the foot of Arthur's Seat and had returned the barrow to Mr Brown. Mr Brown had given Robbie a simnel cake. 'Fae Essie. Put a wee bittie colour in her cheeks.' And he smiled as he wiped his forehead.

Robbie lingered outside for a moment in the fresh air as it washed off the hillside, bringing the scent of pines and the sea. A faint whiff of gunpowder from the tunnel-blasting. He kicked a stone idly and ran to follow it as it bounced haphazardly, skittering across the rough cobbles. Suddenly, he felt an overwhelming urge to go home quickly, to join Essie and bury himself in his books again.

He began to run, soon coming to the buildings that edged the Royal Park, large mixed with small, the smells of burning metal from a smithy mixed with sweeter toasted smoke from the brewery. Across the main street, up the Cowgate with its buildings tottering above his head. He wanted to get home. He took a short cut, running up a steep dark alley, dodging the rubbish piled against the walls, the sewage in the gutters. A shout from above but, before he could move, a bucket of filth sloshed just behind him, its stinking contents splashing his trousers. Leaping aside, he rounded a corner too fast. Coming towards him were two men pulling a cart. There was something jumpy, something secret, about their actions, and Robbie slipped into a doorway, intending to hide until they were past.

The cart had almost come level with his hiding place, when one wheel hit a stone and spun off-centre, tipping the load on to the ground. Both men cursed, and ran to the cart, looking around them. Both had squashed misshapen hats pulled down over their eyes and the collars of their baggy coats turned up. One held a lantern with a tiny guttering flame. He put it on the ground. They crouched over the fallen load. It was a large barrel. One of the metal strips around it had slipped and two of the laths had sprung away. The ropes that had tied it to the cart hung slackly. The cart leaned at a useless angle.

Robbie gasped, and slapped his hands to his mouth to silence his own noise. He could hardly believe what he saw. Through the broken laths of the barrel, an arm, a human arm, hung, swinging stiffly like a broken pendulum, its fingers clawed.

One of the men stuffed the arm back inside and tried to push the slats roughly back into place, sliding the metal strip downwards. Together they hauled the barrel upright and as they did so the lid sprung off.

Robbie held his breath, his thoughts racing. But it was the words he heard them speak which sent his heart spinning crazily and all the strength washing from his legs.

The words flew clear as glass, the rolling Irish accents shattering the sheltered silence of the alley, smashing any traces of the peace that Robbie had conjured during the last days.

'Mary, Modder of Jesus! Knox'll no be pleased, an' he won't. Wid ye look at that?'

'For sure and how'll he pay us a full price for that?' muttered the other man more quietly.

'Bastard! Never needs an excuse to rip us off. And look, wid ye – head smashed. Bastard'll never pay up now.' The voice was snarling, low, as the man looked inside the damaged barrel.

The first man spun round. Then the other. They had both heard it: a gasp from the darkened doorway. The first man ran over to where Robbie was hiding. A knife glinted in a hand. He grabbed Robbie's jacket and dragged him out, peering at him in the shadows. Robbie could not see where the knife was.

The man pushed his face close to Robbie. He was chewing dried fish and the stink of it swam from him. The second man leapt round and both of them pushed Robbie backwards to the ground, his body pressed over the barrel. Robbie's head was inches from the smashed human contents. The first man held him by the throat with one hand, the knife in the other, held so that its cold edge pressed into the skin lower down on Robbie's neck. Dark-ringed eyes inches from Robbie's. Tiny red veins across the sticky-rimmed eyeballs. One eye larger than the other, and higher. Beads of sweat springing from a thin face iron-black with bristle. And scars, twisted across his forehead.

'What have we here?' The man's full red lips were spittled. He chewed slowly on his fish, making a sticky sound. Through the open wet mouth protruded two front teeth, unusually huge, and crossed. It made him look like a rat, with a mouth that could never quite close. The knife rested against Robbie's neck. He could hardly breathe.

The second man spoke, his voice softer, smoother, his pale eyes narrowed so that the near-white lashes almost hid their rabbit pinkness. His pale skin was covered in light-brown patches, freckles merged into each other like pools of wet sand. 'Wid ye get rid of him, William? We've no time for gabbing. Kill him quickly and quietly, afore he gets us killt.'

Robbie struggled to speak, his voice squeezed. 'Please let me go. I won't say anything. I have a sister to look after.'

'Sister eh? Pretty as you, is she?' The scarred man's wet lips turned up into a smile.

'Get rid of him, William. We can't keep the good doctor waitin', for sure. The boy is not'ing to us, but Knox is our wages.' The pale eyes were looking down the street, wary. Briefly, the moon appeared and shone through the thin hair wisping from under his squashed hat. His neck was tree-trunk thick, but his body and limbs were thin and skin-lagged.

Someone came round the corner but doubled back and walked away quickly. No one was going to help Robbie.

'Could be anodder body to sell. And sure, such a fresh young body at that. Not a mark on it, will ye look at it?' It was the rat-toothed man who spoke, greedily.

The other man looked at Robbie and was silent for a moment, thinking. Robbie knew they could kill him easily. Even apart from their strength and his helplessness as he lay forced over the broken barrel, the knife-edge against his neck left him paralysed. He could not even turn his face from the spittle and open lips and foul fish breath. From their leering faces he knew they would do it as happily as they would kill a rat.

'I won't talk. I can help you. I . . . I know Dr Knox. I've seen where he works.' He had no plan. He just said it to show that he had some weapon, that he was not just any boy. He said it to make them pause. They froze. Then the one with the knife drew his face closer and the knife pressed harder until Robbie thought it must break his skin.

In a whisper as smooth and quiet as blood, the sandy-haired man spoke softly, bringing his mouth close to Robbie's ear, the sick-sweet breath warm over his face.

'So? You know Dr Knox? Friend of his, we're thinking? What would the so-clever Dr Knox be doing wit' a friend like you?'

'No, not a friend. I hate him!' The one holding Robbie loosened his grip. They both studied him more closely, their eyes narrowing. Then they stood up straight, and let go of him, though they stayed close. Watching him. Thinking. But slowly. He breathed, dared to move his hand to touch his throat.

Robbie could perhaps have made his move then. Could have leapt to his feet and run away and put them behind him. Could have returned to Essie, to his sensible hard-working life. But once more he had come across that name. Dr Knox. He could not turn away.

Suddenly, he realized exactly what Dr Knox had to do with these men. Robbie knew who they were. Not their names. But what they were. Resurrection Men. Everyone had heard about, and learned to fear, the Resurrection Men. Men who robbed new unguarded graves at night and then sold the bodies. And who bought these stolen corpses? Surgeons. To cut up and explore the workings of the human body. Surgeons like Dr Knox. The law only allowed them the body of one hung criminal a year, Robbie remembered hearing, but one body was not nearly enough for some of them – men like Dr Knox.

So, this was how Dr Knox found the material for his evil hobby. This was how he practised, on stolen bodies, as well as on the living. Robbie's head spun. Dr Knox paid these men, he said to himself. How apt if Dr Knox were to pay him, too. Here was a way to enter Dr Knox's life and, this time, Robbie would not be the victim.

'I can help you,' he said quickly, rubbing his throat. 'You need me. I can help you pull the cart, or I could be your lookout. I'm fast.' He scrambled to his feet, and saw out of the corner of his eye the smashed head squashed inside the barrel, twisted at its neck to make it fit. The stench of fish and the sea swept across Robbie's face. It was a herring-barrel, he realized, its sides slimy with silver scales.

The man with the sandy hair and pale-lidded eyes spoke, in little more than a whisper, taking one step closer again.

'See that body? You set one step out o' line, you so

much as whisper a word o' what you've seen, and the next body will be you, so it will. And your friend, your friend what you say you hate, he'll be the one to cut you up, to slice off the skin from your legs, to open up yer gizzard like a herring, to lift out yer eyeballs one by one and pin t'em to a table. We seen it done, boy, and we'll see it done to you, sure we will.' The words oozed slow and sinister as blood.

Robbie somehow stood his ground. 'I won't talk,' he promised, his voice no more than a breath.

'Now, be getting that wheel on,' continued the man. Both men leaned all their weight against the cart while Robbie positioned the wheel and slid the bolt through. The scarred man spun it fast a few times. It wobbled but it would do. The pale man forced the lid back into the mouth of the barrel and then the three of them lifted it back on to the cart, tying it down as firmly as they could with the ropes.

The two men looked at Robbie, then at each other. The scar-faced one raised a hand and passed the knife across his own throat in a slitting motion. 'No,' cautioned the other man quietly but firmly. ' 'Tis better this way, so 'tis.'

His companion looked at Robbie and made the same throat-cutting motion again, slowly. 'One step out o' line, boy, an' you'll go the way of the horse. We had a horse what pulled the cart, did we not? But the bastard horse had no stomach for pulling dead bodies and it would not move. An' we killt the bastard horse, so we did, shot it through the eyes wit' a pistol. One step out o' line, boy . . .' and he spat the gob of fish on to the ground at Robbie's feet and wiped his lips with his hand.

The pale man laid a large freckled hand on his companion's shoulder and spoke to Robbie, his hard eyes penetrating. 'Knox's place, boy. On wit' you.' The man picked up the lantern and they set off, Robbie running ahead, peering round corners and checking for constables or bailies or soldiers before beckoning to the men to follow with the cart. He did not think about what the cart was carrying. Or of Essie waiting at home. He thought of nothing but Dr Knox and as he did the anger burned. Excitement, too. Now he was doing something.

As Robbie turned into the steep hill leading to Infirmary Street, he heard a whistle. He looked round. The two men were in the shadows, gesturing to him. 'Not up dair, eejit. The back,' urged the sandy-haired one. Robbie was confused. This was the way to Knox's anatomy school, was it not?

The other man snapped, his voice spittled with tension, 'Mary, Modder of Jesus, wid ye jist get a move on? Down there, round the corner and in the Fludden Wall . . .' but before he had time to finish, Robbie spotted the tall figures of two constables. Coming their way.

'Move! This way!' His voice so urgent that the men did not question him. He grabbed the cart himself, hauled it with them up the steep slope. Quickly to the left, into the small courtyard of a building. In the shadows. Silent except for breathing. Robbie squashed against the barrel. Trying not to smell it. The three of them. Mingled sweat stench of bodies too close together. Fish whisky breath. Wide eyes. Fixed on each other. Not daring to move. Or look into the street. Footsteps. Approaching. A sudden crunch as the cart shifted, settling. Do not breathe. Go away. Go away. Go away. Please God, go away. Going away. They breathed again. Wild-faced, the two men began to move. 'No, wait,' said Robbie. He moved out of the courtyard, down the slope and cautiously peered into the main street again. The danger had passed. They had not been seen.

The sandy-haired man clapped Robbie on the back, his hand powerful despite his small size. Robbie would not like to fight a man with such hidden strength. 'Good work, lad, to be sure.' The other man wiped his wet mouth with a sleeve and held out a hand to Robbie.

Reluctantly, but with a strange excitement, even pride, Robbie took his hand and felt its limp bony coldness as he shook it. The man smiled, those teeth like crooked gravestones in the glow of the lantern. When he smiled, his lop-sided eyes remained dead, brackish, the smaller one closing further, the larger one remaining open, watching.

They all moved off again, Robbie in the lead. The Flodden Wall towered above them, its ancient stones thick and strong. Where now? The two men gestured to Robbie to wait on the other side of the road, out of sight. He stood pressed against the side of a building and watched.

There was a doorway, low and dark, set deep into the wall. Robbie had never noticed it before. He looked up. Above the wall rose a tall narrow building . . . and then he realized. This was the back of Knox's anatomy school. After looking round to make sure no one was approaching, one of the men knocked on the door. A moment later, it opened and Dr Knox himself came out, looked around. Robbie's heart began to race. The dark-haired man used his knife to prise the lid away from the barrel. Dr Knox looked inside it, poking the contents with his fingers. The conversation became angry. The two men began to replace the lid and move away with the barrel still on the cart. Dr Knox followed them.

Robbie could see his face, yellow under a nearby gaslight, pitted like curds. Some more words and Knox pulled something from his pocket. He began counting money into one of the men's hands.

The man held his hand out for Knox to shake, but Knox turned away with a casual gesture of his arm, his lacy wrist turning with swan-like grace, his tapering fingers softly curled as if playing a violin. Two more men came out, young men, perhaps students, and hefted the barrel off the cart before rolling it carefully indoors. Knox followed. The door closed firmly.

Robbie walked over to the men, who were crowing over the money they had been paid. Robbie had never seen so much money at one time.

'More t'an ever, stupid bastard!' The man's pale eyes gleamed as he handed money to the other one.

'Easy money! Bee-oootifully easy money,' laughed the wet-lipped one, his tongue sticking out as he counted his share. Robbie stared at it.

'Want some, boy, d'ye? What d'ye tink, William? Will we be generous?' the pale-haired man seemed relaxed now, louder, buoyed up by their success.

'Sure, we can afford to be generous, William. And anyways, he needs feeding, so he does. Skinny as a rat, he is. Pull the cart, boy, and ye'll get yer pay when we get home.'

Robbie pushed the cart the whole way back, lighter now with just rope for its load, through the Grassmarket and into West Port, the two men leading the way in high spirits. They came to a stop outside a crumpled inn. The door opened and a wave of noise and light and warmth spilled on to the cobbles. A woman came out as soon as she saw them, shouting at the two men.

'Where've ye bin, ye lousy bastards? What took ye so long?' But she was smiling, her lips wide and loose.

'Trouble wit' de cart. The lad helped.'

The woman peered at Robbie. From her dress, Robbie had at first thought that she was young, but her skin was mapped with broken veins and her hair, uncovered, was grey and dry. Her cheeks were streaked with vermilion, carelessly applied. Her low-cut dress revealed her upper chest and throat, its skin wrinkled like a dirty sheet. Her bodice had slipped sideways, exposing more of one breast than the other, but she did not notice. Lurching slightly, she moved too close to Robbie, stretching her eyes wide as she struggled to focus on him. She reeked of used sweat.

'We have money, Margaret. Would ye look at this? An' the boy needs a drink, so he does.' The rat-toothed man flung his arms round the woman, who grinned slackly. Before Robbie could stop them, he had been swept into the tavern. Inside, all was noise and steam, bodies and confusion. A swollen roar of voices. The smell of roasting meat. A warm fug enveloped him.

Someone thrust a lidded pewter tankard in his hand. He looked around. Faces, shouting, laughing faces everywhere. He did not know where to go, what to say, who to look at. He caught the eye of a girl across the room. She stared straight back at him, long black curls spiralling over her eyes, pink roses on her cheeks, and opened her little red mouth, sticking her tongue between its lips suggestively. He blushed and lifted the tankard's lid with his thumb before burying his face in the ale. He had had ale before but this was more bitter, stronger, darker. He drank more, felt its warm strength gushing through him, welcoming.

He leaned against the wall, his head against the stone, and let the noise wash over him. He drank again. The warmth was in his stomach now, spreading outwards. He watched the swarming faces until they all merged together. It seemed as though everyone was laughing, heads thrown back, mouths gaping. Voices became louder and louder, each competing to be heard.

There was something comforting about so much laughter. Robbie began to smile too. He closed his eyes and just bathed himself in the warm chaos around him. He need do nothing, think nothing, just close his eyes and relax while the voices ebbed and flowed around him.

Suddenly he felt a hand on his arm. He opened his eyes. It was the darker of the two men. He smiled through spittle-lips, and swung one arm round Robbie's shoulders as he spoke, his voice softened by drink.

'Wha's yer name, boy?'

'Robbie.'

'Well, Robbie, how'd ye like to work for us again? Next time we have a . . . delivery, for your friend – sorry, not friend – Dr Knox? There's good money in it, so there is.'

Why not? It was, as the man said, good money, and easy work. Surely Dr Knox owed them, Robbie and Essie, for what he had done?

'Aye,' said Robbie. 'Where will I come? And when?'

' 'S not reg'lar work. Come here every day, after dark, and we'll tell ye if there's work, so we will. Ask at t' door for us.'

'Wha's your names?' slurred Robbie.

'William Hare, at your service,' replied the man, his hand to his scar-twisted forehead in a mock salute. When he smiled, his black eyes gleamed and his wet lips curled out to reveal their shiny pink insides. 'And my quieter friend is William Burke.'

Hare fumbled in his pocket. Bringing out a handful

of coins, he pressed four into Robbie's hand. Robbie stared at them. He closed his fingers round them and felt their solid metalness. This was more than he would earn in a week at Mr Brown's. Even with tips and Essie's smiling face.

Hare then shifted his face closer to Robbie's. In the hazy distance, Robbie could see Burke walking towards them, pushing his way across the room. Before he arrived, Hare's black eyes drilled into Robbie's. 'Now listen. And listen good, boy. Now ye've been paid, ye'll no' talk. Ye're in this with us and if ye talk ye'll hang with us, I swear to the good Lord, so you will. We hang, you hang.'

Before Robbie had time to think, Burke was with them, pressing one of three small, thick pottery cups towards Robbie. Robbie put his tankard, now empty, on the ground and took this new drink. Burke gave another to Hare, leaving one for himself. 'Here's to us, my friends,' he said, raising it and looking straight at Robbie, his pale eyes watering in the smoky air. They were thinking eyes, without emotion.

'And to the good doctor, to be sure,' added Hare. 'May he continue to need our work for a long time to come. Drink up, Robbie boy.' Robbie looked for a short moment into the whisky. As he drained it back, an image of his father came unwanted into his mind, but the burning liquid drowned all such thoughts as the fire hit his stomach. For a few seconds he could not breathe or swallow, but soon his face emptied into a grin and the blood spun through his body, giving him a strength he had never felt before.

Later that night, much later, he stumbled dizzily up the stairs to his room. Two of the sewing-women sat on the stair, one puffing on the pipe that stuck from her mouth, both slack-jawed with gin. They swayed towards him with a lewd laugh. His reactions were slow and he felt his leg grabbed. Angrily, he kicked his foot from their grasp and stumbled up the stairs, followed by their wheezing laughter.

In his room, he could remember little about anything that had happened in the inn, except the warmth, the money in his pocket, and the fiery strength the whisky had given him.

As he fell fully clothed into their bed, only stopping to kick off his boots, he did not notice that Essie was still awake. He did not notice her lying there like ice.

6

Sliding

Robbie woke early with a stagnant mouth. His head throbbed sickeningly as he sat up, his eyes hot and metallic. He fumbled to light a candle from the orange glow of the ashes and the damp wick fizzled before it lit. His urine was dark, the stream seeming to go on for ever. Steam rose from the chamber pot into the icy air.

He shuffled back to bed. The next thing he knew, Essie was shaking him.

'Get up, Robbie.' She shook him again. 'It's morning and it's the Sabbath.'

'Go 'way.' He did not want to speak. Every word tasted foul. He could smell his own breath.

Essie pulled her clothes on quickly, her fingers fumbling in the cold. Kneeling by the fire, she blew gently on the embers, feeding them tinder and then larger sticks until they burst into flame. She picked up the jug of water and poured some into the broth pot,

121

which she hung from the grease-caked hook above the fire. They had no kettle any more – when the old one had a hole in the bottom, Robbie had taken it to the blacksmith, but the blacksmith, instead of repairing it, had offered him money for it. He would melt it down and make horseshoes. Robbie had taken the money, though it was little enough. So now they boiled water in the broth pot and all their food tasted of old grease and kail. Essie mixed oatmeal into the warmed water, stirring the thin brose with a cracked spurtle. She ate in silence, quickly.

She watched Robbie, strangely wary of him. A tiny splinter of something almost like fear pressed against the fragile skin of her world. She needed him to get up so that this Sunday could be normal.

She was about to go out, when she turned back into the room. Reluctantly, but knowing that it was right and important on a Sunday and that God would be watching, she took a gap-toothed comb and pulled it through her tangled hair, her eyes watering at the tugging. Her hair came well past her shoulders now and the curls hung more heavily than when she was younger. Now they spiralled more than bounced and they sat more obediently under the tattered lace cap which she now attached to her head. She pulled the thin ribbon through the gathered edge and the ribbon broke, as she had been expecting it to do for the last few Sundays. Tying the broken ends together, she mended it as best she could.

Essie looked down at her feet, bare and toughened. Her dress was shrinking. No, she was growing, her legs lengthening and her long scrawny arms stretching through the sleeves like willow branches. Squinting into her broken piece of looking-glass, she looked at herself as though at a stranger. Then grinned and stuck out her tongue. Life was too short to spend time staring into looking-glasses.

Robbie did not get up. Essie went out, leaving her shoes behind – with the sun filtering down to the wider streets, it would not be cold enough to waste good leather. Robbie would be better soon, she told herself firmly. Her father had been drunk often enough for her to know what the morning after looked like.

The early sun was shining wetly on the pavements, the High Street smiling with people in their Sunday best. Girls and boys walking demurely behind their parents, servants too, their faces scrubbed and ready for heaven. The ladies wore long gloves, the cuffs covered by short cloaks, their hair almost hidden by stiff bonnets. And their men strutted, stern in greatcoats.

Familiar faces called greetings to Essie and she waved back. A pie-man, eyes open for any disapproving

Calvinist who might wander by, slipped her a broken pie as she lingered near his barrow, her mouth watering at the beefy steam. She ate it hungrily. A dog began to follow her. She threw a piece of pastry as far as she could and watched a seagull snatch it before the dog could reach it. 'Have tae be quicker than tha',' she told the dog. It still followed her, trusting, before it found a discarded bone and dragged it away somewhere.

She did not follow the Sunday-best crowd to the kirk. Essie's Sunday best was not good enough. The only difference in her clothes on Sunday was her lacy cap. Her dress was as clean as it could be, pummelled in cold weakly-sudded water, and hung to dry on lines between the houses, or by the sooty fire when the rain poured down outside. But it was not nearly good enough for the kirk. No, barefoot Essie was going to listen to a preacher on the Grassmarket. She found herself a position, perched high on the top of the well so she could just see above the heads of the crowd. She could not hear properly everything that was being said, but she liked to watch the drama of the preacher's arms and catch snatches of the familiar words of justice, and see the crowds nod, their heads all turned towards the black-gowned beaky figure in the wooden preaching tent. She liked the way when a drunkard shouted something, the crowd turned on him and some chased him till he fell in the gutter and lay, to become the object of the preacher's fury and the crowd's self-righteous laughter. It seemed right. It made sense.

All morning Robbie drifted groggily on the edges of sleep. It was many hours before he got up and when he did his lips were dry and grey, his stomach empty, his eyes still gritty. He stumbled blearily to get something to eat. There was no milk in the jug on the windowsill. The fire had gone out again and was now nothing but embers. Robbie kicked the table-leg with his bare foot, his vision buzzing.

Footsteps on the stairs. The squeak of the opening door speared his head. It was Essie.

'You better now?' she asked. Robbie mumbled something. 'Where were you last night?' she asked, her voice sharp.

'Mind your own business.' He knew she deserved better. But a whisky head, mixed with his own guilt, made him angry.

'My ain business?' she spat, her words coarse as thistles. 'How's it no' my ain business? We've barely money enough for food. Where'd you get money fo' drinking?'

Robbie looked at her, no words to answer her anger. He rummaged in the pocket of the trousers he was still wearing. He pulled out three coins and threw them on the floor.

Essie leapt on them, her fury blown away. She trod on one with her bare foot and as she bent to pick it up another was hidden under her skirts. Her fingers scrabbling, she picked them up and held all three in front of her, her mouth open wide, almost laughing. 'Where d'you get these? It'd take us days tae earn these!'

'Give them back to me,' he snapped. But Essie was still staring at them, twisting and turning them, wiping them on her dress, looking at each side. For one horrible moment, Robbie pictured himself in the cell again, with the crazy creature eating his coin. He grabbed them from Essie, accidentally scratching her hand.

She drew her arm back as though bitten. She looked at Robbie with disgust. He turned away.

'Take one,' he said, 'and go and buy us some food.'

As she left the room, Robbie lay back on the bed again and closed his eyes against his headache.

Essie would have to grow up, he thought. It was a hard world out there and he was doing his best to survive. For both of them. If they did not help themselves, who else would? They had been deserted, by their mother, by their father, by God. They were up against the world with its injustice and its rich sneering uncaring Dr Knoxes. And there were two choices: fight, or drown in the pig-swill slum. I am older than Essie, he told himself. I understand more of the world. She can go to her Sunday School if she likes, and listen to her preachers, and nod obediently at the words she hears, but I have found another way to fight, and to win.

Next day, ignoring Essie's shell-tight silence, he went about his work for Mr Brown without her. And in the evening, when darkness cloaked the city's limbs, he turned his back on her again and went out. A growing excitement pulsed through him.

The door to the inn was closed but light spilled from the windows. Robbie paused, took a deep breath, and pushed open the door. He was again drawn into the thick warmth of the noisy room. Across the people, he immediately saw Hare, standing with his arm round a woman, his face buried in her ear.

Robbie tried to catch his eye. He felt a hand on his shoulder. Margaret. She leaned towards him, her slack smile revealing her browned teeth and holes where teeth had been. 'Hello, pretty boy. What can I dae for ye?'

'Is . . . does Mr Hare have any work for me? And Mr Burke?'

'Mister Hare? Mister Burke?' she laughed, mocking his politeness. Her breath smelt of sweet ale and fish. He blushed, uncomfortable in her presence, not knowing what to say. She placed one finger on his lips and traced it slowly down his face, his throat, into the smooth cupped hollow in the centre of his collar-bone. Her soft, loose, sweaty body was too close to him. His breathing quickened. She seemed to sway towards him until her full lips were the closest part of her.

He turned away, stepped back. She laughed again, looking for a few long seconds into his eyes. 'Saving yesel', then? For someone pretty?'

'No . . . I . . .'

'You dinnae have tae tell me. Why would I care? Wait here.' And off she went, pushing between the crushed bodies towards where Hare and the girl were. On her way, many a man turned and touched her, whispered in her ear, stared at her breasts, tried to grab her. She dealt with them all with equal ease.

She reached Hare, spoke to him. He turned to Robbie across the sea of faces and shook his head.

Robbie left. Outside, with the door closed on him, he turned and looked through the thick silent window. The warmth, the laughing faces – he wished he could join them again. Wished he could be part of that drifting easy mindless world. Longed to bury his lips in that warm black ale, or to feel the bite of whisky as it flooded through his body and lifted him floating way way way above everything.

He did not go home straight away. He could wait for ever before returning to face Essie's accusing looks. What did Essie understand of anything? She was eight years old. A child.

Robbie walked slowly through the streets. No one looked at him. He could meld into the filth and darkness of the shadowed closes and no one would care what he did. Every now and then, a shaft of narrow moonlight found its way between the tall crazily-stacked buildings, lighting up the ankle-deep human and animal waste which swelled overflowing from channels cut too shallow.

Dr Knox did not live in a place like this. No, his genteel home was a delicate distance outside the skin of the stinking city, away from the houses piled on top of each other, sometimes sixteen storeys high, lightless buildings squashed shoulder to shoulder, tall, thin and struggling to stay upright as they stretched dizzily towards a weak sun. Dr Knox did not have to breathe the diseased stench from the bowels of the streets or dirty his shiny shoes in the blood and slime outside his own door.

And these doctors, these surgeons sauntering and smiling idly in the marbled air of Surgeons' Hall, what did they know of life in the real world? Nothing, thought Robbie, his jaw clenched. But he would make

Dr Knox be a part of his stinking world. He would sully him with the taint of stolen corpses. Robbie knew the corpses were stolen but what did that matter? He had not stolen them. He had done nothing wrong. It was all just part of the world he had been thrown into, through no choice of his own.

A clanging. Clattering, shouting. One of the new fire-carts being pulled at speed by black horses came jangling round a corner, uniformed men running beside it. At the same moment Robbie smelt the smoke. He held his breath while he waited to see which way they would go. Away from his home they clattered, and he breathed again in relief. If you lived in the Old Town you had to fear fire even more than disease. Robbie had his own memory to fuel his fear.

Four years ago now, but he would never forget the deadly roar of the flames as they had swept through buildings and leapt high into the blood-orange sky. As the windows shattered and the wooden roofs puffed into ash, each building became a skeleton, revealing its flimsy structure, the emptiness of its frame. Like a body without its soul. Burning in hell.

They had been let out of school early and Robbie had stood and watched before going home. Transfixed.

Never would he forget the din, a crashing mixed-up chaos of every noise the world had heard of, so loud that for a while he could hear nothing at all, only see people shouting and beams and stone come tumbling silently to the ground. Then there was the confusion, the people running in all directions, the ladders, the human chains with leather buckets of water and dung, different people waving their arms with opposite instructions, even men fighting over who was in charge; the horses rearing, their mouths curled back in terror; women gawping, their silken bonnets protecting their hair from ash; the children staring wide-eyed and wide-mouthed or burying their heads in their mother's skirts. Most of all, he would never forget the sight of two people leaping from a seventh-floor window, holding hands, and their flaming rag-doll bodies tumbling like Catherine-wheels to the ground.

Later, when the delicate tip of the steeple of the Tron Kirk came spinning silently through the flames, a despairing roar went up from the crowd and Robbie thought that truly the world was coming to an end. That nothing could ever be the same again.

Four hundred families lost their homes while the fires raged, and eleven people died. Not Robbie's home, not Robbie's family. The flames did not touch them. But they might as well have done. His father did not come home at the usual time, did not fling wide the door with a comforting smile. Robbie and Essie waited for him, wondering at first what present he might have brought them that day, then just wishing he would come himself, without a present.

Robbie could not bring himself to stoke their fire that evening. Did not dare. He raked the embers and let the glow die down to almost nothing.

They waited for two hours. Night fell. Robbie lit one oil lamp, watching it closely, never taking his eyes off the flame. He moved everything a safe distance from the lamp. He and Essie grew cold. They put on extra clothes. There was a thick mutton broth in the pot, left by Jeannie McKnight, the woman who came to look after Essie. They ate it cold. Just when they thought they could wait no longer, that they must find someone to help them, they heard footsteps on the stairs. Tired footsteps.

He came into the room slowly, his eyes white in a face streaked with soot, one sleeve of his jacket ripped from the shoulder. He went straight to a cupboard and took a bottle of whisky, pouring himself a large measure. His hands were black. For a moment he did not drink, just stared at the golden liquid as if drawing himself down into it. Then, with a deep breath, he quickly lifted it to his lips and drained it, in one desperate fiery mouthful. He squeezed his eyes shut and breathed out. A dribble of whisky trickled down his chin. He did not wipe it away and it left a clean pink channel in the dirt of his face.

Essie, from a dark corner of the room, whispered, 'Father?' Robbie moved a little way towards her. The two children watched their father. Essie without comprehension, Robbie with fear. There was something wild in his father's eyes.

Essie spoke again, unafraid, a black curl escaped from her white ruffled cap. 'Why you all dirty?' Their father did not look up, his head hanging down, the empty glass pressed against his forehead.

'What has happened, Father? We were worried,' said Robbie.

'You were right to be worried,' muttered their father. 'What do you think has happened? Did you not see the fire? Did you not hear it?' His voice rose on a wind of emotion, his accent changing in despair as he spoke. 'Have ye no' seen the buildings, collapsed, destroyed? All destroyed.' He poured himself some more whisky and drank it furiously.

'Yes, I saw it.' Robbie was angry. It was not his fault so why did his father make it feel like his fault? 'I saw . . . I saw everything.' As he spoke he tried to shut out the memories of what he had seen. 'But we' re safe. Our home is safe.'

His father drained his glass and threw it against the

133

wall where it smashed into shocked silence. Then he roared, exploding, his voice thick with Scots now, 'What the deil d'ye ken? It is the end, the end o' us, o' everything, it . . .' and he sank on to a chair, folded himself over and sat with his head in his hands, rocking. Robbie was almost certain that his father was crying.

It was not till the morning that they learnt the whole truth. Their father had left in the early hours and when Robbie went outside to look for him he met only three angry-faced men looking for him too.

'Where's Mr Anderson, lad?' demanded one, coming right up to Robbie.

'Out. He went out. Sir.'

'Aye, weel, he needs tae come back quickly. He owes us money.' The man jabbed a finger towards Robbie's face. Two more men arrived, flat caps pulled down tightly over their tired smudged faces. One had a charred sleeve and a raw black-edged weal on his hand, which he cradled.

'You looking fo' Anderson, too?' one of them asked the first men.

It was Jeannie McKnight who explained. She came early that morning, her kindly face thick with weeping, her red sausage fingers enclosing Essie's startled face, as she looked despairingly at them both, shaking her head with incoherent cries of, 'The puir man! Wha's tae become o' us a'? 'Twas the deil's work, 'twas so!' Once she had calmed down, Robbie began to understand. His father had been the insurer for one of the seven-storey buildings which had collapsed. Of his two business partners, one had died in the fire and the other had disappeared. They owed a small fortune. A fortune which they did not have.

Jeannie McKnight left. How could they pay her now? Many times before she went she took Essie in her saggy arms and wept more snuffling tears. 'I would tak' ye, so I wuid. The baith o' ye. But ye ken I cannae. There's ma' ain family tae think o', an ma' man no' weel.' So she left, leaving them one last pot of rich beef broth before she went. It was the best beef broth they had ever tasted, thick with clumps of barley and stringy with onions, hiding huge lumps of melting beef and dark with a stock cooked for hours over her own hearth.

Now, more than four years after the fire, he could not forget. It was, after all, the reason why he and Essie now lived in a one-roomed hole with the reek of the flesh market beneath them.

As he walked slowly up the stairs once more, he could not ignore the crumbling decay and excrement all around him. He stepped aside to avoid the buzzing remains of a pig's snout halfway up the stairs. On the fourth floor, a door opened as he passed and one of the women fell out, screaming with laughter. She lay there, stranded on her back, one breast like an empty pig's udder hanging from her torn chemise. 'Dinnae jist stand there, pretty boy!' she shrieked. 'Gi'e us a hoist!' The stink of gin rose from her open mouth. As Robbie stood there, two more women lurched out of the room and grabbed the woman by her feet, shrieking with laughter as they dragged her back into the room. A frightened mouse scuttled out of her hair as she slid away, her white legs spilling from her footless stockings as her underskirt rucked up beneath her.

This was not how my life should have been, thought Robbie. It was hard to push the bitterness away. So much easier to be angry.

Next morning, before six o'clock as usual, Robbie made his way to the bakery through sheets of squalling rain. Passing the Flodden Wall, he took a tiny detour to look at the door. It was closed, thick, blank. A dog raised its scrawny leg against the step and the piss steamed in the March morning darkness. Robbie hurried on to the bakery.

Mr Brown looked at Robbie's grey face. 'Ye a' richt, laddie?'

'Wha's tae be a' richt about?' Robbie grumbled.

'Aye, weel, it's a dreich day, so it is,' nodded Mr

Brown, peering out of the dough-steamed windows. 'But it's no like ye tae be so dour, laddie. Ye'll need tae smile fo' the customers.' The light from an oil-lamp glistened on his high-domed forehead, its thick skin wrinkled back as though he had pushed it out of the way of his eyes.

Robbie glared at him and Mr Brown turned away, too soft to speak out. Robbie loaded up all the different wheat breads, oat breads, barley cakes, oatcakes, bannocks, gingerbread with icing stained red with cochineal, pastries twisted and drizzled with treacle, bridies oozing gravy. He fixed the cover on to the barrow and set off, leaving the dough-hearted Mr Brown to beat and pummel the yeasty mixture until the sweat shone rosy on his arms.

The rain seeped down Robbie's face and neck as he wheeled the barrow. He spent the day wet and cold, his mind numbed. His unsmiling face gained him no extra money. He bought a turnip and an old onion on the way home. Told Essie to make them into broth.

The broth was thin and grey. He added more salt from the wooden saut bucket crusting on the hearth. Wet wind blew soot back down the chimney into the room. The fire spluttered blue flames. Essie coughed, the phlegm black on her hand.

That night, Hare shook his head again and Robbie went home angry.

The week continued. Robbie and Essie barely talked, their silence cloud-heavy and cold. Essie watched him, anger gradually congealing into fear. Robbie was disappearing. Her world was changing. She did not understand the change that had come over her brother. Did not know words for what she felt. Just that it was frightening, like walking in a dark unknown street, faster and faster, far from home.

She did her best to keep their room clean, bring food back, wash clothes and hang them from the lines that cats-cradled the narrow space high between the buildings. At first, she emptied the chamber pot in the proper way, walking downstairs whatever the weather, down the narrow wynd, and carefully tipping it into the communal midden. Soon she gave that up, tipping it out of the window like everyone else, her small voice shouting a warning with an increasing lack of care.

She stopped asking to go with Robbie on his rounds. His surly face and snappy voice were no pleasure to be with. Instead, she hung around the fires of the potato-braziers or the chestnut sellers in the Grassmarket, with the other street children. She left her shoes at home. No point in wearing them out. Besides, the other children had none. And so she hardened, built a shell around her fear. But as she did, the sparkle in her magpie eyes dimmed, its energy burning up until it was little more than an ember.

Sometimes in the evening, when Robbie was not there, she took out her battered kaleidoscope from its hiding place under the bed and stared into its spiralling patterns until her head was filled with colour. Then the ember in her eyes glowed more brightly, for a moment, before dying down again. Each time dimmer than before.

Each evening, Robbie went to Hare's inn. Each evening, he watched the crowded room of open-mouthed faces, smelt the swill of ale and whisky and warmth, felt the easy touch of slack-lipped Margaret's hand on his arm and the conflicting feelings she aroused. Each evening, his heart sank as he saw Hare shake his head and turn back to his friends. And each evening, Robbie walked slowly back home, with nothing changed except his anger grown more bitter and more aimless.

He bought whisky and drank it under Essie's tight-lipped gaze. What did she know? A part of him, somewhere inside, remembered what they had both felt when their father drank whisky, and he knew Essie probably thought the same now. But that part of him, the part that had cared, was shrivelling.

Then, at last, one night Burke met him at the door to the inn. His pale eyes were snake-slits, his body rigid with tension, as he beckoned Robbie to hurry to the back of the building and meet him there. Excited, Robbie obeyed.

There was Hare, his lips wetter than ever, his arms jangling and restless. His right hand hovered near his coat pocket, sometimes resting on the knife hidden in it. His left tugged sometimes at his ear, then at his lip, then pummelled the edges of the twisted scar that ran past the corner of his smaller eye. He chewed frantically, the smell of dried fish salty on his breath.

There was the cart, a new herring-barrel fastened with the rope. Robbie looked at it, fascinated. He thought of what was going to happen to the body inside it. He thought of a smiling Dr Knox slicing smoothly into its cold flesh and peeling back the skin. His breathing quickened through his nose, and his lips tightened. A feeling of lightness threatened to lift him away and he tore his eyes from the barrel.

As before, Robbie ran in front of Hare and Burke, peering round corners, beckoning to them or halting them with gestures of his arms. Soon they were in front of the Flodden Wall. High up, the fluttering light from a window of Knox's anatomy school wavered as someone passed by. They waited till Robbie gave the all-clear, then he hid as before and the two men pulled the cart to the door.

As before, Knox came out, the deal was done and two students rolled the barrel into the building, nervously looking around as they did.

Yellow gas-light fell on Knox's face as he turned. He looked like a corpse himself. Robbie's hatred was something hard and physical inside him. It seemed to grow, feeding off itself. He let it grow, needing it to create a meaning for what he was doing.

The three of them made their way back to Hare's inn, spirits high, drunk on success and on the money in their pockets. Robbie laughed with them, joking about the evil doctor and his disgusting habits. They all knew what he did, despite his fastidious clean fingers and the perfect elegance of his bejewelled velvet clothes, his delicately curled and pomaded sideburns and his musical voice. His pitted skin told a truer story, as though each scar was the outward sign of evil within.

What did he do with the parts when he had cut them into bite-sized portions? they wondered aloud. Did he serve them up to his guests? Hare acted the part of a butler, serving up a tray of delicacies to a lady, a part played with skill by Burke, who, with unusual jollity, stuck his chest out and wiggled his hips as he pretended daintily to eat an eyeball. They laughed. Robbie laughed too.

At the inn, they left the cart behind the house and went inside, arm-in-arm. Robbie felt himself folded into the warmth of the crowd and a smile spread through him as he flipped the lid of his tankard up and dipped his top lip deep into the ale. Noise steamed around him, wrapping itself about his ears, his head, his whole body, as he gave himself up to its holding arms.

The three of them joined Margaret, and Burke's wife, Nelly, a cold dark-haired woman with sandpaper skin and bristles on her upper lip, whose eyes watched Robbie with something like mistrust. Robbie did not care. He did not care about anything, and soon Nelly's narrow eyes swirled into a haze, just like everything else. When someone spoke, the others laughed, about anything or nothing. It was the laughing that mattered. Laughing was belonging.

After the ale, the whisky, rich, amber and warming. Robbie fell easily into the cocooning arms of whisky and laughter. Arms that held him tightly, as if they would never let him fall. This was better than anything he could remember. Or there might have been something better, something warmer and more real and more important, but if there was he had forgotten it.

He rolled home a long time later, stumbling up the stairs in the pitch-blackness. The room was dark, too, the fire glowing dully. Essie was in bed. He climbed into their bed still clothed, his mouth leathery, his head spinning with something which had felt like happiness and now began to feel like something else, something heavier.

Essie turned aside and pulled the blanket over her head, shutting him out. She curled up in a ball. In the dozing moments before Robbie fell asleep, he could sense her wakefulness, could hear her fast breathing above the quiet hissing of the fire. He ignored it.

Next morning, Robbie was woken by Essie shaking him. It was daylight. He blinked, confused. 'Wake up! Get up, Robbie!' she was shouting.

He groaned. A dangle of sticky saliva hung from his mouth. 'Go 'way, Essie.'

'But Robbie, you're late for work! What'll Mr Brown say? I woke you afore and you went back to sleep while I was out getting water.'

'Who cares?'

She shook him again. 'Robbie, get up!'

Robbie sat up, clutching his head as he did so. He swallowed, wiped his mouth on the greasy sheet. 'Can't you see I'm sick? Go and tell your Mr Brown. He'll believe it from you.' He lay back down again and pulled the blanket over his head.

'You're no' sick! You're drunk! You're nae better than our feckless father!' she shouted, her shoulders sharp under her dress as she tried to shake him.

There was no movement from the bed, no sign that he had heard. She ran from the room, crashing the door behind her. Robbie was alone.

Essie ran down the stairs, up the narrow wynd, her bare feet cold on the wet cobbles. The wind sliced through the watery sunlight and she wished she had brought her shawl or stopped to put her shoes on. Down the High Street she ran, made faster by anger and the need to act. She had to save Robbie's job. They needed his job. If he lost it, what would they do? How would they survive? Man did not live by bread alone, Essie knew from her Sunday School. But they would die without it, she knew for herself.

Into the Canongate now, past the prison on her left. She recoiled when she thought of Robbie locked in there. Then, nipping into a tiny street on the right, she wound her way round corners and came to the road where the baker's shop sat, its sweet malty smell making her mouth water. She slowed to a walk and approached the door, her chest heaving.

There was no barrow outside. She went in. Mr

Brown looked up, expecting a customer. His face fell when he saw Essie. He turned away, blushing, flustered. Wiped his fat fingers on the white apron wrapped around his barrel stomach. Reached for a piece of unbroken gingerbread, white-iced, snow-capped. And then a black bun, thick, warm, its rich fruitiness wrapped around by thin pastry. He handed them to her, not meeting her eyes.

'Ah'm sorry, wee Essie.'

'Robbie's sick, Mr Broon. He said tae tell ye. He'll be a' right the morrow, ye'll see.' Like Robbie, she had the ability to change her accent on demand.

Mr Brown, wiping his forehead, came round the counter. He crouched down with difficulty, hunched on his fat thighs. He avoided her face but he took her hands in his. He paused. 'Nae, Essie. There's nae job for Rabbie. It's no your faut. It's Rabbie. He's no bin working weel, the past week or mair. The customers are no' happy.'

'But Mr Broon!' Essie's voice rose. 'He's no weel. Let me dae his work. I could dae it. He's no' that much stronger 'n me! Where's the barra? I'll show ye!'

Just then the door opened and they both turned. In the doorway stood a boy of about twelve, his nose dripping, crusted sores around his lips. A gallus grin, wide mouthed, hang-jawed. And Robbie's barrow in his hands.

'Done it, Mr Broon! Quick, wis ah no'? An' I got ye a new customer. Hoose o' la-di-dah English lady an' all.'

Mr Brown stood up, dizzy from sitting on his thighs. Essie darted towards the door. Mr Brown picked up the gingerbread and the bun. 'Essie, no! Dinnae go. Mebbe I could . . . Tak' these at least. I'll no' hae ye starving.' But Essie was gone, leaving Mr Brown standing agitated on his doorstep as he watched her run, bare feet flashing, towards the Old Town.

She did not go back home straightaway. The city was stirring, with people on their way to work in the icy early morning gloom, and sprawling drunks rousing themselves and groaning. She wandered around the streets, cold to her bones. Drawn by the warmth, she stood near a potato-brazier, forcing a smile to her face as she spoke to the pipe-smoking woman who handled the potatoes as though her hands were leather. The woman saw her red raw feet and stick-skinny arms and let her stir the fire with a metal rod. She gave her a large potato steaming from a slit in its skin.

Later, Essie found some of the street children she knew. Three boys were drinking gin from an earthenware flagon, tipping it into their mouths from a height. One of them threw a stone at an old lady passing. The boys laughed when it hit the old lady's ankle and she cried out in pain. Essie left them and went home.

Robbie said nothing at all when she told him about his job. He merely emptied the contents of his pockets in front of her and watched her face as she saw the coins fall. Her face showed nothing. She did not know what to think. Except that they would eat.

And so the days went by, unthinking. The weather lightened, the sun lifted itself higher, clouds whitened and dissolved, the distant sky between the towering houses deepened into a hopeful blue. Robbie noticed none of it. Every morning, he woke late, dragged himself headachey from his bed, spat thick phlegm out of the window, ate little, washed rarely. Sometimes Essie was there. Sometimes she was not.

His mind silted up. He was trapped in the airless narrow veins of the Old Town, under the weight of cold stone and sunless wet walls that ran green with bile. The city was sick and he had caught its sickness.

Sometimes, very occasionally, Robbie realized that this was not how his life should be. But none of it was his fault, he told himself. And if it was not his fault, what was he to do about it? So much easier just to chase the happiness that came from the whisky that he drank each night now in Hare's inn, because nowadays when Hare shook his head, Robbie just came into the warmth and drank late with the rest of them.

One night, in the inn, as his mind wandered during

Hare's vitriolic ranting about his dismal life back home in Ireland, Robbie's eyes drifted round the room. He caught sight of a thin, hollow-eyed boy of indeterminate age gazing at him, his fair hair a tangled web on his shoulders, dirty strands dangling in his eyes, shadows on his skin. Though hard-faced, almost cruel, the boy did not look part of the crowd, his mind elsewhere, his smile unfelt. The boy looked lost.

Robbie took a mouthful of whisky. As he did, the boy took a drink himself, a large mouthful, gulped quickly and desperately.

As Robbie lowered his drink, so did the boy.

It was not a boy. It was a looking-glass.

Robbie drank again and tottered home alone. Drunk though he was, as he climbed the stairs, he realized suddenly that what had felt like happiness before was nothing like it at all. He sat on the edge of the bed, his head in his hands.

Essie stirred from where she lay. 'Robbie?'

'Go to sleep,' muttered Robbie. He lay down. He did not allow himself to wonder what she was thinking.

He closed his eyes and let his thoughts drift amongst the background noise of the night. Like an aged man, with grumbling stomach and stertorous breathing, the Old Town was never silent, and through the thin partitions and shared walls and damaged floors the shouts and crashes and wailing of babies mixed with the creakings of the rafters and the rattling of loose doors and windows. But Robbie was used to it. Soon he was asleep and the city breathed on.

The next time Hare and Burke had work for him was perhaps two weeks later. By now it was the end of April, not that Robbie noticed the increasing lightness of the evenings or the growing warmth in the sun by day. He simply stirred himself dully at the end of another day of blankness and left to make the familiar journey to Hare's, below the sullen shoulders of the castle.

At the inn that night, Robbie's heart leapt when Hare beckoned him round to the back again. Already, he felt the thrill of what they would do. Already he imagined the warmth of the extra whisky he would drink, euphoric once they were safely back at the inn, much richer.

Behind the building, there was no cart. No herring-barrel slimy with fish-scales. Hare and Burke seemed more nervous tonight, fizzing with needled tension. Their heads flicked from side to side, never resting. Even Hare, usually flushed with excitement, looked drawn and white as he chewed nervously.

Robbie began to speak, 'Where . . . ?'

'Shut up and follow us, wid ye?' hissed Hare, his black

eyes slits in the dark. 'Not too close. We want to know if anyone's following.'

Robbie knew better than to ask questions. There was something rat-violent in Hare's face tonight and Burke's eyes were little more than pale slits, his silence menacing. He followed at a distance as they walked, shoulders hunched in baggy coats, misshapen hats pulled down and collars high, through the streets, slippery shadows in the still night. He stopped at a corner, slid round it, waited, looked back. No one. No one other than those who should be there, going about their business.

Something stirred in a doorway. A bundle, shifting. A foot stuck from it. Just a drunk, relaxed as a rag-doll. Nearby, a dead cat, stiff legged. Robbie moved on.

Eastwards they travelled, along the Grassmarket, then into Cowgate and under the new bridge, its graceful arches sweeping over the dank street towards the distant New Town. At first Robbie thought they were going to Surgeons' Square and Infirmary Street. Without a body for Dr Knox? But no, they passed by and moved on swiftly.

Once, Robbie thought he had lost them. His heart pounded as he peered through the gloom. What would they do to him if – ? But no – there they were. They took a narrow turning to the left. Up a steep slope, round a corner. Soon they were in the Canongate.

There, to his left, its windows like eyes frowning at him, was the Canongate Tolbooth, where he had spent a night he would never forget. He did not want to find himself inside again. He felt a prickling on his back.

Soon, the two figures stopped at a house, low and slumped, its roof sagging, its walls thick and uneven. They looked around, quickly opened the door and slipped in. The door closed behind them.

What now? Robbie waited for a minute, looking around, hiding himself. No one had followed, he was sure. There were people passing, scurrying, heads down in the falling darkness. Two men shouted drunkenly at each other, face to face as they swayed closer. A woman picked through some rubbish a few yards away. But no one was watching Robbie. No one had noticed Hare and Burke go into the house. Quickly, he crossed the road. Knocked on the door. It opened immediately and he was pulled inside.

'Well? Anyone see us?'

'No, no one.'

'You sure?' Hare's face loomed spittingly close. Robbie could see the fish rolling around his yellow-furred tongue. A blister seeped at the corner of his mouth.

'Yes, I'm sure. There was no one.'

Hare let him go. 'Margaret thought someone had followed us. Doesn't trust you, she doesn't. Sure, an' I might be agreeing with her. You wi' your lah-di-dah voice. And mind this,' he said, pointing his finger within inches of Robbie's eyes, 'ye're in deep as us, so you are. We hang, you hang.' His face oozed sweat. His breath made Robbie gag.

Burke took over. He held Robbie's gaze with pearl-pale eyes, the near-white lashes almost invisible against his sallow skin. He looked like a slow-worm, but with snake's venom. 'Listen, we're nervous, is all. And wit' good reason, to be sure. We work from here now. Each night, you go to the inn as usual, but if Margaret or Nelly gives you the nod, you come here. You come here and you wait outside, hidden. You don't go in the house. You never go in the house if we're not here. You wait. And you don't get seen. Got it?'

'Let's git to work, an' fast,' muttered Hare, wiping his hands on his trousers, over and over again. Burke led the way upstairs and Hare and Robbie followed. The wooden stairs, little more than a ladder, creaked as they climbed. The walls were damp, and the smell of cod-liver candles and rotting vegetables sat in the air.

In a room upstairs a pile of straw lay in a corner, a grey pillow tossed on the floor beside it. Hare kicked aside the straw. There lay a man, a large man, slumped face down, one knee forced beneath him, his arm twisted unnaturally out to the side.

'Help us wrap it,' said Hare, picking up a large sack. 'We've no barrel today.'

Robbie's feet refused to move.

The two men were trying to turn the body over.

'Mary Modder of Jesus, wid you git over here and help us?' growled Hare, sweat breaking out again on his face.

Robbie moved, slowly as though in a trance. He grasped the man's jacket and tried to heave. The body was rigid. Suddenly, it moved, flopping over like a pig, and the trapped leg snapped free. The hand slid over Robbie's arm and, gasping, he picked up the wrist and flung it away from him. It hit the floor with a slap.

Hare had opened the sack and they began to pull it over the body's feet, bending the knees to force it in. Freed from its slumped position, the body flopped stiffly. The face stared up at Robbie, its eyes still open, the eyeballs webbed with broken veins, the tongue protruding through lips tinged with a blue-greyness. Or not really any colour at all, just ghostly. As Robbie helped pull the sack up around the body, his fingers inadvertently touched the skin, the cheek, and he pulled his hand back quickly. The coldness shocked him, not the coldness of marble or anything hard – the coldness of earth. Not smooth or rough, not soft or hard, just dead.

They struggled to stuff the heavy body into the sack, bending the stiff limbs roughly, and while they did so, Robbie noticed something. He stopped. The men looked at him.

'What's the matter? Too lah-di-dah for dirty work?' Hare looked darker than ever tonight.

'No,' said Robbie, his thoughts whirring. 'I . . . I was only thinking . . .'

'Aye, well, you'll leave thinking to others, so you will,' snapped Hare.

'No, wait,' said Burke, watching Robbie. 'What were you thinking, I am wondering?'

'It's so clean,' said Robbie.

'Clean? Stinks, so it does. Filthy, dirty tramp. Gutter food. Worth nothing alive.' Hare kicked the body with contempt.

Burke put his hand on Hare's arm to silence him. He had not taken his eyes off Robbie.

'Why should it be dirty?' he said, his eyes straight slits, snake-still.

'I thought . . . because. From the grave.'

'We are not grave-robbers,' said Burke slowly. 'We wouldn't do that, so we wouldn't. Why would we be wanting to do that?'

Robbie was flustered. 'I thought . . .'

'Aye, well, wid ye leave the thinking to others?' said Hare, stuffing the head into the sack and tying it with rope at the neck end. He was sweating, his eyes wild.

'Why do you tink the lovely Dr Knox pays us so well?' continued Burke, still watching Robbie. 'Would he pay us so well if the body was half-eaten by worms, now? And he needs the bodies clean, fresh, so that he can do his bee-ootiful scientifical work. His careful and most expert cutting and slicing and pinning, sure an' he does.'

'So, where . . . ?' asked Robbie.

'What you don't know about, you can't tell about,' snarled Hare. 'Mary, Modder of Jesus, wid ye jist git a move on?'

'Sure, an' we get them from elsewhere. They had useless lives but they can be useful in death, so they can,' Burke continued, still looking very carefully at Robbie.

'You mean . . .'

'Yes?' asked Burke, his hands slightly in front of and away from his body, ready. His eyes motionless.

'The gallows?'

'For sure,' said Burke, his shoulders softening, his breath a gentle whistle. 'The gallows. Criminals they are, layabouts, worth nothing alive. That's why they are so clean. They wash before they hang.'

Not grave-robbers then, realized Robbie. Not

Resurrection Men. Somehow, Burke and Hare bought the bodies of hanged criminals and Knox was happy to buy the bodies to furnish his gruesome occupation. Because one body a year was not enough.

The man's neck had been covered, wrapped in a scarf. Robbie was glad. He had seen what happened at hangings. He would not like to have seen the neck.

With difficulty, the three of them carried the sack down the stairs. The limbs had started to loosen and Robbie could barely hold on to it. He was at the head end, and it lolled, leaden, flopping. Twice he heard a crack, felt the crunch of bones in the neck breaking under the head's own weight. He kept his lips clenched, his throat pressed tightly shut, his breath as thin as thread.

They heaved it on to the cart. A noise, a scuffling down an alley. They looked at each other, froze. Burke gestured with his head to Robbie. Robbie ran to a corner. In the distance, in the darkest shadows, perhaps he saw something, the flick of flying feet maybe, a scampering. Or nothing. Then silence once more. Or not silence. The city was never silent. Faraway shouting, the crashes of haphazard activity, singing, the rise and fall of human noise, footsteps ebbing and flowing. But nothing that concerned them.

'It's nothing,' said Robbie. 'No one.'

'Mary, Modder of God, will ye hurry?' muttered Hare, pulling his hat as far down over his black eyebrows as it would go. Both men grabbed the cart. Robbie ran ahead. Everything as before.

Once, when Robbie looked back to beckon them forward, for a moment he could not see them. They had stopped, had pulled the cart into the shadow of an archway. With frantic gestures of their arms, they beckoned him over.

'We're being followed!' hissed Hare.

'Over there – round that corner,' Burke pointed to a turreted building, its steepled windows leaning out over the street, no lights burning inside. Cautiously, Robbie walked towards it, slid with his back against the wall and peered round. Nothing.

The wind whipped some paper fidgeting over the cobbles. A rat scurried from nowhere and disappeared behind an overturned box, rubbish spilling from it.

Distant noise and nearby nothing. Only Robbie's breathing. And now a wind which was rising fast, swishing in his ears and making it difficult to hear anything else. He turned his head this way and that, trying to catch any other sounds. Once he thought he heard something – footsteps? – but the possibility was whished away by the wind. Besides, why should there not be footsteps?

He turned back and retraced his steps to the men. They were worrying over nothing.

'There's still no one,' he said.

On they went, quickly and silently, ears straining.

At the back of Knox's anatomy school, the usual routine – but this time with Knox looking inside the sack to inspect the body. This was now the third time Robbie had watched Dr Knox hand over the money for his filthy trade. Each time, it seemed, his hatred grew. This time it rose like bile. Perhaps it was the extra tension of that night, perhaps it was that Robbie had seen, had felt, the body which Dr Knox's knife would soon cut into. A cold wetness on his back and the smell of sweat from his own armpits.

As he watched Knox's mustard ugliness under the gas-light, it was all Robbie could do to stop himself running over and hitting him, hitting him, hitting him until he was as dead as the corpses he defiled.

Knox was arguing. Burke's face loomed towards Knox's, his neck rigid. The two students stood near the bundle, glancing at each other. They moved to pick it up. Hare leapt towards them, as if to kick their hands away. They rose angrily, bristled, moved forward boldly.

Burke pulled something from his pocket. A glint under the gas-light. It was a knife. He held it close to

Knox's neck. Robbie's insides shrivelled. He shrank further behind a tree, held his breath.

The students stopped, stepped slowly back, their palms facing forwards. Hare had pulled his knife out now, Robbie saw, and it sliced the air between one student and then the other. Hare moved towards them so that he was standing over the body. Voices rose but still Robbie could not hear what was said. Why were they not handing the body over? What was the arguing about?

The scene was frozen. Robbie wanted to run. Surely someone would pass by at any moment?

Dr Knox moved his hand to his pocket. Burke grabbed his arm. Did Knox have a knife too? He would not hesitate to use it. Why should he hesitate? He cut into bodies every day, dead and alive.

Knox only smiled. Robbie could see his teeth. With his other hand, Knox slowly lifted Burke's hand from his arm, distastefully, said something which Robbie could not hear, and pulled something from his pocket. His purse. He gestured to Burke to move back. Hare still stood poised with his knife pointing towards the students. Burke moved slowly backwards, watching closely, as Knox counted money from his purse. To Robbie, it seemed like more money than usual.

The scene melted: Hare moved back, and the

students hefted the body and took it quickly inside. With his casual swan's neck wave of the wrist, Knox slowly followed his students. Burke and Hare picked up the cart handles and ran together. Robbie followed. Through the streets they all ran, trundling the cart behind them. Only when they were far away from the Flodden Wall did they slow to a halt and turn to each other, roaring with laughter. They slapped Robbie on the back, their crazy laughter infecting him until all he could do was laugh as well, without knowing why.

Then they told him. Knox had paid even more money that night. They had told him they wanted more, that it was all too risky, that they had had to go to greater effort. They had reminded him that no one else could provide him with so many bodies, such fresh clean bodies, and that if he wanted them to take risks he would have to pay extra for it. And he had – they had frightened him into it, boasted Hare.

Leaving the cart round the back of Burke's house, the three of them went on to Hare's inn, arm in arm, laughing, shouting raucously, weaving, dancing over the cobbles, jeering at passers-by. People glanced at them and hurried on, heads down. It was as if they were drunk already, Robbie too.

Soon, they were. Robbie fell into the warming chaos of the inn. He was one of the crowd, welcomed, and he laughed with the rest of them, throwing his head back as he drank. The storm of noise rose and faded, washing around him. He could not feel his legs, his arms, any external part of his body, only the fiery rush of the whisky as it flooded his insides. Quickly, his mind began to float and any fear, pain and sadness spun away into the distance.

Robbie stayed drinking long into the night. Why should he not? What was there outside those four walls? In here was shelter. In here he did not have to think about anything else. He drank more, though now it seemed harder to stay floating on that cloud-soft happiness.

Now the only way out was sleep because, asleep, floating or sinking made no difference. So, eventually, he slept, slumped on the floor of the inn, against the wall, his mouth hanging open, a string of saliva gently moving as he breathed. A man tripped and fell on top of him, a boot kicking his face as he rolled away. Robbie felt nothing. A dog urinated on him. He did not wake. Finally, as the other drinkers drifted home, a hand crept inside his clothes and stole the money from his pocket, all the reward for his night's work. He was unaware of any of it. He could have been dead.

In the early hours of the morning, he woke, rigid with cold. He was lying outside in the gutter, though he did not remember how he got there. Pain shot up his arm as he freed it from under his head. His eyes throbbed and his stomach heaved. He vomited on the ground and the smell of it, whisky and vomit, made him vomit again. He retched and spat, while his head roared like waves.

Shivering and wet, he stumbled home. The night was still, the moonlight slicing between the buildings, and a slow floating smurr fell on his face.

By the time he reached his tenement and climbed the stairs, he was half sober. When he saw that Essie was not there, he became, suddenly, completely sober. Panic. The bed had not been slept in. His thoughts swirled and he struggled to make sense out of them. For a moment he stood, heart and mind racing but body paralysed.

His own voice screamed inside his head. What had he done? He rushed down the stairs and back out on to the street. The rain now fell in cold sheets, a new wind whipping it around his face. Where could Essie be? In the grimy close, he called her name. The name echoed into the dripping emptiness. A dead cat stared up at him, its frozen eyes open.

On the High Street, he rushed from corner to corner, peering into every dark doorway. He saw a shadowed bundle curled under an archway. He ran, stooped over it. He pushed it and a white face peered out. A woman, quite young, stared at him with frightened eyes as though she was waiting for him to hit her. He covered her up again.

Out of the corner of his eye he saw it. A flash of brown as it flew towards his hand. Its eyes tiny circular beads. A rat, its yellow teeth bared. It leapt. He whipped his hand away. The rat missed his hand but landed on Robbie's chest with a shriek. Swiping at it with his arm, he stumbled, fell backwards, putting his other hand behind him to break his fall. As he landed, he felt, almost heard, something slice into his hand. He looked. Blood. Pumping, flooding from a deep cut at the base of his palm, towards his wrist. Mixing with the rain. Behind him on the ground a piece of broken pottery, one jagged peak covered in his blood. The rat slithered away and slipped over a wall before disappearing.

For a moment he was too shocked to act. He stared at the blood bubbling out of his hand. It seemed to be flowing faster. He wriggled out of his jacket and wrapped it tightly around his whole hand, feeling a sickening almost crunch as the flesh came together. Held his wrist across his chest. Stumbled to his feet. Took a deep breath to steady himself. Pushed the pain away. And ran back out on to the main street.

A few people were beginning to stir, workers who

had to rise early, shopkeepers, traders, hunched under the rain. He saw a man he recognized.

'Have you seen my sister?' he asked.

'Who're you?' asked the man.

'Robbie. Anderson. Fleshmarket Close. Top floor.' The man sniffed but said nothing. 'My sister? Essie? Small, thin, 'bout eight years old, curly black hair?'

'Ah've no seen her. An ah dinnae ken ye,' muttered the man, and hurried away.

Robbie ran to the next close. The world was a tunnel, black, jumbled, the pinpoint of light at the end disappearing. He searched everywhere, running, his thoughts shrieking. Essie! Where are you? Essie, I'm sorry! I'm so sorry! He did not know whether he spoke aloud or if the cries were in his head.

Driven by a fear that was a million times worse than anything Dr Knox could do, he ran into every close, almost blind with panic. He bumped into people, grabbed strangers and asked if they had seen his sister. Everyone turned away, hurried on, disgusted by the dishevelled blood-stained boy who reeked of whisky and vomit, whose hair covered his face, whose clothes were sodden and whose eyes burned like a madman's.

Eventually, there was nowhere else to look. He slowed to a halt and slumped in despair. His mind in an exhausted blur, he put one foot in front of the other and made his way home. There was nowhere else to go. Perhaps she would be there. She must come back. He thought his heart would crack.

His hand throbbed inside the jacket. He barely noticed.

As he approached the building, he stopped. Dimly, confused, he realized that two people were walking in front of him, starting to go up the stairs before him. He stopped, focused. One was Essie.

7

Joseph

'Essie!' he shouted and began to run. Essie turned. The young man with her turned. Robbie stopped. He looked from Essie to the man. Essie stood in silence, as if torn between emotions. She walked hesitantly towards Robbie. He wanted to sweep her in his arms but there was too much now between them. He knew exactly what he had done. A river had been crossed.

'Essie,' he said. 'I have been looking for you. I see that this gentleman has brought you home safely.' The formality of his words disguised the earthquake inside.

'I suppose you are Robbie?' asked the man. Young, perhaps eighteen, tall, straight-backed, his dark polished hair tied behind him, clean-shaven. A student, from his clothes. He stared straight at Robbie. As if assessing him.

'Yes – and you are?' asked Robbie, a wary politeness while he felt his way.

'My name is Joseph. You should take better care of your sister.'

'Essie is tough,' said Robbie.

The young man laughed. 'Tough? Tough enough, for certain, to pick a poor student's pocket!'

'Essie!' exclaimed Robbie. She stared back at him, her chin jutting.

'It is not Essie's fault. What is a child to do for food when her mother is dead, her father has disappeared and now her brother, who used to care for her, has run off without a thought? Yes, I know all that. It was two days ago she tried to steal from me. This morning I found her picking food from the rubbish in the gutter.'

Robbie felt exhaustion overwhelm him. His hand had begun to hurt properly now, pulsing with pain. His head swam and he wanted to sit down. He wanted to put everything back together again. But how was he to start?

'I'm sorry,' he said to Essie, weakly, broken into tiny pieces. 'I'm sorry, Essie. Now, shall we go inside?' He stood at the door and turned to Joseph. 'Thank you – for bringing Essie back. And for not . . .'

'What has happened to your hand? You are covered in blood.'

'It's nothing. Just a cut.'

'Let me look.' Joseph walked towards him. His eyes were narrow and gouged deep above high-set cheeks.

168

His face was chiselled, carved from granite, perfect, symmetrical. He was different from anyone Robbie had met. Strangely confident. Simple clothes, yet an aristocratic line to his jaw. His coat, though long and well-cut, was not new-looking. His waistcoat was a sober grey, his cravat unfussy, without a jewelled pin. And yet his voice suggested a wealthy education, its vowels long, its accent as English as was fashionable.

Robbie just wanted him to go. He did not want to owe this man more. 'It's nothing, I told you.'

'There's blood a' over, Robbie,' said Essie, looking closely at his jacket.

'I am a medical student,' said Joseph. 'Let me look. You can die from a cut if it is deep enough.'

Robbie stood still. 'No, I can't . . .'

'If you are fretting about payment, think nothing of it. I am a student, I told you – I would welcome the practice. Most patients insist on an experienced doctor.' He took Robbie's arm and held it up as he began to unwrap the jacket, with long delicate fingers. As he peeled away the last bit, his eyes narrowed. He wrapped it up again quickly. 'That requires to be sewn. I shall fetch what I need. Which floor are you on?' Essie told him, and he nodded, as though he had guessed.

They watched him go, picking his feet around the rubbish at the bottom of their steps.

Robbie and Essie went up the stairs in silence. Robbie had to hold the wall as he went, fighting back nausea. His head pounded.

Their room was a mess, crusted with neglect. Rubbish on the floor, an unwiped wooden brose bowl on the table, the bed a limp grey tangle, one candle slouched in a greasy tin. The ashes damp and cold in the grate. The window clouded, sunless. The smell of old food, something dead, whisky and vomit. What have we come to? wondered Robbie. What have I come to?

He sat down, cradling his hand against his chest, shoulders slumped. Essie stood warily, wordlessly, near the door, her face streaked with exhaustion. Robbie tried to gather together some words, though none could describe what he felt.

'I'm sorry, Essie. You will never know how sorry I am. I don't know how this has happened. I'll change, Ess. It will all be all right, you'll see.'

'So, you'll no' drink any more? You'll no' come home drunk again?' Mistrust in her face, her clouded face, the eyes dull now as the ashes in the grate.

'No, I promise,' said Robbie, as he had heard his father say before. Meaning it, perhaps as much as his father, perhaps more, perhaps enough.

'And you'll no' do that work any more?'

'It's good money, Essie. We need the money, don't we?'

'What's on the cart?'

Robbie held his breath. 'What do you mean?'

'What's on the cart?' Essie said more loudly, as though it had been kept screwed up inside. 'Who're they two men?'

For a few seconds, Robbie could not speak. Then, slowly, quietly, 'You followed me.'

'Aye,' came the small strong voice.

'Do not ever follow me again,' said Robbie. He stood up and towered above her. His voice rose. 'Do not ever follow me again! Do you hear? Stay away from those men. Stay in the house at night and don't EVER follow me again!' Fear made him angry.

But Essie did not flinch. She stood as tall as she could and shouted back, 'Why? What's so secret that it has tae be done in the middle o' the night and makes you so feared?'

He breathed deeply. He walked over to the bed and sat down. It felt as though the strength was washing out of him, leaving him hollow. 'I'm so tired, I can't think.'

'But what were you doing, Robbie? What were you doing with the men? An' who's the man what came out o' the wall? You must o' been doing something bad.'

'Trust me, Essie. I did nothing wrong. Anyway, it

171

doesn't matter because I'm not going to do it again. I'm not going anywhere near those men again.' As he said it, he felt his mind lifting. A haze of light in the distance.

Essie was looking at him, wanting desperately to trust him. Robbie went over to her and met her eyes and suddenly pulled her to his chest with his good arm and held her tight. Her cheek lay against his blood.

She struggled. 'You reek!' she said.

Robbie knew that he did. 'Well, we'll need water then, won't we? And a clean shirt. And after that, food. Well, food for you. I'm not hungry. I need your help, Ess.'

'I'll get water,' said Essie, glad to be able to act. She fetched the buckets and ran out of the door to go downstairs, her tiredness falling away. Robbie was back and he said everything would be all right. She wanted to believe him.

Robbie sat down again. Exhausted, weak. His head drumming. Weighed down by something that once again seemed too heavy to lift. And then another feeling, a feeling which snuffed out the shimmer of hope which he had seen in the far distance. He needed a drink. He went over to where his whisky was kept. Took a quarter-full bottle, and pulled out the cork with his teeth. With a shaking hand, he poured a measure into a dirty cup. His body began to calm, to slow, to warm, as he thought of the flying feeling that would come soon after the fire hit his stomach. But as he lifted it to his mouth, he saw in the corner of his eye a movement. He had caught sight of himself in their piece of looking-glass. There was that filthy, lost, sad boy, the one with serpent hair and dead eyes and white teeth in a dark face, like bones dug from the ground by a dog.

He looked at the cup in his hand, stared into the golden drink. He saw in it his father, a broken, useless man. That was what he would become if he did not grasp hold of himself.

He forced his arm to pour the contents of the cup into the chamber-pot and tipped the rest of the bottle after it. And as he poured the whole pot out of the window with a loud cry of warning, the weight lifted further and there was suddenly just a little more light.

Footsteps on the stairs. Essie and Joseph. Joseph carried a brown leather bag, which he set down on the table, sweeping aside the dust and rats' droppings and the oatmeal-encrusted bowl.

'Get the fire going and some water heated, Essie, please, if you will.'

'What's that for?'

'For your brother to wash himself. He reeks like your streets.'

Essie set to work setting the fire in the hearth, her

shoulders softening as she did her familiar work. She worked quickly, her fingers skilfully building a tiny mountain of straw and dried heather and striking the flint until the sparks caught the tinder.

Joseph opened his bag and took out a leather pouch. He began to unwrap it. Robbie spoke 'You said, "your streets". Are you not from Edinburgh?'

Essie spoke up, her face shining. 'Joseph comes from the country, Robbie. He's from a place called the Kingdom o' Fife. Everyone in the Kingdom o' Fife has houses, with more 'n one room each. An' they grow food in a garden, an' Joseph's house has water inside, that comes from the wall whenever you want it.'

'I think you have your answer, Robbie,' smiled Joseph.

'Essie seems to know you well,' said Robbie, wondering how she could have found out such information.

'I confess that I have given Essie more than one meal in the last two days. You may wonder why I did not call a constable when I found her hand in my coat pocket. Usually, I would have done so. But Essie is . . . I can only say that I could no more have done so with Essie than I could have handed my own sister over to the magistrates. I had a sister once. She would have been Essie's age now.'

They watched Essie hanging the pot above the crackling fire.

'Typhus,' said Joseph, his face unmoving, staring into the flames. 'She fell ill on a visit to an aunt in your town. The aunt died too. And two of her own children. It was a long time ago.' Robbie said nothing. What could he say? It was a common story.

Joseph moved, shook his head, relaxed his face. 'Sit down, Robbie,' he said. 'Move your arm as slowly as you can. Close your eyes and keep still.' His voice was calm, reassuring. Robbie sat on the bed, his free will gone. He was happy to be doing what he was told. It was like being stroked inside his head, mind-melting, fuzzy-edged. He could feel his arm being unwrapped gently, sense the trickle of blood along his wrist, feel it wet on his leg. As his back sagged and his shoulders relaxed further, he could hear sounds of Joseph searching for what he needed. Heard the table being pulled over towards him, felt his arm being placed on the table. Then some tugging, pulling, on his wrist. No pain. A tiny stinging sensation that seemed to come from somewhere else. Somewhere drifty. Somewhere warm.

Sounds of another world clattered in the distant streets below, in other rooms, on other stairs, through other windows.

'Essie, if the water is warm yet, mix a little with this, please.' A minute later the sensation of something sticky being pasted over his hand. Still he kept his eyes closed. He felt his hand being bandaged tightly.

'I have finished. You should eat now. And wash.'

Robbie opened his eyes. His hand was cleanly bandaged. He did not know when he had last seen a cloth so white. Soon the water was hot enough and Essie brought it, her tongue poking out as she concentrated on not spilling it, and he washed as best he could, stripping his shirt off in front of the fire, carefully easing it over his bandaged hand. Essie passed him everything he needed, knowing without being asked.

Joseph spoke as he put away his equipment in the leather pouch. 'You live alone?'

'Yes.' Little point in mentioning a father who was more useful gone. 'But we manage.'

'Is this what you call managing?'

'No, this is . . . This is not how it is.'

'But what about Essie? She needs . . .'

'Yes, I know what Essie needs,' snapped Robbie, shame making him angry. 'I am sorry. But you know nothing about us.' He felt awkward in front of this confident young man who was only a few years older and yet seemed to know so much more.

'I know what I can see. I can see you were drunk last night. I know you leave your sister alone at night. I can see that you live on the rotting top floor of a crumbling tenement, where typhus killed twelve people last winter, where humans and rats and pigs and dogs live as though none was a jot better than another. Where I come from, you would have a minister or some good lady of the parish calling at your door to save your souls. If not your bodies. God will provide and God will punish, they would tell you.'

Robbie curled inside. He tried to keep his voice level but mention of God goaded him. 'God? Where is God? What does God care about the likes of us?'

'Robbie!' shouted Essie, shocked. People burnt in hell for less than that.

Joseph picked up his bag. He turned to Robbie and looked at him closely. 'Difficult questions, Robbie, but exactly the ones I would ask if I were in your position. Just where is God in all this?'

Essie's cheeks were white, her eyes wide. Robbie's thoughts raced, faster than he could grasp. Here was someone who was daring to voice his questions aloud.

Joseph was speaking again. 'A baby died in the next building last week. Her older brother came to me, crying, to ask if I could do anything. A rat was eating the baby's face while it was still alive, the mother too weak to notice. The baby's breath reeked of gin and it was too drunk to care what was happening to it. There was nothing I could do. Where was God then?'

Joseph walked to the door. He turned to them. A smile, so straight, so slight. 'Are you waiting to see me struck by a thunderbolt?'

Essie's hands were clenched. 'God is watching. He is watching all o' us.'

'You may be right, Essie.' His voice was level but Robbie could tell he did not believe what he was saying.

'We don' understand everything,' insisted Essie. 'God decides, that's all.' Robbie was silent.

'Take care of that hand, Robbie,' said Joseph. 'And of your sister.'

Before Robbie had a chance to thank him, Joseph had left. Essie made herself busy at the fire, a frown clouding her forehead, her jaw tight. She said nothing. Robbie looked at the closed door and listened to the footsteps as they went down the stairs. He wanted to call Joseph back. He wanted to ask the questions which for so long he had kept inside.

Essie found Robbie his other shirt. The cloth was crumpled and thin, but clean, the worn threads soft and familiar. She held it out to him and he put it on.

He went to the window and opened it. The sunlight slanted on to the building, just a few inches from their window. It never quite shimmered into their own home, throwing its warmth into the spidered corners. A pair of curlews swung fast above his head, their mewling cries soaring, flying free. Down below, the street was in shadow; all the streets he could see were in shadow, darker and darker as they moved further away into dismal alleys and stinking gutters which the sun never reached. But up here you could see the sunlight, and freshness, and warmth, and smell a promised summer.

Essie handed him a bowl. Brose again. He was not hungry. He took a few small spoonsful of the watery oatmeal, under Essie's dull eyes. Soon, he stood up. Still they had not spoken about what they had heard. For both of them, it was too enormous.

'I have to go out, Essie.'

'No!'

He turned away from the pain in her face. 'I have to go and say thank you to Joseph.' It was true – he had not thanked Joseph.

'I don' like him.' She scowled.

'You liked him fine before, Essie. When he helped you. Besides, you're not coming to see him.'

'Be quick, Robbie, an' don' . . . don' listen tae his bad words.'

'A fine one to talk about bad words, you are! You've

been stealing, Essie. What do they teach you in Sunday School? Thou shalt steal?'

'It's different. Where am I tae get food for the both o' us when you're drunk?'

'Just tell me where he lives, Essie. I'll be back before you've read a chapter of your Bible.'

Reluctantly, she told him and he left her standing there, silent and confused.

Only two streets away, another narrow close. The second floor. The stairs clean. Robbie knocked on the door. Joseph looked at him, without seeming surprised. 'Do come in, Robbie.' His confident politeness was unsettling. His eyes always steady, direct.

The room was clean, with thick green curtains pulled back from a wide window. Sunlight cutting through at a sharp angle. A dark polished table, four chairs, no bed to be seen. A strong fire crackling, a copper kettle hanging above the flames from a shiny clean rantle-tree.

'I came to say thank you. For this,' and he held up his hand.

'I told you,' said Joseph. 'I was content to have some practice. My needlework needs improvement.'

'And for not taking Essie to the magistrates. She . . .' But Robbie's voice tailed off. His eye had been caught by something.

A violin. Lying on a table. Joseph saw where he was looking. Robbie spoke, the breath hovering in his throat. 'Do you . . . do you play the violin?' Not taking his eyes from it. Wanting it. The memory so strong that it hurt.

'No, it is not mine. It belongs to someone else. I took it to be repaired nearby and the owner has yet to collect it.' Joseph watched Robbie, seeing his fascination. 'You can touch it if you like, but be careful. It is valuable.'

Robbie touched its shiny yellowed warmth. He picked it up in his left hand, tucked it under his chin in one swift movement. He closed his eyes to the feel of it, the rosin smell, a memory of his mother. He opened his eyes again. If only his right hand was not stiff with bandages.

'You have played a violin, have you?' said Joseph, surprised.

'A long time ago.'

'If it were not for your hand, you could have played that one.'

'Whose is it?' asked Robbie. Wishing he could be that person. Could touch his world.

'Dr Robert Knox. He is an . . .'

The power of that name! The breath spun from Robbie's body until it was as thin as spiderweb.

If he could, he would have gathered up that name and

hidden it in his hands, squashing and squashing and squashing until it was tiny as a speck of dust, until it crumbled into nothing and was no more. He would have turned back time, not to hear Joseph say that name.

The violin slipped slowly from Robbie's hand. Joseph leapt to catch it before it fell. He put it carefully on the table. Now Robbie could see that it was familiar. His mind was numb.

Joseph spoke. 'You know the name?'

Robbie nodded.

'How do you know Dr Knox?' His voice light, simply interested.

Robbie hesitated. 'He killed my mother.'

There was a silence. Then Joseph's voice cut coolly through it, his dark eyes hooded. 'Dr Knox is a skilled surgeon. If your mother died, it was despite Dr Knox's best efforts, I am sure.'

'He killed her! He cut into her alive and she screamed and screamed and I heard her. I was outside the room. I was eight years old. Dr Knox killed my mother!' His voice rose, its notes lifting to a childlike pitch.

'Dr Knox is the best surgeon in Edinburgh. Perhaps even Scotland. Surgery is dangerous. More than half of all patients die. We do not know why. I am sorry about your mother, but you cannot rightly blame Dr Knox.' Joseph's back was to the window. He was silhouetted.

The spring sunlight sliced through the clean glass.

'I can blame Dr Knox. I do.' Robbie's voice grew louder on his anger. 'He is the cause of everything that has happened to me. And to Essie. We had good lives before. We didn't live in a – what did you call it? – a rotting tenement. We were moving, to the New Town. To a house like the one your Dr Robert Knox lives in. Everything would have been different if he had not . . .'

'He performed an operation on my mother, too.'

'And he saved her life, did he?' Robbie snapped.

'No, she died. That is why I chose to become a doctor. To try to save lives. Heal people. Like other doctors.'

Silence. A red mist swirling. The words he needed were stuck somewhere. His thoughts tumbled between guilt and anger.

'But he doesn't care about people!' Robbie struggled to find a reason to heap the blame on Dr Knox. He needed that. 'He cuts into bodies. Dead or alive – he doesn't much care. He only cares about the noise they make. I heard him say so. He digs his fingers in dead men's bodies. He cuts them open and pins the skin back and leaves them lying for men to peer into. I've seen it!'

'It is called anatomy, Robbie. You know nothing about it.' Joseph's cheeks were tight, clenched, angry. There was a sharpness to his voice now. 'You people know nothing about what we do. How else can doctors learn how to cure people if they cannot know what is inside a body? I have been to his demonstrations. I have even helped him. He teaches students. And he is the best teacher we have. He is inspiring.' His voice ringing out, strident, enflamed.

Robbie could not speak. He needed his hatred of Dr Knox, needed the knife-sharp anger to keep away the pain, but Joseph was blunting it. If he could not hate Knox, what would that leave him with?

Into the silence, Joseph continued, his voice softer now, his anger quickly gone. His calm control back. 'So, what do you intend to do with your life, Robbie? You are clever. I saw the books – Latin and Greek. They are not your father's, are they? Essie would not tell me how you earn your money, only that you lost your job in a bakery. So, what are you going to do? Are you going to settle into the filth, and scrabble for your food under the feet of other people?'

'What choice do I have? What is there for someone like me?'

'There is always a choice.' Joseph walked over to the fireplace. He was busy with something, lifting the kettle, scooping something from a tin.

Into the empty moment, the small space between them in this room, Robbie found himself speaking. It did not sound like him. It was as if the words were being pulled smoothly from him on a thread. Or someone else was saying the words while his mouth moved.

'There was something else.'

'Yes?' The quiet sound of water pouring.

A deep breath. 'What you said. About God.' Silence. Robbie continued, fast now, words tumbling. 'I can't talk to Essie. She goes to Sunday School and she can read the Bible. She seems to understand. But I don't. It was what you said about the baby. The one who died, eaten by a rat. What sort of God would let that happen? What sort of a God would take my mother?' The sentence hung in the air, dangling like a noose. At last, he had said it. The question he had kept buried for six years. What would happen to him now?

Joseph came over to Robbie, holding two steaming cups on saucers. The same blue and white pattern he had seen at Knox's house. 'Sit down. Drink this tea.'

The thin porcelain edge of the cup slipped between Robbie's lips. His tongue touched the smoothness of it. The tea was strong and bitter, but sweet too.

Joseph trapped him with those steady eyes, smiled again that perfect smile. 'How do you know it was God?'

'How could it not have been God? God decides, makes everything.'

'No, I am asking you, how *could* it have been God?'

'I don't know. I don't understand the question. That's why I've come here. Because you seem to know.'

'No, I do not know. I do not know what God is, or if he is at all. I will tell you what I *do* know. I know that I have not been struck by a thunderbolt, though plenty of people would like to see it happen when they hear what I say. I know that it makes no sense to me that God controls everything and yet rats eat a baby. How can a world so full of horror and mistakes be created by God?'

'But if God didn't make the world, who did? How could something so complicated create itself? Someone must have designed it.'

Joseph's eyes shone. 'Hah! You are using a well-known argument. You think because something is complicated it must have been designed. Why?'

'Because it makes sense!'

'The fact that it makes sense does not make it true. Let me tell you a story. It is not my story. A great philosopher, Mr Hume – a native of Edinburgh, I may add – relates it. There was once an Eastern prince, he said. One day, a traveller from Europe told this prince that in his country the water in canals becomes solid when it is very cold. So solid that an elephant could walk on it. The prince was angry and said to the traveller, "I used to believe everything you told me.

Now I know that you are just a liar." Do you see the point?'

'No.'

'The only way the prince could make sense of what the traveller told him was to assume that he was a liar. The truth – that water can freeze solid – made no sense to him. So he chose to believe that it was not true.'

Robbie's head was spinning. 'But perhaps God is the truth, and the truth just doesn't make sense to you? You just can't imagine God, like the prince not being able to imagine the ice. You might be wrong, like the prince.'

Joseph grinned. He hit the table with his hand. 'Clever lad! Perhaps you are right. However, I cannot go through my life struggling to believe something which seems to me to make no sense, and have no value. I avoid religion. I do not trust it. And now, Robbie, you should go back to Essie. She will be wondering where you are. Look after her – there is something special about her. Something in her eyes. Any other girl would have been in front of the magistrates long before now.'

Robbie stood up. 'I don't want her to know I have talked to you about this. She needs to believe.'

'That is true for most people, Robbie. As Mr Hume said, man created God for his own comfort. If Essie is comforted, then God has had some purpose.' He followed Robbie to the door. 'What are you going to do?'

Robbie looked around the room, at the books, the solid furniture, the sunlight. He looked at Joseph, the medical student who was making something of his life. He looked again at the violin, remembering his mother. 'I have not decided. But I know where I shall start.' And he did. He knew what he was going to do that evening.

'Goodbye, Robbie. Come again. Take care of your hand. Do not try to use it. Keep the bandage on – the air is full of evil. If the wound begins to smell, come back to me. Remember – I need the practice.' Joseph smiled. Robbie had forgotten about his hand. It did not hurt at all.

Walking up the stairs to his room, Robbie was hit by exhaustion. Everything had washed out of him and he felt as weak as skin.

Essie looked up as he came back in. She was stirring something in a pot.

'I've made you some broth, Robbie. An' I've no' burnt it. An' there's bread, too.' For Essie, survival was measured in food. But there was more to living than that. Man does not live by bread alone, as he remembered from his Bible. He smiled to himself with the beginning of understanding.

He did not want to eat, though he found that when he did he was hungry. 'It's good, Essie.'

'It's the best I've ever made,' she said, spooning it fast into her own mouth and wiping the back of her hand across her lips. In the familiar act of eating, something of her strength and hope returned. Something in her began to shine again.

Afterwards, Robbie climbed into bed and let his body sink on to the familiar straw-rustling mattress. He closed his eyes. At first he could not sleep – his thoughts were webbed like veins. It was hard to shake off completely the hopelessness he had felt only a few hours before. But now it was possible to believe that all would be well. That he could begin to climb back up to the air, to the rooftops, away from the slime and the sewers.

He knew what he was going to do.

He would go to Hare and Burke and tell them that he could not be involved any more. He would say that someone was suspicious of him, had spotted him – which was true enough. They would surely not want him to work with them if he had been spotted?

Everything could go back to the way it was before. He would find new work, return to his studies, prepare for university, move towards a better future. For him and for Essie. As Joseph said, there is always a choice.

And so, believing, Robbie slept a dreamless, peaceful sleep.

8

A Glimmer of Light

Much later that day, Robbie woke. At first muddled. Then everything swirling into place. He rubbed the sleep from his face, and got up. The room was transformed. Books in piles, their few kitchen items on a shelf. Rubbish gone. The table almost clean, the window open and air washing through, catching the flames in the fireplace and making them lean as they fluttered.

Essie saw him. 'I've some more o' that broth,' she said. The sparkle kindled briefly in her eyes again. And then was gone, replaced with a memory of caution.

'Thank you, Essie. And well done – our room looks fit for a lord now.'

As he ate, she sat on a stool nearby and slowly, with unpractised fingers, braided her black hair into a thick uneven plait. She had not cut her hair for months and the curls had become waves, hanging down her back. Now, trapped by the braid, the waves were still. Her face seemed longer, her jaw stronger. When she smiled, her mouth moved more slowly than he remembered, as though she had to think through the act of smiling. 'What're ye going to do?'

'I'm going to tell those men I'm not working for them any more.'

Relief leaping in Essie's face. Then fear again. 'What happens if . . . ?'

'Nothing can happen. I'll just tell them that my family are suspicious. They won't want anything to do with me then. There's nothing to worry about – you'll see. Stay here until I come back.'

Robbie picked up his jacket and, taking one last look around his home, he left the room. He turned again and smiled at Essie before he disappeared down the stairs. His last sight was her worried face, the braided hair flat over her ears. Somehow, he had to make it right for her. He could not watch her lose her trust, her spirit.

Once out of the building, he stopped. His hand throbbed. He leaned against the wall and breathed some strength into his body. It was late afternoon, and the grey April sun hung low in the sky, thinly veiled by cloud, but just visible between the zigzag leaning walls of two buildings. Time to go. Time to tell Burke and Hare that he could not, would not, help them any more.

He moved off quickly, in the direction of Hare's inn.

He did not know which house he would find them in but Hare's was nearer. The streets were noisy, filled with the jangled clamour of people's lives. From each direction, men and women of every class, clattering carriages, horses, dogs, all melded together. Children ran barefoot, or stood mucus-faced on corners, staring emptily. Soldiers sauntered, muskets loose against their chests, red coats splashed like blood across the rat-grey streets. A drunken woman lay sprawled against a wall, glassy-eyed, her baby weakly wailing as it tugged at her limp breast. Muscled Highland porters, strong as ponies, shouted as they pulled the sedan chairs weaving through the crowds, the wooden staves resting across their shoulders. Traders cried their strange advertisements, their voices like trumpets over the sea of people. 'Strongest whisky here! Drunk for three bawbees! Cold deed for five!'

Above all this rose the castle, sprouting from its rock like a giant's head above a diseased body. The veins of the city's streets pulsed filth, its buildings sweating waste, so that the whole creature reeked of illness.

Hare's inn, the windows cold and empty. Robbie knocked on the door. After a few moments, a woman came out, bleary-eyed, her clothes hanging loose, one shoulder bare. Not Nelly or Margaret, but whoever it was recognized him. 'Ye want Hare? Try William Burke's hoose.' And she closed the door.

A fast walk uphill, and then downhill. Soon, he stood outside Burke's house. Its windows quiet, its insides dark. He knocked on the door. The silence grew.

He knocked again. Waited. Nothing.

He looked upwards. Something moving in a window?

There was someone in the house. He felt it. He knocked again, as loudly as he could. The door swung open, pushed by the force of his knocking. No one stood behind it. Robbie stepped inside. 'Mr Burke?' he called, but quietly. And listened. Nothing.

He was about to leave when he heard something. Unmistakeable. A thud, followed by a scuffling sound upstairs. What was happening? Without thinking, Robbie ran to the wooden stairs and climbed them quickly, in one breath.

Flung open the door.

A frozen scene. Wide eyes, wild faces. Hare and Burke, standing, crouched, staring at Robbie. A chair on its back. Someone – a woman – lying on the floor, shoeless, yellowed feet and toenails hooked like a bird's talons, hairy twisted legs exposed, skirts rucked up from a struggle, head covered by the grey pillow which Burke held forced to her face. Arms outstretched, crucified, the hands in claws. A whisky bottle on the floor, knocked over, its contents soaking into the wood.

Burke's jacket pulled off his shoulders. Hare's face etched with long red scratches.

Robbie knew then. Knew what he should have known all along. Knew why the bodies were so fresh.

A frozen moment. But then smashed into action. Hare got to the door before Burke, but Robbie was halfway down the stairs, clearing them in two leaps. He ran from the house, followed at snapping distance by the two men.

Blindly running. Unbreathing panic. Robbie faster, younger, gaining ground. People leaping aside. Angry noises. Shouting from the chasing men, 'Thief! Stop the thief!' A man trying to trip Robbie but Robbie leaping aside, as though carried by the wind.

Homewards. Could he reach it? But no – they would see where he lived. Where else to go? No time for choices. He simply ran, flew, sliding round corners. Sometimes left, sometimes right. Doubling back, a random route. Anything to shake them off. Suddenly he fell, tripping over a loose stone, but he was flying so fast, so smoothly, that he simply rolled, almost somersaulting in the air, landing on his feet and running as if nothing had happened, as if nothing could ever stop him.

A narrow passage. Robbie ran into it. Steps, a long steep flight of steps, slippery with grime. Robbie stumbled down them, three, four, five at a time, one hand grabbing a flimsy wooden rail. A curse as one of the men tripped behind him. But still the gasping, the shouting, the pursuing footsteps. Robbie leapt the final flight and took the corner sharply.

Uphill now, heading into the sun. The castle swayed over him, as if it must surely topple. Still, he ran. His tongue stuck dry to the roof of his mouth. A pain in his side now. And in his hand. Empty weakening legs. His breath in tightened gasps. He must not stop.

Footsteps still behind him.

He slowed to swing round another corner. As he turned, he glimpsed their snarling faces. Saw the thick club in Hare's hand. They were closer. How could they still be there? Would they never tire? He could hear their laboured breathing, imagine Hare's evil spittle on his neck. They were going to catch him. Any moment now. The air like knives inside his chest.

It happened in an instant. As he swung round another corner. In front of him. A man, old, holding a pistol. His startled oyster-pale eyes. Robbie dodging, twisting. Slipping. Falling. A sickening rip in his bandaged hand. A crack as his head hit the wall. Black.

Into the storm roared endless noise and crashing stars and rushing black water. He had no feet. Hands huge. He was everywhere. Black again. Then jumbled shouting. Tongue fumbling. Tunnel swimming. Up downing. Drowning.

His mother floated by. Waving. Smiling. He dived to reach her but their fingers, miles long, stretched and stretched and stretched until they were only lines that went forever towards a point they could never reach. He called to her. She smiled back. She beckoned with a finger. He tried to go towards her, but his legs spindled in the air and she drifted further and further away. 'Come back!' he tried to call, but heard only a moaning wind disappearing into never.

He tumbled into waking and found himself groaning. His head throbbed. Two faces swam above his head. No, one face. An old man, his wispy white hair like fog around his ghost-thin skin.

Quickly, Robbie realized where he was. Lying on the street where he had fallen, a crashing pain in his head. Hare and Burke nowhere to be seen.

'Are ye hurt, laddie?' The pistol was steady in the man's frail-looking hand.

Robbie got to his feet with difficulty, leaning his left hand heavily against the wall. His eyes swimming. His head thick thunder. He looked down at his bandaged hand, now dirty and wet. Blood spreading through the dirt.

'No. I'll . . . I know a doctor.' Almost. He had to find Joseph as quickly as possible. He felt his head, moving his fingers carefully through his hair. Found the swelling. He winced. Looked at his fingers. No blood.

'Who was chasing you, laddie?' He waved his pistol.

'I don't know. Thieves? I don't remember.'

'Aye, well, this soon frightened them off. I'll wager they thought they'd get the better o' me without it. There's no powder in it, o' course. Cannae keep it dry.' His quavery laugh fluttered. 'I've killed Frenchmen wi' more courage than them.'

Robbie leant against the wall, waiting for his strength to return. The old man sucked air through toothless gums. 'The revolution, laddie, the revolution. I was there, at the barricades, helping the poor people o' France. And where did it get them? Deed, that's where. Aye, and then when a few brave Scotsmen tried to rise and fight agin their country's own injustice, where did it get them? Eh? Hanged. Hanged or transported. Hanged or transported.' Spittle flew from the man's mouth as his eyes blazed. 'And now look at us, look at our city. It's nae more than a midden. And what are we doing? What are ye young people doing about it? Why d'ye no' fight agin it? Agin the injustice?' A tear gathered in one pink-rimmed eye. He stabbed the air with his pistol, before tucking it into his belt.

Robbie's hand was hurting properly now. He rocked it against his chest. He shook his head. The bandage was almost completely red. He needed to go. 'I'm sorry,' he said. 'I need to . . . my hand.'

'Aye, laddie, off ye go.' And the old man shook his head and tottered slowly on his way, muttering and shaking his fist against the world.

'Thank you, sir,' called Robbie after him, before hurrying towards the street where Joseph lived. He kept watching for Burke and Hare, but there was no sign of them. As he neared the end of Fleshmarket Close, he heard his name. 'Robbie!' It was Essie. He looked up. She was hanging out of the window. A few moments later she was running towards him, saw the blood immediately.

'Your hand! You need a doctor.'

'I'm going to Joseph.'

'No! No' Joseph! A proper doctor!'

'Essie, he can do it just as well. And he's closer. By the time I found another doctor, it would be worse.'

'So I'm coming wi' you.' And she marched in front of him, quickly hurrying him. He shivered in the cooling air and the blood from his hand dripped on to the ground. Soon they turned into the archway that led into Joseph's close. Drying clothes swung high above them, like seagulls. The wind washed through the close from north to south, carrying away some of the stench.

They began to climb the stairs.

Somewhere in the distance a violin sang, rising and falling, its gentle arpeggios rocking like a lullaby. It was a long time since Robbie had heard a violin played like that, like the song a swan might sing. Its sad sound glided, hovering in the twilight.

The sound grew closer as they approached Joseph's floor. Robbie stopped. It was coming from Joseph's door. But Joseph had said he did not play the violin. And in that same moment, Robbie realized. He stepped back, away from the door. Turned to go down the stairs.

'Where're you going?' said Essie.

'There's someone with him. I can't go in.'

'Aye, you can. You're a muckle great fool. Look at the blood. You'll die if you don' go in.' Essie stretched up to the heavy iron knocker and let it crash three times. The violin stopped. The door opened. Joseph came out, surprised. 'What is it, Essie? Robbie?'

Robbie was leaning against the wall, the blood drained from his face. Joseph moved quickly towards him. 'What have you done? You will need to come in.' Robbie had no choice. He allowed himself to be led inside the room, followed by Essie.

Dr Robert Knox stood with his back to the fire, the yellow violin under his chin giving his face a buttered glow. The bow rested in his right hand, the fingers curled delicately around, the little finger hovering like

200

mist. He lowered the instrument when he saw them come into the room. Laid it gently on the table. He brushed some specks of rosin from the sleeve of his shirt, the lacy cuffs flapping. A jewelled brooch spangled on his throat and several golden chains hung in perfectly-spaced arcs. Near him across a chairback lay his coat, wine-dark in the firelight. The floral perfume bloomed in the warmth of the room.

Joseph was talking. 'This is Robbie, Dr Knox. He . . .'

'We have had the pleasure already.' Dr Knox bowed. Essie and Joseph looked surprised. Robbie's heart thumped hard. 'Robbie was interested in this,' Knox gestured to the violin lying on the table, shining softly. 'My friends thought he was intending to steal it. He meant no harm.' He turned to Robbie. 'I did not know you were acquainted with my best student, laddie.' His eyes, black against the firelight, held Robbie's gaze, and his mouth twisted in a small sardonic smile.

Robbie dared to breathe.

Joseph spoke. 'He has cut his hand quite deeply and I have already repaired it, but he appears to have damaged it again.'

'No doubt the result of your unpractised handiwork, young man,' said Dr Knox, his voice still lightly smiling. 'Never trust a man whose face is so perfectly formed, Robbie. It is a face that has not learnt the lessons of life.'

201

Joseph bowed slightly, at ease in Knox's presence. Knox walked towards Robbie. Pulled out a chair. Gestured for him to sit. Robbie obeyed. He looked down.

'Put your hand on the table, laddie.' Knox rolled his white sleeves back, tucked the lace away. Robbie watched the pumice-stone forehead, the dark dusty hair swept back in ridges. The thick volcanic skin. Knox began to unwrap the wet bandage carefully. Joseph opened his bag and brought out fresh bandages. Curved needles. Steel scissors. Other metal tools of different shapes. A brown glass jar with a cork gummed with something black. He put a bowl of water on the table. Its steam danced slowly upwards.

The surgeon's scent drifted over Robbie's face, into his nose. His thoughts raced. This man, with his breath so close, this was the man who bought the bodies of murder victims. Did he know that people were dying in order for him to practise his godless art? Surely he could not know. He must surely believe they were hanged criminals. As Robbie had believed.

Someone must stop the murders. Who else but Robbie could do it? And how could he? The only way was to inform Dr Knox that the bodies he bought were innocent murder victims. Then, surely, Knox would act. Surely. Would he not? But what if Knox already knew about the murders? Then Robbie would be entirely in his power.

Yet Robbie had to act. There was no one else. He had to do something right. Otherwise how could he live with himself? How could he move forward as he wanted? For himself and Essie. His mouth was dry. He felt paralysed in this man's presence.

Joseph was lighting three oil-lamps. He placed them on the table where Knox sat facing Robbie. Eels of inky smoke swam towards the ceiling. In the sallow glow, Robbie could see the one flaccid eye, the one piercing one.

Essie had been standing silent during this time. She looked from Joseph, to Knox, to Robbie, as if wondering what they all were to each other. Suddenly she spoke. 'I've seen you somewhere afore,' she said to Knox, boldly. Robbie's heart beat faster. The Flodden Wall! She was there. She must not say it! Please let Essie not say it.

'No doubt you have. Edinburgh is a small place. I am quite often to be seen.' Knox did not look up from what he was doing. His legato voice soothing.

'But . . .'

Robbie spoke quickly. 'Essie, you should go. I'll see you at home. Buy us some food. Make some of your broth.'

'We've nae money left.'

Joseph took a coin from his pocket. Essie looked away. 'I wan' tae stay.'

'No, Essie. Go!' Robbie snapped staccato words. He did not want her here. Did not want Joseph here either. Did not want anyone to hear what he had to say.

'The little girl should go,' said Knox. Essie's spell did not work on him. To him, she was perhaps nothing more than a scraggy child with a dirty face and clouded, hostile eyes. 'Joseph, would you take her? I cannot work with a child watching me.' Essie bristled, her skinny fists clenching, but Robbie met her eyes with a glare and she followed Joseph out, her bare feet slapping the floorboards. The door closed behind them and Robbie was alone with Dr Knox.

Knox's fingers, long and spiderlike, continued to ease the bandage away, while pressing hard on Robbie's wrist. The bandage became cleaner, redder. Robbie squeezed his eyes shut. Knox could do anything now, had him utterly in his power. Into his head flashed the sickening image of those three knives. But he had to speak.

He opened his eyes again. 'There is something I must tell you.' The words spurted out. 'About the . . . bodies you dissect.' Robbie stopped and took some breaths, his vision swarming. 'The bodies you think are from the gallows? The bodies you buy?' he added when Knox said nothing. A hesitation before Knox removed another layer of bandage, while keeping pressure on the wrist.

Robbie continued. 'They're not . . . they're not from the gallows. They're murdered. The men . . . aaagh!' A sudden shooting pain. He looked down. The bandage had come away and the edges of the wound were ragged, with blood welling from deep within. Brown strings curled from the edges.

'Look away,' ordered Knox. Robbie turned and continued, through the pain which sliced his breath away as Knox worked. 'The men . . . you buy . . . the bodies . . . from . . .' Robbie fought to push away the dusk which smurred across his eyes. 'They kill them. They killed a woman today . . . I saw her.'

A pause, long and still, poised. The pain less now, dull. A pressing inside. 'You saw them kill this woman?'

'Yes!'

'You actually saw them kill her?'

'I saw . . . no, but I know . . .'

'You know nothing. You saw nothing. Nothing but a dead criminal.'

'But I know . . .'

'You know nothing, I said!' snapped Knox, his living eye sharp. 'I buy the bodies of hanged criminals. It is permitted. Close your eyes.' He continued to work on Robbie's hand. Robbie could feel tugging, dully unpleasant, nothing more.

'If it is allowed,' said Robbie, 'why is it so secret?

Why is it done in the middle of the night?' He could no longer feel what Knox was doing.

Knox paused before answering, his voice cello-sounding, soft as plums. 'Because I buy more bodies than the law allows. That is all. I need them. I need them for my work, work that saves lives. Your life, perhaps. Everyone knows what I do. Everyone knows of my skill. People may not like the idea of anatomy but they all too quickly forget their qualms when I save their lives.'

'Don't you mind where the bodies come from? Don't you mind who they were?'

Robbie thought of the innocent victims stuffed into herring-barrels. And the one he had helped carry down the stairs, its neck bones snapping under his hands. His stomach turned over at the thought. How could this man not mind?

'Why should I mind? Look at your hand.' Robbie looked. His hand and wrist were crusted and smeared with dried blood. But from the cut, at least three inches long, sewn together by yellowy-brown thread, not a drop of blood oozed. 'I stopped the blood vessel inside your wrist. Joseph had stitched the edges of the wound, with admirable competence – though no more than one would expect from a pupil of mine – but this time it was not enough. I, however, have stopped the bleeding. So, do you mind whose body I was cutting into when I discovered new facts about the anatomy of the blood vessels of the hand and arm? Do you mind whose body I cut into to learn what I needed to save your life? For save your life I have. You would have bled until you died, without my skill.'

'I mind when someone dies for you to learn these facts.' Anger made Robbie bold.

'You do not know that. I told you – you saw nothing. You saw nothing.'

Robbie was not reaching this man. He might as well have stood at the foot of the Castle and beat his hands against the rock. 'I am not talking about that.'

Knox said nothing. Gently he wiped the blood from Robbie's arm with a cloth soaked in warm water from the bowl.

'I am not talking about that,' repeated Robbie after a moment to take his breath. To prepare for what he was going to say.

'I assume you are going to tell me what you are talking about?'

'My mother died.'

Knox's face remained unmoved as he wound a new bandage tightly around Robbie's hand. Robbie stared deep, ugly deep, into Knox's face. Into the living eye like coal. Into the dead eye like pig fat. Felt himself outside that cold closed door again, listening, rocking, rocking, rocking. He continued.

'She had an operation. She screamed in pain. I heard her. I was only a child. I was outside the room. She died screaming, five days later.'

'It happens. It happens often. I do not know why it happens sometimes and not others.'

Robbie knew what he wanted to say. It shrieked through his body. But somehow, he could not say it. Could not say, 'You were the surgeon. You were the man who killed her. Do you not even remember?' A stupid heat swam behind his eyes. If he had spoken, he would have cried.

He could not reach this man with his heart of rock. Could only hate him.

Knox stood up. 'I have finished. Your hand will heal. Keep the bandage on for four days. It is well known that air contains poison. Rest, eat little. If you have a fever, go to the Dispensary. Cupping will cure fever. Or go to Joseph if you are concerned. He has been well taught but he requires practice and will likely not charge you.'

Robbie's good hand flew to his pocket. Money! He would need to pay Knox. Yet he had none. Knox waved his arm dismissively. 'It is nothing. I am a guest in Joseph's home. You are a friend of his. I would not take money from you.'

208

Now Robbie was even further in the man's debt. He recoiled at the thought. He needed to hate him, not feel grateful to him. Again.

He had to ask. 'Why did you have me freed before?'

Knox looked at him. 'I have no idea what you are talking about.'

'When I was thrown in the Canongate Tolbooth. After Professor Syme caught me – in Surgeons' Hall. You had me released.'

That musical laugh again, the head thrown back. The sound that had curdled Robbie's blood a few weeks ago on a darkening street. 'That was you? I had no idea! It did not concern you. It concerned only me and Syme. Anything Syme wants, I fight against. I cannot abide the man! Boring, pompous, arrogant – I could go on.' When he laughed, his face moved thickly like leather pocked by mildew. Robbie spat inside. It was when Knox laughed that he could hate him most.

So, thought Robbie furiously, Knox had only had him freed because of hatred of another man? Was he himself worth nothing in this man's eyes?

Knox straightened his clothes, flicked away a fleck of something on his trousers, tugged his cravat and smoothed the perfect points of his collar. He twirled the edges of his sideburns. 'I believe you have a home to go to, young man.' Still smiling, he clicked his heels together sharply and bowed to Robbie, one arm swirling through the air towards the ground. The lacy cuff danced as his wrist curled, and his fingers spiralled.

Robbie walked towards the door, turned, forced himself to express his thanks. As he walked out, the perfume followed him and hatred welled inside him, as natural as blood. Hatred for the man who had saved his life.

As he walked the short distance home, through a freshening breeze, leaving that scent, that face, behind him, he knew one thing for certain. It was hatred of this man which had almost destroyed him before. For his own good, and for Essie's, he must never see Knox again. Must clean him from his mind completely. The thought of his fingers touching him, his corpse-skinned face looming over him . . . No! He must move forward and wipe the man away, leaving him like a trail of dirty footprints behind him. He had done what he could to stop the murders. He had spoken out, told the truth. Now, if Burke and Hare – and Knox – wanted to hang themselves, how could he stop them? And why should he try? All he could do was have nothing more to do with any of them.

He walked away and left Knox's face behind him.

That night, his sleep was long and deep. But

somewhere deeper, a tiny flicker of something not quite known. Far away in his sleeping mind, spinning upwards. What was it? The truth? That it was not enough? That there was something more that he should have done? But he was asleep. It wisped away.

He woke in the morning, clear-headed. Out of the window the crystal air rippled around an early buttermilk sun. Move forward. Shut the past away. Stamp quickly on any darker thoughts.

He would throw himself into his studies again. He would make something of himself. Something that would make Essie happy. Go to university, as Joseph had suggested. He would push away the thoughts of Knox and what was happening in another street.

He would need work. 'I'll find work, too!' said Essie, mixing some weevilly flour with the last of yesterday's milk and spooning it sizzling on to the girdle hanging over the fire.

'Oh, and where will you find someone who will pay you?' he teased.

'Easy. And I'll wager I'll find work afore you!' She flipped the sizzling pancake with a bannock spade and a few seconds later she picked it up with her fingers and tossed it from hand to hand until it cooled enough to eat. Robbie thought she would never outgrow her pleasure in food. Faintly, the magpie sparkle was returning. It was like a star which, when you look straight at it, is not there, but when you look away it twinkles at you, teasing.

A few minutes later, she left the room, crumbs still on her lips. 'I'll have work afore you, Robbie!' and she danced out of the door. 'Nothing dangerous, Essie!' he shouted as she ran down the stairs.

Where could he start? He was not as confident as Essie about finding work. But perhaps Mr Brown was tired of the crusty-lipped boy who had taken Robbie's place. Perhaps he could have his job back? It was a good place to begin. He set off towards the bakery, towards Arthur's Seat. He could smell the salty seagull tang already. Taste the yeast from the bakery and the hops from the brewery.

To avoid going anywhere near the Flodden Wall, he wove his way through other streets. Past stalls selling fish, the cobbles slithery with cod-heads and scales and smashed oysters, shops touting buttons and silk, ostrich feathers dyed every shade of pink and blue, perfume in thick glass bottles with silver stoppers. Past a bookshop, where a large notice in the window proclaimed a new work by Mr Walter Scott. *The Fair Maid of Perth*, read Robbie as he passed. He could not read the author's name without thinking of the King's visit six years before. And he did not want to think about it. He must move forward.

In the next . . . Robbie stopped. How could he move forward now? He had not passed this window for a long time. And now, his eye was drawn, pulled by something he loved, whether from the past or the present. How could he not look?

Violins. Violins everywhere, their mottled yellow varnish bright in the sunlight. In the window, the instruments were ranged perfectly, hanging from hooks, neatly spaced. They were of different sizes, from the tiniest almost toy-like versions, to their elegant full-size cousins. Bows, too, their gentle parallel curves ranged along a wall beside the window. His face pressed against the glass, Robbie could see, on a table further into the shop, the jumbled paraphernalia of creation. Strings and bridges and pegs and half-carved scrolls – Robbie knew them all. Could feel them in his hands.

He went in. A bell jangled somewhere and a round bespectacled man came out from a door at the back. Robbie remembered him. He looked flustered, annoyed. He wiped his hands on an apron smeared with yellow and orange and brown.

'Aye, what d'ye want, lad?'

'I . . . I just want to look.'

'I know your sort, lad. You cannae fool me. It's

thieving ye'll be after, no' looking. Now, be off wi' ye.'

Robbie looked around the room. In contrast to the window display, the inside of the shop was confusion. A cacophony. Shelves on the back wall hung open, their labels flaking. Strings spiralled on the floor like hairs in a wig-maker's. Through a doorway into the back, Robbie could see sawdust and shavings on the floor, a workbench with a violin mould held in a clamp, slivers of wood, shelves with bottles of varnish, their sides stained every shade of brown, red and yellow.

'Be off wi' ye, I said. Before I throw ye out.'

'Please sir,' said Robbie, with all the gentle politeness he could find, 'I am not a thief. I was only looking. When I was younger, I had a violin from this shop.'

The man peered at him through tiny wire spectacles halfway down his nose. 'You would like to buy a violin? Ye'll no' mind if I say . . .'

'No, I have no money. I am looking for work. I am studying to go to university.' The words came out suddenly, without planning.

The man pushed his spectacles up his nose. There was a smear of white powder on his shoulder. One collar of his black coat stuck up, trapped by the string of his apron. He wore a white cravat, its wrinkled ridges lopsided. The flesh of his neck was loose, chickeny, and his remaining hair sat around the back of his head like a

214

white crescent moon. He looked at Robbie, weighing him up. Robbie kept his bandaged hand behind his back.

'I can tidy your shop for you. I can run errands. And I can read and write, do arithmetic. I can look after your shop while you work on your violins. Stradivarius models, are they not?'

It was that which persuaded the man to take Robbie on.

'I cannae pay ye very much,' he warned, 'but if ye work hard, show me I can trust ye . . . Aye, I'll gie ye a chance. My name is Mr Blair.'

Robbie had found himself a job. And as he spent the morning sweeping, tidying, sorting, he smiled at the thought of Essie's face. He breathed in the rosin dryness, the heady varnish smell of the shop. Each time he picked up a violin, as his hand cupped the scroll, the perfect-seeming spiral at the end, he wanted to hold it to his cheek and once or twice he did so, when he knew Mr Blair was not looking, and closed his eyes and smelt his mother.

His hand did not throb at all. By the time Mr Blair had noticed the bandage, Robbie had transformed the appearance of the shop. He could not question Robbie's ability to help him. And the boy spoke well, as though educated.

Mr Blair even told him the secret of the Stradivarius

scroll, the perfect God-given mathematics that made the twist curl round and round and round, in perfectly reducing spirals, to an endless place which could only be imagined. Like a shell, he said, made by God. If you try to copy it by art, you will fail. Only with perfect mathematics can you achieve the perfect shape and the perfect sound. The Golden Mean, this mathematical miracle was called. Robbie listened and watched, transfixed.

At the end of the day, Robbie said goodbye to Mr Blair. He left the shop, with smears of varnish on his hands from the untidy bottles. Their names rolled around his head: gamboge, oak pigment, yellow aniline and, best of all, the fiery orange of dragon's blood. He walked west towards home, with the late afternoon sun warming his face. Essie was there first, her face shining.

'I got work afore you! I telt you I would.'

'Well done, Essie! But it is "told", not "telt". And I'll not be long behind you. I'll have a job tomorrow.' He had no desire to take away all her pleasure.

'So, are you no' going to ask what it is?'

'Tell me then, Essie. What job did you find?'

'Mr Brown, Robbie! He gave me your old job! I telt – told – him about your hand an' he said you can work for him again when you're all better!'

Essie was almost dancing with excitement and pride.

God was looking after them, just as she always believed He would.

Robbie threw himself into this new life, blocking out anything else. He kept well away from Hare's inn and Burke's house. More than once he saw a woman he remembered from the inn, but she passed by and did not notice him. Perhaps did not recognize him, now that he was clean and upright and clear-eyed. His jaw, too, was more square. There were shadows that had not been there. No longer a boy.

His hand healed easily. After a few days, it was itching unbearably and he took the bandage off, though Knox had told him not to. The edges of the cut had knitted together and there was no oozing, though the whole hand was white and wrinkled with dampness from the now-dirty bandage. He left the bandage off and very soon the air had dried the cut and he was left with a thin scar which faded daily.

'You'll want your job back,' said Essie, hesitantly, when she saw how his hand had healed. But he was happy to let her keep the job. He was content amongst his violins.

May melded into June, the summer days hazy. Ladies sweated in their long dresses and layers of petticoats.

Robbie and Essie went barefoot every day now. Robbie's hair was too long, sticking in his eyes, so he borrowed a sharp knife from one of the women in the flesh market and cut it as neatly as he could.

Midsummer Day, eye-squintingly hot. Mr Blair let him finish early and he walked out on to the humming streets. He looked up. The blue swam away for ever. A gull wheeled, little more than a tiny tick in the distance. Arthur's Seat danced in the faraway heat. An idea came to him. How Essie would like it! He hurried to their home to fetch what he needed, and then to the bakery, to catch her before she left. On the way, he stopped at a market stall. He put his purchase in his pocket, wrapped in several layers of old paper.

Mr Brown looked up when Robbie arrived through the door. His face split into a broad smile. 'Rabbie! Is it Essie ye're aifter? She'll be here in a wee bit.'

'Guid afternoon, Mr Brown. Aye, I came fo' Essie. Will she be ready fo' hame soon?'

'Aye, she will so, Rabbie. A richt guid worker she is. Not that ye'd ken it, fae looking at they skinny arms.' Mr Brown wiped his hands on his apron and swept some pieces of warm oat farl into a twist of paper, which he gave to Robbie. The heat spread through the paper.

'Thank ye, sir!' said Robbie. He helped Mr Brown

tidy up, sweeping the flour and crumbs and dried mud from people's feet out of the door.

There was Essie. Cochineal-cheeked in the heat. Her face lit up when she saw Robbie. They said goodbye to Mr Brown.

'This way, Ess,' said Robbie, turning the other way, away from the town and away from home, towards Salisbury Crags and Arthur's Seat.

'Where are we going?' she asked.

'You'll see soon enough.'

They stopped to drink at a public well and went on. Past the grazing sheep. Past the railway workers, brown muscles glistening as they hefted huge rocks on to horse-drawn wagons with levers and ropes. The tunnel entrance seemed deeper, darker each time Robbie came this way, blasted by regular powder-charges. Essie waved at the men and they waved back. They were used to seeing her, with her bread barrow.

'Where are we going?' asked Essie again.

'I told you – you will see soon enough.'

Further along the track, they came to the loch. Robbie turned away from the path, towards the steep slopes on the left. Together they climbed through the heather, scrambling over stones. Away from the people. Away from all the noise and smell and taste of the city.

Higher they climbed, until the people were ants

below them. Breathless, they lay down, the grass beneath them springy, softer than any mattress they could imagine. On their stomachs they lay, chins on hands, staring at the city to the west. A visitor could only marvel at the dramatic silhouette. From here, outside, they could almost forget its real character. It was like a royal portrait, showing only what the sitter wants to reveal.

The sun was sinking, but slowly, and on this longest day of the year it would cling on for as long as possible. The evening rays were still hot, and the hours of lightness stretched ahead.

'I'm hungry,' said Essie, her cheeks pinked by the sun and the climb.

'You are always hungry.' And he pulled the package from one pocket but did not unwrap it. 'First, a fire. We need something for tinder, and sticks.'

'What'll we light it with?' asked Essie.

He pulled flints from the other pocket.

'What's the fire fo'?'

'There'll be no fire at all if you witter on. We need sticks, Essie, and grass for tinder.' She ran off and within minutes had returned with an armful of dry grass and wood.

She stacked it expertly and he struck the flint again and again until one spark and then another jumped into the grass. Shielding it with her hands, Essie softly blew and they watched the tiny flames lick the dry twigs and flare up. More sticks, and soon a good blaze was going. 'Now, stones,' said Robbie, and he searched until he found two flat stones. He put them in the fire and piled more sticks on top.

'What now?' asked Essie.

'Now, you wait,' he replied.

She stared at the flames, the firelight bright in her eyes. They were silent in their own thoughts. Robbie lay back on the grass and chewed a piece of clover, tasting its sweetness. Essie picked petals off tiny flowers and watched them flutter down into the fire. Eventually, once the flames died down, Robbie unwrapped the package. Her eyes opened wide. Beefsteak! Purple with freshness! It was months since she had had meat like that. Her mouth watered. With a stick they raked the burning wood aside and laid the steaks on the stones. A sizzling sound. And almost immediately the smell of roasting meat. After a minute or two, they turned them with a stick. Smoke stung their eyes and blackened their faces.

They ate the steak with their fingers, red juices running down their chins. Essie laughed and told him he looked like a Highlander.

Afterwards, they wiped their hands on the grass. Essie

lay back against the cushioning ground and smiled with content. Her stomach full, her skin warm, all fear forgotten. God was watching over them, she knew.

'Thank you, Robbie.'

Robbie sat for a while and watched her as she fell asleep, the bird-like movements of her face slowly quietening. Now she looked fragile, her cheeks poppy-red.

Later, as the fallen sun chilled the air, he woke her. Drowsily, she allowed him to help her up and lead her down the slope again. They walked slowly back into the town, and came to Fleshmarket Close in near darkness, the smell of the smoke hanging in their clothes.

The weeks, months, passed. Summer swelled, bloomed, pulsed with mist. Flies swarmed amongst the filth of the streets, and the stench blossomed, but in the distance, if Robbie looked high enough, far enough, the days stretched into a hazy blue somewhere, where the bees swam sleepily and the heather blushed on the faraway dancing hills.

It was almost possible to imagine that this was how it would always be. Moving forward, moving upwards, as though all the darkness was left behind for ever.

9

Discovery

Soon summer was past and autumn's fingers had crept into the cockroach darkness. A chill draught rattled the windows and blew across the table as Robbie worked at his books late one evening, while Essie slept. The candle flickered, sizzled, and went out, drowned in its own liquid. He moved to relight it and as he passed the window, he happened to look out. It was the moon that he looked at first, its huge perfect globe hanging as if by magic. By its light, he could see the twisted cliffs of leaning tenements and the tiny houses crumpled between them. He looked down.

It was then that he saw it. Out of the corner of his eye, movement. A cart. The familiar shape of a herring-barrel rocking under its ropes. Trundling fast. Pulled by two men. His throat contracted and he shrank back from the window. Sat down, breathing fast. Sick. He knew who it was. What it was. There had been another murder.

It was then that he realized, suddenly, something which deep down in that deepest darkest part of his mind he had known all along. Something he had tried to shut out. He had tried to hide from it by burying himself in his studies, in the rosin-dusted haven of the violin shop, in his tidy routine life of the last few months. He must stop the murders. There was no one else. Meanwhile there had been another victim. He had not done enough. This time it was his fault.

As he climbed into bed later that night, carefully so as not to wake Essie, he knew what he would have to do. He would have to report Burke and Hare to the authorities.

How? If the constables went to Burke's house, they would find nothing. Nothing but a pile of straw and a dirty pillow. And Burke and Hare would know they were under suspicion. Perhaps that alone would be enough to stop them? No. They would find somewhere else to do it. They were too greedy to stop. And they would certainly come searching for Robbie.

There was only one way. Robbie would have to wait until they were about to do it again. He would have to watch the house. Every day until he saw them bringing a new victim to their murder house. He felt cold at the thought. He did not want to see their faces again, to be reminded of what he had done. Or to think of Knox buying the bodies, sallow in the gas-light.

The next morning he told Mr Blair that his sister was ill. He needed to be with her until she was better – if she was ever better, he said. Mr Blair's kindly watery-blinking concern when Robbie told him about Essie made him feel guilty. But it was the only way.

Ten days it took. Ten days during which Robbie haunted the Canongate, taking every opportunity to pass the house where Burke lived, always with his collar pulled up, always holding his breath as he walked past. The tattered winds of autumn whipped his cheeks. Icy rain dripped down his neck. Each morning, the daylight shrivelled a little more, the darkness creeping in as if a tombstone was slowly sliding over the city. Several times he saw Burke, always walking carefree, smiling greetings to someone he knew, or touching his hat when a lady passed, or lashing out with his foot at a dog. Sometimes from across the street Robbie even saw his freckled skin, the wet pale eyes.

Once he saw Hare with him, walking towards Burke's house. His heart tripped. This was it! But no – there was no one with them and they came out again immediately.

At last, inevitably, the moment came. Robbie was some yards away when he saw them, walking towards the house. With another man, stooped, slow, tottering. An old beggar, chewing, weighed down by his brown layers of cloth. Hare led the way, his eyes darting around, his wet mouth open. Robbie shrank around a corner, peered back. Burke's hand was on the beggar's shoulders, pushing him along. He smiled down at the man, agreeing with some rambled comment, soothing. Robbie's skin contracted. Hare fumbled at the door; it opened; they led the man in. Robbie's last sight was Burke's milky eyes looking out into the street before the door closed.

Robbie ran. Towards the Canongate Tolbooth. He needed a constable. Quick, before it was too late! Or a soldier would do. There! But he could not do it himself. Too dangerous. He would be questioned and remembered. He looked around. A boy kicked stones nearby, oblivious to the cold. Robbie, head turned away from the soldier a few yards away, walked up to the boy. 'See this coin, lad?' The boy's eyes were fixed on the coin as Robbie twirled it in front of him. The boy tried to snatch it but Robbie was too quick and held it high. 'You would like to earn this coin, would you not?' The boy nodded, staring at it. 'Now, listen carefully. You see that soldier?' The boy nodded again. 'Now look down the street, two houses past where that grey horse is standing, the low house with the sagging roof?

Now, you go to that soldier and you tell him – and listen carefully,' and at this Robbie put his face close to the boy's face, 'you tell him that in that house there's a murder happening.' The boy's eyes opened wide. He swallowed. 'You understand?' urged Robbie. The child nodded and held out his hand. Robbie placed the coin in the small palm and the boy started to move away. Robbie grabbed his wrist. 'Not so fast. I haven't finished yet.' He took another coin from his pocket. The child stared, his eyes red-rimmed in the cold. 'This coin is for you too,' he said, 'when I see the soldier going into that house. Now go! Hurry!'

The child ran, barefoot in the cold, and Robbie watched from round a corner while the boy talked to the soldier. The soldier did not seem to listen. He seemed to laugh, and turn away. Robbie's heart raced. The boy persisted and the soldier called another soldier from inside the Tolbooth. The two of them looked at each other, spoke again to the boy, and then moved quickly down the street towards Burke's house. Robbie held his breath as they knocked at the door, waited, knocked again, and then hurled their shoulders at the heavy door.

The boy was running towards him. Robbie threw the coin at his feet and ran away himself.

Home. Light-footed he sped, the weight falling from

him. He could have sung as he ran up the stairs. Could have danced with relief. It was done! No more murders. Now justice.

The feeling of relief did not last long. What about the man? The beggar who had followed Burke and Hare, trusting, unknowing. Had the soldiers reached him in time? Or had Robbie watched the man walk to his own death? Robbie had set a trap and the bait was an innocent beggar. Had he cared enough about the new victim? Did this not make him just as bad as Knox, who believed that it did not matter how he obtained bodies if his purpose, his motive, was for the benefit of medicine?

But no! He could not think like this. If this beggar had indeed become the latest murder victim, there was nothing else Robbie could have done to stop it. His whole aim had been to stop any more murders happening. And to bring the murderers to justice. There was no other way he could have achieved that. Now Hare and Burke would hang. Maybe Knox too. At the thought, Robbie stopped. What was it Hare had said? 'We hang, you hang.' They would not do it. Surely they would not? Besides, they would have no idea that it was Robbie who had reported them. It could have been anyone. And who would listen to them anyway?

Trying to reassure himself in this way, he waited for something to happen, for news of their arrest.

He did not have to wait long. The next day. The noises of the street floating upwards, distant-sounding, muffled. His skin cold with sweat. He went to the window and looked down. Was there something different? Something buzzing, something shocked about the way the people met and bent towards each other and parted and met someone else? Was that what rumour looked like? A whispering game.

He looked up. The air still and thick. Cold and heavy-looking. Then snow, floating flecks of snow, the first snow of winter. He shivered.

Then he heard it. Spun round. Footsteps, running up the stairs. The door flying open. Essie. Her cheeks red from the cold. Her eyes wide. Her hair wind-wild.

Her voice was spiky, frightened. 'Two men've been arrested, Robbie. For murder. They selt the bodies. An' d'you ken who tae, Robbie?' Her eyes flamed. Her arms were taut by her sides. Robbie said nothing, his words trapped. 'Dr Robert Knox!' She spat the words out. 'I said I'd seen him afore. An' I ken just what was on that barrow! It's murder, Robbie! You'll go tae hell!' She was shouting now, lashing out her anger and her fear.

'I didn't know they were murdered!' he shouted. 'You can't imagine I would . . .'

'I don' believe you!' There were tears in her eyes.

'Believe me, Essie. Before God, I swear I did not know. And when I found out, I tried to stop it.'

'I don' believe you.'

He felt sick. Shaking all over. Cold with a new fear. Everything was falling to pieces again. How could he have thought it would not?

What if Burke and Hare named him? 'We hang, you hang.' What would it be like to hang? Robbie had watched a few hangings. Had seen one where it did not work first time. He remembered the angry roar of the crowd when the victim dangled with his legs more than twitching, his whole body in spasm, kicking, silently except for the sawing laugh of the rope as it jerked. Had seen when they cut him down, hacked away the rope from his neck, revived him in water and hung him again, screaming before he dropped. And afterwards the crowd had stoned the hangman, would have killed him if the soldiers had not dragged him away.

He could do nothing but wait.

Essie climbed into their bed fully clothed. Made mute with fear, she pulled the blanket over her head. It was cold in the room. The fire was dead and damp with spluttered soot. No light came from outside. A gale began to blow, battering the windows and the roof and the door. The candlelight shivered. Shadows crept across the ceiling.

Robbie sat. Waited. He knew Essie was not asleep. He could tell by her rigid silence. He went over to her, knelt down by the bed. 'Essie,' he whispered, pushing a drift of hair from her forehead.

'Believe me, Ess,' he said. 'I didn't know. I have done foolish things, but I did not know about the murders. Not until it was too late.'

She spoke through tight lips. 'You see what happens when you say bad things about God? You shouldn't o' said what you said. Tae Joseph. God is punishing us.'

'No, Ess. Look at all the bad things that happened before that. Think about all the people who die, babies, innocent babies. I don't know what the answers are, but I do know it is not so simple.'

Essie was silent. Then she spoke, her voice stronger. 'God will care for us, Robbie. I know he will. Everybody says so. 'Cept Joseph. Mr Chalmers said, at Sunday School, "God is the only father o' the fatherless". God is our father.'

If only it was so simple, thought Robbie in the darkness beside her.

'Robbie? If you swear it's true, that you kent nothing 'bout the murders, I'll believe you,' said Essie at last.

'I swear it, Essie.'

'Everything will be all right now, will it no'?' And she pushed the blanket back and got up. Robbie nodded, silenced by her bright and desperate faith.

With difficulty, Robbie went about the evening routine, prepared food, fetched water. But part of him hung in the air, helpless. Later, Essie slept quickly, reassured. Robbie lay awake. Each time he nearly drifted away, a sudden heartbeat would wake him again. The city, too, pulsed with silent wakefulness. Could it ever sleep again? But, somewhere in the deepest part of the night, he must have slept.

In the morning they were woken by rain smattering on the window. The sky was a swirling sea-grey. The clean mint snow had gone. Rain churned the mud.

Inside, water began to seep through the ceiling, and he moved a bucket to catch the drips.

It was Sunday. Essie went off to her Sunday School, cheeks scrubbed in cold water, hair forced beneath the once-white cap. With her gone, Robbie's thoughts darted without control. Panic grew. How should he spend the time before the trial? Go about his normal work? Do everything as usual? Just keep away from Hare's inn and Burke's house.

If only he could have spoken to Joseph. But how could he? Joseph was part of Knox's world. Joseph had cut into dead bodies himself, had admitted it openly. Perhaps Joseph knew as much as Knox? Perhaps he was involved? After all, two students had helped unload the cart. Perhaps Joseph had done that too? Besides, if he did not know, he also did not know of Robbie's involvement. Whatever the case, it was not possible for Robbie to speak to him about it.

When he went outside to get water from the well in the High Street, the streets were clotted with groups of huddled people, their Sunday clothes hurriedly pulled on. People looked over their shoulders, spoke with eager frowns, spat their self-righteous anger into the cold air.

'They're saying sixteen people was killt, mebbe more. Men and women. Bairns, too.'

Robbie tried to grasp the enormity of sixteen murders. Into his head again came the sight of that woman's twisted legs, her rag-doll damaged body. Guilt. He would never forget it. He wondered if he could ever be clean of it. Of the bodies he had carried. Of the beggar he had seen walk to his death. Of the money he had earned.

'Aye, an' it's tha' doctor I blame. Cutting intae deed bodies like tha'. It's no' right! No' natural.' The man had a growth spreading over his face, cupping his chin and jaw with its grotesque mass.

'Aye, Dr Knox. He shuid hang wi' Burke an' Hare, so he shuid.'

'Aye an then they shuid tak' doon his body and cut it

233

up for a' the world tae see. See how he likes it then.'

Robbie's hatred of Knox was growing back, sending its bindweed roots to catch him again. The feeling was sleet-cold, and shaking, and full of darkness. Why, whenever he seemed to have put the past behind him, did that name rear up again? He could not shake the man off.

Alongside this hatred, lurked the increasing fear that Burke or Hare would name him, drag him with them to the gallows. There seemed no choices anywhere any more, whichever way he turned.

Desperately, he threw himself into routine. Surviving, working in the violin-maker's shop, trying to keep Essie at her books. What else could he do? How else could the days pass before the trial? If he did nothing, time would stand still.

Through all this, Essie's frightened face accused him. How could he reassure her when he could not reassure himself? Often he found her sitting staring into nothing. One day he found the kaleidoscope grimed in dust under the bed. It was broken, its cylinders sliding uselessly past each other, and when he looked through it he saw only a mess of tumbled shards.

Every day that passed was a day nearer the moment when Hare and Burke might name him, calling him to hang with them. Perhaps he deserved it? He was weighed down by events that were heavier than he could measure. The world was not right. Perhaps it could only be right when Hare and Burke were punished, hanging till they were dead. And then, what about Knox? His jaw clenched. Perhaps it would not be all over until Knox had paid a price? Perhaps Robbie, too, would have to pay. His neck cringed at the thought.

Sometimes, as he walked along a street, he would hear children chanting the new rhyme as they skipped or played their endless clapping games:

> '*Doon the close and up the stair*
> *But an' ben wi' Burke an' Hare*
> *Burke's the butcher*
> *Hare's the thief*
> *Knox the man who buys the beef!*'

It was difficult not to believe that they chanted it at Robbie as he hurried past.

At last, the day of the trial. 24th December. The day before Yuleday. In most years, a passing day like any other. Today, crisp, cold, clear, blue. A day drum-tight. A day of brittle fear, light-headed, breathless. He waited. Waited for the word to spread.

Countless times, he went outside the violin shop, looked up and down the hushed streets, watched the faces of the few people who shivered by. Mr Blair had begun to teach him how to scrape and shave the wood from the back-piece of a half-made violin. Today, he took no pleasure in the tiny curls that dropped to the ground at his feet. He could not hold the tool steady. He overheated the red-hot bending iron and dropped it on the floor, where a tiny fire blazed up amongst the shavings. Mr Blair's voice rose in exasperation as he threw water on it.

But it was not until the early hours of the following morning that the word came. The city woke to whispers. Soon the news was everywhere. William Hare had been freed. He had agreed to give all the information that would send his friend to the gallows, in return for his own freedom. William Burke would hang, just over one month from now, and when he was dead he would be taken down and dissected. In public, for all to see. It was only right, everyone said. Only right that his body should be sliced and opened and split and gouged and laid bare to the mob. It was justice, they all said, their eyes bright, sneering in self-righteous disgust.

Knox's name was kicked about in the grime. The evil doctor who had bought the bodies. He must have known, they all said. If he had not known, he should have asked. Robbie's hatred grew on the wind of their anger. It mattered nothing to him that Knox had saved his life; he had forgotten. Or that Knox had freed him from prison; it had been for his own twisted ends, in any case. The hatred was something in Robbie's guts, outside his control. If Knox had asked, had cared, had given a single thought to the living instead of burying his arms in corpses, none of this would have happened. Robbie would not have been tainted and now be in fear of his life.

Knox cared for no one. How could he make Knox care? How could he make him be sorry?

But first, the hanging. There was still time for Robbie to be dragged to the gallows himself. Only when Burke was dead could he be sure that the risk had passed.

10

Hanging

Over a month to wait, a month during which Robbie had no time, no space for anything except that date, hanging in the wintered air like icicles. A frozen day mired in the dead darkest reaches of winter. Sickness settled on the city, creeping around the stinking streets, picking off the weakest, the gin-drowsy babies, the young mothers hollow-eyed with disease. Some died of cold, too weak to shiver in their damp rooms, the fires dead in the grates, rain or snow dripping down the chimneys. They slipped away unnoticed, perhaps being discovered days later, rigid. People walked quickly from place to place, hunched against the cold, stiff-shouldered in the wet wind, scarves moist over noses, sweat clotted into frosty sideburns.

Beneath all this the city's anger grew, fanned by rumour, by horror at what had been going on unseen in their streets. William Hare was forced to flee for his life.

Eventually, word came that he had been seen in an English city, and someone had thrown lime in his eyes, blinding him. Knox's name was still kicked around. The more that other doctors and surgeons defended him, the more the mob considered him guilty.

At least Hare was gone. He could not drag Robbie into it now. Who would listen if he tried? But there was still Burke. What would he have to lose in those last moments before the hangman put the noose around his neck? He could name him and the mob would turn on Robbie.

At last, the hanging day. Robbie woke early, the darkness still deep, a cold wind rattling. Somewhere nearby, a door banging. A baby crying. He lay still, his heart thumping already.

The city buzzed from the early hours.

Essie wanted to watch the hanging. Robbie refused to let her, his face so frosty that she could not argue. She went to her work at the bakery in the early darkness, looking back at Robbie as she left. They had barely talked since the trial, the air between them brittle.

Robbie paced about in the silence. He could not go to work today. He was cold, sweaty, the muscles in his face rigid. He kept looking out of the window, looking for a sign, a sign of anything that he wanted or did not want to hear. It was still dark outside, the northern daylight nowhere near. But he could hear unusual noises and imagine crowds already sweeping towards where the hanging would take place.

There was no air in the room. Robbie could not take a full breath in. Each time he tried, it was as if something sat in his throat.

He had to get out. Pulling on his boots and his jacket and turning the collar up, he left the building, running down the stairs. Once on the High Street, he stood leaning against a building, brushed by the crowds all moving in one direction. The street was clogged with eager people, their faces angry but excited, grey-lipped with cold. Robbie closed his ears to the chatter, the speculation. He breathed in the frosted air. No one noticed him. He wished he could vanish entirely. For ever.

For a while he stood there, torn. What should he do? Should he join the crowds, be a part of their anger, see justice done? Or should he turn in the opposite direction and run and run and run?

It was almost light now, the sky a scudding charcoal. Robbie clenched his hands, palms sweaty. He pushed himself away from the wall and blended into the crowd, carried along by them. They were the blood in the veins of their city, pulsed along without choosing.

The crowd thickened, slowed. They were nearly at

the cobbled square by St Giles' Cathedral, the heart of the city, where the hanging would take place. He could imagine Burke now, being led, slow with fear, towards the platform with its hanging rope. What was in his head? Just fear? Or anger, too? Would he name Robbie, use his last few moments of life to do what he had promised? We hang, you hang. Robbie's throat constricted, his breath now as thin as spider silk.

He stopped. Shouts around him, jostling. 'What ye doing? Git a move on, will ye?' But he was barely aware of it. He turned and fought his way to the side of the street and pressed himself breathless against a wall again. He could not go on. Could not watch the hanging. How could he have thought he might?

He went the other way. Walked fast. Away from the hanging.

Soon, only stragglers were passing him. The roar of the crowd moved on. Robbie walked faster in his new direction. He did not know where he would go. Perhaps to the Royal Park, Arthur's Seat, anywhere away from here. As he walked faster, his shoulder knocked hard against someone. A woman's voice cried out, 'Watch what ye're doing!' Robbie turned briefly to look at her, to mutter his apologies. She looked at him oddly. Did she know him? No, it was just something in his own eyes which disturbed her.

In the pause, he became aware of something. A silence. Utter silence. The city was holding its breath. The woman was still, her face frozen. Their breath clung in the cold air, waiting.

At that moment, they both turned their heads towards the same sound. A roar, a huge surging storm of noise in the distance, a whole city shouting as one. The hanging. It was over. Into Robbie's mind flashed the vision of Burke's body dangling, his legs jerking, his lips hanging open, tongue sticking out. Turning blue. He closed his throat, tightened his stomach. How much pain had Burke felt? Not enough, too quick, nowhere near enough pain.

A spinning feeling in his head. Blackening rain over his eyes.

The woman was speaking, 'So, it's o'er. Ye all right, laddie?'

He mumbled something and walked on, slowly at first. It was over. But it did not feel over. Still it did not feel over.

Knox. The hatred was still there. Knox still did not understand the enormity of what he had done. He must be made to know and to care. Knox was the man who was everything that Robbie hated. Still. The man who represented pain, and anger, and fear, and failure. He would show him what he had done. He would make

243

him understand. He would make him, at the end of it all, be sorry.

Robbie began to hurry again. Soon he was running through almost empty streets. Faster and faster. Towards Surgeons' Square. Towards Knox's anatomy school. And if Knox was not there he would go to his house. Wherever he was, he would find him. The rain slanted, sleeting into his face, sliding freezing down his neck.

Rounding a corner, he lost his balance, fell hard on the ground. Pain shot through his hip, his breath pumped from his body. He squeezed his face shut against the pain. He had to get up. Covered in mud, he struggled to his feet, put his foot on the ground, tried to put weight on his leg. He winced. It would do. He ran on, limping heavily. His breath rasped in his throat.

'Robbie!' A shout. He ignored it. 'Robbie!' He slid to a stop and turned, the rain dripping off his nose and down his chin.

'Go home, Essie! Go home!'

'No! I'm no' going home. I'm coming with you. You'll no' leave me again!'

'You can't come. Go home!' Robbie yelled.

But Essie ran right to him, looking up at him, her hair plastered on her forehead, her eyes blazing through the rain. 'I can so! Whatever it is you're going tae do, I'm coming too. You're no' leaving me again.'

'No, Essie. Go HOME! This time, you can't come.' And he ran, as fast as he could. Faster than Essie could run.

Her anger grew fainter until he could hear it no more. She melded into the pulse of the city.

Round another corner. Infirmary Street. The hospital in front of him. Not far now. He ran faster.

Three men, collars turned up against the rain, hunched shoulders, standing still, their faces sheltered by umbrellas. A conversation, snatched words. The hanging. Was that Knox's name he heard? One man looked towards him, his face wide with recognition. Professor Syme! The man said something. The other two looked up. One old, round, angry-faced even before he saw Robbie. The other – Joseph! Syme began to move towards Robbie. Instinctively, Robbie sprang away. He leapt into the street.

'Robbie!' A shout. He stopped, twisted. 'Robbie!' It was Essie, running towards him on the pavement. Suddenly, a clattering. A carriage speeding round the corner. He saw it from the corner of his eye. Saw Essie's silent scream. Hurled himself aside.

Then confusion. The cobbled crashing, metal screeching. Through the squeal of horses, something huge, something hard, hit him and he was flung into the air, landing twisted on his back.

In slow motion, thinly through a veil of pain, he saw a carriage wheel buckle, turn in on itself and fall slowly. And as it fell, and as he lay, he watched the jagged broken spoke slice through the air towards him. As it tore through the flesh and muscle of his shoulder, he was pinned like a fluttering insect to the ground. Then he tumbled down into the blackness and slid away, dropping into nowhere.

Into the nowhere a scream. Shaking him. His own scream, he realized in a blur. Voices all around him, hands touching him, rain on his face. Someone crying.

The pain was paralysing. He knew it was in his shoulder but every tiniest part of his body was trapped in it. He could not move even a finger. Breathing was difficult. Only shallow breaths. Each a struggle. Not enough air. Blackness. Spreading. Vision. Going to die. Like his mother. God's last word. His punishment.

A splintering sound. His own screaming again, from somewhere that did not feel part of him. Then he was being lifted. On his back he was cradled in many arms and then he felt a rush of wet wind over his face as he was carried away somewhere. He tried to open his eyes but everything was blurred and frightening, upside down and full of strangeness. Every movement was agony.

Then a rattling, more shouting, and he was lowered on to something hard. He floated into the air, lifted again.

Suddenly through the chaos, a voice, strong and sure. 'Robbie, it's Joseph. And Essie's here. Try not to move. You chose a good place to have an accident. You are near the Infirmary.'

'No!' breathed Robbie. 'Not the Infirmary!' But no one seemed to hear.

Through his pain he could hear arguing. Professor Syme's voice. 'For God's sake, man! He's nothing but a common thief. Should be dangling from the gallows, not cluttering up our hospitals. Leave him, I say.'

Joseph. 'I know him, sir. He is not a bad lad.'

'Aye, well what would you know? Did you know he was thrown in prison not so long ago? For stealing? From Surgeons' Hall, would you believe?'

Another voice. 'Let the young man deal with this one, Syme, why don't we? See how well he has learnt his lessons.'

Robbie felt himself being carried upwards, at an angle – steps? – and soon they were indoors. He opened his eyes and through a mist saw marbled columns, lamps everywhere, distant like stars. Suddenly, he came to a halt. A pause. Then, slow, semi-breve footsteps, approaching. A shuffling of feet as the men moved aside to let a newcomer near. And then a deep, rich, musical voice.

'What is all this commotion? Causing trouble, are you, Professor Syme? What? Again?' An amused, lyrical tone. The lowest warm tones of a violin.

Through the blackness in front of his eyes, Robbie could not see the man who spoke. But he knew who it was. His heart skittering, pinned like a moth, he looked into Dr Robert Knox's eyes. This was pure fear. Nothing he had felt before came anywhere near this. If he had had the strength he could have summoned up the anger, too. But what would be the point? He was paralysed, useless, speared through the shoulder by a piece of wood which was going to kill him.

But Knox only turned to Syme and smiled at him, nose high, eyebrows raised, a delicate tapering finger stroking the side of his chin. A floral scent draped itself over Robbie's face and he breathed it in, wanting to drown in it.

Knox spoke. 'My dear Professor Syme, surely you would not turn away this young boy who is so gravely injured? This would not be the mark of a distinguished and virtuous man. But, since you no doubt have a great deal of exceptionally important work to do, I am sure you will allow me to care for this boy. We have met before. I will perform the operation at my own expense,

248

as I so often do. With young Joseph as my able assistant, of course.'

Professor Syme, his face purple with anger and unable to look Knox in the eye, turned away with a flick of his hand. 'Please yourself, Knox. You always do. No doubt, once he is as dead as your other patients, you will have some use for him.' And he walked away, his shoes echoing in the corridor.

Voices swirled around Robbie, snatches of words and sentences, Knox's name several times. A coldness swept through him, numbing his thoughts. Only fear and pain remained. Fear and pain without words. Raw, unbreathing.

He was moving again. As he was carried away, somewhere, he tried to die. Tried to shut everything down, to clamp his heart, to stop breathing entirely.

Through the darkness another voice. Essie. 'Robbie! Hush, Robbie. It's going tae be all right.' And he felt her warm hand holding his, felt its bird-like lightness. 'We're nearly there.' No! He tried to squeeze her hand. To tell her that he must not be there, must not go to the Infirmary. But his fingers did not work. He was drifting. Floating towards a place where nothing meant as much as it should.

Along corridors, endless turnings, up stairs, along, around. Now a room, high-ceilinged, wide wet windows. With a searing pain he felt himself being moved on to a table. He did not know if he cried aloud. He was exhausted by the effort of being in pain, of struggling to breathe through ice.

He looked at the ceiling and grew colder. A large spider hung briefly on its thread above him. Watched him watching it. It scuttled back towards the safety of its web. The voices of everyone in the room drifted into the distance. He began to fade, retreat. He could almost believe that this was not going to happen.

He could not hear Essie. Where was she? He began to panic. He tried to move, felt steel hands on his head, his legs, his face, a palm on his forehead, a cloth going over his eyes. His breathing shallowed, quickened, gasping. He was suffocating. It was coming. Whatever it was, it was coming.

Through the fear, that voice. Knox. 'Be calm. I have not started yet. Stay very still and very calm. It will soon be over. Breathe slowly and deeply.'

The voice barely reached his terror. He wished someone would hit him on the head, knock him out. A pounding in his ears. Every muscle stretched. His head forced into the hard table. His eyes were squeezed shut and the blood danced purple behind them. His legs shook with cold, jerking.

He could only wait for what was to come.

The pain was one shattered scream, shooting into a million splinters in his ears. Something was stuffed between his teeth. Every muscle in his body, every joint, jerked into spasm. Something rasping was inside him, scraping against the bones in his shoulder, digging into him, tugging, ripping. He felt blood flow down past his neck and towards his back.

Into space he dived, scrambling away from the fear, scrabbling in the emptiness, struggling to find solid edges to push himself against. But all was vapour beneath him and still fear clung to him. Then, as he tumbled towards cave-cold nothing, suffocating, he saw a glow in the spiralling distance, a misty, growing whiteness. He spun towards it. Fear fell away from him. As if in a dream he flew towards the whitening light, stretched from head to toe on a silver arrow, spiralling unbreathing, silent screaming. As long as he could hold his breath, he would fly towards the light. And he could hold his breath for ever, for ever and ever and ever. He could stay out here, up here, and never go back. How easy it would be, how dizzyingly easy just to float away.

He watched with detached pity the dwarfed figure of himself pinned on the table in the room below, like a poor damaged butterfly specimen not quite dead.

There was Knox, working fast. He smoothly pulled the wooden spike from Robbie's shoulder and pressed his fingers into the wound to stop the spurting blood. Joseph also had his fingers in the wound, pinching vessels. Between them their hands and knives worked with spiderlike speed and skill and Robbie felt nothing, only watched from afar. Another man held his head, firmly, the hands over his ears.

Robbie floated away, flying higher towards the whiteness. Towards forever. Into his mother's arms.

Robbie smelt her breath on his neck, noticed the sparkle in her angel eyes. She held and held and held him. Together they flew. She did not drop him.

In his head as they spun, floated the one question he had wanted to ask. Wanted for so long to ask. 'Why did you drop me?' She answered his unspoken question.

'It is simple, Robbie. I had no choice. In some things we just have no choice. In others we do. It is telling the difference that matters. Look down.' Robbie looked down, and there was Essie, outside the room. Her hands were over her ears. Her face was screwed tight, her eyes shut, as though by shutting her eyes she could block the sound of Robbie screaming. He moved to go down to her but his mother's voice in his hair whispered, 'No! You must not take her with you. She will find her own way.'

Floating free in the whiteness, in a place where everything made sense, Robbie understood. He had to finish the journey on his own, as his mother had done.

From somewhere far away, yet somehow deep inside him, came his mother's voice. 'You cannot choose what happens to you. But you can choose how to live. You can choose who to be.' Still she held him. Until he was ready. Then he let her go.

As she floated away, their fingers parted, slip-sliding, tip-touching, and she was gone, leaving behind the memory of her star-bright eyes. As he drifted alone, he allowed himself another floating moment before returning. Taking a lungful of air, he dived back into the pain and fear.

Controlling his breathing, slow, slow, slow, he hovered somewhere inside himself. His body was a mass of fire, white-hot, as though real flames were eating his skin. He felt his flesh being tugged, pulled, drawn together. Sensed something sharp piercing the skin at intervals. But, strangely, no fear. It was only pain and what was that? He let all his limbs go limp and sank into the table. The cloth had fallen from his face.

Opening his eyes, he saw a man's face above him. The man's hands held his head, but gently now. And there was Joseph, his high cheekbones shadowed in the lamplight, meeting Robbie's wakening eyes. Robbie looked to the left. There was Knox. Concentrating. His one good eye focusing on what he was doing. The other useless eye dead. The pitted face taut. And then a smile. A relaxing. Knox looked at Robbie. 'Well done, lad. You will soon be good as before.'

Strong hands raised him upright. The pain was dull. His head felt heavy and he let it drop. He let his whole body relax as caring hands bandaged his shoulder tightly, fastening his arm across his chest. Gently, slowly, they lowered him back down again. He closed his eyes, drifting.

He slept.

When he woke, he was alone. The calmness he had felt before he slept had gone. His shoulder throbbed and waves of heat swept over him. His skin twitched, his muscles jerked. He moved his head from side to side, for no reason that he knew.

Through the fevered thoughts, one stood strong and bright. That he had not finished the journey. There was more still to do. Perhaps, even, it was only the beginning.

The door opened. Soft footsteps across the room. A hand on his forehead. Knox, smiling with his cloth-like skin, but never, never smiling with his eyes.

Robbie spoke, his mind suddenly quite clear, his voice like glass. 'Do you remember me?'

'The boy with the injured hand? The boy who spied

on me in my own house? Who gazed at my violin? The boy who picked up a knife, with God knows what intention? How could I forget you? And your questions.' He gazed at the diamond ring on his finger, as he held the pulse in Robbie's wrist.

'No, from long ago. Six years ago.'

'Should I?'

'My mother died.'

'I know. You told me.'

'You were the surgeon.'

Robbie watched Knox's face. Saw a muscle in his cheek cringe. Felt the stillness of his body. For a long heavy moment, the earth stopped spinning.

Then Knox dropped Robbie's wrist, turned away, walked to the window. He looked smaller than Robbie remembered. His velvet jacket hung unevenly from his shoulders. When he turned back, Robbie saw that his watch-chain was caught on a button and made two unbalanced loops. Vermilion streaked one cheek. 'That is why you were outside my house,' said Knox, in a level voice. 'It was not the violin.'

'I followed you,' said Robbie. He continued, through the light veil of pain. 'And that's why I mind, mind whose body you cut into. That's why I mind how those people died.'

'And that is why I must not mind,' said Knox, coming

back towards him, his face framed by the moonlight now shafting through the window, his voice burning with a passion Robbie had never heard. He spoke to Robbie, spoke to him properly. 'It is a choice I have made. Because if I minded, nothing would ever be learnt. I mind about curing people, any people. What else is my life about but that? I saved you. And I have saved countless others. But I could not save your mother. I failed. I regret that most deeply. I regret every life I cannot save.'

Robbie could not speak into the silence that followed. This was what he had waited for so long to hear. Dr Knox was sorry. Yet it did not seem to be the most important thing any longer.

He was tired. Very tired. It hurt to talk, but he had to ask. He turned towards Knox. 'I heard you say something once. You said pain was God's will.' He began to feel faint. 'That it was wrong . . . to try . . . to take it away.' He was exhausted.

Silence, followed by a roar of laughter. 'Good God, you make me sound like a Calvinist minister!' His voice took on a mocking quality, as if play-acting. 'A shocking idea, quite shocking. To eliminate pain? Pain is God's will, His gift! How could we mortals be so audacious as to consider going against God's will? We should welcome pain, as God's gift to us.'

'That was it!' gasped Robbie. 'I heard you.'

'You heard me!' agreed Knox, still smiling. 'You heard me mocking the views of those pious fools who think God would put us on this earth to suffer. God put us on this earth to exercise our own free will, to make choices and to live by them. I am a surgeon. Everything I do is designed with one thing in mind, and one thing only – to find ways to cure patients. When they die, I have failed. I failed your mother. I am sorry.'

The memory of his mother floated by, her soft hair trailing, the way she used to stroke his forehead, to kiss him every night, to say she loved him. The way when she smiled a tiny dimple appeared on one cheek only. The sunlit apple warm smell of her. The way she held him and never, never, never let him go. And the sparkle in her eyes. How could he have forgotten the fire-bright sparkle in her eyes?

Knox was sorry. It was what Robbie wanted. But did it matter? What did it matter what Dr Knox did? It only mattered what he did himself. What choices he made. His mother had said, 'In some things we have no choice. In others we do. It is telling the difference that matters. You cannot choose what happens to you. But you can choose how to live. You can choose who to be.'

Joseph came into the room with Essie. Through the fragile strength of her bright magpie eyes, she watched

257

Robbie carefully and when he smiled, she smiled too, a tiny dimple on one cheek only. How had he never noticed that before?

11

A Few Years Later

Another summer humming towards its hazy end. In the distance the heathered hills, a faraway blush. A hanging sun warming the city.

Some students, laughing, clutching their books. All in black coats, sharp white collars, carefully rumpled cravats pushing their chins high.

A building with spires that stretched into the misty blue. Carvings, intricate patterns, an impossibly symmetrical design of arches and curves. A doorway, enormous. From the doorway, a young man, perhaps twenty, perhaps slightly more, hurrying down the steps. A kindly face, but focusing on something important inside himself.

Another man, a little younger, perhaps eighteen, something burning in his eager eyes, running down the steps after him. The younger man overtaking the other, running in front of him, stopping him with a hand on his arm.

Robbie spoke. 'Sir, please, Dr Simpson, sir.'

The other man stopped, turned towards this student. He smiled, waited, as though he could spare any amount of time.

'I was at your lecture. I need to ask. What you were saying in there, sir. About surgery without pain, about patients being asleep while they are operated on. Do you really believe it is possible? In our lifetime?'

Dr Simpson smiled. 'Of course I do. It is what I am working on. It will happen one day, mark my words. And, God willing, I will be there when it does.'

'Will you let me help you, sir?'

Dr Simpson looked at him, considering. Then smiled. 'Would you like to help me now? I am meeting some colleagues. We have been trying a miraculous substance which sends us into a deep sleep from which needles and any manner of pain will not wake us. But we must try it many times on different people, because the required dosage seems to vary. Are you willing?'

'Certainly, sir!' Robbie's heart flew. Clutching his books to his chest, he walked away with the young man, burning with questions.

Epilogue

Many Years Later – Edinburgh 1862

The elderly surgeon, distinguished-looking, walked down the marbled corridor, calmly. He opened the thick, heavy door at the end. The hum of many voices rose, and fell as he entered.

The surgeon removed his jacket and rolled up his sleeves. He washed his hands roughly. Dried them on a cloth which had been clean only the day before.

He walked over to the table set in the middle of the room. A wooden table. Nearby, some bottles, cloths, metal instruments. He smiled at the patient lying on the table, covered modestly by a sheet. She looked nervous, her face sheeny with sweat. 'Do not be frightened,' he said. She closed her eyes and unclenched her hands. A muscle in her face softened.

There was silence in the room. Though when you listened, focused, you could hear breathing, the occasional rustle, and distant sounds, birds, carriages, a train, a city calling. A tiny clink of metal on metal as the surgeon sorted the instruments. The sunlight danced drowsily on the walls. A cobweb hung across the ceiling, a spider watching.

The door opened. Footsteps across the floor. The surgeon looked up. A man was coming towards him, his face serious. All eyes turned towards the man. He whispered something in the surgeon's ear. The surgeon's shoulders slumped. Silence. He stared at the knife in his palm.

'Is everything all right, sir? Dr Anderson?'

The surgeon looked up. 'Yes, thank you. Thank you, yes. It is only that I have heard some bad news. Someone I knew, a long time ago, has died. He became a good friend.'

Taking a deep breath, he smiled again at the patient. 'Now, let us begin.' She shrank. 'Be calm. You will feel nothing. I shall put this over your face. Just breathe in as deeply as you can.' He held a cloth in front of her, dripped some drops of colourless liquid from a bottle. Turning aside himself, holding his breath, he held it gently over her mouth and nose. Her muscles relaxed into a peaceful drifting faraway smile. He lifted back the sheet.

As Robbie sliced smoothly into the soft flesh, calmly, carefully, holding the razor-thin blade firmly, strongly, he heard it: floating somewhere above the woman's faraway dreaming, rising and falling, like the last song a swan might sing, the distant arpeggio sound of a violin.

Author's Note

Dr Robert Knox was the real surgeon who bought the murdered victims from Burke and Hare. No one ever proved one way or the other whether he had known or suspected that they were murdered, but the mob was furious and attacked his house. He stayed in Edinburgh for some years, but his career was ruined, and he left for London, where he spent the rest of his life caring for cancer patients, often working amongst the poor and charging no fee. He did play the violin expertly and his love of music was one of the many cultured aspects of his life. His arrogance made him many enemies – such as Professor James Syme, his perpetual rival – but his brilliance as an anatomist, surgeon and lecturer made him many friends and admirers.

Professor James Young Simpson is famous for his pioneering work with chloroform, for use in surgery as well as childbirth. He fought against the belief that pain in childbirth was God's will, His punishment to women for their disgrace in the Garden of Eden. Many times he was found unconscious on the floor, after experimenting with ether and chloroform with his friends and colleagues.

The debt we owe to these surgeons and inventors is boundless. The admiration we should have for the patients is immense. They dared to be operated on without anaesthetic, knowing that there was a very good chance of dying. Only through such sacrifice were the surgeons able to increase their knowledge of disease and the human body.

The scene I describe at the beginning of this book is closely based on a true story. I dedicate my story to that woman.

N.M.

Praise for *Mondays Are Red*

'A brilliant adaptation of the Faustian legend. Nicola Morgan is a fresh and original voice.'
'. . . The pace and excitement of this unusual story . . . builds to a gripping climax.' *Bookseller*

'. . . synaesthesia is very rare indeed but its use in a teenage novel is a stroke of genius and Morgan weaves a compelling and disturbing tale around it.' Anne Johnstone – *The Herald*

'A stunning, extraordinary debut.'
'An outstanding novel that rewards rereading.'
Lindsey Fraser – *The Guardian*

'This is a novel to brood over, written by a new and original talent.' Nicholas Tucker – *The Independent*

'. . . oddly brilliant . . .' Dinah Hall – *The Sunday Telegraph*

'. . . very creative, the plot utterly absorbing, disturbing, exciting and page-turning. Nicola Morgan is a great new children's author for older children (and adults!)'
The Children's Bookcase, website

'. . . extremely impressive debut . . .' Michael Thorn – *The Scotsman*